THE HEAVENSTONE SECRETS

V.C. Andrews® Books

The Dollanganger Family Series
Flowers in the Attic
Petals on the Wind
If There Be Thorns
Seeds of Yesterday
Garden of Shadows

The Casteel Family Series
Heaven
Dark Angel
Fallen Hearts
Gates of Paradise
Web of Dreams

The Cutler Family Series
Dawn
Secrets of the Morning
Twilight's Child
Midnight Whispers
Darkest Hour

The Landry Family Series
Ruby
Pearl in the Mist
All That Glitters
Hidden Jewel
Tarnished Gold

The Logan Family Series
Melody
Heart Song
Unfinished Symphony
Music of the Night
Olivia

The Orphans Miniseries
Butterfly
Crystal
Brooke
Raven
Runaways (full-length novel)

The Wildflowers Miniseries
Misty
Star
Jade
Cat
Into the Garden (full-length novel)

The Hudson Family Series
Rain
Lightning Strikes
Eye of the Storm
The End of the Rainbow

The Shooting Stars Series
Cinnamon
Ice
Rose
Honey
Falling Stars

The De Beers Family Series
Willow
Wicked Forest
Twisted Roots
Into the Woods
Hidden Leaves

The Broken Wings Series
Broken Wings
Midnight Flight

The Gemini Series
Celeste
Black Cat
Child of Darkness

The Shadows Series
April Shadows
Girl in the Shadows

The Early Spring Series
Broken Flower
Scattered Leaves

The Secret Series
Secrets in the Attic
Secrets in the Shadows

The Delia Series
Delia's Crossing
Delia's Heart
Delia's Gift

The Heavenstone Series
The Heavenstone Secrets

My Sweet Audrina
(does not belong to a series)

V.C. ANDREWS®

THE HEAVENSTONE SECRETS

POCKET BOOKS
New York   London   Toronto   Sydney

Pocket Books
A Division of Simon & Schuster, Inc.
1230 Avenue of the Americas
New York, NY 10020

Following the death of Virginia Andrews, the Andrews family worked with a carefully selected writer to organize and complete Virginia Andrews' stories and to create additional novels, of which this is one, inspired by her storytelling genius.

First Pocket Books hardcover edition January 2010

V. C. ANDREWS® and VIRGINIA ANDREWS® are registered trademarks of the Vanda General Partnership

POCKET and colophon are registered trademarks of Simon & Schuster, Inc.

For information about special discounts for bulk purchases, please contact Simon & Schuster Special Sales at 1-866-506-1949 or business@simonandschuster.com.

The Simon & Schuster Speakers Bureau can bring authors to your live event. For more information or to book an event contact the Simon & Schuster Speakers Bureau at 1-866-248-3049 or visit our website at www.simonspeakers.com.

Designed by Esther Paradelo

Manufactured in the United States of America

10 9 8 7 6 5 4 3 2 1

ISBN 978-1-4391-5496-0
ISBN 978-1-4391-6682-6 (ebook)

THE
HEAVENSTONE
SECRETS

Prologue

LIKE MOST ANY other girl my age, I was afraid of the darkness when I was alone. I was afraid of mysterious sounds, curious shadows, and all the other assorted Halloween creatures that populate our nightmares. More important, perhaps, I was not afraid of admitting to those fears. It was comforting to know that so many others my age shared them with me and so few would deny it. But I did have one fear that I was ashamed to admit or reveal to my friends, or anyone, for that matter, and I did the best I could to hide it, even though, at times, that seemed impossible to do.

I had always been afraid of my older sister, Cassie. As long as I can remember, Cassie made me tremble inside when she looked hard at me or came toward me quickly as someone angry might. There was nothing grotesque or immediately frightening about Cassie, either. Anyone who heard me say I was afraid of her would surely tilt his or her head and smile with some skepticism. But none of them was her younger sister, and none of them lived with her.

Mother once told me that she thought Cassie, even though she was only about three at the time, deliberately caused me to fall off the diaper-changing table, which resulted in a fracture in my right leg. To this day, Cassie denies it and insists that Mother was just not watching me properly and had put me too close to the edge. Although Mother blamed her, she excused it with something called sibling rivalry. She even made it sound okay.

"Until the day you were born, Cassie was the precious princess in the family, especially for your father, and then you came along and nudged her off the throne. It's only natural that she would have been terribly jealous and disappointed, but smother your worries. Sisters grow out of such things as soon as they are confident about themselves," Mother told me, and then ran her fingers through my long golden-brown hair, which she said was softer than silk. I could see the pleasure in her face, and I was happy that I could bring that look of pleasure into her speckled green-blue eyes simply by being me.

Unfortunately, I would immediately wonder if she had felt that way about Cassie's hair when she was my age. Cassie didn't take as much pride in her hair as I did, and she certainly wouldn't let Mother run her fingers through it that way anymore, if she ever had. She always hated Mother touching her and especially hated her hair being brushed or changed from how she wanted it. Still, I was afraid she would be envious of how much attention Mother or Daddy paid me, whether it was because of my hair or my clothes or some clever thing I had said.

Maybe Mother could see that fear in my face. She leaned down to whisper, her lips tickling my earlobe, and added, "And you and I know, Semantha, that Cassie is the most self-confident girl her age for miles and miles and miles around us. She doesn't have to be jealous of anyone anymore. There are few her age or even older who are as intelligent and as competent as Cassie. Cassie is a born leader. She'll make us all very proud someday. I'm sure of it."

There was always a lot of whispering going on in our house. Soft words flew through our rooms on butterfly wings. Our parents whispered to each other often, even if we were too far away to hear their exact words. However, Cassie was the champion whisperer. That was because whenever she wanted to impress me with something, she would whisper it. It was a way of stamping it *Secret,* just the way a letter or a package might be stamped *Priority Mail.*

And there was no greater sin in Cassie's Ten Commandments than her First Commandment: Thou shalt never reveal a secret, especially if it was a Cassie Secret.

Over time, her other commandments would come raining down upon me as if from the lips of some deity. Eventually, I came to believe that Cassie had her own private religion, her own personal god. I watched her carefully in church and saw how her eyes would blaze with defiance whenever we were asked to speak directly to God. She wouldn't speak. She wouldn't sing a hymn or chant a prayer. She wouldn't even bow her head. Neither Mother nor Daddy ever seemed to notice, or if they did, they didn't seem to care, and ours was a very religious community.

We lived in the Bluegrass region of Kentucky, because that was where Daddy's ancestors had come to live when they left England. Our triple great-grandfather, as Cassie liked to call him, built the Gothic Revival mansion in which we lived. Daddy, being the oldest son, inherited it. He had one brother who was five years younger, Perry. He worked in the Heavenstone company, but he lived in Lexington. He was a bachelor and lived alone in a townhouse.

Our house had ten rooms. Five were downstairs: the large living room with the original fieldstone fireplace with stone up to the ceiling, a large dining room with a grand teardrop chandelier that had been imported years ago from France, a kitchen that had been renovated five times to provide for more modern appliances, twice alone after Daddy and Mother married, a dark oak den that was our entertainment center, and Daddy's home office with a library with leather-bound first editions. Behind his large desk, built from the same dark oak that was used to make the library shelves, were bay windows that looked south on our property, so he was never bothered by the direct sunlight. His office had a slate floor and an alcove that housed all the modern machinery any business office would have.

There were ancestral portraits everywhere. Daddy's favorite was of one of our triple great-grandfather's son, Asa Heavenstone. Asa was a hero in the Civil War who was killed only a week before the war ended. His portrait with him wearing his Confederate uniform still hangs in the living room next to portraits of our great-cousins, -uncles, and -aunts, as well as

Grandfather and Grandmother Heavenstone. The people in Kentucky weren't all in favor of the Confederacy, so we had cousins who were in the Union Army as well—only none of their portraits were hung on our walls. Daddy told us his grandparents were always terrified that someday, the family would learn that one of those in the Union Army had killed Asa.

Daddy has a large portrait of his father in the office, angled so that it always seems he's looking down at him. I have often seen Daddy looking up at his father and nodding slightly, as if they had just had a serious conversation about the business. He often looked at Asa's portrait the same way.

Mother often said that if one of us had been a boy, she would have named him Asa. When Asa was killed, our triple great-grandfather went into a very deep depression from which he never recovered. Even though he had two other sons and a daughter, he never got over Asa's death, because Asa was his oldest and his favorite. His own death was a deep, dark secret. Mother feels confident that he drank himself to death in this very house. She envisioned him spending hours looking up at Asa's portrait as his heart continued to shatter. Maybe that great sadness was what Daddy felt when he looked up at the portrait. I thought he imagined himself in Asa's father's shoes and tried to feel what he might have felt.

Many times, I have stood in front of Asa's portrait, studying it for any possible resemblances to my father or myself and Cassie. Daddy had a similar beard, but other than that, I didn't see much similarity. I could see some resemblances in our other relatives but none in him. Cassie says that was because Asa looked too much like his mother. She says his father loved him the most because he looked so much like his mother, "and after all, that was where his father's romantic love had gone. Husbands favor the child who looks the most like their wives."

The Heavenstone family lost much of its land and wealth after the Civil War, but Great-grandfather Patton Heavenstone restored much of it through the fortune he made with his general stores, which eventually became the Heavenstone Department Stores our family now owned. There are ten throughout the state, with an eleventh being developed in Lexington. There is a statue of Great-grandfather Patton Heavenstone in the lobby of the first Heavenstone Department Store in Danville. His first two wives died, one of typhoid and one because of a heart defect, but his third wife outlived him.

I knew all this because Daddy said learning our family history was more important than learning the history of our state and country.

"What is a country if not for its families?" he emphasized. "And what is a family without children?"

We weren't expected to answer any of these questions. It used to be difficult to tell the difference between questions Daddy wanted us to answer and questions he wanted to ask and answer himself. Even questions about us weren't necessarily the ones we were to answer, so his pausing for a moment after asking meant nothing.

"Why are you not working harder and being as good a student as Cassie, Semantha? I'll tell you why you're not," he would say before I had a chance to protest and tell him that I really was working hard at being a good student. It was just impossible for me to be as perfect as Cassie. I know I spent more time on my homework than she did. Whatever I would say wouldn't matter anyway, I supposed. What Daddy believed was already, as Cassie would say with one of her dramatic gestures, "a fait accompli."

Because Cassie could frighten me, she could easily command and hold my attention. Besides, it was fascinating to watch her parade about with her mother-perfect posture and cast her deep and serious pronouncements at me, as would someone tossing flower petals while riding in a parade. Cassie was always either in a parade or on a stage, and I was always on the sidelines or in the audience.

Many of those solemn declarations that she made were about being perfect for our parents.

"We have to be better in every way than other children would normally be for their parents, Semantha. We're a famous family here. We have a real history, a rich heritage. Few families do. There is no official royalty in America as there is in countries like England, but there is in the minds of Americans. What that means," she quickly added, because she could see I didn't understand her—she claimed my face was so easy to read that it could have a library card—"is that people still look way up to certain other people, people with a history like ours, and think of them as something special. We truly are something special, so you can't be ordinary. It's absolutely forbidden for any of us Heavenstones to be ordinary," she emphasized, which was Cassie's Second Commandment.

"We have to say double the clever things other children would say. We have to make our parents laugh twice as much as other parents laugh. We have to give our parents twice as much love, too, especially our daddy, who has been handed down all this grand heritage."

"I give them all my love," I said.

"It's not enough. You're not enough, I'm not enough, as we are. We must . . . rise to the occasion. We must be like angels, so much like angels that Mother will swear she sees wings on us both. Daddy already sees them on me, as you know, and that's not by accident." She paused and turned to me as if she had just remembered she was speaking to me and not to herself. I would swear that the way she held her shoulders when she said that actually made me think I did see wings on her, too. "Are you listening?"

I nodded emphatically, but the more Cassie talked about being more than perfect for our parents, the more worried about failure I became. How can I be twice as much as I was? I wondered. I didn't doubt that maybe Cassie could. She was so intelligent and clever and read far beyond what girls her age would or could read. She was far more mature than her classmates, too. However, I knew that her teachers weren't all fond of that. Some complained that she was racing through her childhood too quickly. She should play more, enjoy more, they said.

"Cassie is Cassie," Daddy would reply, as if that explained everything.

Sometimes, however, I thought Mother was really becoming more and more unhappy about Cassie, rather than taking double pleasure in her. Ironically, Cassie had a personality that resembled our mother's more than mine did, and I was sure Mother saw things in her and about her that she didn't necessarily like in or about herself.

For one thing, Cassie was too quick to see and point out weaknesses and flaws in other people, and once she rendered a judgement about someone, she couldn't be moved from it, even, as Daddy might say, with a bulldozer. I sensed he actually liked that about her. "Too many women are flighty," he said. "Their minds are tied too tightly to their erratic emotions and go from high notes to low notes like some out-of-tune piano."

But Cassie was so particular, especially about her classmates, that she had no real friends, just casual acquaintances she tolerated. She wasn't just a snob. She was "a snob's snob."

Although Daddy didn't come right out and say it, I was sure he thought Mother was a snob, too. Mother didn't belong to any clubs or organizations, and whenever Daddy asked her why not, she always answered with a complaint about the other women. "They gossip too much," or, "They are obsessed with the wrong priorities." They were too materialistic or simple. She also said many of them were "vague."

What did she mean by that? I asked Cassie. Cassie would never refuse to answer a question. She liked being asked, and she liked my listening to her. She would widen her eyes and put her face so close to mine, I could see the tiny specks of green in her eyes. I was jealous of those specks. They were Mother's specks.

"When Mother looks at these vague women, she doesn't see anyone. They are so vapid and empty she looks right through them. They simply don't exist."

I shook my head. It made no sense. How could they not exist? They were standing right there in front of Mother, weren't they? I pointed that out and said, "They eat and talk and walk."

"So do insects," Cassie said. "That's what they are, merely insects."

Like Mother, she had a way of pursing her lips after she was critical of someone or something. It was as if they both decided that they would say no more on the subject, not that they didn't have more to say. They just didn't want to waste another breath, and as Daddy would say, "When those two get that way, you can't pry an additional word out of them with a crowbar."

Both Cassie and Mother were very efficient. From the moment she rose in the morning to the moment she went to sleep, Mother had something to do. She hated wasting time, which was another reason she had so few friends. She told us that most of the women she knew loved wasting time, spending hours and hours at lunch, sipping coffee, pecking at their food like birds, and then shopping even if they had nothing for which to shop.

"Leisure," Mother would say, "has not given these women opportunities to do something significant with their lives. On the contrary, it has taken those opportunities away. They are no longer important to their families, especially their children. They have nannies when the children are young and, of course, maids and cooks to clean and prepare the meals. They make sure their children are fully occupied with piano lessons or dancing lessons, and if they need help with schoolwork, they hire tutors. They don't realize it, but they've replaced themselves.

"But perhaps they're too selfish to care," she concluded after thinking about her own words for a moment. "Their homes are simply . . . private hotels."

Consequently, despite the size of our home, we had no maids or cooks, and neither Cassie nor I had a tutor. Even if Daddy complained mildly about my average grades, he couldn't deny that I had the best tutor possible already with us: Cassie, who in my mind knew as much as, if not more than, my teachers did. Before Mother would agree to either piano or dancing lessons, we had to demonstrate to her that we wanted them very much ourselves first. Cassie didn't want them, but I did. All of my friends were having lessons.

"I don't know why you practice the piano and go to dance class, Semantha," Cassie told me. "You'll never be a pianist, and you'll never dance in a professional show. It's a waste of precious time."

I didn't reply. I tried not to contradict Cassie, but even my silence was defiant to her. She'd go, "Well? Well? Well?" until I had to say, "I guess you're right."

I did eventually stop taking my lessons. Neither Daddy nor Mother tried to get me to change my mind, especially when Cassie pointed out to them that I might better spend my time trying to improve my grades. The extra time didn't make much difference, however.

Somehow, even though she had no piano or dance lessons, Cassie was always very busy. She loved organizing, whether it was her own clothing, groceries in the kitchen pantry, or Daddy's magazines and newspapers. She inspected our house every day, looking for something out of place or some reason to rearrange things. For this, Daddy or Mother always paid her great compliments. They were both very proud of her.

Cassie was, of course, an excellent student. She just didn't do anything else at school, because nothing else was really worth the time or more important than helping Mother look after the house and Daddy. As far as I could tell, that meant boyfriends and school dances weren't important to her, either, whereas I couldn't wait for them. It puzzled me that she could be so disinterested in these things. Although we were sisters, we were so unalike.

Someone merely had to look from her room to mine to see the vast differences between us. My clothes were often not hung up or put away neatly. I had papers, magazines, and dolls scattered like the end-of-fall leaves everywhere. Often, I'd forget and leave the remains of something I had eaten on the plate for a day or two, and I never made my bed as well as Cassie made hers. Mine always looked slept in, while hers looked unused. Our bathrooms were the same way. Mine had towels unfolded, often on the floor, the soap streaking the sink, shampoo bottles open and leaking in the shower, or washcloths crumpled on the vanity table. My mirror usually had spots on it because I stood too close to it when I brushed my teeth vigorously.

Across the hall in her suite, Cassie's bathroom looked as if it had just been built and had yet to be used. Everything sparkled, and Mother never looked in on it without declaring how spic-and-span it was, loudly enough for me to hear, even through a closed door.

Once, when I was much older and thinking back on all of this, I decided that I was the way I had been simply because I didn't want to be at all like Cassie. I deliberately did things that were opposite to what she did. It was important to me that everyone saw and knew that I was her sister, yes, but we were as unalike as any two unrelated strangers, and I wanted people to see that.

To her credit, Cassie didn't try to make me into a carbon copy of her. I think she was happy that there were so many differences between us. She didn't want to share a compliment or any praise, especially from Daddy, but, more important, she didn't want anyone to believe that what she had accomplished and what she could do was so easy that even someone like me could accomplish it or do it. I sensed how little she respected me for who I was.

Does all of this mean I didn't love her? Can you still love someone who frightens you? She was my sister. We were part of the same family and had the same loving parents. If something happened to her, I would certainly be unhappy about it. I thought.

And I hoped she felt the same way toward me, but did we love each other the way other sisters loved each other? Sometimes I thought we did, and often I thought we didn't, but in time, I would learn that Cassie's way of showing her love or feeling love was so different from mine, from everyone's, that it was easily unseen and unfelt.

Maybe that was the tragedy of Cassie Heavenstone.

No one could ever see how she really was capable of loving someone else.

It's the only soft and forgiving thing I can say about a sister who nearly destroyed me.

1

An Announcement

WHEN I WAS just fourteen years old, my world began to sink in and collapse like a punctured balloon. Whatever happiness I enjoyed slowly leaked out and disappeared. It took me a while to notice and realize it. I was just like someone who, gazing at his car one day, saw that he had a flat tire. When did that begin to happen? he might wonder. I knew when it had begun to happen for me.

One night at dinner a week after my birthday, Daddy put down his knife and fork, folded his hands, and cleared his throat. Cassie and I believed that whatever he was about to say had nothing whatsoever to do with his business or his finances. There was a rule at our table that none of that would be discussed at dinner. And that was true even if Daddy had something wonderful about the business to announce to us, such as a large increase in the profits of one of our stores or our stores beating out the famous chain stores nearby. Whatever the good business news was, he wouldn't say a word about it until after dinner or maybe not until breakfast the following day. For some reason, breakfast was not as sacred a meal as dinner. Of course, dinner was more elegant, with our expensive china and silverware, linen napkins, and the imported tablecloth that Mother had bought on one of their European trips.

My responsibility was to set the table, light the candles in the gold candle holders, and after dinner put everything away or in the dishwasher and washing machine. Cassie helped Mother prepare the food, and I helped both of them serve it. Mother was an excellent cook, always coming up with new and interesting recipes, and Cassie was a quick study. She could replicate almost anything Mother had made a day after she had made it. Twice when Mother was sick with the flu, Cassie "leaped to the helm," as Daddy would say, and created dinners that were as wonderful as what Mother made. Even I had to admit it, although Cassie was far more interested in Daddy's opinion.

At the beginning of dinner, we were to lower our heads while Daddy recited a prayer, but Cassie never lowered her head. I knew both of my parents were aware of it, just as they were in church, but neither forced her to do it. It suggested to me that maybe they were as afraid of her as I was, which, of course, made no sense. How could parents be afraid of their own daughter?

"Your mother and I have an announcement to make," Daddy began this particular evening, and then he stroked his perfectly trimmed and groomed rust-brown goatee. It was a gesture that was always followed by a very serious pronouncement. Another sign was the way his emerald-green eyes brightened.

At forty-eight, he was by anyone's measure still a very handsome man, with a perfectly proportioned straight nose and firm lips. He kept his hair a little longer than most businessmen his age, but it was always trim and neatly brushed. Even though he didn't work outdoors, he had a robust complexion, and because he was six feet two inches tall with wide shoulders, he looked fit and strong. Mother always said that when he was wearing jeans and a short-sleeved shirt instead of his suit, he looked like a lumberjack.

His father had named him Teddy after Teddy Roosevelt and, according to family history, made sure he understood that he had to be as courageous, as loyal to the truth and to what was right, and as strong in body and mind. He was fond of telling Daddy, "Charge up that hill! And no matter what, never surrender!"

Daddy's pausing made what he was about to tell us even more important. I held my breath and glanced at Cassie, who sat with a smirk on her lips. She looked as if she knew what he was about to say and already did not approve.

"Your mother," Daddy continued, reaching to his right to take her hand, "is pregnant."

I know my mouth widened with surprise, and I was sure my eyes swelled, but Cassie's smirk only grew deeper. She leaned slightly forward, folding her hands on the table the way Daddy folded his before a serious pronouncement.

"Is that wise at your age, Mother?" she asked very calmly. "You're forty-two."

"Women in their forties are having children. Your

mother is in perfect health, Cassie, and Dr. Moffet is very optimistic about her having a healthy and successful pregnancy," Daddy replied before Mother could.

"Of course, Dr. Moffet would say that. We're good customers."

Daddy sat back, displeased with her, which was very unusual to see.

"Doctors don't have customers, Cassie. They have patients, and a good doctor is not motivated by profit the way a businessman should be."

"Then there are no good doctors," Cassie said.

Cassie never backed down from what she said or believed. When she was very little and she was reprimanded or forbidden to do something, she would hold her breath until her face reddened so that Mother would relent or to get Daddy to compromise. She once went two days without eating a morsel because she was in a sulk.

"I was hoping you girls would be as happy about this as we are," Mother said, battling back the disappointment I could see she felt.

"I am," I said, perhaps too quickly.

Cassie glared at me for a moment and then formed her smile mask. "Of course, we're happy, but naturally, we're worried, too, Mother."

"Don't be," Mother said firmly. "I'll be fine. It will all be fine."

"We hope so," Cassie said, but the way she said it made it clear that she was full of skepticism. She always managed to speak for me, saying "we" whenever she was going to offer an opinion about something that could have an effect on us both.

"In any case," Daddy continued, "I would like both of you to take this into consideration and do whatever you can to make things easier for your mother during the next seven months. I know you both already do quite a lot, but . . ."

"Then you are already two months pregnant?" Cassie asked quickly.

"Yes, Cassie, I am."

"Why didn't you tell us earlier?" she followed sharply, her eyes narrowing. "There are so many ways to confirm a pregnancy earlier."

I suddenly felt as if the table had been spun around, and Cassie was the mother and Mother was the daughter. When Mother didn't answer, Cassie continued, "Why didn't you let us know you were both thinking of having another child?"

Mother looked at Daddy. They both seemed flustered.

"We weren't . . . it wasn't something we were sure we . . . what difference does that make?" Daddy shouted. "We're telling you how things are now."

"Obviously," Cassie replied. "But why didn't you decide to do this years ago?"

"The truth is, Cassie, I've been trying to get pregnant for some time now. I've been to see fertility doctors and specialists, and finally, something has worked," Mother told her softly. She smiled. "With the two of you young adult women now, things will actually be much easier. You can help me take good care of the new baby, be like two little nannies. When you're able and free, of course," she added.

"Why shouldn't we be able and free?" Cassie retorted.

"Oh, you both will have your own busy lives, I'm sure. Actually, I'm not worried about it. It's a good time for me. I look forward to it," Mother added. She smiled at Daddy and took his hand again. "Of course, we're hoping . . . we'll soon know whether or not . . . if . . ."

"If it's a boy," Daddy said, smiling. He turned to Mother, and they looked at each other as if they were alone and both twenty years younger.

"We've already decided we will name him Asa. Nothing would please your father more," she told us.

They continued to look at each other with such love and gratitude that it brought tears to my eyes. I glanced at Cassie. She looked as if she would set the house on fire. She jerked her eyes toward me and I looked down quickly. Later, she told me our parents had no idea what they were getting themselves into, what they were getting us all into.

"I don't understand," I said. "Why do you say that?"

"This world we're in will be turned topsy-turvy," she said, "so get ready to stand on your head."

Then she marched off to her room and shut the door.

Which reminded me of Cassie's Third Commandment: Don't ever do anything to make her unhappy.

However, Cassie wasn't wrong. No matter what I thought about her and what I think about her now, she really wasn't wrong very often. Our house and our lives did start to change, but I didn't think they went topsy-turvy. On the contrary, to me, it was as if a brand-new sunlight was streaming in through our windows, lighting up the dullest corners, brightening colors, and making furniture and artifacts sparkle. I think Mother thought that, too, because she went about the grand house as if she were seeing it for the first time. During the next two months, she changed the arrangement of some furniture and worked harder at polishing and vacuuming and having Cassie and me polish and vacuum. She had window cleaners and rug cleaners, painters doing touch-ups. She bought new lamps and even some new kitchen appliances, and took more interest in our landscaping.

"Why is all of this suddenly so important? She acts as if the new Messiah is coming," Cassie muttered.

I nodded, not because I, too, saw it as being over the top but because I saw it as wonderful. Cassie looked at my face and added, "She's being ridiculous, behaving like some newlywed. If all of these things had to be done, why weren't they done for us as well?"

"Maybe they were," I dared to suggest. She pursed her lips and pulled back her head. "I mean, right before you were born and then right before I was."

"Nothing was changed then, Semantha. Daddy used to think this house was as sacred as a church. You know how he feels about our family's history. Most of it is exactly as it has been for nearly eighty years. No new bride, no matter how she was supposedly loved, would dare interfere with that. We are the Heavenstones!" she declared, as if that explained everything.

"Oh," I said.

Of course, I thought then, Why is Daddy permitting her to do all of this now? But I didn't dare ask. I didn't have to ask. Cassie was prepared to give me an explanation.

"Men," she continued in one of her loud whispers, "can suddenly become boys so easily and quickly that it would make your head spin. Their wisdom evaporates," she added with such confidence. It was as if she really was older than our parents, growing up so quickly that she had passed them by years ago. "They get so infatuated with their women that they'll fall over themselves trying to please them. Women are stronger when it comes to that sort of thing," she said, nodding. "You don't see as many making fools of themselves when they're older. There are some who do, of course, but not as often as men."

How do you know all this? I wanted to ask her. *You never go out on a date. You've never had a boyfriend or, as far as I know, even had a crush on a boy. Did you learn it all from books?* I didn't ask these questions, because I was sure she would see it as some disagreement, and I didn't want to do anything that would bring unhappiness into our home right now. Even I, who didn't know half as much as Cassie knew about the emotional and physical changes a woman goes through when she is pregnant, could see that Mother was often on the verge of tears for what looked to be no real reason whatsoever.

"We simply have to hope Daddy comes to his senses and reins in this wastefulness and unnecessary expense," Cassie concluded, but everything went contrary to what she hoped, especially when Mother and Daddy were told there was no questions about it: she was going to have a boy.

When they came home that day, it was as if they had won the biggest lottery. Daddy was practically floating, and Mother's face was so radiant she really did look twenty years younger. They talked about having a party to celebrate but agreed to be cautious and wait.

However, they now decided they were going to renovate one of the upstairs bedrooms to create Asa's nursery. Not only were carpenters, electricians, and plumbers brought in, but Mother decided, with Daddy's approval, of course, to hire an interior decorator.

"An interior decorator for a baby's nursery!" Cassie cried when she heard about it. She came rushing into my bedroom one Saturday morning to tell me.

I was seated at my vanity table, brushing my hair and thinking about Kent Pearson, who was in all of my ninth-grade classes except home economics. We had been classmates since the seventh grade, but suddenly, one day, when I looked at him, I saw him differently. He seemed to have become this handsome young man behind my back. He caught me looking at him with interest and blushed, but since that day, he had begun to pay more attention to me, finding every opportunity he could to talk or walk with me.

This caused me to wonder more deeply what it was that actually happened between a boy and a girl.

Was it something magical, mysterious, or was it, as Cassie would probably say, simply the burst of hormones? If that were true, however, I'd have feelings like this for almost any boy, but I didn't. I thought only of Kent, dreamed only of Kent, and was excited to be only with Kent. Were we too young to have experienced love at first sight, even though it wasn't really our first sighting of each other?

"Did you hear what I said?" Cassie continued. She stood beside me with her arms folded under her breasts, her shoulders back.

Although Cassie was only two years older than I, she was nearly five inches taller and had what I had heard referred to as a full figure. She wasn't at all matronly-looking, even though she often acted as if there was not even a foot left in her journey to maturity. However, no one simply seeing her would think of her as anything but a pretty teenage girl. She didn't spend as much time on her hair and makeup, nor did she care as much for what was in fashion, as I did, but she never looked unkempt, and she did have our mother's perfect facial features, with the same exotic speckled green-blue eyes and light brown hair that glistened golden in the sunlight. She kept her hair shorter than mine and Mother's and wasn't fond of wearing earrings. She didn't want to pierce her ears, but when she heard Daddy compliment Mother on a pair of pierced earrings, she went ahead and had hers pierced and now always wore earrings.

"What?"

"What? What? How can you sit there for hours

and look at yourself? The way you brush your hair makes me think you're in some kind of a trance."

"I'm not sitting here for hours. Mother brushes hers this way and this much every day."

"Whatever. That's hardly important. Didn't you hear me? I said they've hired an interior decorator for the nursery. All they really have to do is put a crib and some other things in the bedroom, but now they're going to change the wallpaper, the floor, maybe even the ceiling, and definitely all the lighting fixtures. I heard them say that they may even replace the windows to make the room brighter! That means busting out walls!"

I nodded. I didn't know what to say. It all sounded fine with me.

"You know how much all that will cost? They'll spend more money on this nursery than most people spend redoing a whole house. Before our brother is even born, they're doting on him, spoiling him. You can just imagine what's going to happen when he is born."

I couldn't help but wonder if this was the sibling rivalry Mother had told me Cassie had had when I was born. If it was that, why didn't I have it, too?

"They're both so happy about it," I said.

She stared at me and then shook her head. "Listen to me, Semantha. Read my lips if you have to, but listen. Sure, they're happy now," she said, "but wait until they have to go through all that parents go through with infants, waking up all hours of the night, changing diapers, fighting baby rashes, worrying over every possible infant illness, doctor visits, on and on and on."

"They went through it with us," I reminded her.

"Are you a total zero, Semantha? They were both sixteen years younger then. They're so used to their own time and interests now, especially Mother. She, especially, will be overwhelmed. What it means is I'm going to have to do more, and so will you.

"Don't you realize what the age difference between Asa and us will be?" she continued so intensely that I could see the veins in her temples. "By the time he's ten, we'll both be well into our twenties, maybe going to graduate school or married. Why, people might even think he's my son and not my brother. They could even think it of you!"

"Oh, yes. I never thought of that," I said, and she calmed a little.

"In any case, who will be here to help raise him?" she added, nodding.

"They won't need us for that by then, will they?"

"Of course, they will. It's harder when children get older. You know what Daddy says: little children, little problems, big children . . . understand?"

I nodded, again not looking sufficiently upset for her.

"Okay. Just wait," she said. "You'll see."

She paused and looked at me in the mirror and squinted as if it was a window and not a mirror and she was looking at someone else some distance away.

"There's something different about you these days. What is it?" she demanded.

I raised my eyebrows and shrugged. "What?"

"I don't know. You're acting flighty, like you're always thinking about something else. I see the way you float through the halls and up and down the stairs like you're in some kind of a movie hearing your own theme music." She paused and narrowed her eyes again. "Are you interested in some boy? Is that it? Do you think you're in love? Well?"

"No," I said weakly. She smirked.

"Who is it? C'mon, out with it," she said. "Who is this love of your life?"

"I'm not in love."

"Semantha Heavenstone. This is your sister, Cassie, who's talking and to whom you're talking. You know we're too close for you to hide any secrets very long from me. Your forehead's like a neon sign flashing your thoughts. Well? Who?"

"Kent Pearson has been paying a lot of attention to me lately," I confessed. Just as she said, it was impossible for me to hide things from her.

"Kent Pearson," she repeated, chewing over her knowledge of him. "Yes, I know who he is. He has an older brother a year ahead of me, Brody. He's a very poor student. I heard he might not even graduate. As I recall, the Pearsons aren't very well off, either, so there's no money for tutors."

"Kent's very smart," I said. "He won't need a tutor."

"Um . . . be careful," she said. "Don't give him the impression that you like him too much."

"Why not?"

"You might as well get used to the idea, Semantha. There will be many boys after you, hoping to get into this family and this wealth. That means you have to be extra, extra cautious."

"Is that why you don't have a boyfriend?" I asked, maybe too quickly.

"I haven't seen or heard anyone worthy of my interest yet," she replied without skipping a beat.

I wanted to ask her more about the boys in her class and the classes above hers. How could there be absolutely no one worth her interest? There were many boys from well-to-do families, families as respectable as ours, but before we could continue the discussion, we heard Mother calling on the intercom to tell us Uncle Perry had arrived.

"Great," Cassie said, dropping the corners of her lips. "He's here."

She was not nearly as fond of Uncle Perry as I was, and he knew it. I knew he was flamboyant and quite different from Daddy, but I enjoyed him, enjoyed what Mother called his joie de vivre. I couldn't remember a time when he had been unhappy or depressed. He always dressed in bright colors and wore glittering gold rings, bracelets, and necklaces. He often teased Daddy about his stuffy clothing, calling him too conservative, boring. Daddy merely shook his head, as if any comments Uncle Perry made were simply full of air.

I had to agree that he took after their mother more in his looks than he did their father. He was good-looking but in a pretty-boy sort of way, concerned about his complexion (he went to tanning salons), his hair (never out of style), and his nails (always manicured). He had eyelashes any woman would envy, a nose a little too small and dainty for a man, and thinner lips than Daddy's. Cassie and I had visited him in his townhouse in Lexington only twice, but both times, we were impressed with how neat and organized everything was. He paid great attention to the slightest detail. When Cassie looked at something such as a vase or a small statue and put it down just a few inches from where it had been, he immediately returned it to that place.

The second visit had occurred only a little more than a year ago, but when we left, Cassie leaned over in the limousine hired to take us and whispered, "I don't think he lives alone."

"What does that mean?"

"When I was in his bathroom, I looked in the cabinet and saw two different toothbrushes and different men's colognes. There were other clues," she added.

"Men's colognes? Don't you mean perfume if it's someone else?"

She smirked. "Hardly. Uncle Perry is gay, Semantha."

My face was surely awash in astonishment. That had never occurred to me, and I had never heard either Daddy or Mother say such a thing, even suggest it.

"But . . ."

"Why do you think he has never brought a girl-friend to our house or even mentioned someone? Why is he still unmarried?"

"I thought he was simply a bachelor."

"Christmas trees, Semantha, you're so naive for your age, especially nowadays. Sometimes I wonder if Mother faked your birth and you were left on the door-step. I suppose you've never noticed his pierced ear."

"What? No."

"He doesn't always wear it when he comes to our house, but next time we see him somewhere else, look at his right ear. The left is not pierced. Duh."

I shook my head, still amazed. "Wouldn't Daddy be upset?"

"Who says he isn't? He has simply chosen to ignore it, and Uncle Perry has the sense not to flaunt his homosexuality in Daddy's presence. It's a forbidden topic in our house, so don't dare mention it. You'd only upset Daddy."

"No, I would never . . ."

I remember thinking how slow I really was in comparison to Cassie. Was it simply her two additional years of age? Maybe I really had been left on the doorstep.

Regardless of what she had told me, I couldn't be any less warm to Uncle Perry. I thought he was truly a very creative man. He was in charge of the Heavenstone Department Stores' publicity and promotion as well as designing an entire line of Heavenstone fashions for both men and women and, lately, even children. The line was very successful.

We both went downstairs to join him, Daddy, and Mother. He had come for lunch but had also brought a portfolio of new fashion ideas for teenage girls and wanted our opinions. The three of them were in the living room, and Uncle Perry had his portfolio opened on the large glass coffee table. Mother was looking down at it, and Daddy was sitting in his favorite easy chair, puffing on his meerschaum pipe, which had been his father's.

Uncle Perry was wearing a bright blue blazer

and light blue slacks with blue boat shoes. He wore a cravat and looked as if he had just stepped off the cover of a fashion magazine himself. The moment we entered, he brightened, but I felt he was looking mainly at me.

"Ah, the infamous Heavenstone sisters," he declared. Mother laughed. "Just in time, girls. I'd love for you to peruse my new creations. Your father has yet to groan or moan, which usually means I'm right on track or, as he would say, still in the black."

"Lucky is all you are," Daddy said.

"What difference does it make if the bottom line is where you want it, Teddy?"

Now Daddy grunted.

We both looked at the portfolio. Uncle Perry stepped back, and Cassie began to turn the pages. I thought everything looked terrific and couldn't wait for some of it.

"They look sloppy to me," Cassie said coldly.

"Sloppy is in, Cassie. You should know that better than I," Uncle Perry said, turning his attention to me. "Besides, it's not really sloppy. It looks like it's sloppy, but everything is coordinated, all the layered clothing, the shoes, the hats."

I nodded. "The girls in my class would love it all," I said. He beamed.

"She's right. The girls in her class would," Cassie said.

"Well, they are the ones with the discretionary income, according to our marketing analysis, Cassie," Uncle Perry said softly.

"I wouldn't buy them."

Uncle Perry held his smile, but I could see the pain in his eyes.

Cassie looked at Daddy and added, "But I don't follow the flock, so I'm not really a good judge when it comes to what will and won't sell. I'm sure all this will do fine."

"Thank you, Cassie. That's almost a compliment," Uncle Perry said, and Mother laughed.

Cassie was not one to blush or redden, but she did this time. It made my heart thump. Would she say something nasty? Uncle Perry turned back to me.

"In two months, you can start wearing some of this, Sam."

Sam was the nickname Uncle Perry had given me from the very first day he learned my name was Semantha. Mother thought it was cute. Daddy never told him not to call me that. In fact, I sometimes felt he wished he had come up with it first. Cassie hated it. Now that she had exposed Uncle Perry's sexual preferences, she would whisper later on, "He likes to turn everything into his way of seeing the world. Sam is more of a man's name. Get it?"

I shook my head.

"You will," she promised, and left it at that.

Later, at lunch, Uncle Perry talked about his upcoming vacation. He was going on a Caribbean cruise. He loved traveling and had gone to far more places than Daddy and Mother. Mother had many questions about his trip, but Daddy seemed reluctant to ask or hear any answers.

Cassie leaned over to whisper, "It's probably a gay men's cruise."

I nearly choked on my salmon.

"So," Uncle Perry said after Mother and Cassie had brought out coffee and some Danish for dessert, "how do you girls feel about having a new little brother?"

"How should we feel?" Cassie replied. The way she looked at him made it seem she really wanted to hear his answer. I could see it threw him off. He looked at Daddy and then smiled.

"I would imagine excited," he said.

"Well, of course," Cassie said. "And we're happy for our parents, too."

Uncle Perry nodded. He drank his coffee, glanced at me, and looked now as if he couldn't wait to be on his way. After lunch, however, Daddy took him to his office to discuss some business. Later, after we helped Mother clean up, Cassie told me to follow her up to her bedroom. Even though she closed the door behind us and we were far from anyone who could hear us, she still whispered.

"Now you should have no trouble understanding why Daddy wanted Mother to get pregnant so much."

"What do you mean?"

"Christmas trees, Semantha. Figure it out. Who will take over the Heavenstone Corporation in years to come? Not me, and certainly not you."

When I didn't respond, she raised her voice. "Uncle Perry will never have a son, much less a daughter, unless he adopts one, and that child won't have any Heavenstone blood in him!"

"Oh."

"Yes, oooooh." She flopped on her bed. "Every generation of Heavenstones has always had a male to take control of what had been built by his father and his father's father. Daddy must have nightmares about it. He's not happy with the prospect of some other, bigger corporation taking us over, but without a son, what else could happen? You see what Uncle Perry is like. Even if he outlived Daddy by years and years, he couldn't handle the responsibilities. He knows nothing about real business."

"But why couldn't you run the company someday, Cassie? You're the smartest girl I know."

"I don't want to," she replied sharply and slowly. "I'm more like . . . like a wife. Goodness knows, I do half of Mother's work here, don't I? Well? Don't I?"

"Yes, but I thought . . ."

"Don't think."

She sighed and then looked at me harder. She nodded to herself.

"What?" I asked.

"I suppose you could, with great care and guidance, someday find the right man to marry, a man who might be able to be work in our corporation. But," she added, shaking her head, "I have grave doubts about your taste when it comes to the opposite sex. I see how infatuated you are with Kent Pearson. Don't deny it. He'll be lucky to attend a state university and probably won't have a head for business anyway, if he's anything like his brother. Therefore, even if you have a boy, he might not have the wherewithal to inherit control of our empire."

"Empire?"

"Don't you see?" she cried. She actually pounded her own leg for emphasis, so hard it made me wince. "You can't just go flouting about with anyone who pees standing up."

"What?" I started to smile.

"Any boy, Semantha. You have to realize your responsibility to our heritage."

"What about you, Cassie? You might find the right man if I don't."

She looked away for a long moment. I thought she might have nothing else to say.

And then she whispered as if she were talking to herself, "I can't possibly leave Daddy, especially now."

Before I could ask her what she meant, we heard Mother calling us in the hallway. I went to the door.

"What, Mother?"

"Your uncle Perry's leaving, girls. I just showed him Asa's nursery and some of the renovations."

I looked back at Cassie. "Uncle Perry's leaving."

"I'm devastated. Go say good-bye for me," she told me. Then she rose and went into her bathroom.

Her whispered words seemed stuck in my ears: *"I can't possibly leave Daddy, especially now."*

I would hear them often in my mind.

And I would struggle to understand them as if my life depended on it.

Little did I know that it actually did.

Only the Beginning

THAT EVENING, I thought I was dreaming it, but I soon realized that Cassie was kneeling at my bedside and whispering in my left ear. I opened my eyes and continued to listen before I turned toward her. I wanted to be sure it wasn't a dream, and I was terrified that it might be a ghost, one of the Heavenstones, of course, maybe even Asa Heavenstone, since his namesake was soon to be born. It wasn't the first time I had thought I heard voices in this historic house. There were even times I had thought I had seen something ghostlike moving in the shadows.

I turned slowly and saw Cassie in her nightgown.

"She's doing it again," she whispered.

"Who?"

"Mother."

"Doing what?"

"Crying, moaning, complaining. You'd have to be dead not to hear it. She's walking the hallways, and Daddy is pleading with her to go back to bed."

I sat up and listened. I didn't hear anything.

"What do you mean, she's doing it again? I don't hear her," I said.

"She's not doing it now. He got her to go back to their bedroom," Cassie said. "I told you, didn't I? I told you this would happen. She doesn't have the temperament for all this, for having a new baby. She's too much into herself, into her own life."

"How can a mother be too much into herself to have her own baby?"

"You really are so naive, Semantha, especially for someone your age. You ever wonder why our mother hasn't ever been involved in Daddy's business? She hardly visits one of our stores. You know why he really never talks about business at dinner? He knows she's not in the slightest interested. Haven't you noticed how much of an introvert she's become?"

"What's that? I'm not sure," I admitted.

"Christmas trees, Semantha. You're in the ninth grade. If you'd read more, you'd have a decent vocabulary."

"I read."

"It means she won't belong to any club or go shopping with friends and always gives Daddy a hard time about going to social events. She's happy just doing her housework and her jigsaw puzzles. Why do you think she has so few personal phone calls? She'll never call anyone back. She'd rather be by herself than with anyone else, even Daddy."

So that's what it means, I thought. Of all people to call someone else an introvert, Cassie shouldn't. She could easily be describing herself, not Mother.

"Daddy doesn't seem unhappy with her," I offered.

She stood up, towering over me now. In the

distorted shadows carved by a half-moon glowing through my curtains, Cassie seemed to rise above her height and expand. Her face looked covered in a silvery-gold mask, with her eyes dark, vacant sockets.

"He would never come right out and tell us something like that, Semantha," she whispered.

Whenever she whispered like this, I automatically whispered back. "Then how do you know it's true, Cassie?"

She looked as if she was smiling.

"I know Daddy better than anyone, Semantha. I can tell immediately when he is happy and when he is not. He shoots me certain looks from time to time, looks he won't permit anyone else to see, not even you, because he doesn't want to upset you. He knows how fragile you are."

"I'm not fragile."

"Of course you are, Semantha. You know it's because you were a premature baby, born nearly six weeks too early. You were kept in the hospital for almost three weeks. Everyone expected you would die."

"But I thought the doctor said I would do just fine."

"Of course, he would say something like that. He didn't want to frighten and worry our parents. But think, Cassie. Haven't you been ill with all the childhood diseases? You have much thinner bones than I do. When you're naked, I can practically look right through you. The smallest, most insignificant little things get you upset or nervous. I know you're afraid of almost everything, including your own shadow. That's why I try to look after you as much as I do."

I didn't say anything for fear she would think I sounded ungrateful, and I did feel more secure knowing she was keeping an eye on me.

She leaned down again, kneeling slightly. Now I could see her eyes clearly because of the way they glittered in the moonlight. She looked very excited and, in an odd way, happy.

"Mark my words. This is only the beginning. Prepare yourself for a great deal more difficulty to come," she said, then rose and slipped out of my room as quietly as she had slipped in. It was almost as if I had dreamed the entire thing. My heart was thumping. I had to take deep breaths. Cassie was always saying I probably had asthma, but Dr. Moffet said it wasn't so.

In fact, this wasn't the first time Cassie had told me I was fragile, weak, and prone to illness. Whenever I did get a cold or a bellyache, she was always there, nodding her head as if she had expected it. Maybe she's right, I thought. Maybe I am fragile. I had to admit she hardly ever got sick. She had gone years without missing a day of school. When I had asked Mother about it once, she had said, "Cassie just has a better immune system than most people. She's lucky, but don't worry. There's nothing terribly wrong with you. You're a normal young girl."

What did that mean? Cassie wasn't normal?

I lowered my head to my pillow again but kept my eyes open. Was Cassie right? Would things get worse? What could we do about it, anyway? And why hadn't I ever noticed how Daddy revealed things to her but not to me?

I had a hard time falling back to sleep, but I finally did, and when I woke up, dressed, and went down for breakfast, I was surprised to see Cassie already in the kitchen making breakfast. I glanced into the dining room and saw Daddy at the table reading the morning paper. This morning, he looked as well put together as ever in his pin-stripe suit and tie, his hair as perfect as usual. There was no evidence in his face or demeanor that he had suffered a horrible night with Mother.

"Where's Mother?" I asked Cassie.

She continued to work, preparing some soft-boiled eggs the way Daddy liked them, all mashed up. She flitted about to get the toast, cream cheese, and coffee set up on a tray. Daddy liked his toast cut into perfect quarters, and she cut it as if she had a ruler in her head. Finally, she turned to me and grimaced.

"Mother's not feeling well this morning, Semantha. I'm getting Daddy his breakfast first because he has to get to the office, and then I'll look after Mother. Make your own breakfast. Squeeze your oranges for your juice. Also, I won't be going with you to school today, so you'll have to take the bus. Well? Get moving. Don't dilly-dally."

"Why aren't you going to school?"

She glanced at the open doorway to the dining room and drew closer to me.

"I'm staying home to look after her," she whispered. "Daddy can't miss work."

"Oh. Should I go up to see how she is?"

"She's still asleep, which is not surprising. Just

take care of your own needs for now, and behave yourself in school," she added, as though she were decades older than I was, not just two years. I started to say something to defend myself. I always behaved in school, and except for the one time I was reprimanded for talking too much to Darlene Gavin, I never was sent to the dean's office or assigned detention.

But the moment I opened my mouth, Cassie shot daggers from her eyes, and I snapped my mouth shut and went to squeeze my oranges. I watched how perfectly she continued to arrange Daddy's breakfast, with the eggs placed at twelve o'clock, the juice at three, and the coffee at nine. The plate of cream cheese was at six. It looked good enough to be a picture in a food magazine. She smiled at me and then took it out to him. I hurried to join him with my juice and cereal.

When he smiled and said, "Good morning," to me, I looked hard for some subtle message, but I didn't see anything like the suggestions of unhappiness with Mother that Cassie had described to me the night before.

"Mother's not feeling well?" I asked.

"Oh, just some typical pregnant woman stuff," he replied, not sounding at all concerned, and surely nowhere nearly as concerned as Cassie was. "I see here in the paper that your school's basketball team is contending for first place."

"Uh-huh."

"First time in nearly ten years. You and Cassie should go to the next game on Friday night, a home game. It's the big one, according to this article. It should be exciting. I was on my school's basketball team, you know. We went to the finals when I was a senior."

"I want to go," I said quickly.

Kent had asked me if I was going. He wanted to sit with me. I was afraid that if Cassie did go with me, however, she wouldn't let me sit with him.

"I'm not interested in the game," Cassie said, coming in quickly. "It's noisy and crowded and a waste of time."

Daddy shrugged and smiled at me. "Well, I guess not everyone's into sports."

"I'd like to go," I said.

"And how do you intend to go, Semantha? I'm not driving you," Cassie said, "and Daddy's certainly too busy to—"

"No, that's fine. I'll take her and pick her up," he offered.

Her face reddened. "You don't have to do that, Daddy," she said. "If she's so intent on going, I'll take her."

He continued to eat his breakfast. "Whatever you girls decide," he said. "What a beautiful breakfast! These eggs are perfect, Cassie. Just like your mother makes them."

Her hard, angry look softened into a smile.

Later, before I went out to walk to the corner to meet the school bus, Cassie popped out at me from the living room, where she was dusting and polishing furniture. She grabbed my arm and tugged me closer to her. Daddy had already left for work.

"How could you do that to Daddy at breakfast?" she asked.

"Do what?"

"Be so selfish. With all that's happening with Mother, how could you think only of yourself?"

"What did I do?"

"What did you do? Trying to get Daddy to take you to that stupid basketball game? He has no time to do those things now. What if Mother isn't any better by Friday?"

"He didn't think she was so sick, Cassie. I asked him, and—"

"I told you," she said, shaking my arm. "He would never tell you how worried he is. He'll always try to protect you from bad or sad things."

"He's the one who asked me about the game," I said, rubbing my arm where she had grabbed it. I was sure I had a black-and-blue mark, but if I mentioned it, she would only tell me that was proof I was so fragile. "He was urging me to go, urging us both to go."

"He was just being . . . nice. Being Daddy," she said. "And with all that's going on here, it's a wonder he can do that. He's so strong. Now you can see why he's so successful in business, and you can certainly see the differences between him and Uncle Perry, can't you?"

"Well, what should I do?" I asked.

"Nothing. It's too late to do anything. It doesn't matter. I'll take you, but I'm not staying there. If you can't arrange for a ride home, I'll have to go back to get you. Next time, think about others before you speak," she said, and returned to the living room.

"What about Mother? Did you bring her break-fast? Is she awake?" I called after her.

"Just go to school, Semantha," she replied from inside the living room. "If you miss the bus, you'll have to hitchhike or walk. I can't leave now to take you. I have too much to do here, because Mother is too sick to lift a finger. Don't forget. I predicted it. I predicted everything that's happening and will happen."

I looked back at the stairway. I should have gone to see Mother myself, but now I didn't have enough time. I had to hurry out and down the long driveway to get to the bus stop. Since Cassie had gotten her license and Daddy had bought her a car, we drove to school, but now that she wasn't going today, I had no choice but to take the bus. If I didn't get there before it arrived, the driver wouldn't look for me. He didn't expect me to be there waiting. I reached the corner just in time.

I sat with some of the girls from my class, and we got into so many conversations I began to regret having to go to school and back with Cassie. She hardly even spoke during the trip, and if she did, it was rarely about anything fun at school. It was usually just one of her many lectures on boys or behavior, lectures full of dire warnings. The way she spoke and described all the dangers and traps in the world, it was a wonder she ever left the house.

The girls were all eager to talk to me. They had lots of questions about my house and the depart-ment stores, but their real curiosity was about Kent Pearson and me. Everyone had seen us together in the hallways and at lunch. Almost all of them thought we were a perfect couple, but I could tell that one girl, Meg Stein, was jealous. That didn't bother me. If anything, it made me prouder.

Kent was very happy to hear that I would be at the basketball game on Friday. At lunch, he asked me if it might be possible for me to go to a party at Eddie Morris's house, another boy in our class who had gotten permission from his parents to have an after-game party.

"It's just until midnight, and my father will drive us there. I'm sure he would be happy to drive you home as well," he said.

I could just imagine how Cassie would react. I wanted very much to go, but I didn't know how I could manage it. It was very hard to lie to Cassie. She had eyes like X-rays, and, as she always said, my face was an open book. Anyway, it was hard to lie to someone you feared, whether he or she was good at seeing into your heart or not.

"I'm not sure," I said. "My mother is having a hard time with her pregnancy, and—"

"Your mother is pregnant?" he asked. It sounded as if he was asking if my mother had the plague. I simply nodded. "Wow. How come you never said anything?"

I shrugged. How could I tell him my sister forbade me to tell people, especially my schoolmates?

"Well, anyway, try to come," he urged, and I promised I would.

It was on my mind the rest of the day. I didn't think at all about Mother. Did that mean I was as selfish as Cassie accused me of being? She had me feeling guilty about so many things I was afraid to do more than tiptoe around her these days. Her whole personality seemed to have hardened ever since Daddy had announced Mother's pregnancy.

On the bus ride home, some of the other girls mentioned the after-game party and asked if I was going. I could see Meg Stein was hoping, maybe even praying, I would say no. That would give her an opportunity to steal Kent away from me.

"Of course," I said bravely. "Kent has already arranged our transportation."

Meg's face sank in like a heavy rock in quicksand. I sat back nervously, wondering how I would ever manage getting to this party.

Semantha Heavenstone, you have to develop the courage to stand up to your sister, I told myself. She shouldn't be able to boss me around like this. Just because socializing wasn't important to her didn't mean it couldn't be to me. She was fond of saying we were different. Okay, fine, so let it be that we were different.

As I walked home and then up the driveway, I kept firming up my courage, imagining how I would ask Daddy and Mother for their permission and then somehow avoid Cassie for two more days. Once she did find out, it would be just like her to find a reason she couldn't take me to the game, and then I would be stuck. *Semantha, if she does that, you'll ask Kent to have his father come by to pick you up,* I told myself defiantly. That would solve the problem. It would really enrage Cassie, but surely she would get over it. It was time I struck an independent note. Other girls my age had a great deal more freedom and wondered why I was still treated as if I were in elementary school.

I was so excited about my new courage that I didn't notice Daddy's car until I was practically upon it. Why was he home so early? Of course, my first thought was that something was wrong with Mother. I rushed into the house. Normally, I wasn't bothered by the quiet, the stillness, but right now, it felt ominous. I hurried up the stairway, but before I could turn to go to Mother's room, Cassie called to me. She had to have been standing there in the shadows like one of the Heavenstone ghosts, waiting for me.

"Why is Daddy home?" I asked.

She was standing with her back to the wall, her arms folded, and her head down. She didn't look up until I was right upon her.

"We had a little crisis here today, not long after you left for school, Semantha," she said.

"What crisis?"

"Mother began to bleed, hemorrhage. She said she was calling on the intercom for me, but I was in the shower, and I didn't hear her."

I stood waiting for more. She looked down the hallway toward Mother and Daddy's room and then added, "I found her on the floor with a towel between her legs, a bloody towel."

"Oh, my God! Is she all right? What about the baby?"

When she answered, she didn't look at me. She looked across the hallway and spoke as if she were reciting.

"Naturally, I helped her back to the bathroom,

and then I rushed to call Daddy. He called Dr. Moffet, who was here a little before Daddy arrived. Daddy was at our store site in Lexington. We're building one there, you know. It's absolutely the worst time for Daddy to be so burdened."

"Of course, I know we're building one there." How curious that she would think she had to tell me that, but she did look dazed. "I know how busy he is, Cassie, but Mother . . . what happened then?"

She turned back to me and quickly molded her face back into the adult face she always assumed around me.

"Daddy arrived, and we waited for Dr. Moffet to examine Mother. He said she was all right for now, but she has to remain in bed for at least forty-eight to seventy-two hours. She isn't to move, and he meant *move*. I have to bring her all her food, even a bed-pan. Daddy wanted to hire a nurse immediately, but I talked him out of it. I can get my schoolwork sent home. It's not a big deal."

"Maybe I should stay home, too, and help."

"Absolutely not. If you did that, it would make them both feel terrible. They would clearly see how disruptive this foolish pregnancy really is."

"Foolish?"

"Of course, foolish. What else can we call it, Semantha? She is simply too old, and her body is re-minding her of it. I don't understand what possessed them to decide to do this."

"But Dr. Moffet said it was all right, and you said Daddy . . . the Heavenstones needed a boy, needed someone to manage it all after Daddy retires."

"Yes, but," she added, looking toward Mother and Daddy's bedroom, "not with Mother now."

"What? What does that mean?"

She looked at me as if she'd just realized I had been standing there listening to her.

"Nothing. Except it means we're all in a crisis now for months and months, so don't cause anyone any more trouble or worry," she told me, then turned and started for the stairway.

"What trouble have I caused?"

"Do your homework," she muttered instead of answering, and descended the stairway.

I watched her for a moment and then went to Mother and Daddy's bedroom. I knocked on the open door and entered. Daddy was seated right beside the bed, holding Mother's hand. She was lying back on her pillow, her hair down, her eyes closed, and a cool cloth compress on her forehead.

"Oh, hi, Semantha. Come in, come in."

Mother opened her eyes and reached out for me. I hurried to take her hand.

"What happened?"

"A little incident," she said. "I'll be fine. I didn't lose the baby," she added.

"Just lucky Cassie was home," Daddy said. "Your mother wanted her to go to school and not bother," he added, giving her a look of chastisement.

"I could have stayed home, too," I said.

"There's no need for both of you to do that," Daddy said. "Cassie's quite capable of handling it all." He smiled. "So. Is there a lot of excitement about the basketball game Friday?"

"Very much. No one's talking about anything else."

"These are your best years, Semantha," Mother said. "Enjoy them, and don't dare worry yourself about me. It will all be fine, just fine."

"There's a rally the last period of the day on Friday. The whole student body will be brought down to the gym, and the coach will speak, and the cheerleaders will cheer."

"How exciting," Mother said. "Your father told me Cassie's taking you to the game."

I nodded. Was it terribly selfish of me to mention the party now, considering what had happened? Once again, my open-book face spoke for me.

"What is it, Semantha?" Mother asked. "Is something wrong at school?"

"Oh, no. It's nothing."

"It's something," she said.

Daddy nodded.

"It's just that I was asked to go to an after-game party," I said, trying to make it sound insignificant so neither she nor Daddy would think I was being self-centered.

"Where is this party?"

"At the home of a boy in our class, Eddie Morris. His father owns that big pharmacy."

"Oh, yes," Daddy said. "He's always in politics. Very respectable people."

"This boy I know, Kent Pearson, has asked me to go. He said his father would take us and take me home afterward, but it's not important now."

No one spoke for a moment, but they both

smiled at me. I looked toward the doorway, terrified that Cassie might have come back upstairs and overheard me.

"Well, it sounds fine," Mother said. "One thing is for sure. Of course it's important. I don't want anyone moping about and wringing her hands over me while she could be enjoying herself. That goes for both you and Cassie."

"I don't have to go," I said.

"Of course you do," Mother said. "If there's any problem, your father can pick you up as well. I don't want him thinking only of me," she added, now giving him a look of chastisement.

He laughed. "Okay, Semantha, it's settled. Now, why don't you do whatever you have to do before helping with dinner," Daddy said.

"Wipe that look of worry off your face, honey," Mother told me. "Everything's all right. Go on."

I leaned over to kiss her and then left them. I could feel the tugging emotions inside me, the battle between happiness and fear. It actually made me shiver a bit. I hurried to my room and tried to concentrate on my homework, but my eyes kept leaving the pages of my textbooks and looking with anticipation toward my bedroom doorway. Cassie never came, so I finally closed my books and went downstairs to help with dinner.

She had already done quite a bit. She had prepared a pot roast and potatoes, begun to steam some vegetables, and had the ingredients for our salads neatly arranged on the center worktable in the kitchen. Before I could say anything or ask anything, she turned to me and snapped, "Set the table for the three of us. Put my setting in Mother's place tonight."

"Mother's place?"

"Yes. I don't want Daddy looking at her empty chair all through dinner and feeling terrible. It will hurt his appetite, and I've prepared this pot roast exactly as he likes it. Don't just stand there gaping at me, Semantha. Get moving. It's almost dinnertime, and we'll eat on time, despite Mother."

I nodded and hurried to do what she asked. When I returned to the kitchen, I saw she had Mother's tray all ready to go up to her room.

"Should I take that up to Mother?"

"No," she said. "I will. Go dress for dinner."

"Dress?"

"Put something much nicer on, Semantha. I am. Let's do all we can to make Daddy happy tonight. He's had a terrible day because of her."

She lifted the tray and started out.

He's had a terrible day because of her? I thought. What about Mother's day? She was the one who had almost lost the baby, not Daddy.

I kept it all bottled up and walked behind her to get dressed for dinner. Daddy met her in the hallway outside his and Mother's bedroom.

"Cassie, how wonderful!" he cried. She handed him the tray.

"Your dinner will be ready on time, Daddy," she said. "Semantha and I will get dressed and be down in fifteen minutes."

"Thank you, Cassie. You are a terrific guardian angel," he said, and kissed her on the cheek.

She stood there looking after him until he went into the bedroom. I saw her bring her hand to her cheek and pause as if some king or even the president of the United States had just kissed her.

When she turned and saw that I had watched and heard everything, she pulled her shoulders back and lost her look of joy instantly.

"What are you doing dilly-dallying there, Samantha? I told you to get ready for dinner. Do I have to tell you everything twice?"

You're not my mother, I wanted to say, *so stop acting like it.*

But the words collapsed before they reached the tip of my tongue. I swallowed them back and hurried to my room. I looked through my closet. Almost any choice I started to make didn't look good enough. It was as if Cassie's eyes had somehow snuck into my head, and I was seeing everything the way she would see it. Finally, I decided on a dress I had worn to Daddy's birthday dinner last year. It still fit perfectly, which probably would have made any other girl in my class happy, but to me, it meant I had not grown very much or gained much weight. I was back to thinking about my fragility again. Was it all because I had been born prematurely? Was Cassie right as always?

I fixed my hair and put on a little lipstick. Daddy liked me to wear a little lipstick, but he didn't like much more makeup on our faces. Cassie wore lipstick, too, but she put it on so lightly it was often hard to see. I couldn't help being nervous about my appearance. I stepped out of my bedroom and walked downstairs gingerly. The moment I entered the kitchen, Cassie turned to inspect me. Incredibly, she was wearing the dress she had worn at Daddy's birthday, too, but she didn't think it wonderful that we had both thought to do the same thing. On the contrary, she looked upset.

"Why did you choose to wear that dress tonight?" she asked in an angry tone of voice.

"I thought it was my nicest, and you said—"

"You know Mother bought that for you and bought this for me just for Daddy's birthday dinner."

"Yes," I said, still confused about to why it would upset her. "And you're wearing yours."

She stared a moment. "Go back upstairs, and change into another dress," she said sharply.

"What?"

"Do you want Daddy to think we're both so happy Mother's too ill to be with us that we conspired and wore our nicest dresses? Have some sensitivity. Go on. I'll do your dinner chores. Go!"

I turned and hurried out. What was she talking about? How could this make us look insensitive? I was confused, but Cassie was so much smarter than I was and knew so much more. I had to listen to her and go by what she said. I changed into a more ordinary dress and returned to the kitchen. She already had done everything.

"That's better," she said, looking me over. "Now, just go in and sit," she ordered.

"But shouldn't I help you serve?"

"I have it all well organized, Semantha. Sit," she commanded, as if I were her pet dog.

I joined Daddy at the table. He smiled as soon as I sat.

"Look at how you both have taken charge when it's needed. It's a great lifting of the heavy burden from my shoulders to have two daughters like you and Cassie, Semantha. You both have the Heavenstone resourcefulness and sense of responsibility. We're going to be fine."

He turned as Cassie entered with the pot roast.

"Well, well, now, look at this. I smelled how wonderful it was when you brought it up to your mother."

She set it down and brightened with one of her best smiles for Daddy.

"And look at how beautifully dressed your sister is, Semantha. Isn't that the dress you wore to my birthday dinner?"

"Yes, it is, Daddy," she said, nodding at me.

"I don't deserve such a daughter. Thank you, Cassie. Your mother will be quite happy to know you're filling in so well for her."

Cassie looked as if she was simply too happy to speak. Finally, she managed, "It's not anything, Daddy."

"It is to me," he said. "Well, let's begin."

Cassie served him his pot roast and the vegetables. She poured him his glass of red wine, standing at his side and looking like a professional waitress. She even waited while he smelled it and sipped it, pretending he was in a restaurant.

"Perfect," he told her.

"Very good, Mr. Heavenstone," she said, and

Daddy laughed the way I remembered him laughing when he and Mother were much younger and still behaved like newlyweds.

Cassie sat in Mother's place. Daddy didn't seem to notice or care. He said a prayer that included wishes for Mother's and the new baby's health. Finally, we began to eat.

"So," Daddy said, nodding at me. "Your sister has been invited to her first party."

"What?" Cassie looked at me. "When?"

"After the big ball game. I know the people well. Very respectable," Daddy said, as if he thought she had to be the one to grant me permission.

"You're going to a party after the game?"

I nodded, almost too slightly to notice.

"How come you never told me?"

"It just happened."

She looked annoyed but then turned to Daddy and smiled. "Well, if you and Mother approve, I'll be happy to take her and pick her up."

"Apparently, all the transportation has been arranged to and from the party. You need only take her to the game, Cassie," Daddy said.

"It has?" She looked at me again. This time, the smile on her face was one of her masks. It was a smile that gave me the feeling there was no one under it. "Who's taking you?"

"Kent Pearson's father," I said.

She held the smile, but her eyes darkened.

"My two grown-up daughters," Daddy said. He lifted his wine glass. "Here's to you both."

Cassie continued to smile and look pleased, but

that didn't stop me from trembling inside. Afterward, I expected she would say something to me in the kitchen when we cleaned up, but she worked silently.

"You can go up," she told me. "Spend some time with Mother, but not too much. We aren't supposed to make her tired. Then go to your room and finish whatever you have to do for school." She looked down at the sink and not at me.

"Okay." I started to turn away.

"And then," she said, "I'll come talk to you."

"About what?" I asked.

"Sex," she said.

"Sex?"

"Apparently, I have to do it. It is something a mother is supposed to have done by the time a girl reaches your age."

How did she know our mother hadn't, even though that was true? What I knew came from other girls and from what I had learned in school and had read myself.

I was going to say something, to tell her it really wasn't necessary, I knew enough, but she looked away, and I thought retreat was much easier.

I always did.

Maybe that was why all that happened to me happened. Maybe I had no one to blame but myself.

3

The Talk

I LOOKED UP from my homework the moment I heard my door being opened. I was so full of nervous anticipation I had trouble concentrating on my assignments, anyway. I wasn't comfortable with the idea of Cassie teaching me about sex, but I couldn't help wondering if she knew something very important about it that I didn't know. After all, she seemed to know about anything and everything adults were supposed to know. What good was it for me to have a sister like her if I didn't appreciate her and take advantage of what she could offer me?

She slipped in as if she were sneaking into my room and closed the door very softly behind her.

"Did you go to see Mother?" she asked softly but not quite in a whisper.

"Yes. She kept closing her eyes, so I didn't stay long. She didn't eat all her dinner."

"I'm not surprised," she said, and sat on my bed. She gave me one of her small-eye studied looks as if I had already done something terrible. "Now I want you to be absolutely, completely truthful with me, Semantha. If you're not, it will only come back to haunt you, and by then, I might not be able to help you at all."

"Truthful about what?"

"What you've already done with boys, Kent Pearson in particular," she replied.

"I haven't done anything with boys. When could I have done anything?" I followed, because now she wore a skeptical expression.

"Don't try that sort of an excuse, Semantha. I know how girls your age behave nowadays, and believe me, boys can find the time and the place when they've a mind to. I know most girls go along, either because they don't want to be considered immature or because they let their own curiosity get the best of them. Do you know what willpower is?"

Girls my age? I thought. She's only two years older than I am, but, just like always, she makes it sound like two decades.

"Willpower? I think so."

"In this case, it means having the strength to resist not only the boy but yourself, Semantha."

"Myself?" I shook my head. "How—"

"Don't sit there and tell me you haven't had sexual thoughts and haven't touched yourself and discovered . . . pleasure."

I felt the blood rush up my neck. Had she been spying on me?

She smiled. "It's okay," she said. "It's natural to a point. If Mother had done her mother job, you'd know all this by now, but I can see you don't. I'm not surprised. She never did her job with me, either."

"Then how did you learn all this, Cassie?" I asked.

"Never mind how I learned. It's how *you* learn that matters now, so pay attention." She stood up.

She paced for a moment silently, as if she had to be sure she used the right words. When she spoke, she didn't look at me at first. It made me feel as if I were in a classroom.

"Our bodies are built to make and carry babies and then deliver them whole and healthy into this world. It's natural to our female selves. Our bodies don't care how young we are. When all of our hormones and development are aligned, it's as if some switch were turned on. In fact, there are some girls who get so mature so early that they have big psychological problems."

She paused and looked at me.

"Remember that girl I pointed out to you, Donna Wellington, the girl in the fourth grade with breasts as developed as a girl in eleventh or twelfth grade? Remember? We saw her on the playground, and she looked so out of place."

"Yes."

"Can you imagine what's been happening to her? She's probably terrified of herself. In a sense, we should all be a little terrified of ourselves, because, as I said, our bodies don't think about consequences. We're little baby-making machines, that's all."

"You make it sound as if we're all two different people fighting with each other."

"We are," she said, spinning on me. "That's the point, Semantha. There's you in your developing body, and there's you in your mind, which doesn't always keep up. You already know where to touch yourself to feel the excitement, right? Right?" she asked again sharply, stepping toward me.

"Yes," I said. She looked as if she would pounce on me if I hesitated one second.

She nodded and sat on the bed again. "Now, I'm sure you've been lying here," she said, her voice growing softer as she ran her hand over my bed, "dreaming of what it would be like to have Kent Pearson touch you in those places."

I started to shake my head.

"Don't!" she snapped. "Don't be dishonest with me, Semantha. Not for a second, not an instant. Tell me the truth right now. You have, haven't you? Well?"

I took a deep breath. Despite my age, my youth, I still felt there were things that should be private and only mine. She was reaching so deep down inside me, reaching to explore places I hadn't explored myself. She was crawling into my fantasies, my dreams. Even the closest of sisters, brothers, even husbands and wives, can't possibly share all that.

"You don't have be ashamed with me, Semantha. I'm your sister, your only really faithful companion. No one will care for you as much as I do. Being sisters, we can share the most intimate things, and now that you're obviously at the age when you will have more intimate things to share and explore, I'll be here for you. So, admit it. Am I correct about your thoughts concerning Kent Pearson? Well?"

"Yes," I said, barely above a whisper.

She nodded, smiling with satisfaction. "That's good, Semantha. It's good that you trust me. You know I trust you, because I've told you things I wouldn't tell Mother. I knew you wouldn't go running to her to tell on me, either. You're my best friend in the world." .

That took me by surprise. Of course, I knew she had no real friends. She talked to other girls about schoolwork and did hang around with some girls at school, girls I thought no one really wanted to have as friends, but I never dreamed she would tell me that I was her best friend. Sisters didn't have to be best friends. I knew many other girls and boys, for that matter, who wouldn't consider their sisters and brothers best friends. Most were always complaining about them.

"Now, then," she continued, returning to her mother demeanor, "since you've already fantasized, imagined Kent touching you in places that would get you excited, the danger of your actually permitting him to do so is that much greater. It might even seem as if you're still dreaming, and don't forget that there is that terrific curiosity in you, that thing about your body I described, its craving, as I put it."

"Craving?"

"It craves to be touched, to be riled up and brought to that point where it can welcome more. It's the *more* that's most dangerous."

"Oh. I know about how we get pregnant and all that, Cassie."

"You know nothing," she said sharply. "You've never been fondled, kissed passionately, touched, and driven toward an orgasm. Yes, you've read about it in your textbooks or those silly romance novels on your shelves there. My God, *The Taste of Love, The Deepest Kiss, Under My Secret Heart?* Give me a break. None of those books will tell you the absolute truth, help you to understand yourself."

"What is the absolute truth?" I asked.

"Simply this, Semantha. No matter how nice Kent Pearson is to you or any boy is or will be, he wants only one thing: to satisfy his own need."

I nodded. Should I tell her what Gloria Benson had told me about herself and Donald Marcus, how they had agreed not to do it but she satisfied him a different way? It had shocked me when I first heard it, and despite what Cassie had just said about us being best friends, I couldn't get myself to share it with her and describe it.

"So," she said, "you can go to the party with Kent. I'm sure he'll try to get you to go to a private place in the house, and then he'll kiss you and touch you and try to get you to let him insert himself inside you, and if you're not careful and if you don't have the willpower to resist, you could be very, very sorry. It could ruin your whole life!"

I shook my head. "Don't worry, Cassie. I'm not going to do that."

"You say you won't, but when you're there in the darkness, alone with him whispering all sorts of things in your ear and touching you, and you're thinking about your fantasies . . . it could happen. I won't be there to protect you. No one will."

"It won't happen," I repeated more firmly. "Don't worry."

"Because you can ruin yourself for more

important things, Semantha," she continued, as if I hadn't spoken. "You're a Heavenstone. You have a major obligation to our family, our heritage, to all Daddy has been building for our family."

I nodded, but I wanted to ask her why she didn't think of her own obligation, too. She told me before I could ask.

"Just as I do," she said. "Why do you think it is that I'm so particular about whom I see? I have control of myself, and I want you to have control of yourself. Do you understand me? Do you understand the things I've told you?"

"Yes, Cassie."

She pulled herself back and tucked in the corners of her mouth as she looked at me. "I wouldn't have to do this if our mother had done her job with you," she said again.

"She's done her job. She's told me about sexual things, Cassie," I said.

Her eyes grew colder, darker, as her cheeks sank. She turned in her lips so tightly that little white lines ran above her top lip and below her bottom lip. "Mother told you? What sexual things?"

"Things. When I got my first period, she spoke to me about what was changing in my body and what I had to think about and what not to worry about."

She relaxed again. "I'm sure. That's Mother. Always looking for things not to worry about, instead of facing the things that we should worry about. Did she tell you what not to do with boys? Well? Did she? Because, as I said, she never did with me."

"Not exactly," I said. She had suggested some of

it, but I didn't want to tell her that or say anything that might make her jealous. "Not the way you just told me."

Her face softened even more, and she smiled.

"Of course not. Anyway, I want you to come right to see me when you return from the party Friday night. You come to my room, no matter how late it is, understand? And you tell me exactly what you did, what he did, what happened between you. You've got to trust me, trust and believe that I will help you. Okay? Will you do that?"

I nodded, but I couldn't help the way my forehead folded as I imagined telling her every nitty-gritty detail of what went on with Kent.

"I don't want you to be unhappy, Semantha, and I don't want to stop you from having fun. I care about you, about us, about our family, that's all. All right?"

"Yes," I said.

"Good."

She stood up and looked at me for a long moment, so long that it made me nervous.

"You're prettier than I am, Semantha, so all of this is more important for you than it is for me."

I started to shake my head. I had always believed I was, but I never wanted to say it or have anyone else say it in front of us.

She smiled. "I'm not jealous or unhappy about that. We're two different people. You have your good qualities, and I have mine. Some girls, pretty girls like you, have to depend more on their looks than anything else. That's fine for them. The only problem with depending on your looks is the problem of age. Looks degenerate, change, like a lightbulb dimming and dimming and dimming, until it goes out completely.

"But don't worry. You'll always have me beside you, helping you, caring for you. I'll be even more loyal to you than the man you eventually marry," she added, and then she did something she rarely did.

She hugged me and kissed me on the forehead, just the way Mother always did.

"Good night," she whispered, and left, closing the door softly behind her.

I didn't know why, but I was trembling. She had left me with words that should have made me happy, but they didn't. And even worse, whenever I had a thought about Kent, about the things she described, I immediately felt terribly guilty. I would have gone to sleep dreaming of sitting next to Kent at the game and then going to the party with him. I would have imagined us dancing, everything, but the moment one of those thoughts came into my mind, I did everything I could to chase it away. I even imagined Cassie next to me as I slept, just waiting for a fantasy to come into my brain. As soon as it did, she would nudge me to make it leave.

I would have been nervous when Friday came, anyway, but after Cassie's little mother-daughter-like talk, I was practically trembling all day. She made sure to put reminders in my head, too. On our way to school, she said, "I hope everything I told you is still fresh in your mind. I know how easy it is to forget when you get excited."

"I won't forget," I said.

"Good." She smiled at me. "We'll be perfect, as perfect as I planned for us to be. Remember, we are the Heavenstone sisters. That means a lot around here. I can almost hear people thinking it whenever they see us together. 'There they go, the Heavenstone sisters.'"

She laughed. She seemed to be in one of the best moods I had seen her in since the night Daddy announced Mother's pregnancy. Mother had gotten strong enough to look after herself. She didn't want Cassie to miss any more school. Daddy said he would hire a nurse if we had to, but Mother insisted she was fine, and Cassie agreed.

"I'll be coming right home from school, anyway, Daddy," she told him. "No need to bring a stranger into the house. I can do whatever has to be done."

"Well, I don't doubt that," Daddy said. "I can't think of too many women who are as reliable as you, Cassie."

Cassie beamed. That helped put her in the good mood, I thought.

We entered the school building together. Because she was two grades higher than I was, Cassie and I rarely saw each other in the building, even at lunch, because there were two lunch rooms, one for students in grades seven through nine and one for tenth through twelfth. I don't know if it had been designed to be that way or just turned out that way. Rarely did she come looking for me, but this particular lunch period, I looked up from my tray of food and saw her in the doorway, obviously searching for me. I was sitting with Kent, two other boys, and two other girls. The moment I saw Cassie, I felt my face flush, as if I had been caught doing just the things she had warned me against.

"What's wrong?" Kent asked, seeing how I had stopped eating and listening to everyone.

"My sister's looking for me. I'd better see what she wants," I said.

I rose because I saw she had spotted me and was heading in my direction. I didn't want anyone else to hear what she might say. She paused when she saw me heading for her.

"Something wrong with Mother?" I asked quickly.

"No." She looked past me at my table. "Do you have lunch with him every day now?"

"Sometimes," I said. I really did, but one day he had missed lunch.

She leaned toward me to whisper. "Listen carefully to the way his friends talk. It will tell you a lot about him. If they make sexual references in your company, and he lets them, that will tell you something important about him and how much he really respects you. Understand?"

I nodded. Had she come here just to tell me this? It made me feel as if the relationship between girls and boys was really just some game, some contest, and she was assuming the role of my coach. In a real sense, I realized that she was.

"Same with the other girls in your company," she said, still looking past me at my friends. "If they giggle or don't seem embarrassed, you know they've been promiscuous. You remember what that means?"

"Yes, Cassie. Don't worry so much."

She pulled her face back. "Don't tell me not to worry so much. What happens to you happens to me. I thought you understood."

"I do. I'm just . . . it's all right. I'm being careful."

"Um," she said, looking past me again at the boys and girls at my table, as if they were all part of some gang doing sex and drugs. I felt like bursting into tears. She was embarrassing me. I could see other students starting to pay attention to us. "Okay, we'll talk later." She turned and walked out.

I stood for a moment, trying to catch my breath and calm down. On the way back to the table, I fumbled for an explanation. They were all surely going to be curious.

"Anything wrong?" Kent asked immediately.

"My mother had a little setback a few days ago, and my sister stopped in to tell me she had gone to the doctor and all was well," I rattled off. I started to eat again to make it seem like nothing.

It worked for a while. My girlfriend Bobbi talked about life with a much younger brother, and Kent's friend Noel described what it was like for him to have a much older brother. Then Kent said, "Your sister's pretty tough. My brother Brody says most of the boys in her class and his are afraid of her. But she's the smartest kid in her class, so maybe she knows something the others don't." Everyone laughed.

Noel changed the conversation, and we didn't talk about Cassie anymore. On the way back to class, Kent repeated how much he was looking forward to seeing the game with me. "And afterward," he added with a smile that a few days ago, I would have welcomed, would have warmed my heart, but today put little butterflies in my stomach. I only nodded and went into the classroom quickly, feeling terrible that I hadn't seemed more enthusiastic. I tried giving him a warm smile, but I could see he was concerned.

The moment I got into the car with Cassie at the end of the day, she began her cross-examination.

"So tell me," she said, "was I right? Did you hear and see what I anticipated?"

"No," I said, and then I thought I would get her off the topic quickly by telling her the things Noel and Bobbi had said about having big differences in ages between themselves and their brothers and sisters. It worked, because it got Cassie back to one of her favorite topics: The Foolish Pregnancy.

"People live as if they'll live forever, be young forever. They don't plan their lives intelligently. Everything was going just fine in our family."

She ranted and raved about it all the way home. I didn't have to say anything. Then she surprised me by telling me not to worry about my after-dinner chores tonight.

"Just get yourself ready to go to the game and your party. I'll take care of everything after I bring you to the school."

"Thank you, Cassie."

She seized my arm as I started to get out of the

car. "You know I only want what's best for you, Semantha, because what's best for you is best for me and for the Heavenstones."

"I know, Cassie. Thank you," I said.

She held on to me a moment, as if she could read my inner thoughts through my arm to see if I was being honest. I didn't doubt she could. Finally, she smiled and let me go. I got out quickly and hurried in, first to see how Mother was and then to go to my room to choose what I would wear. I found Mother in the kitchen, up and about and preparing dinner. Cassie came flying in behind me.

"What are you doing?" she cried. "You know you shouldn't be on your feet this long, Mother. I told you I would prepare dinner tonight. I can do those veal chops just the way Daddy likes them."

"Oh, I felt a lot better, Cassie. I've been putting too much on you. I know you have your own work to do," Mother said, smiling. She did look a lot stronger.

Cassie seemed to deflate with disappointment. "You're disobeying the doctor's orders," she said. "Daddy will be mad at me."

"Oh, no, he won't, honey. He's been here twice today checking up on me," she said.

"Twice? How can he do that and be overseeing the new store in Lexington?" Cassie asked, as if she were Daddy's boss and disapproved. "This is taking him away from important work." That wiped the smile off Mother's face so quickly it was as if she had dipped her head into the path of a raging tornado.

"Don't worry," Mother said. "He said he had to spend his day at the local office today."

Suddenly, she looked as if she had lost her renewed energy, and she put her hand out to brace herself on the counter.

"Mother, are you all right?" I asked.

"I'm fine," she said.

"No, you're not. I can finish here, Mother," Cassie said, throwing her books down onto the table. "You just go back upstairs and rest. Go on. Do it!" She was so gruff that Mother recoiled. Cassie smiled quickly. "Daddy will be relieved to know you didn't overdo it, and this way, you can enjoy dinner with us later." She sounded as if she were talking to a child.

"Maybe you're right," Mother said.

She described what she had done and what was left to do. Cassie whipped the apron off the closet door and practically charged at the food.

Mother smiled at me. "I'll go up with you, Semantha. You can tell me all about tonight, the game, the party."

I took her arm, and we left the kitchen.

"Your sister is such a workhorse. She's a wonder. I'm so lucky to have a daughter like her. And like you," she added quickly. "Two beautiful young women. As your uncle Perry says, the infamous Heavenstone sisters, although I wouldn't say infamous. I'd say fabulous."

She leaned over to kiss my cheek, and we walked up the stairs together to her room. All the while, I was boiling with the thought that I should tell her about the conversation I'd had with Cassie about boys and sex. Something inside me told me she should be made aware of it all, but something else, something stronger, warned me of how Cassie would react once she found out. To her, it would be a betrayal of the special relationship she believed we had. She had talked so much about trust and how we kept things between us, kept them even from our parents. It would be devastating to her if I told Mother about it all now. Maybe later, I thought. Maybe I would tell her after it was all over.

I helped her get back into bed.

"This is good. I should rest. Your sister is such a realist. She always makes me look past the dreams and the fluff to see the truth. Maybe she'll become a doctor. She's not afraid to tell anyone what she believes. That's the self-confidence I described. She's a strength in this family, Semantha. You should rely on her as much as you can."

"I rely on you, too, Mother."

"Of course, but sisters have a special bond. I always wished I had had a sister. You can confide in each other and share so much. Especially about boys," she added, smiling.

I was about to say, *But Cassie has never had a boyfriend*. The first words were forming. I would tell her everything now—but before I could speak, she closed her eyes.

"Okay," she said. "I'll just take a little rest before dinner. Go on and do what you have to. I know you want to prepare for the game and the party. I'm fine," she said. She looked as if she fell asleep instantly. I stood there a moment, and then I left, closing the door softly behind me.

I ended up choosing one of the outfits Uncle Perry had designed last year. It was a silver metallic minidress with a pair of ankle-length black leggings and black platform shoes. Cassie hated the outfit, but even Daddy said I looked terrific in it, and he usually didn't go overboard when it came to giving Uncle Perry's designs compliments. I had had little opportunity to wear it before this.

Because of the time factor, I had to wear it down to dinner. There was no time to prepare and change afterward. Fortunately, Daddy saw me before Cassie did. He lavished compliments on me immediately. When I looked at Cassie, I could see she was full of disapproval, but Daddy's comments blocked any criticism she could express. When Mother came down, she, too, expressed delight with my appearance.

"You look so grown-up, honey," she said.

Cassie was as quiet at dinner as I had ever seen her. As soon as we were finished eating, she practically leaped up to declare that we had to leave immediately to get me to the game before it began and get herself back to clean up. Daddy once again suggested that Cassie go, too. He even said he would handle the dinner cleanup, but Cassie again refused and expressed her disinterest.

"I have more important things to do, Daddy," she said. No one dared ask what was more important.

As soon as we got into the car, Cassie let me know her opinion of my outfit. "You might as well wear a sign around your neck," she said, "a sign that says 'I'm looking for trouble.'"

"Why? Mother thought it was nice, and Daddy loved it."

"Of course, Daddy loved it. He's a man, too."

"What do you mean, Cassie? He's my father, our father."

She looked at me and shook her head. "A man is always a man first, whether he is a father, a brother, or an uncle. Don't think I'm oblivious to the way Daddy looks at me, too," she added.

I felt a cold, electric sizzle around my heart. What was she saying? The way he looks at her too? She glanced at me and saw the look on my face and certainly, as always, read my thoughts and feelings.

"Don't look so worried. It's all only natural. Remember what I told you about willpower? Well, it certainly applies to men as well as to women, Semantha. A father, brother, or uncle has to depend on it as well, and most of them are usually successful. Of course, most of them don't have attractive and competent, mature daughters, sisters, and nieces to tempt them."

We pulled into the school parking lot. It was jammed with cars. She stopped near the entrance. I opened the door slowly, still confused by all that she had just said.

"Now, go have a good time," she told me, "but remember, you're a Heavenstone."

"Thanks, Cassie."

She leaned over to hold the door open so she could call out to me as I walked toward the gym.

"We're sisters, Semantha. What happens to you happens to me!" she cried.

I didn't turn around. I kept walking, even though I didn't feel my feet hitting the ground.

A cheer bursting from the overflowing crowd washed it all away as I opened the door and began what I hoped was to be an exciting night.

4

The Game

THE MOMENT I entered the gym, I saw Kent waving madly from the stands. Although the crowd was beyond capacity, with throngs of adults and students rushing in to grab whatever seats remained, he had obviously been watching and waiting eagerly for me. The roars of the crowd were already loud enough to drown out your thoughts. It was impossible not to be immediately lifted into the excitement.

I saw that Meg Stein had somehow wangled a seat just behind him and was leaning over to whisper in his ear. She pulled back as soon as he spotted me. The cheerleaders came out, and the fans on our side began to chant along with them as I made my way up to the row and squeezed in between Noel and Kent. I glanced at Meg, who looked pretty unhappy that I had shown up. I deliberately smiled at her to force her to smile back.

"Wow, you look great," Kent said.

"Thank you."

"My father will be waiting for us outside after the game. Eddie has about thirty coming to his party. His parents paid for all the pizzas, and Dustin

Dylan has already set up his DJ equipment in the house."

I nodded. It was exciting to me. It would be the first real party I had been to without adults looking over our shoulders, but I couldn't shake off the feeling that Cassie was looking over mine. Even here, even in the gym, the feeling was so strong, in fact, that I actually looked for her somewhere in the crowd. What if she had lied to me and remained for a while to watch me? However, the moment our team took the court, all those feelings flew away. The anticipation was too great, and I was determined to have a good time.

I hadn't attended many basketball games, but this was the most nerve-wracking I had seen. The lead kept bouncing from our opponent to us right up until the middle of the fourth quarter, when our team seemed to get a surge of new energy and pulled ahead by nearly eight points. When the final buzzer rang, we had won by three, and the cheers threatened to lift the ceiling off the gymnasium. Everyone was hugging and kissing. Kent embraced me and kissed me full on the mouth, and then he and Noel hugged. I stood there dazed for a moment. When I turned to Megan to hug her, too, she looked as if she would burst into tears. I just smiled at her.

"Wasn't that great?"

"Yes. Have a good time," she muttered, and rushed down the stands to leave. The kiss had apparently convinced her that she had no chance to steal Kent away.

But I thought the kiss had been so quick and so short that it almost didn't seem to have happened.

Kent was certainly not fazed by it. Exhilarated, he grabbed my hand. "C'mon. This is going to be a real celebration," he said, and we made our way into the wave of students rushing out to celebrate the school's victory. He was frustrated by how long it took us to exit.

"Take it easy. We'll get there," I wanted to say, but I didn't want to appear any less enthusiastic.

Out in the parking lot, it felt like New Year's Eve, Christmas, and all my birthdays wrapped up into one night. People were honking their horns and shouting. They were still hugging and congratulating each other, as if they had somehow been responsible for the victory. Afraid to miss something, everyone was rushing about in all directions. Some actually looked dazed.

"There's my father!" Kent cried. He led me to a black sedan. He opened the rear door for me, and I got in quickly.

"Well, I guess I don't have to ask what happened," Kent's father said. "Look at this place. You'd think we had won the NBA championship or something."

"It was a terrific game, Dad."

"I imagine so. Hello there," he said, turning to me. In the vague light, I could see that he was a tall, thin man with dark brown hair. Kent was also tall, but he had a fuller, rounder face and lighter hair.

"Hello, Mr. Pearson. Thank you for taking us to the party."

"You're quite welcome. I don't know whether Kent's been talking more about the game and the party or more about you," he teased.

"Dad!"

"Okay. I'll shut up and be a chauffeur." He turned around.

"You know how to get to Eddie's house, Dad?"

"Your mother and I have been there a number of times, Kent. Don't worry."

Kent shrugged and smiled at me, and then he reached for my hand. "Wasn't that great?"

"It was the best game I ever saw," I said.

"We weren't favored to win, you know." He took a deep breath and sat back. "You haven't been to Eddie's house before, have you?"

"No. My parents might have."

"They have," Mr. Pearson said. "At a fund-raiser. Oops, I forgot. Chauffeurs aren't supposed to listen to their passengers' conversations."

"Very funny, Dad."

I laughed. I was glad Mr. Pearson had a sense of humor. I had been afraid I would be very nervous being driven to a party by Kent's father. I had never met him, and I couldn't help but imagine he was wondering what sort of girl his son had chosen. If Cassie had overheard my thoughts, she would surely have bawled me out for not thinking he should be honored to have a Heavenstone in his car. But despite our family's success and our obvious great wealth, I couldn't sit high on that pedestal Cassie imagined. If anything really made me nervous, it was people thinking that I thought I was too good for them.

The ride wasn't long, and when we turned down the street on which the Morrises lived and Mr. Pearson pointed out the house, I could see that Eddie

Morris's home wasn't as grand as ours. Cassie would say it had no history. Not that it wasn't an impressive home—it was a large, recently built three-story set on the crest of a little knoll and surrounded by at least four or five acres of gently rolling hills.

"Here's a druggist who owns property any horse owner would covet," Kent's father said.

"They have horses, Dad."

"Not racehorses," his father said, winding up the long, tree-lined driveway to stop in front of the house. It had a beautiful entry, approached through elaborate landscaping. "I pick you up at midnight?"

"As long as the car doesn't turn into a pumpkin," Kent said, and his father laughed.

"Never mind, Cinderfella. You behave yourself. We've had our talk about—"

"Dad, please."

"Okay. You're on your own. If you want me here earlier because you are bored . . ."

"I doubt that, Dad."

"Have a good time," his father said. "Make sure he behaves, Semantha."

Kent shook his head and got out to hurry around and open the door for me.

"Oh, sorry. I forgot to be a chauffeur again," his father called.

Other cars were arriving, some approaching too fast. His father looked at them, and for a moment, both Kent and I wondered if he was going to get out to bawl out the drivers, but he just started away. Kent released the breath he had been holding. He didn't want his father embarrassing him.

"C'mon," Kent said, taking my hand. I had to run to keep up with him.

Eddie Morris greeted us. He was the star of the junior varsity basketball team and would surely be on the varsity next year. He was a six-foot-four ninth-grader with a shock of coal-black hair that he liked to keep long. It was the source of lots of humor, because he was always brushing it off his face. During basketball games, he kept it tied behind his head in a thick ponytail. I didn't know him all that well, but he was always polite and friendly whenever we did speak in school. He had a younger sister, Amy, in elementary school, who had apparently been shipped to her cousin's house for the night.

"Hi, Semantha. Welcome. How did this goofball get you to be his date?" Eddie asked. He and Kent playfully punched each other's shoulders. "The pizza's already been delivered. You guys should get some before it's all gone."

Others were coming in behind us, and he went to greet them as well. The music blaring from the living room was so loud everyone had to shout to be heard, even if he or she was only a few feet from the other person. I was surprised to see a number of students from tenth and eleventh grade, as well as a dozen or so from our class.

"I'm starving," Kent said. He led me right to the kitchen, where the open boxes were spread on the long white-tile counters and the tiled butcher's table in the center. There were paper plates and plastic forks, but everyone was mostly just holding a piece and gobbling it down as if he had been on some deserted island for months. I saw plenty of soda, but it wasn't until we went into the living room, where Dustin Dylan had set up his disco equipment, that I saw anyone drinking liquor. It was the older boys, who slipped it into their sodas and then offered it to the girls they had brought. I didn't see anyone turn it down.

"Remember, no smoking," Eddie warned his guests. "Of anything!" Everyone who heard him laughed, but he made his next warning very seriously. "And don't forget. My father's a pharmacist, so there's no drugs."

Noel and Bobbi had somehow beaten us to the house and were already dancing. Kent and I had a piece of pizza and drank some soda, and then we joined them. I wasn't very confident of my dancing. I had done so little in front of other people. Of course, I practiced in my room at home whenever I could. Cassie always teased me about it. I never saw her dance, even at weddings we all attended, unless Daddy asked her. Those were only slow dances, however.

Kent was a good dancer, and he kept complimenting me on my dancing. As my confidence built, I felt myself relaxing more. I had left Cassie's warnings back at the gymnasium, and for the first time, I felt I could enjoy myself. Here I didn't have to keep remembering that I was a Heavenstone. No one seemed to care who anyone was, least of all Kent. His friends kept kidding him about having to have his father drive him on a date.

"At least he made a great choice," Noel said, coming to his defense. He winked at me.

"Yeah, well, what's he going to do, ask his father to take them behind the football field later?" Sammy Duncan asked.

"As long as he doesn't turn around to look, it's all right," Kent fired back.

It made me blush. Bobbi grabbed my arm, and we went off to the bathroom together to talk.

"Don't listen to those idiots," she told me. Then she smiled and said, "Noel says Kent is head over heels in love with you. He's going to ask you to go steady with him. Nothing as corny as giving you a school ring or something, but, you know, promise to be only with each other. What will you do?"

"I don't know." I really didn't, but she mistook my hesitation for something more.

"That's good. Play hard to get. Boys say they hate it, but they really don't. It makes you more . . . more of a catch when you do give in."

"My sister says it's not good to move too quickly with any boy."

"She's right. Though who am I to agree? I lost my brake pads a while ago."

I suspected what she meant, and I suppose the look on my face caused her to laugh. After she repaired her lipstick, we returned to the living room and the dancing.

"I hope none of that joking bothered you," Kent said.

"No, of course not," I said as strongly as I could. I didn't want him or anyone to think I was so dainty. I had enough of that with Cassie constantly reminding me how fragile I was. I knew almost everyone thought I was overprotected because we were so wealthy. I suppose we were. I wouldn't doubt that I was the most innocent and unsophisticated of all the girls in my class.

An hour or so into the party, one of the varsity basketball players, Martin McDermott, arrived, and that created a new wave of excitement. He started to describe the game from the team's perspective, and the music was turned down. Everyone listened, and then Martin, who was treated like a returning war hero by everyone, especially Eddie, started to dance with one of the girls from the eleventh grade who had already consumed a lot of alcohol.

We could see how all those who had started slipping liquor into their sodas were acting a bit wilder. The dance floor became more and more crowded, and the music got even louder.

"There are definitely more than thirty people here now!" Kent shouted.

"I know!" I shouted back. My throat started to ache from shouting to be heard.

"This is a wild party!" Kent said.

"Yes."

We tried to keep dancing, but everyone was beginning to bump into everyone else, especially the girls who had drunk too much liquor.

"Let's take a little walk," Kent said to me when someone had offered him liquor to mix into his soda and he refused. "It might get ugly here soon. I've been drunk only once in my life." He led me away quickly. "And it wasn't pretty. I think I threw up my insides and had to grow new organs."

"I've only had a little wine," I admitted. I didn't want to sound so protected, but he was being truthful, so I thought I should be.

He looked at his watch. "My father will be here in less than an hour," he said. "C'mon." He tugged me along faster.

"Where are we going? How do you know where to go?"

"I've been to Eddie's house many times. We've been friends since fourth grade. Let's go look at his horses. We ride them sometimes."

He led me through the kitchen to a back entrance. We went down a small stairway and turned right to the barn. Even this far away from the living room, we could hear the music and the laughter. We heard what sounded like something falling, too.

"Eddie's parents will kill him if anyone breaks anything," Kent said.

He opened the barn door and flipped a light switch to give us more illumination. The two horses in their stalls turned with interest.

"He calls this one Chesterfield, and the other is Comet. Chesterfield was his grandfather's name," Kent explained.

"They're both beautiful."

"American quarter horses. Well trained, too. I'm not much of a rider, but on Chesterfield, I look like a real cowboy."

He walked down to a little area toward the rear of the barn, where there was equipment, saddles, and a small, well-worn leather sofa. He sat and looked up at me.

"I'm really glad you came with me," he said. "I've had a crush on you for a long time, but I was always too afraid to talk to you. Until just recently, that is."

"Why?" I asked, prepared to hear about the grand Heavenstone name or something.

"I didn't want to be embarrassed if you didn't like me. I was a coward!" He laughed. "C'mon." He patted the sofa. "Sit for a little while, and then we'll go back to the party and watch everyone make fools of themselves."

I looked at the horses. They were both watching us with what looked like real interest. When I didn't move fast enough, Kent rose a little, leaned forward, and took my hand, tugging me to the sofa. I sat beside him.

"I was honest about myself, so how about you, Semantha? Have you been with other boys, boys maybe from other schools?"

"No."

"I'm surprised you don't attend a private school. Everyone is surprised about that, actually."

"My sister, Cassie, wanted us to, but my mother was against it. My father never went to a private school. I like our school."

"Yeah, me, too. Are you shy, too?"

"I guess so," I said.

"Let's find out."

He leaned toward me to kiss me, and I pulled back.

"You didn't complain when I kissed you at the game," he said.

"I'm not complaining," I said.

He smiled and moved faster this time to bring his lips to mine. It was a long kiss.

"You're the prettiest girl in our class, Semantha," he whispered. "Maybe even in the whole school."

I started to shake my head. He kissed me again. I knew he expected me to kiss him back as hard and as long as he was kissing me, but when his lips touched mine, I didn't do that. I couldn't help it. When I closed my eyes, all I could see was Cassie's disapproving face.

"Don't you like me?" he asked, obviously disappointed in my reaction.

"Yes."

"You don't act like it," he said.

"I'm a little nervous, Kent."

"Sure. Me, too," he said. "But you can't let that stop you from having a good time, right?"

"I don't know."

"I do," he said. He kissed me on the neck and brought his hands up the sides of my arms to put them behind my back and pull me closer to him so we could kiss again. This time, I really tried, and he liked it. "Semantha," he said. "Semantha. You have the nicest name, too."

I was beginning to wonder if he was as shy as he claimed to be. In one of the romance novels I read, the novels Cassie mocked, there was a man who pretended to be shy and awkward, and that way, he always managed to get the girl he wanted to be more cooperative.

"I'm glad you're as shy as me," he said as if he

could read my thoughts as easily as Cassie could. "That way, we'll both help each other, discover each other. You want us to do that, right?"

Before I could respond, his hands came around my shoulders and quickly slipped over my breasts. When he pressed his palms to my nipples, the tingle shot through me with electric speed. As if she was part of the lightning, Cassie's face flashed in front of me.

Instantly, I jumped up.

"What's wrong?"

"We'd better return to the party. Your father will be here soon."

"Not that soon. Don't you want to be alone for a while?" he asked, his voice full of disappointment. "I thought you'd want to be alone with me, and that was why you agreed to come with me."

"It's getting late. I think we'd better return to the party."

He looked at me with confusion. "Why are you getting so upset? All I did—"

"Let's just go back, Kent. Please."

He smirked, looked down a moment, and then stood up. "Yeah, let's just go back," he said, and walked quickly toward the door. I had to hurry to keep up with him, and he was silent all the way back into the house.

The party did seem to be getting more raucous. Someone had talked Eddie into spiking his soda, too, and he looked dazed and unaffected by the way the older students were banging into the furniture and spilling drinks. The kitchen looked as if it had been hit by a hurricane—the plastic forks on the floor as well as the counters, the garbage can overflowing, half-eaten pieces of pizza on the counters and even one smashed into the tile.

"Eddie's parents are going to be pissed," Kent muttered. He looked at his watch. "Maybe my father is here. Let's take a look."

I followed him to the door. We heard Noel call to us, but Kent ignored him and walked out. We stood in the entryway, looking down the driveway. One of the older boys was kissing Kaley Lester by a parked car. Kaley was in our class and usually very quiet and to herself, but the boy she was with was all over her, and even from this distance, we could see that his right hand was under her skirt.

"I guess she's not as shy as we all thought," Kent muttered. I was going to suggest that someone might have spiked her soda, but before I could reply, he said, "There's my father."

We walked down the sidewalk to the driveway, and Kent practically lunged for the rear car door when his father stopped. I got in quickly, and he followed.

"How was it?"

"Okay," Kent said.

His father hesitated and then nodded at the house.

"Everything all right in there? The music sounds pretty loud."

"They're celebrating a great school victory, Dad," Kent said sharply.

His father nodded and started away. The silence between us made him uncomfortable. "You guys tired?"

"I guess," Kent said.

"The great thing about being young is that you can burn the candle on both ends for a while, but believe me, it catches up with you."

"Dad . . ."

"I know, I know. You guys have a right to make your own mistakes. Is that what you tell your parents, Semantha?"

I looked at Kent, who was looking out the window. "No, Mr. Pearson."

"Good for you," he said, and we drove almost the remainder of the way in silence. When we turned into our gated entrance, Kent muttered under his breath.

"What?" I asked.

"No wonder you're a princess. You live in a castle," he said.

I felt tears coming, but I swallowed the lump in my throat.

"I'm not a princess, Kent."

Before he could get out to open my door, I opened it myself this time.

"Good night, Mr. Pearson, and thank you."

"You're welcome, Semantha."

I went up the steps and didn't turn around until they were nearly at the end of our long driveway. The moment I entered, Daddy came up from his den office.

"Hey, honey, how was the night? I heard we won the game?"

"It was exciting, Daddy."

"And the party?"

"Okay," I said.

"Well, I promised your mother I would wait up for you. Let's get to bed," he said, putting his arm around me. "Was it a big party?"

"About thirty, I think, but more and more kids began to show up, so it might be a lot more now."

"Some of them get out of hand?" he asked softly as we reached the top of the stairway.

"Some," I said. "Not us," I added.

"I didn't have any doubt about it," he told me, kissed me on the cheek, and went to his and Mother's bedroom.

I started down the hallway and paused when I reached Cassie's room. She had deliberately left the door open. I didn't feel much like spending any time talking about the party with her, but I knew she would only come into my room and wake me if I didn't go into hers. I took a deep breath and entered. She was sitting up in her bed, reading, and slowly put the book down on her lap.

"Good," she said. "Come in." She patted her bed.

"I'm tired, Cassie. Can we talk in the morning?"

"Absolutely not. People forget important details when that much time passes. You want to talk when everything is fresh in your mind. Come here," she said firmly.

I approached her bed and sat at the foot of it. I didn't look at her.

"Something happened, something bad?"

I shook my head, but then I nodded. "Kent's mad at me."

"Oh? Start at the beginning."

I began to describe the game, and she stopped me.

"By beginning, I mean after the game, Semantha."

"His father drove us to Eddie Morris's house. There already were a lot of kids there, dancing, eating pizza . . ."

"And drinking and smoking?"

"I didn't see anyone smoking. Eddie warned them about that and about drugs."

"But they were drinking?"

"The older students were."

"No one tried to offer you a drink or a pill or anything like that?"

"They offered us, but Kent refused. He said he still remembered getting sick from drinking too much."

"Umm," she said.

"We danced and were having a good time. There was a professional DJ."

"Never mind that. Did Kent try to get you alone somewhere? Well?"

"We took a walk because the party was getting too wild."

"To where?"

"The stables to look at the horses."

"Go on," she said. "Don't make me pull teeth, either, Semantha. Just come out with it."

My throat closed up. I felt as if I were suddenly standing naked. Why did I have to tell her all this?

"Nothing happened!" I cried. "I'm tired. I'm going to bed."

I leaped off the bed and charged out of her room, but my heart was thumping so hard when I went into mine that I thought I would faint. Quickly, I went into my bathroom and locked the door. For a while, I just stood there, looking at myself in the mirror. Then I undressed, brushed my teeth, and washed my face. When I came out, I thought I would just go right to sleep. For a moment, I didn't see her. I got my nightgown out and put it on and pulled back my blanket, and then she stepped out of the left corner where she had been standing the whole time watching me. I nearly jumped out of my own skin.

"Cassie, I'm tired!" I cried. "It's very late."

She didn't speak. She stepped toward me. "Get into bed," she said. "Go on."

I crawled under my covers, and she sat on my bed and fixed the blanket around my neck and shoulders the way Mother always fixed it. Then she stroked my hair just like Mother, too.

"Poor Semantha," she said. "Your first bad sexual experience."

I turned away.

"It's so much better if you talk about it, Semantha. It's like eating heavy food before you sleep. It will lie on you all night. He took you somewhere where he could be alone with you, and then what?"

"I think I got him angry because I was so nervous about being alone with him."

"I'm not concerned about his being angry, Semantha. Actually, his being angry tells me quite a bit about him. What exactly did he do? I'm sure he tried to kiss you, right?"

I nodded.

"And you like him, so you kissed him back. We already expected that."

What we? I wanted to say. *It was me, me! I was alone with Kent, not we.*

"And the kissing was exciting," she continued, "and he got excited because you were being so . . . what shall we say . . . cooperative? That's a signal for boys. What did he try then? Did he try to get under your dress? What?"

"No. He just . . ."

"Just what, Semantha?"

"Brought his hands around over my breasts."

She nodded. "Of course he did. And what did you do? Did you moan and groan?"

"No, Cassie. I jumped up."

"And that's what made him angry?"

"Yes."

She smiled, and then she grew serious again. "How did you feel, Semantha? I mean, how did you really feel?"

"I felt bad."

"Because you wanted him to touch you, right?"

"No. Well, maybe, but I felt bad because he was so upset. I felt like I had tricked him."

"That is exactly how boys want you to feel. Exactly," she said, and stood up to pace as she talked. "They get you feeling guilty for being sensible, for being cautious. These days, boys think if you smile at them, you want to go to bed with them immediately, and if you prove otherwise, they accuse you of being a tease.

"Don't you fall for that, Semantha," she warned, waving her right forefinger at me. "You have your self-respect. Good for you. Now, when the time comes, when the right boy is there, then things will be different."

"How do you know who's the right boy?"

"Don't worry, we'll know. This is good," she said. "This is all very good. You listened well. I'm very proud of you. Tonight you were a true Heaven-stone. Now, don't you dare go to sleep feeling guilty about anything, understand? I won't permit it."

I said nothing. She paced a little more, looking as if she was talking to herself, and then she stopped and abruptly said, "Good night."

She walked out and closed my door.

What did she mean when she said, "Don't worry. We'll know?"

What we?

Was she going to hold my hand throughout my whole teenage life?

What would she do when I went off to college and she was at her college?

I wasn't going to sleep feeling guilty anymore. I was going to sleep feeling terribly confused.

And, without knowing exactly why, feeling a little afraid, too.

5

Tease

CASSIE SAID NOTHING more that weekend about my night with Kent, but when she looked at me, I could see she hadn't forgotten a single detail. I wasn't as angry at him as she wanted me to be, despite how he had behaved at the end of the evening. All weekend, I was hoping that he would call me to apologize for his behavior and maybe suggest that we try to be together again. I did feel bad about how I had behaved. I could just imagine how I had looked to him when I jumped up like that and insisted on leaving the stable. If I had a chance to explain, maybe he wouldn't be so angry. Every time I heard a phone ringing, I prayed it was mine, but the only time mine rang was when Bobbi called to tell me how much she had enjoyed Eddie's party and asked me how I had liked it.

I said, "Yes, it was fun."

"It was fun? You don't sound enthusiastic about it," she quickly replied. I wasn't sure if she was fishing for information or not. She gave me the impression that Noel had not spoken to Kent and then called her, because she seemed to know nothing about the way my night had ended. I kept wondering if this was an act, so I wasn't very responsive to her questions.

"I guess you're used to more elaborate, expensive parties, huh?"

"No."

She waited, but I didn't know what else to say.

"Okay. I can see you're not in the mood to talk," she said, and ended the call quickly.

I couldn't help being very nervous on Monday morning. Surprisingly, Cassie was in one of her buoyant, happy moods. She was as nice to me as could be and even seemed pleased that Mother's pregnancy apparently was back to being okay. She had nice things to say about the redecoration of what would be Asa's nursery, too. Afterward, when we were on our way to school, she told me Daddy had promised to take her to see the work on the new store in Lexington very soon. She knew he hadn't asked me, and Mother wouldn't be going.

"It's going to be our special day," she said. "We'll go to lunch, of course. And he'll introduce me to all his important friends."

She saw the look on my face and added, "And maybe next time he'll take you."

I wasn't jealous, so I said nothing, not that she would have noticed if I had. She was on a tear about the Heavenstone business and how hard Daddy worked, and how little appreciation Mother showed him. She said the truth was that he talked to her more about the business than anyone, including Uncle Perry. This was one of Cassie's favorite topics, and if I had heard it once, I had heard it a hundred times. I was still in deep thought about Kent and really wasn't listening all that closely to what she was saying, anyway.

When we arrived at school, I hurried in, hoping to see and speak to Kent before the bell for homeroom sounded. We were in different homerooms. I did see him talking to some of his friends. He turned and saw me, and I started in his direction but stopped when he turned away abruptly and started down the hall.

After that, I wasn't going to initiate any conversation with him. I wanted to wait to see if he would speak first to me. He didn't. In the classes we shared, he went directly to his desk and afterward either left before I did or after and didn't catch up with me.

I was afraid it would be this way all day, and sure enough, at lunch, he sat at a different table and didn't acknowledge me at all. By this time, everyone's curiosity was at high pitch. Bobbi was the first to ask what had happened. The way she asked me caused me to think she already had Kent's answer, an answer that certainly didn't flatter me.

"I had the feeling you weren't happy when I called you," she said when I didn't respond quickly enough. "Apparently, Kent didn't have that good a time, either. Why not?"

I thought hard for a moment and then said, "I think he was disappointed."

She smiled. "I'll say. Too bad. You two looked good together. Maybe you just aren't ready for a mature relationship." She left to join Noel.

After that, the buzz began. Whispers, like hummingbirds, fluttered about the ears of others in my class. Before the end of the day, I understood I had been accused of being a tease, a girl who promises more than she will ever deliver and enjoys tormenting boys. Most blamed it on my being a spoiled rich girl who always got what she wanted when she wanted it.

Moving in like some parasite, Megan Stein was all over Kent whenever she had the chance. Maybe to hurt me more than to please himself, Kent behaved as though he had just discovered her. I saw him talking softly to her at her locker between classes, his lips so close to hers they were already kissing each other's breath.

As I was walking out of the building, Bobbi's final comment to me for the day was, "You know that this makes it harder for you to get another boy in our school interested in you."

Instead of showing the sadness and pain that she and the others expected, I simply said, "I'll survive," and walked away from her. I knew this would just reinforce their idea of me as being stuck-up and arrogant. Since Cassie already had this reputation, it was easy for them to paint me with the same brush.

I didn't think that Cassie had ruined things for me with the other kids in school. In fact, I suddenly was prouder of her than ever. As I made my way out to the parking lot, all I could think was that Cassie was especially right about boys. Cassie was still the smartest person I knew. As usual, the moment she set eyes on me, she knew I had gone through a difficult day.

She said nothing until we drove away from the school. I was looking out the side window but seeing nothing.

"You don't have to say anything, Semantha," she began. "I'll tell you what happened. Your wonderful new boyfriend treated you like horse dung all day."

I turned to her and nodded.

"And he made sure everyone knew it was all your fault, right?"

"Just like you said, Cassie."

"It's so typical," she muttered, shaking her head. "Most of the boys in this school are the same. They don't have class. They're not up to being with you and me, Semantha. This is why I wanted us to go to a private school. They're all riffraff. Don't you spend a second regretting anything. None of this is your fault, Semantha."

"I won't."

"Good, good. Don't worry. The right young man for you is out there, so get that sad look off your face. We certainly don't want Daddy to see it. The worst thing for you right now is pity, and that's what our parents would feel for you, especially Mother. She would make you feel even worse doing that. Don't act any differently from the way you've been. If you think you are going to be sad, walk away and come see me, okay?"

"Okay, Cassie."

"I just knew something like this would happen. I could tell what sort of boy he was just by looking at his older brother. What they say about the apple not falling far from the tree is correct."

"His father was very nice, Cassie."

"You haven't met his mother, and you don't know their family background. They're common people, Semantha. We're the Heavenstones. Don't ever forget it, even for a moment. You won't be able to forget it. It's in you, and it's stronger than anything else in you.

"The Heavenstones," she muttered, and drove on. I was beginning to hear myself chanting the same thing.

Because Daddy was so excited about his new store in Lexington, when we arrived at the house, it wasn't difficult for me to hide my social and emotional disappointment. He was so excited that he broke his rule about not talking about business at dinner. Mother had prepared a delicious stuffed pork roast and her special mashed sweet potatoes, but she looked tired to me and even a little pale. She put on the best face she could because of Daddy's enthusiastic description of everything.

"There's a very good chance that the governor himself will be at our opening gala," he revealed, "and at least one of our United States senators, not to mention a herd of other important local politicians, businessmen, and just about all the television and radio media available.

"Your uncle Perry has come up with what I must say is a brilliant public-relations idea, as well," he added, looking at Cassie and me.

"He has?" Cassie asked. "What?"

"Customers in all of our other stores are filling out coupons. We're having a drawing the night of the gala opening, a lottery, and the winner gets to spend one thousand dollars in any of our stores. It will bring in tons of publicity," he said.

Cassie returned to eating without any comment. I was happy for Uncle Perry, and Mother said she thought it was brilliant. When Daddy asked Cassie to think up some additional good ideas to make the gala as exciting as possible, she brightened again and told him she would make a list and bring it to him in his office later.

I could see that despite her efforts to hide her fatigue, Mother was too tired to help with the cleanup or do anything more. I pleaded with her to go up to bed, and she finally relented and did just that. Cassie surprised me by chastising me for persuading Mother to rest.

"Don't you know that when you tell someone she looks sick and tired, she'll feel sick and tired? Daddy spoils her too much as it is, especially now, when he has all this important business to do."

"But—"

"Never mind, Semantha. I'll take care of it. Go do your homework. I'll do all this."

"I can help you. I can—"

"Just go up to your room and do your homework," she said. "I know you've had a very trying day, and you hid it well from Daddy. Go on," she repeated, and turned her back on me.

I watched her for a moment and left. As I was walking toward the stairway, however, I heard Daddy ask her why she was doing everything herself.

"Oh, Mother was too tired, Daddy, and Semantha has a load of homework. It's all right."

"You're an angel, Cassie, an angel," he said.

I didn't have that much homework, and I was so disturbed by what had happened at school that I probably wouldn't be able to concentrate. I could have helped her finish. I wanted to run back and tell that to Daddy, but I also imagined how angry Cassie would be if I contradicted her, so I continued up the stairs. I went to see how Mother was doing. She was already in bed. I had been right to send her up.

"Mother, are you feeling ill?"

"Just a bout of nausea suddenly. I was a little dizzy, too, but it's passing. I'll be fine," she said. "Don't worry, honey."

She smiled at me, and I went to her and hugged her. She stroked my hair and smiled.

"When are you going to another party? Doesn't the school have parties, too? I bet there's something for the holidays coming up."

She was right. There was always a holiday party before the break for Christmas vacation, but I had no expectations. Bobbi was probably right. None of the other boys would ask me to go with him.

"Yes, there's a party before the holiday break."

"Well, maybe I'll take you to look for a new dress. We haven't done that for a while. Maybe this weekend," she said.

I didn't want to tell her anything unpleasant or sad, and I remembered Cassie's warning about attracting pity, so I just smiled and nodded.

"Do you need anything?" I asked.

"No, I'm just going to rest. Go on and do your homework, honey."

"I'll come back to say good night," I promised. She nodded, and I started away. When I reached the door, I looked back at her and saw she had closed her eyes and looked as if she had fallen asleep just that fast.

I don't care what Cassie says, I thought. We have to look after Mother more. I vowed to do just that and left.

Cassie eventually came around to agreeing with me, anyway. In the days that followed, Cassie was doing more and more for Mother, preparing her breakfast and bringing it up to her before she and I left for school, even some days fixing her lunch so all she had to do was warm up something or uncover something waiting in the refrigerator. Despite all of this resting and Cassie's and my assuming more and more of Mother's work in the house, she didn't appear to be improving. She did her best to hide it all from Daddy, who was very busy with preparations for the new store's opening and gala.

All of this weighed heavily on my mind. Half the time, I wasn't listening in school, and I was even embarrassed in social studies class when my teacher asked me a question and I just stared dumbly until Victor Brown, sitting next to me, poked me in the arm. The class broke into laughter, but Mrs. Gerda gave me a zero for failing to pay attention. Of course, everyone who saw it happen and who heard about it later assumed I was in a daze because of what had happened between Kent and me. Kent and, especially, Megan Stein really enjoyed my awkward moment. I saw all the smiling, laughing faces looking my way later at lunch, too.

Cassie's right about this school and the students attending it, I thought angrily. They don't have class. Maybe I'm better off being a snob like she is. I won't beg for anyone's friendship. I even considered going back to Mother and asking her to agree to enroll us in private school. It wasn't a question of the money. We could afford to have both Cassie and me in private school. Mother was just adamant that we would have a better understanding of what she called 'the real world' if we weren't so isolated. If this is the real world, I thought, looking at my fellow students who were enjoying my discomfort so much, then I'd rather be isolated.

I was shocked by Cassie's reaction when I described what had happened to me in social studies class and why. If anything, I had expected she would repeat all she had told me about the public school and might even go with me to plead for our being transferred to a private school, but instead, she blamed me.

"I told you not to dwell on Mother like this, didn't I? I told you that doesn't do anyone any good."

"But . . . you're doting on her, preparing her breakfasts, her lunches, aren't you?"

"I'm doing it, but I'm not behaving as if she is suffering from some terminal illness, Semantha, and I don't think about her all day here in school. You come home with this sort of a long face every day, you'll upset Daddy. Grow up. Be stronger. Everything is going to work out just fine."

I shook my head. "I don't know what to think anymore," I whined. "You always warn me about ignoring reality, putting my head in the sand like an ostrich, living in a fantasy."

"You don't have to do that. Just try to be more mature about it. Don't act like a child and cry."

"I don't cry."

"You look like you're just about to, and Daddy will easily see that, and that will make him worry even more, thank you. Do you want that? Well? Do you?"

"No."

"Then wash off that look of self-pity. Just go through the day doing the things you're supposed to do, and leave Mother's health up to her doctor. They're supposed to be going there this afternoon," she added.

"Oh, good," I said. "I'm sorry. I'll try to be more like you."

"Exactly," she told me.

Neither Daddy nor Mother was home when we arrived from school. Despite what I had said to Cassie, I was on pins and needles waiting for them to return from the doctor. It was getting very late, too. Cassie was downstairs preparing dinner, in fact, and I was getting ready to join her and set the table. Where could they be?

The moment I heard them come into the house, I charged out of my room to the stairway and came to an abrupt stop.

Daddy was alone. One look at his face told everything.

"Where's Mother? What happened?" I asked as I rushed down the stairway.

"She was terribly anemic. Dr. Moffet is puzzled, so he's put her in the hospital for evaluation."

"What does that mean?"

"I'm not sure yet, Semantha." He pressed a smile onto his face, which was obviously reluctant to take it. "She'll be all right. They'll get to the bottom of it quickly."

We both heard some clatter in the kitchen. He smiled.

"Cassie's preparing our dinner, huh? I was thinking of taking you both out, but if she's already made something . . ."

"I prepared one of your favorite meals, Daddy, veal marsala and couscous," Cassie said from the kitchen doorway.

If she heard that, she surely heard what was said about Mother, I thought, and waited for her to ask questions, too, but she didn't. She came out, wiping her hands with a dish towel.

"I imagine you've had a very trying time. You should go up and take a hot shower and get comfortable. You can tell us about it all at dinner. Go on," she ordered, the way Mother would.

He smiled.

"I guess you're right, angel." He leaned over to kiss her on the cheek and then started up the stairs, walking slowly. He seemed truly exhausted.

When I glanced at Cassie, I saw she was close to tears. I couldn't remember when I had last seen her this way.

"Cassie?"

"Poor Daddy," she said. "All this burden on his

shoulders." She turned quickly and went back to the kitchen.

"Poor Daddy? But what about Mother?" I called after her. She didn't stop. "What about going to see her?" I asked, but by then, I was asking myself.

At dinner, Cassie was anything but depressed or worried about Mother. Whenever I said or asked anything about her, Cassie gave me a look of reprimand. When we were together for a moment in the kitchen, she whispered, "Can't you see how he's tottering on the brink of a breakdown? Try to distract him, get him to think of other things, Semantha. Stop asking and talking about Mother!"

"But . . ."

"No buts, Semantha. Christmas trees, you're getting to be more of a burden than Mother," she added.

Stunned, I stood there looking at her. How was I more of a burden, and how could she refer to Mother as a burden, anyway?

She sighed deeply. "Just go back in there and talk about something pleasant. Ask him about the upcoming gala. Talk about Uncle Perry, if you want, but just don't harp on Mother right now. Go on. I'll be right there."

I returned to the dining room, but I was very nervous. Surely, I couldn't hide my feelings and fears from Daddy. Somehow, however, he didn't appear to notice. Despite what I said, he still talked about Mother.

"I'll be going up there right after dinner," he told me.

"Shouldn't we go with you, Daddy?"

"No. You two just take care of your schoolwork. I won't be that long. She has to rest. I just don't understand . . ." he said, shaking his head.

Just then, Cassie came from the kitchen with a surprise. Even I didn't know she had baked Daddy's favorite cake, a chocolate angel-food cake dripping with strawberry syrup. I remembered when Mother had taught her how to make it. A big smile traveled from Daddy's lips to his eyes.

"Cassie, you outdid yourself," he declared. She put the cake down at the center of the table and stood back, admiring it as if it were truly a work of art.

"I hope you like it, Daddy."

"Like it? I love it," he said.

She hurried to cut and serve him a piece and waited as he tasted it.

"It's wonderful, Cassie. If I didn't know better, I'd think your mother was in that kitchen."

She looked at me, and her face blossomed into the brightest smile I could remember. "Thank you, Daddy," she said.

"Semantha, cut yourself a piece," Daddy said. "You don't want to miss this."

I had some, and it was as good as, if not better than, Mother's cake. I couldn't help but continue to be impressed with Cassie. She always managed to rise to an occasion, have a solution. Afterward, she hurried to the front door and stood there, making sure Daddy put on his scarf.

"It's nippy tonight," she told him.

He laughed and kissed her on the cheek. "I'll be

back soon," he said. "I can't wait to tell your mother how well you're taking care of us, Cassie. She'll be very pleased."

Cassie nodded, flashed a look of satisfaction my way, and watched Daddy leave. For a few moments, she just stood there at the door. This time, when she turned around, she looked quite different. She looked as if she had aged years. She pulled her shoulders back and glared at me.

"What are you doing standing there like that? Did you finish cleaning off the dishes and putting them in the dishwasher?"

"Yes."

"Then go do your homework, and don't spend any time on the phone gossiping."

"I don't gossip on the phone. Who would I talk to now, anyway?"

"Never mind what you do and don't do, Semantha. Just go do what you should do. Go."

Why was she behaving like that? I wondered, but I didn't argue. I shrugged and went up to my room. I didn't need her to tell me to do my homework. She knew that. Just for spite, I procrastinated, fiddling with my hair, thinking about makeup, and doing my nails. Finally, realizing I was only spiting myself, I started my schoolwork. I heard her come upstairs, but I didn't hear her going to her room, so I went to the door and looked out. I saw her going into Mother and Daddy's bedroom. Before I could call to her, she closed the door.

What was she doing now? I wondered. I stood there in my doorway, waiting and waiting. My curiosity aroused, I walked down the hallway to our parents' bedroom. I stood for a moment listening. It sounded as if Cassie was talking. Was she on the phone? Was she talking to Daddy at the hospital? Had she gone in there to prevent me from hearing the conversation? I slowly reached for the doorknob, but my fingers trembled. She would hate my bursting in on her. Instead, I knocked. Her talking stopped. I knocked again.

"Cassie?"

She didn't respond, but after a few moments, she pulled the door open.

"What now, Semantha?"

"I . . . why are you in here?"

"What are you doing, following me around the house?"

"No. I heard you come up, and I was waiting for you and saw you go in here."

Looking past her, I saw that the bed was unmade. She caught my gaze and shook her head.

"If you must know every little thing, Semantha, I was in here fixing up the bedroom for Daddy. Obviously, having to take Mother to the doctor and then the hospital, he had no opportunity to get things organized. I'm about to make the bed now. Are you satisfied?"

"I just wondered. Is there anything I can do?"

"Yes, go back to your room, finish your homework, and prepare for bed. I'll come in to say good night."

"What?" What did she mean, she would come in to say good night?

"To calm you down, Semantha."

"But I thought we'd wait up for Daddy."

"Who knows how long he'll be? If he comes back soon, we'll see him."

"He said he wouldn't be there long."

She stared at me.

"He did!"

"He's only trying to avoid telling us how serious things are."

"What do you mean? How serious are they?"

"Serious. The doctor put her in the hospital, didn't he? Now, go back to your room and let me finish up. I'd like to get to my homework, too."

She stepped back and closed the door. The trembling I had felt in my fingers now traveled down my spine. For a moment, I thought I couldn't breathe. I returned to my room, but I just sat on my bed thinking. How come I hadn't realized Daddy was keeping things from us? How serious was it? Could I call the hospital? Again, I wondered why Cassie could see and understand so much more than I could in our father's face. He was my father, too, wasn't he?

I hugged myself and rocked on the bed. Feeling so helpless and alone, I started to cry softly, keeping my eye on my door. If Cassie caught me, she would get hysterical. Catching my breath, I went to my window that looked out on the driveway and watched and hoped for the sight of Daddy's car. It was quiet. Every time I saw a pair of headlights on the road, I held my breath, but none turned into our gateway.

I spun around when I heard my door open.

"What are you doing?" Cassie asked.

"I was just . . . hoping to see Daddy's car."

"Christmas trees, Semantha. I was just hoping to see Daddy's car," she mimicked. "I swear, you're going backward in age. If he knew you were standing there like that, waiting all night, how do you think he would feel? Will you just get yourself to bed? I promise, if he comes home or calls soon, I'll come tell you."

"It's not that late, Cassie."

"Are we going to stand here and argue about something so stupid? I have enough on my mind. Go to bed, Semantha. Or do you want me to come in here and read you a story?"

"Stop it."

"Because I will, you know."

"Stop it, Cassie."

"Then go to bed," she said. She backed out and closed my door.

She did succeed in making me feel immature, so I prepared for bed. Before I got into bed, I looked out the window again. Daddy had been gone for a little more than four hours now. Something wasn't right. Or maybe he just hated to leave Mother there by herself and was staying as long as he could. I told myself I would just doze and keep one ear alert for the sounds of his arrival.

But sleep overtook me, crawling in, over, and around me. It had a good grip on me, too. The emotional roller coaster I had ridden all day was far more exhausting than I had imagined. My fatigue sank me deeper and deeper into the darkness, into a place where even dreams didn't dwell.

When I heard the scream and the sound of crying, I thought some nightmare had worked its way through a tunnel to reach the place in which I slumbered. A second scream woke me, however. It stunned me, too, and for a long moment, I didn't move. I listened. I heard the sobbing clearly now and reached over to turn on the lamp on my beside table. I sat up and listened again. The sobbing was softer, and there were some muffled voices. I threw off my blanket, slipped into my robe and slippers, and went to the door.

The hallway lights were bright.

At the top of the stairway, Cassie sat with her hands over her face.

I shouted her name.

She turned and looked at me, her face streaked with tears.

My heart stopped and started.

"What?" I asked, and even before she replied, I began to cry myself.

"Daddy lost his Asa," she said.

6

A Loss

"WHERE IS DADDY?"

She didn't reply.

I hurried to her.

When I reached the top of the stairway, I looked down and saw Daddy sitting on the small, decorative bench in the entryway. He had his hands clasped in his lap and was staring ahead. I thought he looked stunned.

"What happened? Is Mother all right?"

Cassie shook her head. Then she rose like a woman four times her age and started down the stairs. I followed slowly. My heart was racing so fast and hard I thought I would lose my breath and tumble down after her. When she reached Daddy, Cassie fell to her knees and embraced his legs, laying her head on his lap. He seemed to snap out of his melancholy and stroked her hair. Then he began to speak in a slow mumble.

"They blame the anemia . . . weakened her . . . a miscarriage . . . she needed a transfusion . . . hemorrhaging . . . we nearly lost her, too. It all happened so quickly . . . I wasn't there five minutes . . . rushing her out to the operating room. Dr. Moffet did all he could. I stayed with her . . . held her hand, but she didn't speak, barely opened her eyes . . . emotional . . . traumatic . . . state of shock."

He lowered his head.

"Will she be all right?" I cried.

He didn't reply. Cassie lifted her head and glared angrily at me, her eyes so full of heat and fury that I stepped back. Then she rose and sat beside him, putting her arm around him, pressing her cheek to his shoulder.

"I know you're both terribly disappointed," Daddy said.

"Only for you, Daddy," Cassie quickly told him. "We're worried about you more."

"And Mother," I said.

Finally, he looked at me and smiled. Then he lifted his arms, and I rushed into his embrace. He held me tightly. I had my eyes closed, but when I opened them, I saw Cassie had turned away. Daddy kissed the tears streaming down my cheek, and I stood up, wiping the rest of them away.

"She'll be fine after she rests," he said. "But she'll be . . . very fragile."

I looked at Cassie. Fragile? That was what she always called me.

"We'll take care of her," Cassie told him. "Don't you worry, Daddy. You have so much to worry about. Don't you get yourself sick over this."

He smiled at her and sighed deeply, so deeply I thought his heart had slipped down into his stomach and he would keel over. Then he pressed down on his knees and stood.

"We all should get some sleep. We'll need our strength for the days to come," he told us.

Cassie rose and seized his left hand quickly. He pulled it free but put his arm around her shoulders.

"Yes, Daddy," she said. "Lean on me. Lean on me for as long as you like. I'm strong enough."

"That you are, dear Cassie. That you are."

They started toward the stairway, and then he stopped and turned back to me.

"Come along, Semantha. You should go back to bed."

"She will," Cassie said, her eyes narrowing.

I started after them. I don't think I shall ever forget Daddy walking up the stairway that night. He did lean on Cassie, and he lumbered along as though he had aged centuries. My handsome, robust daddy was reduced to a weak old man. For a moment, when he reached the middle of the stairway, he looked as if he might topple backward. I could see Cassie tightening her grip around his waist. She was strong. She was actually holding him up, helping him climb those stairs. I wanted to do more, but there was no room for me beside him. All I could do was remain as close behind them as possible, maybe to catch him or push him forward.

When we reached the top of the stairs and Cassie had turned Daddy toward his and Mother's bedroom, she paused and nodded at me.

"You go to sleep, Semantha. I'll help Daddy get to bed. Go on. Be a good girl, now."

Not only did she sound like Mother, she even wore Mother's expression. They did look so much alike. She didn't wait for my reply. She continued to guide Daddy down the hallway and turned him into the bedroom as if he had forgotten where it was and was going to walk past it. I stood there until I heard her close the door.

For a moment, it felt as if all the air had gone out of our house and I was suffocating. Images of both Daddy and Mother at the hospital and gruesome, sad thoughts were spinning in my merry-go-round brain. I had to hold on to the railing until the nausea and dizziness passed. Every face in every ancestral painting hanging on the walls was glaring down angrily at me. At least, that was how it seemed to me. The historical family was upset and disappointed. An heir had been lost, a Heavenstone had been discarded like just so much medical waste. Whatever blessings and protection the spirits had given us would be taken away. We were unworthy of their royal support. This was only the beginning of our downfall.

I fled from those looks of condemnation, imagined or otherwise, as I fled from the tragedy that had just unfolded.

After quickly closing my door, I slipped back under my blanket and stared into the darkness. Would Daddy, the strength and power of our family, be so broken and inconsolable that he would be unable to continue? I agreed with Cassie that Uncle Perry could not step into Daddy's shoes. I should have been worrying solely about him and about Mother, but oddly, what I thought about was how pleased all those at school who were jealous of me would be, how pleased those who were frustrated by my not groveling for their friendship would be. I hated the thought of returning to school once everyone had found out that something so terrible had happened to the Heavenstones.

How could I be thinking of myself when Daddy was suffering so and Mother was too weak and sick to speak to him? Look at how concerned and caring Cassie was, how eager, and strong enough to be there for Daddy when he needed support the most. I felt so inadequate being sent to my room. Did everyone still see me as a little girl, inconsequential, just another teenager who still had jelly beans for a brain? In their minds, I wasn't yet capable of being or acting mature enough to handle such a crisis. I had to be protected like a child.

When I thought about how happy Mother and Daddy had been when they had learned she was carrying a boy and Daddy would have his Asa, I broke into a fit of hysterical sobbing. It seemed it would never end. I tried to get hold of myself, but the more I tried, the harder I sobbed. Finally, exhausted, out of breath, my chest aching, I smothered my face in the pillow and forced myself to stop.

I know I slept on and off, twice waking to what sounded like Cassie crying in the hallway. I was too tired and terrified to get up to see, and the crying stopped. I hoped it was a dream. I had never seen Cassie cry. I had seen her have a tantrum, but never cry or whine. Just the thought of her doing that frightened me. What more terrible thing could happen to us?

I didn't want to get up in the morning, and I

hated the thought of going to school. I hoped Daddy would want me to stay home. Maybe all of us would go to see Mother and try to cheer her up. That would be more important than my going to school and being a zombie in my classes. I wouldn't hear anything or learn anything, anyway.

Despite the hour, it was deathly quiet in the house. I rose and dressed as quickly as I could, more out of curiosity than anything else. I imagined Cassie would be preparing Daddy's breakfast by now. Maybe he was up already and downstairs. I just hadn't heard them. I rushed out and down to see, but when I stepped into the kitchen, I saw nothing had been done. Cassie had not been there this morning, and Daddy wasn't at the table, either. Now worried as much as curious, I hurried back upstairs. I practically ran to Cassie's room, knocked softly, and when I heard nothing, I opened the door to see what she was doing.

She wasn't there.

It looked as if she hadn't been there all night. The bed was still made the perfect Cassie way, and no head had creased her pillows.

What was going on? Could it be that Daddy had been called back to the hospital and Cassie had gone with him? They hadn't wanted to wake me up? What did this mean? Had something more happened to Mother? This time, I walked very slowly down the hallway to Daddy and Mother's bedroom, terrified of what new horror I would learn of. I stood outside the door, listening for the sounds of his getting up, but I heard nothing, so I knocked softly on the door and waited.

I was surprised to discover the door had been locked. I listened and knocked again, only a little harder, louder. Finally, I heard the lock being opened. Cassie stood there looking out at me sleepily. She ground her eyes with her small fists and straightened her shoulders. She was wearing what she had been wearing the night before.

"What is it, Semantha?"

"How's Daddy? Why are you still here? Why aren't you fixing him breakfast?"

"Couldn't you do something yourself?" she snapped back at me. "Would it have been so terrible for you to fix us both breakfast and bring it up here?"

"I didn't know you were still in here, Cassie."

"Of course, I'm still in here. I had to stay with him all night. He needed me."

She looked back at Daddy, who was fast asleep.

"I talked him into taking one of Mother's sleeping pills, and it finally took effect, so keep your voice down."

She stepped out and closed the door softly behind her.

"I didn't get much sleep myself," she said. "Forget about school today. Neither of us is going."

"Good."

"I have to shower, change. In the meantime, you prepare the coffee. We'll see if we can get him to eat something. I'll be down in a little while. Go on," she said, waving her hand toward the stairway.

"What about Mother?"

"What about her?"

"Have we heard anything?"

"No."

"I . . . thought I heard you in the hallway last night . . . crying."

"Don't be ridiculous," she said. "You and your imagination. Go on. Do something constructive."

She marched away. I looked at the closed door a moment and then went downstairs to make the coffee as she had ordered. When she still hadn't come down, I started making Daddy's favorite omelette with cheese and put up some toast. I got the tray ready and went out front to get Daddy's newspaper and put it on the tray. As long as I kept busy, I could keep from crying and trembling. Just as I cut the toast in four quarters, Cassie appeared.

"What are you doing? All I told you to do was make the coffee," she said, marching in quickly.

"I thought . . . I'd do more to help."

She poked a fork into the omelette.

"This is way overcooked for Daddy. He hates dry eggs," she said, and poured the omelette into the garbage disposal.

"But I timed it," I protested.

"Obviously, you timed it wrong, Semantha."

She started on a new omelette.

"You might as well eat that toast yourself. It will be cold and dry. Make yourself your own breakfast."

She prepared another omelette, and when she poured it onto the dish, I thought it didn't look any different from the one I had made, but I was afraid to comment. I just ate a little cereal and fruit and nibbled on my toast as she worked. She poured the coffee into a pot, and for a moment, I thought she was going to complain about the coffee, too.

"Is the coffee all right?

"It's a little weak, but he won't know the difference this morning," she replied.

"But I measured it just the way you do."

"You didn't put enough in one or two of the spoonfuls, Semantha. Forget about that for now," she said.

I noticed she had prepared enough toast and enough omelette for herself as well. She started for the stairway.

"You're going to eat up there, too?"

"Of course. Would you have him eat alone this morning of all mornings? Start on the house when you're finished in here," she ordered.

"Start on the house?"

"The dusting, vacuuming, polishing furniture. I want to take the curtains down in the living room today and clean them as well. The piano looked dusty to me yesterday, but I didn't have time to get to it," she added. "It will bring happiness to Daddy when he sees how well we can look after everything, with or without Mother." She continued up the stairway. She had a soft, pleasing smile on her face. Was that for Daddy's benefit, or did she really enjoy all of this?

I moved quickly to the foot of the stairs and called up to her before she reached the top.

"What?"

"What about Mother? Aren't we going to the hospital?"

"We'll see. If she's still in a state of shock or something, there might not be any point to our going. Daddy will be calling the doctor this morning. Just get on to your work. It's not a holiday from school. We're home because we have to be."

"I know."

"Good. I'm glad you know."

I looked up after her for a moment. Why wouldn't we go to the hospital if Mother was still in a state of shock? Maybe our presence, our talking to her, would help bring her out of it faster. I don't care what Cassie thinks, I thought. I'm going to the hospital, with or without her.

For the time being, however, there was nothing for me to do but what Cassie had told me to do. I returned to the kitchen and cleaned up what I could and then got the vacuum cleaner, the polishing cloths, and polish and started on the living room, keeping one eye and one ear toward the stairway, anticipating Daddy's coming down. I couldn't understand his sleeping in this late. I concluded it was because of the sleeping pill, or pills, he had taken.

I had finished with the vacuuming and started on the furniture when Cassie appeared. She had come downstairs so quietly I hadn't heard her.

"How is he?" I asked.

"He's a little groggy, but he's okay now. He ate most of his breakfast, but only because I was there insisting. I told him it won't do any of us any good if he gets himself sick, too."

"That's what Mother always tells me when I'm sick and I don't want to eat."

"Well, of course. That's what a mother should say. He's getting dressed." She started to turn away.

"Has he called the doctor?"

"He has a call in to him. We're waiting for the doctor to call back."

"Did he say we might go to the hospital?"

"We'll see. Just keep working," she said, and left before I could ask any more questions.

I kept working, but I was on pins and needles waiting for Daddy. Finally, I heard him coming down the stairway. I rushed out of the living room. He still looked a little tired, but he was dressed as handsomely as ever. He smiled when he saw me standing there with a polishing cloth. Cassie came out of the kitchen quickly.

"How wonderful to see how you two pitch in to help. Thank you, girls."

"Are we going to see Mother now, Daddy?"

He nodded.

"Maybe we shouldn't go just yet," Cassie said.

"I want to go," I said firmly.

"So do I, but we also want to do what is best," she told me.

"I'm afraid she's not much better than she was when I left her last night. It's understandable that she would be in a depressed state."

"We can cheer her up, Daddy."

"If she can see or hear us," Cassie said.

"It can't do any harm, and Semantha is right. It might help bring her around. I have a few calls to make," he said, looking at his watch. "We'll leave in twenty minutes or so."

He went to his den office.

"Go wash up," Cassie snapped at me. It wasn't hard to see how irritated she was at my contradicting her. "You probably stink of polish and have dust all over you."

I nodded and hurried to the stairway, avoiding her gaze. Close to a half-hour later, we got into Daddy's car, Cassie up front and me in the back, which was usual whenever we went anywhere without Mother.

"When we get there," Daddy began as we drove out our main gate, "try not to let her see how much you're disappointed with what has happened. Talk about other things. If she starts talking, no matter what she says about the miscarriage, change the subject."

"Well, you do have the gala opening next week," Cassie said. "We can talk about that."

"Yes. That's smart," Daddy said.

"Does Uncle Perry know about it all, Daddy?" I asked.

"Oh, yes. He was up there with me at the hospital before I came home yesterday. He practically flew from Lexington when I told him what had happened. Your uncle Perry is quite fond of your mother, and she of him."

"Women are most comfortable with men who don't present any sexual threat to them," Cassie declared.

Daddy turned to her. I held my breath. Was he going to be angry that she had referred to Uncle Perry's homosexuality? He didn't look angry, however; he looked impressed.

"That might very well be true, Cassie. Very astute."

"I've been doing some reading about that," she said.

"You always amaze me, Cassie. There's nothing predictable about you. Someday, some man is going to sell his soul for your devoted attention."

"That's not the man I'd want," she said, and what I had feared might not happen for some time happened. Daddy laughed. In fact, he looked as if he was relaxing, too.

"Maybe we'll go to lunch at a nearby restaurant I know instead of the hospital cafeteria," he said.

"That would be nice," Cassie said.

"How long will Mother be in the hospital, Daddy?" I asked.

"I don't know yet, honey, but I'm sure not very long. Dr. Moffet's building her up quickly. He did say he was having a therapist see her today."

"A therapist?"

"Psychiatrist," Cassie said.

"She needs a psychiatrist?"

"Maybe not a psychiatrist," Daddy said. "A psychologist, sort of a counselor who can help her get over the disappointment. We'll see," he added. "Let's not . . ."

"Get ourselves too depressed about it," Cassie finished for him, turning to look back at me.

"Exactly," Daddy said.

I looked at Cassie. She was still staring at me. I felt as if the two of them were the adults and I was an even younger child. Daddy treated Cassie as if she were close to his age and treated me as if I were too young to understand anything.

Don't look at me like that, Cassie Heavenstone! I wanted to shout. *You're barely two years older than I am.*

I smothered those words almost as quickly as they came to mind, however, and turned away to look out the window. Cassie, as if she was practicing for when we would be with Mother, began to talk to Daddy about the gala and the new store. She had given him a half-dozen suggestions for the party, and he liked most of them. I know he surprised her when he told her that Uncle Perry liked most of her ideas as well. Cassie acted unimpressed or disinterested in that and skipped over it as if he had never said it.

As they continued talking, I let myself drift off to think about Mother. I had to fight back my urge to cry every time I pictured her happy and hopeful. Just thinking about how we would have to dismantle the nursery choked me up. Maybe Daddy would just lock the door and do it all when Mother wasn't paying attention. It had to be very difficult for him, too, though.

I had actually begun fantasizing about having a little brother. I had seen myself caring for him, babysitting, helping Mother raise him. Contrary to the things Cassie had said, I had seen his coming as an exciting thing. I hadn't imagined its turning our world topsy-turvy in a bad way. All I had imagined were good things, happy things.

I wondered if they could possibly try again. I knew it was too soon to ask such a question, but it bubbled about in my brain. Would Mother be too frightened to try again? Would Daddy? What if they did and she had another miscarriage? The consequences of that could be overwhelming. No, I thought, there was no way they would even think about it. The prospect of a male Heavenstone to be born and groomed to take over our expanding business was gone forever. It was more likely that Daddy would try to get Cassie to become more involved. Women were running major corporations all over the country now, and if anyone had the leadership, administrative skill, and intelligence to be a CEO, it was surely Cassie. I had to give her that.

If it was what Daddy wanted in the end, she would do it, I concluded. She lived to please him.

We'll be all right. The Heavenstones will be just fine.

Strengthened by my own theories and projections for our future, I walked into the hospital with Daddy and Cassie unafraid. I told myself that we would help Mother recuperate, and things would soon return to normal. Why, this could all make us even tighter as a family. We'd care more for each other, be more considerate to each other. Pretty soon, I'd be chanting aloud like Cassie: "We're the Heavenstones."

The sight of Mother looking shriveled and small in her hospital bed plugged up my gushing optimism quickly. It was as if she were lying on a mattress full of her own tears. The dark circles around her eyes, the pallor of her complexion, and the weakened appearance she presented practically nailed my feet to the floor. I had to press myself to move to her bedside. Daddy rushed to take her hand. She opened her eyes, and almost immediately, her lips began to tremble.

"Please don't cry, Arianna. We need you to get well and come home," he said, and leaned over to kiss her cheek.

Her lips stopped trembling, but she didn't speak.

"The girls have been terrific. They're taking good care of me, and they've been working on the house, too."

Mother nodded and looked at us and shook her head, again looking as if she would cry.

"You've got to get yourself well, Mother," Cassie said, moving beside Daddy at her bedside. "There's so much to be done for the new store opening. We've got to mend and become the Heavenstone family again."

She stood looking down at Mother, who simply looked up at her as if she didn't know what Cassie was talking about. I hurried to her bedside and kissed her. She smiled finally, but she had yet to say a word to any of us. Instead, she simply closed her eyes.

"She's still under some sedation," Daddy said in a voice just above a whisper. "I'm going out to speak with the doctor. I see he's at the nurses' station. You two keep talking to her."

Cassie waited until he was gone and then looked at me and at Mother and shook her head.

"Mother, we need you to stop this and get better," she said. "It's not the end of the world. Other women have had miscarriages and rebounded quickly. Besides, you were taking a chance getting pregnant this late in life. Surely, you knew this might happen."

"Cassie!" I cried.

She ignored me. "Daddy is devastated, too, but he has to recover and deal with his responsibilities. The quicker you get better, the less pressure there will be on us all."

I looked down at Mother. She didn't open her eyes, but her lips began to tremble again. I couldn't stand it. I walked away from the bed and looked at the floor, with my back to Cassie. She came up beside me.

"Stop behaving like an infant, Semantha. This is how you deal with people in her state of mind. You force them to snap out of it. You don't cater to their self-pity."

"How do you know what to do? You're not a doctor," I snapped back at her.

"I've read about this. In fact, I studied up on it last night. I did a great deal of research on my computer. I'm not doing anything to hurt her or be mean. I'm trying to help her. I'm surprised you would think anything else. In fact, I'm a little hurt, Semantha. I would hope you'd think better of me. I'm always looking after you, aren't I?"

"It sounds very cruel."

"It's called tough love, and it's a proven technique. I'll show you articles on it when we get home."

I nodded, but I still didn't like it. She returned to Mother's bedside and continued to whisper her tough love. I stood back, watching, until Daddy returned and she stopped talking. Cassie shook her head to indicate that there was no change.

"I was right. She is still under sedation," Daddy said. "We should leave and return after lunch. She'll be more alert then."

"Whatever you think, Daddy," Cassie said.

Just then, Uncle Perry appeared in the doorway. "How is she?"

"Resting . . . sedated," Daddy said.

Uncle Perry nodded. He came in and looked at Mother and then at us. "Sorry, girls," he said.

"We don't want to dwell on it," Cassie said. "Especially in front of Mother. She might still be able to hear us, sedated or not."

Uncle Perry looked at Daddy, who nodded, and then we all walked out of the room.

"What's Moffet saying today?" Uncle Perry asked Daddy.

"He has a therapist coming to see her late this afternoon. He wants to keep her a few days."

"What about the bleeding?"

"It's under control. Thank God," Daddy told him, and smiled at me.

Uncle Perry nodded and looked at Cassie and me. "You girls have got to stick together and pitch in."

"Oh, they're doing a great job already," Daddy said.

"We do stick together, Uncle Perry, and we always pitch in," Cassie said sternly. Then she smiled. "Especially now, with all this pressure from the new store opening."

"Good. Well, as long as your mother is on the mend and—"

"I thought you had a very good idea with that

lottery," Cassie continued. She sounded disinterested in talking about anything else.

He raised his eyebrows. "Oh?"

"Only I suggested we don't simply have people fill out a coupon. We automatically include everyone who buys anything at a Heavenstone store that day."

"Oh . . . Teddy?"

"I thought it was a good suggestion, Perry. Helps the bottom line."

"Fine."

"Now, then," Daddy said, rubbing his hands together. "Let's go to lunch."

"Where we can talk more about the opening and get my father's mind off this situation," Cassie added, leaning toward Uncle Perry.

Uncle Perry looked at me. It didn't take a genius to see the difference between Cassie's emotional state and mine. I was still hovering close to tears. He smiled at me. "C'mon, Sam. You can ride with me," he said and put his arm around my shoulders.

I looked at Cassie. She shrugged, and as we walked to the elevator, she whispered, "Better you than me."

"Your sister is one tough cookie," Uncle Perry said when we got into his car. "Your father and I had a great-aunt like her, Great-aunt Agnes Loomis, who was married to your grandmother's brother. He died while they were on vacation in Florida, and she kept him in storage until she finished the holiday. She didn't want to lose the money they had spent. I hated the way she looked at me whenever we saw her. I used to have nightmares about her. I still do, matter of fact."

We saw Daddy pull out of his parking spot, and Uncle Perry started his car and followed.

"If you're in a crisis, however, Aunt Agnes and, I suppose, Cassie are the types of people you want." He glanced at me. "How do you two get along? You're pretty different."

It wasn't the first time I had been asked about Cassie's and my relationship. Another one of Cassie's Commandments was that Heavenstones never say anything about each other that they wouldn't say to each other, especially to someone outside our immediate family.

"Okay," I said.

"Just okay?" he followed quickly.

"Cassie is my older sister," I said. "She looks after me, and she is much smarter than I am."

"There's two kinds of smart," Uncle Perry said.

"What are they?"

"There's book smart, and there's people smart. My guess is you're people smart, which means you'll get along better out there, meeting people, working with people, socializing. Cassie doesn't have many friends, does she?"

"I don't like saying bad things about Cassie, Uncle Perry."

He nodded. "I understand. That's admirable. Loyalty is admirable, but," he said, looking at me again and smiling, "don't forget to be loyal to yourself, too."

I said nothing.

His words hung in the air between us as we drove on, staying close enough to Daddy's car for me to see Cassie talking to him continuously.

Cassie was never at a loss for words when it came to talking to Daddy, whereas she could sit in a room for hours with Mother and not say a single thing.

"You guys will be all right," Uncle Perry said, believing my silence was all worry about Mother. "I'm sure."

It was only the two of us in the car, but strangely, all I could hear was what I was sure Cassie would say: *How would he know?*

7

Hospital Visit

CASSIE KEPT OUR conversation at lunch focused solely on the gala opening of the new Heavenstone store. Uncle Perry looked amused at her determination to control the discussion. Every once in a while, he threw me a smile, but I looked away or down, afraid that Cassie would realize he was including me in his amusement with her. I sensed that Daddy wanted to talk more about Mother and the loss of Asa, but Cassie had probably persuaded him in the car to hold off on any discussion about all that until we were alone. She never recognized Uncle Perry as part of our immediate family.

Afterward, we all returned to the hospital. Mother was more alert now and had eaten some lunch herself. I was so happy to see her sitting up in bed that I could feel the smile bursting on my face. It brought a smile to hers, too, finally that motherly smile that was as important to me every morning as the rising of the sun was to the earth itself.

But almost as soon as her smile came, it disappeared when she set eyes on Daddy, and once again, her lips began to tremble. I could hear Cassie's groan of disapproval.

"Dr. Moffet doesn't think it would be wise for us to try again, Teddy," she said when Daddy took her hand.

He glanced at us and nodded. "That's all right, Arianna. We'll be all right. I told you not to think about any of that right now. Just concentrate on getting yourself stronger and better."

"Daddy's right, Mother," Cassie chimed in. "You want to be able to attend the opening ten days from now. You should be at Daddy's side when he meets the governor."

Mother looked at her as if Cassie were speaking a foreign language.

"And don't forget we have Semantha's birthday soon, too," Daddy added, smiling at me.

Mother gave me another short-lived smile and turned back to Daddy. "I'm tired, Teddy."

"That's the medicine still working," he said. "You won't need much of it soon."

"Sure," Uncle Perry said. "In a day or so, you'll be on your feet, Arianna."

Mother just shook her head. Daddy started to take the tray off her table, but Cassie shot forward to do it.

"That girl won't let me lift a napkin," Daddy told Mother.

She nodded, barely creasing her lips.

Uncle Perry stepped up to the foot of the bed. "Hey," he said. "We need that smiling face of yours, Arianna. You can't expect Teddy and me to make a good impression without you."

Mother forced a smile again but turned back to Daddy, her eyes watering. "I'm so tired, Teddy, and so sorry."

"It's all right," he said, patting her hand. "We'll be all right. It's not your fault."

"Of course it isn't," Uncle Perry added. "You have to tell yourself, if it was meant to be, it would be."

. Behind him, Cassie rolled her eyes. The nurse's aide came in, and Cassie gave her Mother's tray.

"I know you all have so much to do," Mother said "I don't want to bring any more hardship to this family."

"Arianna!" Daddy snapped. "Don't say things like that. You haven't brought any hardship. We're all fine, fine."

I couldn't help myself. I started to cry. Instantly, Cassie seized my left arm at the elbow and tugged me back.

"Stop it!" she whispered. "You'll make things even worse."

I sucked in my breath and turned so Mother wouldn't see. Cassie stepped in front of me and began to talk to Mother.

"Now, listen, Mother, Daddy's right. Semantha and I have things under control at the house. We'll both return to school tomorrow, and Daddy will return to work. We'll come to see you as often as we can while you're here, but Uncle Perry and Daddy are right. We need you well and home." She spoke sternly, then glanced at Daddy and added, "We really need you, Mother. The house is empty without you.

No matter what happened, you still have Semantha and me to care for and love, and we both love and need you."

Daddy nearly came to tears. Mother reached up for Cassie's hand, and Cassie leaned over to kiss her cheek. "Thank you, dear," she told her.

I stood back, watching a little in awe but mostly in envy. I saw the way Mother had almost immediately changed her mood, and I saw how even Uncle Perry looked impressed with Cassie now. He glanced at me and nodded. I could hear his thoughts. *See why I said she's just like my aunt Agnes? If you're in a crisis, they are the types of people you want.*

Cassie stepped back and looked at me. It was her way of giving me permission—no, more like ordering me—to step forward, say my little piece, and retreat.

What could I say after that little speech she had made? Nothing could come up to it.

"Cassie's right, Mother. We need you home. Please get well soon."

I kissed her cheek, too, and then Cassie thought we should let Daddy and Mother be alone for a few minutes. She, Uncle Perry, and I said good-bye and went out into the corridor.

"I hope you really don't mind my correcting your suggestion for the gala, Uncle Perry," Cassie told him as we walked toward the waiting lounge.

"Why should I mind? I can see the point. After all, I want only what's good for our business," he said. "As your father always says, we have to keep our eyes on the bottom line."

"Thank you," Cassie told him. He raised his

eyebrows. "After Mother is home a while, we'll invite you out to the Heavenstone mansion for dinner."

"Don't you two girls become disappointed and nervous about your mother if she doesn't snap back as quickly as you would like. She is in a very—"

"We know, emotionally fragile state. I didn't approve of their trying to have a baby this late in their marriage," Cassie told him. "I was afraid something like this might happen, and it has."

"Sometimes it's not so pleasing to be right," Uncle Perry countered, and Cassie was speechless a moment.

She regained her composure and suggested that Uncle Perry didn't have to wait with us. "We'll be fine. No need for you to waste any more time."

"I'd like to talk with your father before I leave, and I don't consider this a waste of my time," he said curtly.

Cassie shrugged, found a magazine, and sat. I could almost hear Uncle Perry's blood racing angrily through his veins. His face had reddened. He looked at the soda machine and asked me if I wanted a drink. I nodded and walked over to it with him.

"I can tell you this, Semantha," he said, "and you don't have to reply or react in any way. Your sister is worse than Aunt Agnes when it comes to people skills. If she ends up running the Heavenstone Corporation, it won't last."

He punched our drink choices, gave me mine, and sipped his by a window, far from Cassie, who was already absorbed in a magazine article and couldn't have cared less. Ten minutes or so later,

Daddy came out to join us. He told us the therapist had just arrived and was speaking with Mother.

"She's taking it all too hard," he said, shaking his head. "I'm really worried about her. She wanted this baby even more than I did." He smiled at Uncle Perry. "She lives to please me."

"She'll be okay," Uncle Perry told him. "Give it some time, Teddy."

Daddy nodded and looked at us. "Okay, let's go home, girls. Maybe I'll take you out to dinner tonight."

"Oh, no, Daddy. I've already defrosted three beautiful filet mignons for us. I have it all marinating so it will be just the way you like it."

"When did you do that?"

"While Semantha was changing to come to the hospital," she said, making it sound as if I did frivolous things while she did meaningful ones.

"See, Perry, I'm in good hands," Daddy told him.

Uncle Perry nodded and looked at me when he replied. "She's just like Aunt Agnes when Uncle Leo had his first stroke, remember? You'd have thought he had nothing more than a cold."

"Yeah, but she held them all together," Daddy said, smiling at Cassie.

I walked with Uncle Perry, who hugged me and whispered, "Take care of your mother when she comes home, and take care of yourself, Sam."

He kissed me and got into his car. I joined Daddy and Cassie, who were already waiting in Daddy's car. We were all quite silent for a while as we left the hospital. Then, to my surprise, Cassie didn't talk about the gala; she talked about the lost Asa, the so-called forbidden topic.

"You were very brave in there today, Daddy," she began. "I know how much you wanted this baby, how much it meant to you to have a son."

"No, I—"

"Yes, it did, Daddy. I understand. Men might favor their daughters, but they live for their sons, and you've never had one and probably won't."

"Cassie, don't talk like that!" I cried. It came out before I could stop it.

She looked back at me with those dagger eyes and then continued. "I want you to know, Semantha and I understand and will help you with Mother."

"Oh, I know you will, honey."

"Every time she looks at you, she will see the disappointment in your eyes if you're not careful, Daddy."

"I understand. We'll work it all out," he said, and patted her on her knee. "Don't you worry yourself sick, now."

"I just . . . we just don't want you to be dragged down by all this."

Daddy nodded. "Yes, we wanted a son," he said, his voice cracking a little, "but we're grateful we have you two. We're already blessed. Don't worry."

Cassie said nothing, but when she turned to me, she had a smile so deep in satisfaction that it turned my stomach.

However, I knew what was going to happen as soon as we were alone at home. Seconds after I went into my room, she followed and came at me with her eyes looking like egg yolks. I actually took a step back in anticipation of her slapping me.

"How dare you criticize something I'm saying to Daddy like that? Did you think I was trying to hurt him, hurt his feelings? Well?"

"No, but I thought it would."

"You thought? Ha," she said, throwing her head back. "You know nothing about human psychology. Besides, you don't pretend something doesn't exist just because it's painful to acknowledge it. If you do that, it ferments inside you until it does destroy you."

She stared at me a moment and then calmed down.

"What am I doing? You're still a child. Of course, you wouldn't understand any of this. Just remember, keep quiet. If you have any questions, you wait and ask me them later, and I'll do my best to get you to understand. Understand?"

"Yes, but I'm not a child, Cassie. I'm nearly fifteen. My birthday is in two weeks."

"There are grown men and women who are nothing more than children. Age has nothing to do with what I mean." She paused and shook her head at me as if I was beyond help. "Forget it for now. I've got to do some schoolwork and get down to the kitchen." She turned away from me but turned back quickly. "And when Daddy leaves for the hospital after dinner, don't ask to go with him. He and Mother need time alone now."

She left my room, and I stood gazing after her, my eyes burning with tears.

When had I been at a lower moment in my life? I

wondered. I was an object of mockery at school, and with Mother in this terrible state and Daddy acting as if Cassie was his only daughter, I had never felt more alone. But I wouldn't permit myself to cry. Sitting in my room and sobbing would be just what Cassie would expect, would justify her calling me a child. Somehow, I had to become as strong as she was, so Daddy would see that I was just as capable of rising to the occasion. I could be just as mature and responsible and dependable.

The first thing I would do would be to start the housework and chores without having Cassie tell me first. And I wouldn't ask her for anything, especially in front of Daddy. Mother and Daddy need me as much as they need Cassie now, I thought, and so, as Daddy would say, I took a lug wrench to my determination and tightened it so much I could barely breathe.

The next morning, I was up before Cassie. The sight of me in the kitchen stopped her dead for a moment. I already had the coffee made and the table set for breakfast, too.

"What's gotten into you?" she asked with a half-smile.

You, I wanted to say, but I just shrugged and said, "I don't know. I was up, so I started on things." Then I smiled to myself and added, "I know how hard you're working and thought I should do more."

"Well, yes," she agreed, nodding, "you should. That's very admirable of you, Semantha. I guess our little chat last night did some good."

She went right to work preparing Daddy's

breakfast. After my last attempt to do that, I wouldn't try again. I fixed my own cereal and fruit. We both heard Daddy come down the stairs and turned to the doorway.

"Look at my elves at work. I bet Santa Claus doesn't have it any better," he said.

"Well, you are our Santa Claus, Daddy," Cassie said quickly. I wished I could have been that witty.

"Now," Daddy continued, looking at us both suspiciously, "who put out my clothes for this morning, had everything hanging and waiting for me when I opened my eyes, just like your mother always does? Well?"

"Maybe you have an invisible third elf working here," Cassie told him, and he laughed.

"Everything smells good. I have a good appetite this morning."

"Your paper's on the table, Daddy," I said. Cassie had forgotten that. She whipped her head around and looked at me. "I got it first thing."

"Thank you, Semantha."

He gave me a kiss and then kissed Cassie. Usually, he kissed her first. She continued to look strangely at me for a moment after Daddy went into the dining room.

"What's wrong?" I asked.

"Nothing. Go eat your breakfast. I'll bring the rest out to Daddy."

"I called your mother this morning," Daddy told me when I sat at the table. "She sounded a little stronger. I think she had a good session with the therapist."

"When will she come home?" I asked, just as Cassie brought in his breakfast.

"We'll see. She still has to build up a bit. That looks wonderful, Cassie. Thank you," Daddy said when she placed his plate in front of him. She looked at me and shook her head, as if I had already done something wrong. Then she went to get her own breakfast.

"Does the doctor know yet what happened?" I asked quickly, hoping he would answer before Cassie had returned.

"Not exactly. I don't want to have him put her through a series of tests to get to the exact causes, either," he continued.

Cassie returned and took Mother's seat again.

"Tests can wear you down, too," Daddy added.

"What difference would it make now, anyway?" Cassie said. She had apparently overheard everything. "As long as she is no longer in any physical danger."

"My sentiments exactly," Daddy said, nodding. "Let's just get her back on her feet as quickly as we can."

Cassie had that self-satisfied look on her face again. Nothing pleased her as much as Daddy agreeing with something she said or suggested. I finished eating in silence while she and Daddy talked about the Lexington store.

Afterward, I did most of the cleanup, because Daddy wanted to show Cassie a new line of products he was considering for the stores before he went to work. She went with him to his den office. When I was finished, I got my things together for school.

Daddy was already at the front door when I started down the stairs.

"See you guys later," he called to me, and waved.

"Okay, Daddy. Have a good day," I said.

Cassie came hurrying out of the kitchen. "You left the milk out," she said.

"No, I didn't."

"Okay, then the container grew legs, arms, and hands, opened and closed the refrigerator door, and trotted up onto the counter. Let's go."

I followed her out to her car and got in. The moment she started the engine and drove off, she began her ranting.

"He has so much to do. You wouldn't believe the list of things to cover just today. I mean, imagine having to have an entirely new staff of employees trained and ready. Each of our stores employs more than a hundred people in two shifts, you know. Imagine the payroll, the taxes, dealing with the personalities, and then reviewing new products, overseeing the orders, on and on and on."

"You seem to know a lot about it, Cassie. Maybe you should think of becoming the CEO of the Heavenstone Corporation someday."

She whipped her head around. "I told you. I don't want to be a businesswoman. I'm not interested in all that, dealing with all those personalities. Mother really let him down this time," she concluded, nodding.

"How can you say such a thing?"

"Christmas trees, Semantha, my not saying it doesn't mean it didn't happen, does it? Besides, it's only you and me talking. I would never say such a thing to Daddy, and you'd better not ever tell him I did."

"Of course, I wouldn't. I wouldn't want to hurt him and hurt Mother."

She smirked and nodded at me. "I would have preferred your saying you would never betray me, Semantha. That would be the first thing coming to my mind if it concerned you."

"I meant that, too."

"Yes, I'm sure. Anyway, here's the plan now. We're not returning to the hospital."

"What?"

"We're not going to visit Mother there."

"Why not?"

"You want her home, don't you?"

"Of course I do."

"Well, we don't want her to get comfortable there, to think it's all right for her to prolong her stay. This is part of that tough love I told you about the other day. She'll see that if she doesn't come home soon, she'll continue disrupting our lives. It will stop her from feeling all this self-pity, wallowing in it. We won't even call her.

"Now, what we have to do is tell Daddy we have tons of homework every night, tests, term papers. And we have the housework to do as well. He'll understand, and he'll tell her that, and very quickly she'll see that she must get on her feet and put a stop to this 'Oh, woe is me' routine."

"But—"

"Didn't I tell you it would turn our world topsy-turvy? Didn't I?"

"Yes, but whoever thought she would have a miscarriage?"

"Do you want me to quote the statistics of failed pregnancies occurring in women over forty?"

"Dr. Moffet thought it would be all right."

She smiled. "Next time we see him, ask him why he was so confident."

I was silent. I felt very confused. Was Cassie right? Was this the best thing to do? Ignore Mother?

"Remember when I used to tell you how we have to be special, Semantha, how we come from a very important bloodline? How we have to be perfect? Well, here's an example of it. Just pull yourself together and follow me, and you'll be fine. We'll all be fine." She smiled to herself and chanted in a whisper, "We're the Heavenstone sisters, the Heavenstone sisters."

It was still echoing in my brain when we pulled into the school parking lot. Since my incident with Kent and the aftermath, I had a sinking feeling whenever I thought about school. That returned in spades this morning. I hurried to my locker and then to my homeroom, not even looking to see if anyone was interested in saying good morning to me. I took my seat and waited for Mr. Wegman, our homeroom teacher, to begin taking attendance. Roxanne Peters, who sat behind me, tapped me on the shoulder. I turned, and she leaned forward.

"Jami Wright's mother called my mother and told her your mother had a miscarriage. Is that true?"

I stared at her a moment and turned around again without speaking. For a moment, it felt as if all the air had been sucked out of the room. I felt her breath on my neck as she leaned even farther forward to whisper.

"My mother said she wasn't surprised and wondered why a woman your mother's age with two fully grown daughters would start over with another baby. Was it an accident?"

"What?" I cried, spinning on her. Some of the other students stopped talking to each other and looked at us.

"I mean, her getting pregnant?"

"It's none of your business or your mother's business," I said.

When she smiled, I couldn't help myself. Something broke inside me, and I lifted her desk so that it fell back on her, knocking her and her chair to the floor. The noise was like a firecracker. Mr. Wegman stopped taking attendance. No one moved, no one spoke, until Roxanne began to cry. I was sent out with a written referral to see Mr. Hastings, the principal. Referrals from a teacher were like speeding tickets policemen gave to drivers, only we had to stand before the judge immediately. I was trembling so much when I left the homeroom I thought I would faint. Somehow, holding my breath all the way, I made it to Mr. Hastings's office. His secretary took the referral, read it, gave me a look of surprise, and then told me to take a seat and wait. She went into his inner office with the referral.

The threads of all sorts of terrible thoughts spun in my brain. How disappointed would Daddy be when he found out? Would Mother somehow find out, and would that set her back even more? How would Cassie react? What about the rest of my teachers, who all thought good things about me? What punishment would Mr. Hastings dole out? Would Cassie be called out of class to take me home? Daddy was already in Lexington, I imagined. It would be just horrible if he had to turn back because of me.

"Mr. Hastings will see you now, Semantha," his secretary said, and stood back in the doorway to permit me to enter. I did so slowly, probably walking like someone about to go to the electric chair.

Mr. Hastings sat back in his desk chair. I had never gotten anything but a smile or a pleasant hello from him, but I knew from the testimony of other students, students who were in trouble frequently, that he could be more like the warden of a maximum-security prison than a kind-hearted administrator in a public school. At the moment, his face didn't show a tiny hint of disappointment or surprise. It was the face of the executioner, firm and dark.

A tall, stout man, Mr. Hastings had been a college football star. He was as big and as robust as Daddy and held a commanding presence behind his desk. To me, it looked as if he could press a button and drop me into some dark pit for punishment. His thick, dark brown hair was almost military short. He had a nearly square jaw, two piercing hazel eyes, and firm, straight lips, pressing on each other so hard they formed tiny white spots in the corners.

"Sit," he said, nodding at the chair in front of his

desk. I went to it quickly. He looked at the referral again, as if he had to read it many times to believe what it said.

Before he could speak, his secretary knocked on the door and poked her head in.

"What is it, Mrs. Whitman?"

"The nurse says Roxanne Peters has a nasty bruise on her right elbow. She is advising her mother to take her for an X-ray."

He didn't speak immediately. He looked at Mrs. Whitman and then at me and nodded.

"Thank you, Mrs. Whitman. Please have Mrs. Mills inform me about the follow-up ASAP."

"Yes, Mr. Hastings," Mrs. Whitman said. She backed out, closing the door.

"You've been here long enough to know I have a no-excuse, no-defense policy when it comes to anyone being physically violent with anyone in my school," he began.

I didn't sob aloud, but I could feel the tears escaping my lids and starting to zigzag their way down my cheeks. I quickly wiped them off.

"However, considering your history here, I would like to know why you did such a thing, Semantha." He sat back again and waited.

I took a deep breath. "My mother had a miscarriage a few days ago. She is still seriously ill because of it."

"More reason for you to behave yourself," he quickly interjected.

I nodded. "As soon as I sat down, Roxanne

began to say nasty things about my mother, and I just wanted to shut her up. I'm sorry I hurt her."

"What should you have done instead?" he asked softly.

"Ignored her. I tried to do that!" I cried. "But she wouldn't stop."

"What else could you have done?"

I knew what he wanted me to say, but few girls or boys I knew in school would have done it.

"Raise my hand and tell the teacher what she was doing."

"Exactly. Then she'd be the one sitting here in front of me, and not you."

Yes, I thought, but afterward, every student who still liked me would hate me for being a rat. They would even begin to tease me more every chance they had, especially all of Kent's friends. Why didn't Mr. Hastings know this himself? He was a student once, and I was sure he had been harassed by someone and hadn't just turned them in to the teacher.

"As I said, no matter how good the reason for what you did seems to you or even to someone else in the classroom watching it all unfold, it was still absolutely forbidden in my school. Small acts of violence have a way of becoming bigger and bigger acts, until someone gets seriously hurt or killed. We see it happening everywhere these days."

He leaned forward, glaring at me.

"It won't happen here. Not on my watch," he said. He sat back again, pausing to calm himself. "Is your father at the hospital with your mother?"

"No, he's in Lexington. We're opening a new store there. Then he'll go to the hospital."

"What is his cell-phone number?" Mr. Hastings asked. "Or the number at the store?"

"I don't know the store number. His cell phone is 555-5454."

Mr. Hastings jotted it down. "Your sister's name is Cassie, correct?"

"Yes," I said. I couldn't help looking more frightened of her than of my father, and I saw how that surprised Mr. Hastings.

"Is there anyone, another adult, at your home now?"

"No, sir."

"Not even a housemaid?"

"We don't have a housemaid."

He raised his eyebrows, then opened one of his drawers and took out a file. He flipped through it and nodded. "She has permission to drive to school and park in the lot. Did she do that this morning? Drive here with you?"

"Yes."

"Unfortunately, then, your sister will have to take you home and remain with you until your father makes other arrangements. I don't send students to an empty home or one where there is absolutely no supervision. I'm suspending you for one week, and you will not be permitted back until your father brings you back and we have a meeting with you in my office.

"I'm sorry for your family's trouble, but if

anything, that should have given you more reason to behave yourself. There are no mitigating circumstances when it comes to violence in my school, and no one is treated any differently from anyone else when it comes to that."

My tears came again, but this time, I didn't bother to wipe them away. I let them drip from my chin.

"Go back to the outer office, and take a seat until your sister comes for you."

I rose slowly, or it seemed I did. I was in such a daze, so terrified, I wasn't sure of anything. It also felt as if I were floating across his office to the doorway. I returned to the seat I'd had in the outer office to wait for Cassie. I knew exactly what she would say.

"See, see, I told you it would turn our world topsy-turvy!"

8

Topsy-Turvy

CASSIE SAID NOTHING to me when she came to the office. She glanced at me and then went directly to the counter to get the letter for Daddy that Mrs. Whitman had already typed up, copied, and put in an envelope. It was as if Cassie had done this many times. I watched how cool and unemotional she was. Anyone else who didn't know us would surely think she worked for the school and had no special interest or relationship with this particular student being punished.

"I'm Cassie Heavenstone," she told Mrs. Whitman.

Mrs. Whitman explained what was in the letter and that it was very important that our father read it.

"Keeping it from him won't help your sister," she added.

Cassie pulled her shoulders and head back as though Mrs. Whitman had tried to slap her. "Why would I do that? I don't appreciate your insinuation."

"I'm . . . just . . . giving you good advice."

Cassie took the envelope and put it in her purse. "Is that all? Are we finished here?"

"Yes," Mrs. Whitman said.

Cassie nodded at me, and I stood up, glanced at Mrs. Whitman, who looked a little shocked, and followed Cassie out. She was walking quickly toward the exit, so I had to hurry to catch up.

"I really dislike that woman," she muttered as if nothing else had occurred. "As Daddy would say, she thinks her poop doesn't smell." She paused at the door and looked at me. "You don't have to tell me anything. What you did in homeroom shot through this school so fast it might as well have been a breaking news bulletin on CNN."

Before I could respond, she threw the door open and charged out to the parking lot. Again, I had to run to keep up.

"I'm sorry they called you out of class, Cassie."

"I don't mind missing classes," she muttered. "Most of the time, I'm so ahead of everyone else, I have to sit there thinking of things to do for Daddy and the stores. I actually welcome being called out, even for something like this. Get in," she ordered when we reached the car.

I moved quickly. She sat for a moment, thinking.

"I'm not returning to school today. It's my responsibility to remain with you. I'm the only adult available," she said. *Only adult?* I thought. *She's not old enough to be called that.* "All right," she said, starting the engine. "Let's hear about it."

I began to describe what Roxanne Peters had said and how she was persistent and mean. Cassie listened without commenting. In fact, she was silent for quite a while after I had finished telling her why I had done what I had done and how Mr. Hastings had spoken to me. I feared she was too angry at me to speak.

"It's not your fault," she finally began. I breathed a sigh of relief about that, until she added, "It's Mother's fault."

"What? Why?"

"It's what I call an echo." She kept her face forward, talking as if she was dictating to someone. "When you do something wrong, terribly wrong, it has consequences that sometimes don't roll out for a while but nevertheless are directly caused by what you have done. This is, I'm afraid, only the beginning for us, at least for a while."

"Only the beginning? Why?"

"Daddy will have to suffer through all the condolences from his business associates. It will spread rapidly through our employee population, and every time he enters one of our stores, they will look at him with pity. No one will try that with me in my classes, but I know they'll be whispering behind my back. I don't pay attention to any of them as it is, so it will be like nothing's happening, but it's different for poor Daddy. He has to face these people daily, and it will be painful."

She finally turned to me.

"A man like Daddy doesn't ever want pity. It's degrading, especially when it comes from people so inferior. The Heavenstones have always been strong, proud people, even when they lost so much after the Civil War. They didn't grovel or beg for mercy. They grew stronger and stronger, until we became who we are today.

"I'm not saying what you did was okay, Semantha. It was . . . childish. There are so many more sophisticated ways to get back at someone, ways in which you can make that person look like the guilty one, in fact. I hope that when you're older, you'll be more creative. Throwing someone's desk over on them, although satisfying for the moment, is not very effective. You should have bitten down on your lip, waited, and come to me later. I'm sure I could have helped you do something far more effective."

"Daddy will be so upset with me when he hears about all this," I moaned.

"Yes, he will, but I'll handle it much better than whatever Mr. Hastings wrote in his dumb letter. I'm sure it's something standard, a boilerplate discipline letter in which he might just fill in your name. He never struck me as being much of a brain."

I still didn't know whether Cassie was angry at me or simply not in the least concerned about how it would all affect my school life.

"What do you mean, it was an echo? I still don't understand, Cassie."

"Christmas trees, am I talking to myself? The foolish pregnancy, Semantha. That's what's led to this today and who knows what tomorrow."

"Oh. Then Mother will feel even worse now."

"She surely will. That's why you had better listen to me and not go visiting her in the hospital. Even in the state she's in, she'll be able to read your obvious face easily, and you will have no choice but to blurt out everything, which might nail her to that hospital bed for weeks more."

I started to sob softly.

"There's no reason to cry now, Semantha. It's over and done with. Can't you try to act like a Heavenstone, at least make an effort? I told you I would handle this."

I held my breath and nodded. She drove on in silence but wearing a strange smile all the way home.

When we arrived, I went directly up to my room. The fear and tension exhausted me, and I fell asleep for a while. I didn't come out until I was hungry for lunch. I didn't hear Cassie and thought that she might have changed her mind and returned to school after all, but when I was in the kitchen making a sandwich, I heard her come out of Daddy's office.

I poked my head out of the kitchen doorway.

"I'm having a turkey and cheese sandwich. Do you want me to make you one?"

"Yes," she said, surprising me. She usually wanted to do things for herself. "Do it on toast and cut it in fours like I do for Daddy."

I saw that she was carrying some documents.

"What's that?"

"Store business, things for the gala, that sort of thing. I've been studying it. Uncle Perry isn't as successful for us as he makes out to be and Daddy pretends. He's lucky I'm not the CEO. He'd be gone. I'll be in the dining room. Bring a cranberry juice with the sandwich, and don't forget napkins."

Making something like a turkey and cheese sandwich isn't a big, involved project, but because I was doing it for Cassie and knew how she could be, I made it as perfectly as possible. Not a piece of turkey or cheese stuck out, and I actually measured the quarters with a ruler. She had her face in a folder when I brought it to her and set it down. She glanced at it and nodded. Then I got my sandwich and sat across from her.

"Should we call Daddy and tell him anything?"

She lowered the file, picked up one of the sandwich quarters, and began eating without replying.

"I mean, I don't think he can find out beforehand, but maybe I—"

"What did I tell you in the car, Semantha? Didn't I tell you I would handle this?"

"I know. I just thought—"

"Don't think right now. Just do what I say, and we'll get through this . . . this incident."

She continued reading and eating. I finished my sandwich, and when she was finished, I took her plate and glass into the kitchen. I heard her return to Daddy's office. No one could keep herself busy the way Cassie could. On the contrary, despite how unpleasant school had become for me these past days, I realized I was going to be quite bored for a week. I didn't know if my schoolwork would be sent home. I supposed the letter to Daddy said something about it. For now, all I could do was go up to my room to watch television.

Later in the afternoon, I heard our doorbell ringing and hurried out to see who it could be. Cassie was at the door greeting someone. I stood at the top of the stairs, waiting and listening. Moments later, she and a man wearing a cap that said "The Lock Jaw Company" came to the stairway. I stood back as they ascended.

Cassie said nothing to me as she showed him where to go. I followed.

"What's happening?" I asked.

She ignored me and brought him to the door of what was to have been Asa's nursery.

He looked at the doorknob and nodded. "I'll have to replace all this."

"Can you do it now?"

"Oh, sure."

"Then do it," she said. "I'll have a check ready for you when you're finished."

"Okay," he said, and went to get his tools and equipment.

Cassie finally turned to me to explain. "We're locking this door and keeping it locked for a while. Only I will have a key."

"Why?"

"Why? Because it's a constant reminder of the foolish pregnancy, Semantha. When Mother comes home, she'll be bound to go in there and cry and moan. I'm replacing the lock, and we won't give her a key until she is stronger and over it."

"Did Daddy tell you to do this?"

"He didn't have to tell me. I knew it was the right thing to do. Believe me, he'll be very pleased about it. Right now, neither he nor Mother should dwell on this nursery."

I was amazed at how confident Cassie was about the things she decided and did. Why was she so sure Daddy wouldn't be upset and would actually praise her for this?

"I was going to have it done later in the week,

but since you presented me with this opportunity today, I thought, why not take advantage of it? You see, Semantha, you have to find something good and positive in everything that happens to you, even the bad things. That's what we're going to do now. While I'm with the locksmith, you start preparing the table for dinner. I'm going to give you more things to do. I have decided that your problem comes from the fact that we all do too much for you."

"Why? That's not true. I do my chores, help out, don't I?"

"Like a little girl might, yes, but you need more and more responsibility. You've got to be seized by the heels and dragged into maturity. Eighty years ago, a Heavenstone your age would have been engaged, married soon after, and pregnant soon after that. Do you think any of your little girlfriends could manage such responsibility now?"

"But they shouldn't have to. We shouldn't have to. It's not eighty years ago. Things are different."

"Never mind. I don't know why I'm wasting my time talking about it. Put up some potatoes. I want to make Daddy's favorite mashed. We're having veal chops. You'll find them in the refrigerator, and there's a bowl in which I have prepared the sauce to marinate them. Daddy has to eat earlier tonight. He's going to the hospital to meet with the therapist."

"How do you know?"

"I spoke to him an hour ago."

"Did you tell him about me, about what happened?"

"Of course."

"What did he say? Is he very angry?"

"Yes, but thanks to me, not as much at you. Relax. I told you I would handle it. Don't I always take care of you? Well?"

"Yes, Cassie."

"So, why are you still standing here? Go down and get to work."

"Okay," I said, and hurried downstairs, passing the locksmith, who had started up.

Afterward, I was in the kitchen with Cassie when Daddy came home. He paused to look in at us. I had to look down.

"I am really surprised at all this, Semantha."

"The letter is on your desk," Cassie told him. He nodded and walked to his office. I felt my heart thumping. Cassie looked at me and shook her head.

"Don't start wailing like a baby, Semantha. Wait here. Keep everything warm. We'll call you," she said, and went out to follow Daddy.

A little while later, she returned.

"Okay, go to his office. He wants to talk to you now. I'll finish here. We're eating in ten minutes, so don't keep him."

I hurried down the hallway. Daddy was standing by his bay windows with his back to the door, his hands clasped behind him. He turned slowly and shook his head.

"Of course, you shouldn't have been so violent, Semantha. I'm actually quite shocked you were, but Cassie explained what happened. I can understand what you did, but I can't defend it. However, Cassie is right. The principal should be taking our situation into consideration, and what that girl was doing to you was aggressive and violent, too, in its way. This punishment is a bit too much. A week is a long time to miss classes. Cassie has already scheduled an appointment for me with him tomorrow. Fortunately, I'm here tomorrow, so it's no problem."

"I'm sorry, Daddy."

"I know. Cassie is also right to say we should keep this from your mother for now. I agree with her that, for now, the two of you should not come to the hospital."

He smiled.

"I know what you did you did because of how badly you feel for us. Sometimes I want to explode, just start shouting at anyone for anything. We were so close, so close, but we have to swallow and absorb our defeats and disappointments and go on. Next time something like this happens, you'll have to count to ten before you react."

"I will, Daddy."

"I'm sure you will," he said, coming around the desk to embrace me. He kissed my forehead and brushed back my hair the way Mother always did. "Well, I'm starving, and I did smell the aroma of the meal Cassie's prepared. Let's go eat."

I nodded. His embrace restored me. We started out.

"And I must say," he continued as we walked down the hall to the dining room, "your suggestion about the nursery was quite smart and thoughtful."

I stopped. "My suggestion?"

"About the lock. I was thinking about that,

about your mother going in there constantly and crying. It never occurred to me to do something that simple. You girls are definitely Heavenstones through and through."

Later, after he left for the hospital, I asked Cassie why she had told him the changing of the lock on the nursery was my idea. She smiled and shook her head.

"My dear little sister, don't you ever get it? What better time to give you credit for a good idea than when you are at fault for something? It helped bring him to see the goodness in you and therefore want to defend you and forgive you even more."

"Oh. I never would have thought such a thing," I said, more to myself than to her, because I was thinking that it was dishonest, a manipulation. It actually made me feel even dirtier, like some sly, conniving child.

"Of course, you wouldn't. That's why you have me," she said. "Someday, you'll do something for me in my time of need. Won't you? Well?"

"Sure, Cassie."

"Good," she said.

We heard the phone ringing and knew from the number of rings that it was my line.

"So it begins . . . the gossip. Go on, have fun with your little friends. Tell them you don't regret anything and that you'd do it again. They'll be shocked at your courage and respect and fear you more. Go on," she urged.

As usual, Cassie was right. Everyone in my class wanted to know what had happened to me and what was going to happen now. The first call came from

Rachel David, who sat in the row across from mine in homeroom and had witnessed the whole episode. She told me that I was the big topic of discussion at lunch and that even Kent was impressed.

"He said you have more guts and grit than he thought. It sounded like he regretted dumping you," she added.

"Dumping me? Boys always try to get you to believe they did the dumping, but I dumped him at the party," I said, and she laughed. To my surprise, she told me she would call me tomorrow night, too, and report what was said.

"No one really likes Roxanne Peters. She's a real backstabber. Too bad you only bruised her arm and didn't break it."

I laughed to myself. Cassie was so perceptive. She had predicted just how my classmates would think and act. In their minds, I was suddenly someone heroic. I liked Cassie's idea about finding something good in the bad things that happened. I went to sleep that night actually feeling a bit proud of myself and wondering why I had ever shed a tear.

And it was all because of Cassie. If she had ever loomed tall and impressive to me before, she was even greater in my eyes now. And suddenly, maybe for the first time, really, I began to see myself as a true Heavenstone.

She stopped by to say good night. For a moment, when I saw her in the doorway, I thought I was looking at Mother. When she came in, I realized why. She was wearing one of Mother's nightgowns. I recognized it immediately.

And she spoke in Mother's soft, loving tone of voice. "How are you, Semantha?"

"All right," I said, puzzled and even a bit frightened by this sudden change in her.

She came to my bedside and sat with her back to me but turning slightly, just the way Mother always did. Then she reached out and brushed back my hair, and she smiled, not a Cassie smile mask or a smile of skepticism and distrust but a Mother smile, loving, concerned.

I was still holding my breath. This was more like a dream.

"You've had one terrible, terrible day. I'm sure you felt alone and frightened for much of it. You wondered how the people who loved you would react. You worried about being hated, about their anger, didn't you?"

I nodded.

"Just remember, you're always safe here and always loved here and always part of this great family. We might not approve of everything each of us does, but we'll never betray or desert each other, never. Go to sleep knowing I'm here for you and I will protect you as I would myself." She leaned down and kissed me on the cheek. Then she brought her lips to my ear and whispered, "We're the Heavenstones."

I said nothing. I watched her rise slowly and practically float out of the room, turning in the doorway to smile at me and flip off my light the way Mother would before she closed the door softly and left me, only feeling not safe and secure but confused in the darkness.

The following morning, Cassie made a startling declaration to Daddy and me. It rang like that of someone who was putting herself on a hunger strike.

"I've decided that as long as Semantha is prohibited from attending school, I will not attend, either," she announced.

It took Daddy by complete surprise. He looked up from his coffee and his newspaper, and for a moment seemed at a loss for words. "Do you think that's wise, Cassie? I mean, you could fall behind in your work. No sense in both of you having so much to make up, is there?"

"First, I'm so far ahead of everyone else in all of my classes, I could stay home for the remainder of the year and go in to take my finals. Second, we're the Heavenstone sisters, Daddy. We support each other always."

"Well, loyalty is admirable. I can't deny that." He thought a moment and then smiled. "I guess I have my work cut out for me this morning when I meet with your principal."

"He's no match for you, Daddy," Cassie said. "His biggest accomplishment has been getting a new bulletin board for the building."

Daddy laughed. "Okay, girls. You sit tight. I'll call you when my meeting is finished."

I didn't know what to say. If I told Cassie she shouldn't stay home, she would get angry. I was sure of that. It was better simply to show her appreciation. I thanked her.

"You don't have to thank me, Semantha. I am sure you'll be as loyal to me when the time comes, if it should come," she said.

"Oh, yes," I told her, even though it gave me the feeling I had just signed my name in blood. I was still thinking about how she had behaved in my room the night before.

When Daddy left, we went right to work on the house. She said she would do his office, wash the floors and windows, dust and polish. She wouldn't permit me to do anything in there, and when she did do the office, that took most of the day. She pulled every volume off the shelves and dusted each one as well as the shelves. Daddy always complimented her on how she had turned his office from a mess into a picture-perfect workplace.

Maybe because I was so nervous, I worked even harder than Cassie and lost track of time. I was doing the inside windows in the living room when Daddy returned. Cassie had heard him before I did and was there to greet him. They were both standing in the living-room doorway.

"Okay," Daddy said. "You're returning to school tomorrow, Semantha. You are on probation, which means you can't do anything like you did to that girl. If anyone bothers you, you are to go right to the principal, understand?"

"Yes, Daddy."

"I've got to get to the office and then to the hospital. Maybe you two can go with me tonight," he said.

"Thank you, Daddy."

"I know you're a good girl, Semantha, and this was just an unfortunate incident. Carry on, you two," he said, and left.

I sat on the sofa, a little dazed and feeling just how hard and intensely I had been working. Cassie returned from seeing Daddy off. She stood smiling at me.

"Well, now, didn't I tell you Daddy would do it? Hastings probably wilted like a flower in his presence. Daddy could have been a great lawyer, a great anything. I have no doubt in my mind that one of these days, they'll come around to ask him to run for governor."

"Really?"

"Of course, really." She stopped smiling. "We can't go with him to the hospital, however."

"Even now?"

"Especially now. Have you forgotten what I told you? She'll just dwell on our sympathy and languish in that place for weeks."

"But what will we say to Daddy?"

"We'll both be too exhausted from the work and the emotional roller coaster. In fact, neither of us will have much of an appetite at dinner. Eat something before so you really aren't hungry. I'll do the same. He won't insist or be disappointed, and he'll have to say something to Mother. She'll see he's not telling her the whole truth, and she'll get herself together to get out of there and home."

I nodded, but Cassie could see I wasn't happy about it. "I do miss her and want to see her, Cassie," I said.

"Of course you do. We do, but if we don't use tough love and be strong, we'll only do her more harm. You want her back on her feet quickly, don't you?"

"Yes."

"Then it's settled. You might as well go back to work here and really get yourself tired. Then you won't have to pretend so much. In fact, when you're finished here, wash all the floors downstairs and upstairs. I'm returning to the office."

Wash all the floors in this great house? That will take me all day, I thought, and just sat there anticipating how exhausted I would be. I went ahead and began the work, however, breaking only for lunch and then, when Cassie called me down from washing the upstairs floors, to have what she called a snack to kill our dinner appetites. Her plan certainly worked. Daddy only had to take one look at both of us at dinner for him to suggest that we should stay home and get to bed early.

To my surprise, Cassie started to protest, but then she looked at me and said, "Semantha is exhausted. She's had a terrible emotional ride. I couldn't see leaving her alone."

Daddy agreed and was pleased. He left right after dinner and promised to give Mother our love and tell her we'd be there tomorrow.

"Of course, we won't be."

"How will we avoid it tomorrow, Cassie?"

"Don't worry. I'll think of something. She won't be there much longer, anyway, I'm sure."

Still, I went to bed feeling very guilty and twice almost went to the phone to call the hospital and at least speak to Mother, but Cassie had specifically forbidden that, too.

"Mother will see he's making up some excuse,"

she told me before I went to sleep. "She'll realize she should come home. She'll be worried about us instead of herself, finally."

I nodded, but I couldn't help remembering how Uncle Perry had called her another Aunt Agnes. If the world really needed people like that, I thought, it must not be a very nice place.

I was so tired that despite my wish to wait up for Daddy to see how Mother was, I fell asleep almost as soon as my head hit the pillow and didn't open my eyes until the sunlight struck my face in the morning. Realizing I had missed him, I leaped out of bed and washed and dressed as quickly as I could. Cassie was already downstairs, and Daddy was at the table. He had to go to Lexington this morning.

"How was Mother last night?" I asked the moment I saw him.

Cassie poured him some more coffee.

"It was amazing. When I first arrived, she was almost the way she was when you girls were there, but when I told her why you two couldn't come, she seemed to rally. Before I left, she told me she has to get home and get back to taking care of all of us. I was very encouraged."

"That's wonderful, Daddy."

"Yes. Now," he said, looking at me with his chin lowered and his eyes raised, "remember, you're on probation. No funny business."

"I'll remember."

"Good."

Almost as soon as he left, Cassie pounced. "Well? Do you see how right I was now? Do you?"

"Yes, Cassie."

She smiled. "As long as you listen to me, Semantha, you'll be fine. We'll all be fine."

What could I do but agree, yet I wondered if she ever felt arrogant. Mother always said she was the most self-confident young woman around, but when does self-confidence move into the realm of arrogance? When do you become your own worst enemy?

And for Cassie, Cassie as a worst enemy would be devastating, I was sure.

It wouldn't be all that much longer before I would be the one proving that true.

Mrs. Bledsoe

CASSIE DIDN'T HAVE to come up with a new reason for us staying home and not visiting Mother at the hospital. When we arrived home from school the next day, we found Daddy in the hallway speaking with a private-duty nurse. Even without the sight of the nurse being there, one look at his face told me anyway that Mother had been brought home. His smile and robust energy had returned.

It had been a most interesting day for me at school. Again, Cassie's predictions proved to be true. Before I had violently attacked Roxanne Peters, most of my classmates and other students saw me as aloof, rich, spoiled, and snobby, someone who thought she was lowering herself to be in their company. The fact that I could behave more the way one of them would behave won me many new converts and solidified whatever small relationships I had built with some. Even Kent, as Rachel had said, saw me in a new light and was very friendly, to the point of suggesting we go to a movie together soon.

Furthermore, I was granted some sympathy as well. Whether they were afraid to or not, most of my classmates didn't laugh or think of Mother's miscarriage as something funny or deserved. They all wished her a speedy recovery and pounded on Roxanne Peters for being an insensitive bitch. I was wallowing in my newfound popularity. Maybe it was my imagination, but I thought my teachers looked at me differently, too, looked at me with a little more respect. Whatever, it turned out to be one of my more enjoyable days at school, now topped off with Mother's return home.

I was surprised, however, at Cassie's reaction. The moment she saw Daddy and the nurse, she became angry. She recoiled. Her body tightened like a guitar string, and her lips whitened at the corners. I could almost feel the rage in the air between us, but Daddy, maybe because of his happiness, didn't see it or feel it.

"Great surprise for you, girls. Your mother is home. Dr. Moffet decided she had recovered enough to go home, but for a week or so, we'll need the assistance of Mrs. Bledsoe. For now, she'll see to Mother's medications and nutrition and make sure she rests and is doing well. You can go up to see her."

"Give her another hour or so first," Mrs. Bledsoe said firmly. "I just got her to sleep."

"Why would you get her to sleep minutes before we came home?" Cassie asked. "Anyone would realize we'd want to see her immediately, and she would want to see us."

She came at Mrs. Bledsoe so sharply that the nurse was speechless for a moment. Even Daddy looked shocked. He gave Mrs. Bledsoe a small smile that said, *Please excuse my daughter. She's a little overwhelmed.* Mrs. Bledsoe didn't show any anger, but I felt certain she felt some.

I estimated Mrs. Bledsoe to be in her fifties, maybe sixty, but later would learn she was only in her mid-forties. Her hair had turned gray prematurely, and she had done little or nothing to hide the grayness. It wasn't a bright, healthy-looking gray, either. It looked more like dull pewter. She was about five foot six, slim, with rather long, thin arms and hands with long, thin fingers. In fact, thin seemed to be her dominating characteristic. Her nose, although not pointed or too long, was thin. Her lips were pencil-thin. Only her untrimmed eyebrows were thick, but her face was long and looked as if when it was form-ing, two strong hands had pressed on both sides to keep it narrow and her cheeks flat, extending her chin just an inch or so too much. The starch-white uniform washed out what little color there was in her complexion.

"When someone is in the hospital for a while, they are bed-tired," Mrs. Bledsoe explained. "It will take a little time to get her back on her feet. You can't rush it, especially with someone who's been through all your mother has been through. Actually, Dr. Mof-fet wanted to keep her a few more days, but she insisted on coming home today. I hope you'll both be very cooperative," she concluded.

"Oh, I'm confident they will, Mrs. Bledsoe," Daddy said. "Mrs. Bledsoe will be in the guest room right across the hall from our bedroom. I've already told her what a great cook you are, Cassie."

"Of course, your mother will be following a diet plan Dr. Moffet has arranged," Mrs. Bledsoe quickly interjected. "I'll take care of that."

"Fine," Cassie said. "Do let us know when it's all right to see our mother," she added, and headed for the stairway.

Daddy watched her go for a moment and then turned to me, a little suspicious. "How was your day at school, Semantha?"

"It was good, Daddy. No problems."

"I'm sure there won't be any more. I've got to run back to the office for a few hours. Help Mrs. Bledsoe with anything she needs, will you, honey?"

"Okay, Daddy. I'll just go put my school things away and change. I'll be right down, Mrs. Bledsoe."

She nodded and smiled at me, and I followed Cassie up the stairs. She was waiting for me at the top with her shoulders drawn up, which always made it seem as if her head and neck were sinking into her body. One look at her face, and I could see immediately that she was even more enraged, angrier, than I could ever remember. She wagged her head and smirked at me.

"I heard you. 'Okay, Daddy. I'll be right down, Mrs. Bledsoe,'" she imitated. "How nauseatingly sweet."

"What should I have said, Cassie?"

She turned away, started toward her room, and stopped. "Why did he bring her here? We don't need her. I can do everything for Mother. I was doing it before, wasn't I? Now we have a stranger right in the middle of our personal lives and personal business, a stranger in a Heavenstone home. Bledsoe. Her name is quite appropriate, don't you think?"

"Why?"

"Bledsoe . . . bled . . . Mother hemorrhaged. She nearly bled to death. Get it?"

"Oh. It's just a coincidence."

"There are no coincidences in life. Everything has a purpose, a reason. She won't be good for Mother and especially not good for us. Don't be so nice to her. Once she sees how unwelcome she is, she'll leave."

"But Daddy wants her here, Cassie."

"He's . . . just being overly cautious now. It's absolutely the wrong tactic. He's still babying Mother. She won't get stronger if she has a crutch like that hanging around."

"He'll be upset at us," I warned.

She thought a moment and then smiled. "You're right. Forget what I just said. You can be nice to her. Don't worry. Just follow my lead," she said, and went to her room.

Forget what she just said? I had no idea what she meant by following her lead. Confused, I went to my room to change. Afterward, I wondered if I should go down to see what Mrs. Bledsoe needed, as I had promised Daddy, or wait for Cassie. What did Cassie want me to do? I stepped out of my room and looked across the hallway. Her door was open. I went to it, expecting to see her, but she wasn't there. She wasn't in her bathroom, either.

When I came out and started toward the stairway, I heard a door open and close and saw Cassie come out of the guest room Mrs. Bledsoe was using.

"What were you doing in there?" I asked.

She looked at Mother's bedroom door and brought her finger to her lips, waiting to get closer to me before whispering, "I wanted to be sure everything was all right with the guest room. Daddy just assigned her the room without checking to be sure she has everything she needs in the bathroom. We haven't had anyone use that room for some time."

"Oh," I said, surprised that she was concerned for Mrs. Bledsoe now.

She saw it in my face. "This is the Heavenstone house, Semantha. We don't run a third-rate boardinghouse."

"I know." I looked toward Mother's bedroom.

"I checked on her. Don't worry."

"She was awake?"

"She was for an instant but fell back to sleep."

"I thought we weren't supposed to go in."

"No one tells me when I can and can't see my mother. She's groggy, so for now, we'll let her sleep. Let's go down and see what we can do to help Mrs. Bledsoe in the kitchen," she said.

"Help?" I wanted to be sure I heard right, that Cassie really did have a change of heart and maybe was beginning to see things Daddy's way.

She paused and turned back to me. "There are ways to help, and there are ways to help, Semantha," she replied, and continued to the stairway.

What did that mean? Why must Cassie speak in riddles? I followed her down. Mrs. Bledsoe was in the kitchen, obviously searching for things. She was squatting by one of the lower cabinets and was taken by surprise when she turned and saw Cassie and me standing in the doorway, watching her silently. It flustered her for a moment, and she dropped a pan.

"Oh."

"Let us help you, Mrs. Bledsoe," Cassie said in a sweet, soft change of voice that surely would make anyone wonder if she was schizophrenic. "I'm sorry we got off on the wrong foot before. We do want to be cooperative for Mother's sake."

"Oh, thank you, dear. I was looking for a blender."

Cassie nodded to me, and I stepped into the kitchen and retrieved the blender from one of the lower cabinets.

"What are you blending?" Cassie asked.

"I have this nutritional supplement I give all my patients who need to be built up. Anemia can be so devastating. Your mother told me she's fond of apple juice, so I'll blend it with that. I'd like her to have the supplements between meals. Perhaps in a day or so, we'll get her moving about. I'm sure she'll be fine in a week's time."

"Perhaps sooner," Cassie said.

"We'll see."

"I'm going to prepare one of Daddy's favorite meals," Cassie continued. "It's a meat loaf. I'm sure you would agree that Mother could use some meat."

"Maybe in a day or so. I'd prefer she eats a lighter meal for her first day back," Mrs. Bledsoe said. "I'm just going to give her some eggs and toast tonight."

"Eggs. Okay. She likes the way I scramble them. I use just the right amount of milk and cheese and . . ."

"We'll see," Mrs. Bledsoe interrupted, and began to blend her supplement with the apple juice.

Cassie went over to look at the canister of powder. She read the ingredients. "It does have many good things in it. Maybe we should all take this. Do you, Mrs. Bledsoe?"

"Not regularly now. I do take vitamin supplements, however. Don't you girls?"

"Oh, we eat really well here, Mrs. Bledsoe."

"Nutrition is a science," she replied, "and is especially important when someone is run-down, someone like your mother."

"Then we're lucky we have you," Cassie said. If a smile could poison someone, Cassie's could, I thought. Mrs. Bledsoe just nodded and continued preparing her nutritional drink.

Cassie turned to me. "Help me prepare dinner," she said, and started to gather the ingredients for her meat loaf. She kept an eye on Mrs. Bledsoe as she worked and assigned different tasks to me.

As soon as Mrs. Bledsoe left with the drink for Mother, Cassie pounced. "You see? You see how bad this woman will be for Mother? Here I tell her I can make the eggs the way Mother likes them and she hesitates. She wants to be in complete control. 'Nutrition is a science,'" she said bitterly. "I know the type. She lords it over poor, unfortunate sick people who can't put up any resistance and whose loved ones are terrified of disagreeing with her. Mother won't improve at all under her care."

"Maybe she'll change her mind about your preparing the eggs," I suggested.

"The eggs? It's not just the eggs! It's the whole situation, Semantha. Christmas trees," she muttered, and returned to her preparations for dinner, working in silence.

"You girls can go up to see your mother any time you'd like now. She's awake," Mrs. Bledsoe told us on her return.

"Thank you," Cassie said, not in any way revealing that she had already seen Mother. She nodded at me, and we left the kitchen and went up to Mother and Daddy's bedroom.

I hurried ahead to Mother's bedside. She smiled up at me, and I quickly kissed her. Cassie did the same.

"How are you girls?" she asked.

"We're fine," I said. "But we missed you."

"I know, dear. I'm sorry."

"It wasn't your fault," I quickly told her.

She looked at Cassie. "Were you here before, Cassie?"

"Yes, but you were asleep."

"I thought it was a dream."

Cassie looked at me, raised her eyebrows, and then sat on the bed. "Do you think that maybe you came home too soon, Mother?"

"I don't know. I couldn't stay there anymore. I could see what the nurses and the nurses' aides were thinking every time they looked at me. To go so long toward term and then lose your baby . . . I was drowning in their pity."

"Daddy didn't have to hire this nurse. I can take care of you quite well, Mother," Cassie said.

"I'm sure you can, but I don't want you missing any more school on account of me."

"I'm wasting my time there, anyway. I should be taking college courses, and you know it."

"Yes," Mother said. "My brilliant daughter. I'm proud of both of you. You've been taking good care of your father and the house."

"You'll be up and around in no time, Mother," I told her.

Cassie nodded at the drink Mrs. Bledsoe had brought. There was still quite a bit left. "You don't really like that stuff she prepared for you, do you?"

"It's okay. I'm just . . . just still a little tired and have little appetite."

"Well, even though she's here, I'll be nearby if you need me, Mother," Cassie said. She leaned toward her and whispered, "If you want something to eat that she won't give you, just let me know, and I'll see that you get it."

"Thank you, dear."

"I'm preparing that meat loaf you make, just the way you make it. Daddy loves it."

"That's very nice, Cassie. It helps me to know you're so competent and can take my place."

"No one can take your place, Mother," I said sharply, even with a little hysteria in my voice.

"I know, dear. I was just referring to now, when I'm still unable to fulfill my duties."

"You will soon," I insisted.

"I've got to get back to work," Cassie said, standing quickly. "That nurse insists on preparing you some eggs. I know you would prefer the meat loaf."

"It's all right for now, Cassie. I don't think I'll even eat much of the eggs."

"Not if she insists on making them," Cassie muttered, and started out. She paused at the door and looked at me. "Are you coming to help, Semantha?"

I got up from the bed reluctantly. "I'll be back up to see you as soon as we're finished," I promised.

Mother nodded and closed her eyes. I stood there a moment, fighting back tears. I hated to see her so weak and tired and defeated.

"Semantha," Cassie whispered.

I turned and hurried out after her. "She still looks so sick," I said.

"No kidding," Cassie muttered, and hurried down the stairs.

Mrs. Bledsoe was starting up. "I'm just going to check her blood pressure," she said.

Cassie flashed a smile mask and continued to the kitchen. She worked silently, but by the way she kneaded the meat and mixed in the ingredients she had me prepare, I could see that the anger was still boiling in her. I thought I would try to get her to be more reasonable.

"Now that we see how things are, isn't it good that Mother has a professional nurse, Cassie? As Daddy would say, she's still not out of the woods."

She didn't answer. I could see that she didn't even hear me. She was so deep into her own thoughts that the house could explode around her and she wouldn't know it. She didn't come out of it until Daddy arrived. He was very anxious about Mother.

"How's it going?" he asked Cassie.

"Fine. I've made your favorite meat loaf."

"I meant, how's your mother doing?"

"She's still very weak, Daddy. I do hope Mrs. Bledsoe's supplements and care get her on her feet quickly, although Mother didn't like the drink and hardly drank it. She made her some eggs and toast and brought it up to her just now. She wouldn't let me make it, so I don't know how Mother will receive it. You know how Mother hates the gushers in the eggs. I take my time removing any and . . ."

He nodded, smiled at me, and hurried up the stairs.

"Let's set the table," she told me sharply. Then she paused and smiled. "Don't forget to put out a place for Mrs. Bledsoe."

As it turned out, Daddy wanted to have his dinner upstairs with Mother. Cassie carried his tray up to him. I knew she wasn't going to be happy with our having to eat dinner only with Mrs. Bledsoe, but she wasn't unpleasant. She asked the nurse many questions about herself, where she grew up, where she went to college. She wanted to know if she had always been a private-duty nurse and what other work she had done. I thought Mrs. Bledsoe would be upset with Cassie's rapid-fire questions, but she calmly responded to everything.

Finally, Cassie changed the subject. "I know my mother is recuperating from a physical shock to her body, but don't you think she's in a deep depression?" Cassie asked.

"Oh, I think she'll come out of it once her health returns. Life is full of disappointments. We're all more resilient than we think, but we need to be healthy."

"That's encouraging," Cassie said, glancing at me. She turned back to Mrs. Bledsoe and said, "I guess we are lucky having you here, Mrs. Bledsoe."

I didn't speak. I didn't trust the way she was behaving. I kept expecting the floor to collapse under us.

Mrs. Bledsoe complimented her on the meat loaf. She ate every morsel.

"Would you like some more, Mrs. Bledsoe?" Cassie asked. "I can get you a little more." Before Mrs. Bledsoe could respond, she took her plate and started for the kitchen.

"I really don't—"

"Oh, please. It pleases me so much when people enjoy the food I prepare," she said.

"Well . . . just a little."

Cassie smiled and went into the kitchen.

"You sister is quite an accomplished young lady. I understand she is an honor student as well."

"Yes, straight A's. She even helps her teachers correct other students' papers sometimes."

"I was a good student, too, but not quite that good," Mrs. Bledsoe said. "What about you?"

"I'm okay. I get mostly B's. Some C's," I admitted.

"You're both lovely daughters. I can see why your father is so proud."

Cassie returned with her second helping.

"Oh, that's too much, dear."

"Eat what you like, Mrs. Bledsoe. I don't keep food for leftovers. I like making things fresh every day."

"Oh." Mrs. Bledsoe raised her eyebrows and continued to eat. "Wonderful flavor. We get meat loaf in the hospital cafeteria, but it tastes a bit like I imagine cement might taste and sometimes feels like it in your stomach."

Cassie laughed. I smiled, still amazed at how well we were all getting along now.

Despite Cassie's insisting, Mrs. Bledsoe didn't want any dessert and decided to retire to her room, where she said she would watch television until she looked in on Mother. She told us she would check on her a few times during the night.

"How can you possibly get a good night's rest with so many interruptions?" Cassie asked.

"Oh, you get used to it. It's not a problem," she said. "Thank you, girls." She rose and left.

"She doesn't seem to be too bad a person," I said.

Cassie was staring after her. She turned to me slowly, her smiles gone. "Too bad a person? She's pathetic," she said.

"What?"

"Would you like her life to be your life? You heard her. She has little or no family, has never been married, has no children, no boyfriend, if you read between the lines. Probably the most exciting thing she's done is give an enema." She rose. "I'll go up and get Daddy's tray. You clear the table," she told me.

When she came down, she didn't look happy.

"What's wrong? Is Mother all right?"

"She's the same, but look. Daddy hardly ate. He told me he was just too nervous to have an appetite, and this is his favorite meat loaf. I was so careful to make it just the way he likes it. You saw how much time and effort I put into it."

"It's only because he's worried, Cassie."

"I knew he shouldn't have brought her home so quickly. He's sitting up there watching her every breath. I hate to see him like that."

"But it made him so happy to bring her home, Cassie."

"So? It won't do anyone any good if he gets sick, too, now, will it? He has so much to do this week."

"She'll be lots better tomorrow," I said.

She paused and looked at me with an expression of disgust that made me shudder.

"What?"

"You had better stop deluding yourself, Semantha. Grow up. She's never going to be the way she was."

"What?" My lips began to tremble. "Why not?"

"It was too traumatic an experience. It's not like she cut herself or had a minor rash or something, Semantha. There was something living inside her that died, and that something died for Daddy as well."

"But Mrs. Bledsoe said people are resilient, and if they are healthy—"

"Mrs. Bledsoe puts Band-Aids on people, Semantha, takes their blood pressure, and dispenses pills. What would she possibly know about this experience? The most important thing that she's probably lost is her thermometer. I doubt she's lost her virginity. The faster she's gone, the better chance we have to bring back some normalcy into this home. As long as she's here, it smells and feels like a hospital. Daddy will realize that soon. He's pretty smart. You'll see."

I said nothing. I finished my work and then started up to see Mother. Daddy was talking with Mrs. Bledsoe in the hallway. They both turned to me as I approached.

"She drifts in and out," Daddy said. "Don't be frightened, honey. It's all right. She'll soon be up and around."

I looked at Mrs. Bledsoe, who nodded, and then I went in to see Mother. I sat with her and talked about school. Sometimes she listened, sometimes she just stared as if she were alone and heard nothing. I kept expecting Cassie, but she never came up. Finally, Mrs. Bledsoe came in and told me I should just let Mother rest now. She said she would sit with her and that I shouldn't worry. I thanked her, kissed Mother, and left. I thought I would go directly to my room to do my homework, but when I came to the stairway, I heard the sound of Cassie's laughter. It was coming from the living room. Curious, I went down to see.

She was sitting with Daddy, who was sipping some coffee. They both turned to me when I entered. The way Cassie was looking at me made me feel as if I had interrupted two adults having an adult conversation. Whatever it was, it wasn't for my ears.

"How was she?" Daddy asked quickly.

I told him how she did seem to drift in and out.

"Mrs. Bledsoe assures me it's not unusual. In a few days, Dr. Moffet will stop by. Cassie was just telling me about some of the amusing and ridiculous things that happened in school today. I must say we have to reconsider the idea of a private school for you two. I imagine you'd like that."

"Maybe," I said. He looked surprised.

"She'll like it, I'm sure," Cassie said. "For now, you'd better see to your homework. I'm too busy to go over it with you, Semantha. It takes her longer when I don't help her," she explained to Daddy. He nodded.

That wasn't completely true. It was only when I had some difficult math. I started to say something, but she turned away and whispered something to Daddy that made him laugh. Frustrated, I turned away and went upstairs.

Cassie didn't come up until much later, and she didn't stop by my room. I heard her go into hers and close the door. I finished my homework and went to bed. I fell asleep quickly but was woken in the middle of the night by the sound of some commotion. It was just before three in the morning. I heard Cassie's voice and quickly got out of bed, terrified that something had happened to Mother.

Daddy was in the hallway. He was in his robe and slippers. Cassie, in her nightgown, was listening to him. I hurried to see what was happening.

"What's wrong? Is something wrong with Mother?" I asked, holding my breath and pressing my hand over my heart.

"No," Cassie said. "It's Mrs. Bledsoe."

"She thinks she might have a bad case of the stomach flu," Daddy said. "It's terrible, Semantha. My fault. I should have made sure everything she needed was in that bedroom and bathroom."

"What do you mean, Daddy?"

He shook his head.

"Mrs. Bledsoe has the runs," Cassie said, "and there was apparently no toilet paper or tissues. She's messed herself the way some of her patients do. It's quite unpleasant."

"But . . . I thought . . ."

She turned back to Daddy. "If she might have the flu, Daddy, it's very dangerous for Mother in her run-down state. I'll see to Mrs. Bledsoe, but you should make immediate arrangements to send her home. Don't worry. I'll stay home tomorrow and take care of Mother."

Daddy was very flustered. He actually started in one direction and then went in another. "It's so late. We can't send her home in the middle of the night like this," he decided.

"She's a nurse, Daddy. I would think she would be all right."

"I don't know."

"I don't even like you going in there now. Flu can be very infectious, and you could carry it into your bedroom and infect Mother."

He nodded. "But you . . ."

"I won't stay long, and I will be careful not to get too close to her or touch her."

She went to the hall closet and gathered up toilet paper and tissues and some clean towels and wash-cloths.

"Go back to Mother, Daddy. I'm sure she's disturbed. I can handle this."

"Yes, I . . ."

"I'll handle this," Cassie said firmly. "Go on."

Suddenly, Daddy looked like a little boy eager to obey his mother. He nodded and went to his bedroom door. He paused there and looked back.

"Go on, take care of Mother. That's more important," Cassie insisted.

He nodded again and went into the bedroom, closing the door behind him.

"I thought you said you were in her bedroom checking that she had everything she needed, Cassie."

She looked at me a moment. In the dim hall light, her slight smile looked like a devil's grin. "I must have overlooked things. You can go to sleep, too, Semantha. Unless Daddy takes you to school, you'll have to go on the bus again," she said, and went to Mrs. Bledsoe's bedroom door. She squeezed her nose and smiled at me and then went inside, closing the door behind her.

I stood there, amazed. I could never do what she was about to do.

However, Cassie was going to get what she wanted. Mrs. Bledsoe would be gone. I started back to my room, worrying, of course, that Mother might not have the medical attention she needed. Maybe Daddy would hire a new private-duty nurse tomorrow, I thought, and that gave me some comfort. But when I stepped into my bedroom, I also thought Cassie would persuade him not to bother. She was usually very successful when it came to persuading him to do one thing or another.

I started to get back into bed but stopped.

How convenient it was that Mrs. Bledsoe, of all

people, had contracted a stomach flu. Cassie was somehow to blame for this, I thought. But even if Cassie had deliberately taken all of the toilet paper and tissues out of the bathroom before, how did she know Mrs. Bledsoe would have such a nasty flu?

The answer exploded in my head. I froze with my blanket in my hand.

Then I quietly left my room and tiptoed through the hallway and down the stairs. When I flipped on the kitchen light, I really didn't know what to look for or where to look, but I went to the garbage compactor and rifled through some of the refuse. I saw the first one and plucked it out. It was an emptied laxative capsule. I knew what they were. I had once been given one. I opened the cabinet we used for our medicines and saw the bottle. It was nearly empty.

Staring at it, I recalled how Cassie had doled out everyone's meal and then had gone back to get Mrs. Bledsoe more meat loaf.

It stunned me.

"What are you doing?" I heard Cassie ask.

My heart jumped in my chest when I turned and saw her standing in the kitchen doorway.

"Why aren't you in bed?"

She stepped into the kitchen, her eyelids narrowing and her shoulders rising.

Without accusing Cassie of anything, I said, "She'll find out she doesn't have the flu, Cassie."

"Of course, she has the flu, Semantha. It can't be food poisoning. You and I ate the same things, and we're fine. She agrees. She's just about packed. The taxi is arriving any minute to take her away."

She moved closer to me, seeming to grow taller, wider.

"It's best for all of us, Semantha. You agree, don't you? Don't you?"

I looked at the medicine cabinet and then at her. Her eyes followed my moves, but then she stuck her gaze on my face. I nodded.

"Good. Then go to sleep. Everything's okay. I'll see that everything is just fine. I'll have your breakfast ready, too. Good night," she said, closing the medicine-cabinet door. She folded her arms across her breasts and stared at me until I turned and hurried out of the kitchen.

I hurried up, taking two steps at a time and gasping at the top. I didn't stay there long. All I wanted to do was get back into my bedroom before Mrs. Bledsoe appeared. I knew I couldn't look into her face without crying.

And if there was one thing I was afraid to do right now, it was cry.

Cassie wouldn't like it.

10

Sedated

DESPITE THE LITTLE sleep Cassie had, she was up ahead of me and very bright and energetic in the morning. I had heard Mrs. Bledsoe leave her room and go down the stairs during the night. I had gone to my door and listened harder and heard Cassie, too. She sounded very pleasant and concerned for her. Mrs. Bledsoe kept thanking her.

"I'm bringing Daddy and Mother's breakfast up to them," Cassie told me. "Everything you need for your breakfast is right here on the counter."

"Does Mother know about Mrs. Bledsoe?"

"Daddy told her last night. She wasn't very upset about it. I knew she wasn't fond of having her. I can see a change in her already."

"Really?"

"Of course. Being under that added tension only harmed her recuperation. It was too stressful. Hurry and eat, and then go up to say good-bye for the day. You have to make the bus, Semantha, and the clock doesn't wait for anyone," she added, which was one of Daddy's favorite expressions.

She fixed the tray and left. What Cassie had done

to Mrs. Bledsoe frightened me, but, like her, I did feel things were more normal in our home. Because we had never had sleep-in help or even part-time house help as long as I could remember, we were closer than most wealthy families who had servants. Perhaps Mother was right about that. Whenever something made one of us unhappy, the rest of us felt it and reacted and were not ashamed to show it. There was no one here to make us feel embarrassed about our emotions, and nothing about our personal lives could become fodder for gossip.

After school and on weekends, when Daddy, Cassie, and I were here with Mother, our house was more like a protective cocoon. Thinking about all of that now convinced me that Cassie was right when she said there was something special about us, about the Heavenstones. We were like four parts of one person. No family members felt the blood of their ancestors running through their veins as much as we did and only because we were in this great house, this monument to our heritage. When I was younger, I believed I saw different expressions on the faces of our ancestors. I'd glance at a portrait and think, she just smiled at me or winked at me. The house and all that was in it was as alive as we were. It wasn't something I would tell anyone else, but I still had those feelings.

I thought about this as I ate my breakfast, and it had the effect of calming me. Things were tumbling back to the way they had been. It was as if the past months had been erased. It was like the day before Daddy had announced Mother's pregnancy at dinner. Happy and energetic again, I hurried up to Mother and

Daddy's bedroom. Cassie hadn't come down. Daddy, already dressed in his light-blue suit and tie, was standing by the window sipping some coffee. Mother was sitting up, and Cassie was standing by her bed, overseeing everything and looking as if she was in total charge.

"As you can see," she said the moment I entered, "unlike yesterday, Mother has eaten most of her eggs this morning." She nodded at Mother's nearly empty dish. "Mrs. Bledsoe might be a good nurse, but she's certainly no cook."

"What a dreadful thing to happen," Mother said when I kissed her good morning. "That poor woman."

"It's a wonder more medical personnel don't get sick, being around so many infected people. More people get sick in hospitals than out of them," Cassie said, and Daddy nodded.

"Still, I'm not happy about your missing so much school, Cassie," Daddy told her.

"Don't you spend a second worrying about that, Daddy. I'll arrange for Semantha to pick up my work. I usually do the week's work in one day, anyway. Mother," she added, looking at her, "shouldn't need more than a few more days, and then she'll be on her feet again."

"We'll see what Dr. Moffet says. He'll be upset about Mrs. Bledsoe and want me to hire someone new."

"Once he stops by and sees how well I'm taking care of her, he'll change his mind, Daddy," Cassie insisted. "I can make sure she's well fed, much better fed, and rested and takes her medications just as well as Mrs. Beldsoe could. We already see how Mother likes my cooking better."

Daddy shook his head and smiled. "What am I to do with such a daughter, Arianna?"

Mother forced a small, short smile and then took a deep breath. "That's all I can eat, honey," she told Cassie.

"One more bite, Mother, and please finish your juice. As Mrs. Bledsoe would say, you need your vitamin C if you want to get well faster."

Mother smiled a real smile this time. In fact, it was the best smile I had seen on her face since she had gone to the hospital.

"Now I know what an ogre you girls thought I was when I would pester you to finish when you girls were sick," she said.

Daddy laughed. "Cassie did sound like you for a moment there. I'm off, gang. Final preparations for the gala opening. I'll call you as soon as I hear from Dr. Moffet, Arianna," he said, and leaned down to kiss her. For a moment, they just looked at each other. I saw how Mother's lips were starting to tremble. "Now, don't keep thinking about it," he whispered. He held her against him. Her whole body shuddered.

I looked at Cassie. She seemed disgusted, shook her head, picked up the tray, and started out. "You'd better get moving. You'll miss the bus," she told me.

Daddy seemed unable to release Mother. He held her against him so long it brought tears to my eyes. He didn't let her go until I said, "I'm off."

I rushed to kiss Mother good-bye and then

hurried out after Cassie. She was still descending the stairs and waited for me to catch up.

"I can't help crying every time I look at them, Cassie."

"Cry if you want to, but do it in private. One more mourner in this house, and we'll be able to register as a funeral home." She paused on the stairs. "I'll have my teachers send my work to the office. You'll have to speak to that horrible Mrs. Whitman. She can be very nosy, so if she asks you anything, just stare at her without answering and leave."

"Can you really miss all this work in school?"

At the bottom of the stairs, she paused. "I'll tell you a secret, Semantha, and you know how I feel about keeping our secrets."

I nodded.

"I intend to quit school."

"What?"

"I've been thinking more and more about Daddy and our business ever since I began studying the paperwork in his office. He needs me now, especially now. As I've said, Uncle Perry is in his own world and of no help when it comes to administrative matters."

"Quit? But everyone says you will be the valedictorian."

"How would something like that compare to what I can do for Daddy? Do you think I'm that selfish, that egotistical?"

"No, but won't he be very upset?"

"In the beginning, but once he sees how valuable I can be to him, he'll change his mind." She looked up the stairs. "With Mother a real burden now, he needs me more than ever."

She stared up silently.

"He should have left for work already," she whispered. "She's dragging him down."

I stood there, shocked and confused by her words. Suddenly, she turned to me, looking as if she thought I had been spying on her or something.

"Get moving. You'll miss the bus!"

I hurried out, my heart thumping even before I started to run down the driveway. The things she had just told me, especially about her quitting school, were too shocking to put aside, even when I got on the bus and the girls were jabbering with exciting news about the upcoming school party and Billy Stanton, a boy in my class, getting into a car accident last night. He wasn't hurt, but he had been drinking, and he had missed a turn and gone crashing into the wall at a gas station. The chatter was finally too overwhelming to ignore.

At the beginning of my last class of the day, my teacher was given a note that I should go directly to the general office at the bell. I knew that was for Cassie's schoolwork. Of course, I wondered why she even wanted it if she was really going to quit school to work with Daddy. Maybe she was just fantasizing, I thought. Maybe she didn't mean it.

She was right about Mrs. Whitman. As soon as she saw me, she wanted to know if anything was wrong at home. I did as Cassie commanded and stared at her silently. It obviously unnerved her. She handed Cassie's work to me and turned away quickly.

I smiled to myself and hurried to make the bus. I can learn so much from Cassie, I thought. No matter how mean to me she seems to be sometimes, I should remember that. Few of my friends had an older brother or sister even willing to help them as much as Cassie was willing to help me.

Overall, it had been another good day for me. The friendliness I had felt the day before had continued in school. Kent was now pressuring me to meet him at the mall movie theater on Friday night. I didn't want to use Mother's condition as any sort of excuse, but more important, I really did want to meet him. I still felt guilty about the way I had behaved at Eddie's party. I told Kent I would try.

"Try hard," he said.

"What about Megan?" I asked.

"Megan? Megan who?" he replied, and I laughed.

I couldn't remember when I had felt better about myself and the school. This was why I had hesitated when Daddy had suggested he might put us in a private school. Now, if Mother just improved and we got back to where we had been as a family, life would be perfect.

The chatter on the bus ride home was just as loud and excited as it had been on the way to school. At least four of my girlfriends wanted to call me in the evening. I felt as if I had been woken out of a Rip Van Winkle sleep and was finally in this world. With a bounce in my step and a smile on my face, I hurried home from the bus stop, eager to see how Mother was doing. Cassie seemed to be waiting for me at the door.

"How is she?" I asked immediately.

"Resting comfortably. Dr. Moffet came by during his lunch hour. Daddy told him about Mrs. Bledsoe's abrupt departure."

"What did he say?"

"He said Mother's problems are now more psychological than physical, anyway, so it wasn't important whether Mrs. Bledsoe was here or not, considering the good job I'm doing."

"Psychological?"

"Exactly. Just as I told you, she's never going to be the same."

I felt my heart deflate. "Never the same? What does that mean?"

"We don't know yet, Semantha."

"Well, what does Dr. Moffet say to do?"

"He's put her on some tranquilizers, so she'll seem sort of out there to you right now. Ignore it. Don't try too hard to get her to be talkative and energetic."

"Does Daddy know all this?"

"Of course. He was here, too, and he and I and Dr. Moffet had a conference afterward. Is that my schoolwork?" she asked, nodding at the packet in my hands.

"Oh, yes."

She took it. "It will amuse me for a while," she said.

"Should I go up to her now?"

"Why not? There's no nurse telling you when you can see your mother anymore."

She walked off toward Daddy's office. I watched

her for a moment and then started up the stairs. I really didn't understand everything Cassie was saying. How does someone who is psychologically ill get better? Surely not by simply taking tranquilizers. We had to find ways to get Mother to think about other things now. We had to bring joy back into her life somehow. We—

I stopped dead in my tracks and stared.

The door of the refurbished and redecorated nursery, the door that Cassie had made sure would be locked so Mother wouldn't be reminded often of what she had lost, was slightly ajar. It had been opened. But why? Why? And why had it been left open?

I went on to Mother's bedroom. She looked as if she hadn't moved an inch from where she had been when I had visited her in the morning. Her eyes were closed, and she wore an expression of utter sorrow, the sort of expression someone has moments before she begins to cry. I went right to her and took her hand.

"I'm home, Mother," I said.

Her eyelids fluttered and then opened, but not fully. "Oh, Semantha. Was I asleep?"

"I think so."

"Is it morning?"

"No, Mother. It's afternoon. I just returned from school."

"Yes," she said. "School. I must have been dreaming, then, dreaming I could hear Asa crying."

I was still holding her hand, but I froze. How could she dream that? He had never been born. I didn't know what to say.

"It came from right across the hall, from the nursery, the beautiful new nursery."

"Like you said, it was just a dream, Mother. Don't think about it."

"Yes, don't think about it," she repeated. She closed her eyes, and when she opened them again, it was as though she thought I had just entered. "Oh, Semantha. I just realized what you said. You're home from school."

"I'm home, Mother. What can I get you?"

"Nothing. I'm resting. Dr. Moffet says I should rest. How's your father?"

"He's at work, Mother. Remember, the new store opening?"

"Yes, at work . . . the new . . ."

She closed her eyes again and blew air through her lips. The way she was behaving frightened me. I put her hand down gently and quietly left the room, walking to the stairway with my head down, my tears stuck in my throat. Then I hurried down to Cassie, who was reading from a cookbook in the kitchen.

"Cassie, she's acting so strange."

She kept reading as if I hadn't spoken and then put the cookbook down slowly and turned to me.

"Didn't I tell you, warn you, that she was on tranquilizers? I told you she would be that way. Don't you listen when I speak?"

"Yes, but . . ."

"It has to be this way for a while," she said, and reached for the cookbook again.

"But . . . the nursery," I blurted.

"What about it?"

"The door was open. It was unlocked."

She sighed and nodded and then sat at the kitchenette table.

"Why?" I pursued. "I thought you wanted to keep it locked so—"

"There was a bad situation earlier," she began. "Now, don't get all soapy and stupid on me, Samantha," she warned, "or I won't tell you things."

"I won't."

"I heard her screaming and practically flew up those stairs a few hours ago. When I got to her and Daddy's bedroom, I found her out of bed. She was actually crawling on the floor."

"Oh, no."

"Yes. She wouldn't get back into bed. She believed she heard Asa crying in the nursery. Can you imagine? No matter what I said, she wouldn't believe me. The only way I could prove to her that it was just a dream was to take her to the nursery and show her there was no baby. It was so disturbing that I must have neglected to relock the door. It was not very pleasant, but once I got her back in bed, she calmed down and fell asleep again. She had a decent lunch, however," Cassie added. "Now, I'm studying this recipe for clam cakes with lemon sauce. Daddy loves it. I remember Mother made it for him about six months ago but not since. I've already made a chocolate angel-food cake for dessert. He loves that, you know."

"But Cassie, isn't this . . . I mean, what you said happened. Isn't that very serious? How could she think she heard a baby's cry?"

"No. I've read a great deal about it during my spare time. Some women have phantom pregnancies and births, swearing they have a child when there is none, for example. I told you her problems are psychological now."

"But shouldn't we call Dr. Moffet?"

"If we call him for every little thing, he'll think we can't take care of her, Semantha and he'll recommend putting her in the mental ward or something. Would you like that?"

"Of course not."

"Then just relax. I've taken care of it, and I can handle it. Go do your homework or gossip on the phone or something. I'll need you in about an hour to help with dinner. Oh, I think we should work on the living room tonight."

"Didn't we just do that?"

"No, we didn't just do it. I think I know when we should concentrate on one of the rooms in the Heavenstone house and when we need not." She looked past me and softened her lips. "It's as if the house speaks to me sometimes." Then she caught herself and returned to her firm look. "Go on. You're going to be busy tonight. And you should leave her alone for a while. The more rest she gets, the faster she'll make something of a recuperation."

She returned to her cookbook. I went upstairs to my room. I did have homework, and now that I knew I'd have to do housework, I thought I had better get right to the assignments. I wasn't into them twenty minutes before I received my first phone call from one of the girls, Susie Cohen. She was very excited, because Eddie Morris had asked her to the movies.

"Maybe you can double-date with us. You know, you and Kent," she said.

"Maybe."

I had no intention of ever telling any of my new-found best friends anything about Mother and what was happening now. Susie, like the others, was persistent, though.

"Why maybe?"

"My father is preparing the opening of a new store."

"Yes, I know. It's big news."

"I might have to do things with him," I said, making myself sound important. It worked.

"Oh. Yes, I guess you would. Well, maybe you'll have some time off to go on a date. Call me as soon as you know."

Not a half-hour later, Bobbi called to reinforce everything Susie had told me. "Noel and I will be going. We can all have a great time, Semantha. Break out."

I told her I would try. Just before Cassie called me down to help with dinner, Kent called. It felt like a small conspiracy.

"Are you trying hard?" he asked.

"Yes, but there's a lot going on here with my father's new store and all, Kent. I'm not trying to avoid you," I promised.

"That's good news," he said. I knew what his first question would be when I arrived at school the next day.

I joined Cassie in the kitchen and began to set the table.

"Maybe Daddy will want to eat with Mother again," I suggested.

"No. I'm going to feed her much earlier. He won't eat well if he has to eat in that bedroom with her half in and half out of it. I won't allow it," she added, as if she had truly taken over our home. When I looked at her with surprise, she said, "I'm just trying to do what's best for all of us."

I nodded. She projected such strength and authority, it did feel as if I was talking to my mother or father and not my two-years-older sister. I felt I had to get her permission for everything now.

"I want to go to the movies Friday," I blurted. "You think that will be all right?"

She paused and studied me. "Don't tell me that Kent Pearson asked you."

"All my friends are going, Cassie."

"All your friends? Oh, so now you are one of the gang?"

"You said that would happen. You were right," I added, hoping that by giving her a compliment, she would be nicer about it.

"I suppose you should get out of here. Right now, this is Casa Depression. We'll run it by Daddy."

"Thank you, Cassie."

"I know what I told you, but I didn't mean that you should jump right in with them. Be careful. Remember all the things I told you and warned you about, Semantha. You are destined for bigger and better things. You're a Heavenstone."

I nodded, even though I didn't feel that way. I never felt I would have as special a future as Cassie would have. My grades weren't outstanding. I had no unique talents. When I had been in a school play two years ago, I had had a minor part, so minor, in fact, that I had been ashamed to go out on the stage when I knew Cassie was sitting with my parents in the audience. I hated calling myself just average, but I didn't know how to change it. Most other students were like me but didn't seem to care. Maybe that was because they didn't have as exceptional an older sister or older brother and didn't come from a family that was as famous and successful as ours. Sometimes, I wished I had been born into an ordinary family in which no one put too much pressure on anyone or expected any of them to be in *Who's Who*.

"Finish setting the table," she said, and I hurried off, thinking I had somehow slipped out of Cassie's chains of disapproval and control. It cheered me up enough to have an appetite.

When Daddy came home from work this time, I could easily see he wasn't as happy and was quite worried about Mother. Whatever Dr. Moffet had told him and Cassie weighed on him. It was almost as if he carried pounds and pounds of iron on his shoulders. He looked like someone suffering from a terrible migraine, too. He barely smiled at me and didn't even ask how my school day had gone. He always asked that. This time, he nodded, mumbled something I didn't hear, and then went quickly up the stairs to see Mother.

From the look on Cassie's face, I knew she was even more concerned than I was.

"This is all too much, even for him," she muttered. "You know, a man of his age is a prime candidate for a heart attack."

"Why? He's always been so healthy, Cassie. I can't remember him being too sick to go to work."

"This kind of sickness doesn't show itself, Samantha. It wears at him inside, and he won't talk about it. Don't ask him, either, or tell him he looks bad. That would only make things worse. When he tells you he's worried about Mother, just tell him she'll be all right. Tell him to give her time. Understand? Especially, don't break out in tears or even look like you will."

"I'll try not to, Cassie."

"I hate that expression, 'I'll try,'" she mimicked. "People use it to anticipate failure and provide an excuse. 'Well, I tried, didn't I?' What good is that if you fail? Imagine a doctor, a surgeon, coming out of the operating room to tell the man's wife that he tried. The man is dead. That's all that really matters."

I didn't say anything. I supposed she was right. When was she ever wrong?

Later, she brought Mother her dinner. I went up with her. Daddy was still in the bedroom, sitting there looking almost as dazed as Mother. She still seemed dopey to me. How much medicine had she taken? Was it supposed to be this strong?

"Oh, good," Daddy said brightening when he saw Cassie holding the tray. "Maybe food will give her some energy."

Cassie set the tray down on a bed table and

propped Mother up using her big pillows. She opened her eyes and looked at all of us as if she didn't know us.

"You have to eat something now, Mother," Cassie said. "I made you some hot oatmeal and some toast. I put some fruit in the oatmeal and honey, just the way you always make it for us."

Cassie moved the table over the bed and handed Mother the spoon. She took it and just stared at the oatmeal.

"C'mon, Arianna," Daddy urged, moving to the bed. "Eat something."

She looked at him, took a deep breath, and started to eat. Daddy smiled at Cassie. She flashed me a look of satisfaction and pride.

"Why don't you go change and relax for a little while before dinner, Daddy?" she told him. "I'll stay with Mother. I made one of your favorite meals tonight. It's a surprise."

Daddy shook his head. "You're a wonder, Cassie." He watched Mother eat for a few more moments and then nodded. "I'll step back in before going down to dinner."

When he turned to leave, he seemed to just then realize I was there, too.

"Hey, Semantha, how was your day?"

"Very good, Daddy. Everything's fine."

"Great. Uncle Perry will visit this weekend. I told him it would be all right. Might do her some good, too. She's very fond of Perry," he said, and left.

I looked at Cassie. She wasn't smiling anymore.

She pushed the toast on the tray to remind Mother it was there. Mother ate but didn't look at us or say anything. Suddenly, she stopped. Her face looked as if it was shattering.

"Look at me," she said. "Look what's happened to me."

"Oh Mother, you'll get better," I said quickly. "You'll get stronger and better very soon."

"Of course, she will," Cassie said, looking at her. "She wouldn't want to live if she would be like this forever."

Mother looked up at her and nodded.

I knew Cassie was saying that to make Mother eat and try, but the way she said it made me shudder inside. It was as if the two of them had made some hellish bargain, some pact. Cassie smiled at me and winked.

Later, after Mother had eaten and I was carrying the tray out, Cassie walked beside me.

"That's tough love," she said. "See? She ate it all. You just don't stand moaning and crying and making a pool of pity around her bed. You let her know that she can't wallow in this 'Oh, woe is me' attitude too long. Understand?"

"Yes," I said. I really didn't, but I knew she wanted to hear that.

"Good. At dinner, we'll ask Daddy about your Friday night date. I wouldn't want you to get too serious with that boy, but you need to get out of here for a while and have some normal fun with people your age. It will help you deal with all of this more easily, and that will help me."

I nodded, happy about that but also feeling as if I, too, had made some sort of hellish bargain.

The Accident

MOTHER MADE ONLY small improvements by Friday. She was up and about but apparently, from what Cassie told us, got tired quickly. Her disposition didn't seem to improve much, either. It wasn't that she was wallowing in self-pity so much as she looked lost, confused. Even when she looked at me, I had the creepy feeling she didn't know who I was. I wanted to say something to Daddy. Perhaps her medicine was too strong. When I suggested that to Cassie, she got very angry.

"That's all you have to do now is worry him. Did you see him yesterday? He wasn't even able to eat dinner with all that's happening. People are calling him constantly. We're three days away from the gala opening. Besides, she's only taking what the doctor prescribed."

"I'm worried, that's all," I said.

"And what am I, some moron?"

"No, but . . ."

"Go get ready for your hot movie date, Semantha."

"You really think I should go?"

"You should go, but don't come home pregnant."

"What?"

"You heard me, Semantha. Keep your legs crossed, and if I hear you were doing any drinking or any drugs, I'll turn you in to the police myself."

"I don't do that," I said.

"Like you've had so many opportunities to demonstrate your self-control. Remember, you are very vulnerable. Boys can tell. Be alert. Make sure no one slips anything into anything you drink, and if your boyfriend gets too aggressive, get out and call me. I'll come get you. Okay?"

I didn't answer.

"Okay?"

"Okay, Cassie, but you make me feel like I'm going into a war and not on a date."

"Believe me, it's a war," she said.

During the day in school, Bobbi, Susie, and I decided to pressure the boys to take us for pizza before the movie. When I told Cassie that I wouldn't be there for dinner, she did not have the reaction I was anticipating. She actually looked pleased.

"But I can still help set the table and —"

"No. It will be only Daddy and me. Uncle Perry isn't making his duty call until tomorrow, thank heavens," she said.

"I don't think it's a duty call for him, Cassie. He really likes Mother."

"I'm not saying he doesn't or didn't, but no one would enjoy seeing someone in the condition she is in right now, least of all a dandy like Uncle Perry. He gets hysterical if a pimple breaks out on his face."

"He doesn't get pimples anymore."

"Never mind. Just mind what I tell you," she said, and walked off.

Despite the things Cassie had said, I could barely contain the excitement of going on a real date now, which meant no adults driving us to and from the mall, because Eddie had a car and a license. He had an SUV that would hold all six of us. I was the last one to be picked up and ran out to the car as soon as I saw them coming up the driveway. Aside from Kent, none of them had been this close to the Heavenstone house. Their awe at the sight of it and our grounds embarrassed me. I had been so happy finally to be thought of as one of them, and with only one look at my home, that "aura of royalty," as Cassie referred to it, instantly returned.

"You could put all of our houses into your house, Semantha," Susie said.

"How many servants do you have?" Bobbi asked.

"None."

"None? Not even a maid?" Eddie asked.

"No. Cassie and I and my mother do all the work. My mother likes it that way. She's a great cook, and Cassie's a great cook too, so we don't need a cook."

"Lucky you," Bobbi said, and I could feel the underlying resentment of the Heavenstone family slowly returning.

"We inherited the house," I told them, hoping that would make it sound more acceptable.

"My father inherited my grandfather's debts," Noel quipped.

"How is your mother?" Kent asked.

"She's getting better, thank you."

"I would like to see the inside of your house someday," Susie said. They all agreed.

"As soon as my mother's well enough, I'll invite you all to dinner."

"To dinner?" Eddie asked.

"Yes."

"Do we have to wear jackets and ties?" Noel asked, smiling.

"No, of course not."

"We have to mind our manners, though," Eddie said. "No eating with your fingers, Noel, like you do at your house."

"My parents aren't stuffy people," I said defensively, maybe too defensively. No one spoke for a few moments.

"Where we going for pizza?" Kent asked to break the silence. "Let's stop at Luigi's, which is right before the mall. The mall place is nothing."

"Big spender," Noel said. "That is more expensive than the mall pizza, though."

"We could chip in," Susie said.

"I bet Semantha could buy it all," Eddie quipped. To my surprise, even my new girlfriends laughed.

"I didn't bring much money," I said, in a little panic.

"Just kidding," Eddie said. "If we can't afford some pizzas and drinks, we oughtta stay home."

Even so, I felt a combination of embarrassment and annoyance. The conversation moved on to other things, but the echo of their insinuations about me and my family and our wealth hung in the air around me. Once again, I wondered if Cassie wasn't right. We were different, and we should be more discriminating about whom we chose as friends. I hated feeling like this, but I couldn't shake it off. At the restaurant, I know I was markedly quieter than the other girls. Kent kept asking me if I was all right.

"You don't mind eating in a dump like this, do you, Semantha?" Eddie asked with a wide smile.

"Stop it, please, Eddie. I'm not a snob."

Eddie laughed, but that seemed to end the teasing.

Kent whispered an apology for him as we left the restaurant. "He's just feeling his oats because he's able to drive at night and has a new SUV," he explained.

I tried to relax, but no one else but me seemed to be enjoying the movie later. Eddie and Susie talked so much that people around us began to complain loudly. Bobbi and Noel were kissing so passionately that they couldn't have followed the story, anyway, so when Eddie suggested that we leave and go to Cary Lothar's house, they all leaped out of their seats.

"C'mon," Kent urged me. I had no choice but to follow them out. Our leaving brought some applause from the people who were sitting behind and in front of us.

"How can we just go to Cary Lothar's house?" I asked when we all got into Eddie's SUV.

"He's home alone with Nikki Benson and told me we could come over after the movie, but why waste time, especially with this dog of a film?" Eddie said.

I was afraid to say I had been enjoying the movie. As soon as we got into the SUV, Kent put his arm around my shoulders and urged me to draw closer. He kissed my cheek and neck, and then, when I turned, he kissed me on the lips. I was self-conscious about kissing like this in front of the others, but aside from Eddie, who had to drive, everyone else was kissing, too. However, Susie was practically on Eddie's lap nibbling on his ear.

"Oh, boy. You've got my full attention," he said, and sped up.

None of us in the rear could have warned him. We were all too occupied. Susie had apparently put her hand between Eddie's legs, and he wasn't paying much attention, either. The elderly man who backed out of his driveway was either distracted by something himself or was just careless, but his car shot back directly in our path. Eddie hit the brakes hard, but because his eyes weren't on the road, he was far too close by then. We weren't wearing seat belts in the rear, and Noel, who was in a bad angle at the moment, literally flew forward between the two front seats and slammed his head into the dashboard, just as Eddie's SUV crashed into the rear of the elderly man's automobile, spinning it around.

The sound was deafening. The airbags popped out in the front, squeezing Eddie and Susie back. Kent and I managed to hold on to each other and just bang into the back of Susie's seat. Bobbi fell to the floor, twisting her arm but not breaking it.

For a moment, no one spoke. We were all in too much shock. The air around me seemed electric. I felt nauseated and dizzy but held myself together. The echo of the crash still reverberated in my ears. Every bone in my body was still vibrating. I raised myself a little to look out the windshield at the mess. There was a fender on the road, and the entire rear of the other car was bashed in as if it were made of clay. I could see the elderly man was in shock himself but got out of his car and then swayed and fell back against it. The noise of the crash brought people out of his house. I saw an elderly woman and a younger woman hurrying down the driveway to him, the elderly lady screaming. Then Bobbi screamed. She held up her hand to show us there was blood trickling down the side of Noel's head.

Eddie sat there, gaping down at Noel.

"Hey, Noel, hey," Eddie said, shaking him a little. Noel didn't respond.

"He's unconscious. Do something, Eddie!" Bobbi shouted at him.

He fumbled with his cell phone for a moment and then just got out and screamed for an ambulance. The younger woman hurried back into the house. The elderly lady guided the man, whom I assumed was her husband, back into the car to sit and wait.

Kent started to move Noel.

"Don't!" I cried, putting my hand on his arm. "Remember what we were told in class when the paramedics talked to us. He might have a spinal injury that you'll make worse."

He pulled his hands off Noel as if Noel's body had turned to molten steel.

"Is he bleeding badly?" Susie asked through her tears.

"No," Bobbi said, a little calmer. "But he's not regaining consciousness. Everyone else all right?"

"I hurt my arm, but it's not broken."

"We're okay," Kent said.

Both Susie and Bobbi started to cry. I didn't. Maybe I was in a state of shock, but I felt a certain calmness, almost as if I had left my body and was above it all watching, just like some uninvolved observer, detached enough to do and say the right things.

"Put your jacket gently under Noel's head," I told Kent.

He nodded, stripped it off, and did as I said.

"Does Eddie have a first-aid kit in the car?" I asked Susie.

"I don't know."

She shouted for him. He was now screaming at the old man for being an idiot. His wife started shouting back. I opened the door and got out.

"Stop it!" I shouted at Eddie. "You're not doing any good. Wait for the police and the ambulance. Do you have a first-aid kit?"

He looked at me, then muttered some curse words, and returned to the car. I got back in, too.

"No, I don't have a first-aid kit," he said. "They shouldn't let people that old drive. He looks like he's ninety."

"You weren't watching the road, Eddie. None of us was," I said.

He spun around. "Bullshit. The guy just backed out without looking."

"Forget about it," Kent said. "Just let Eddie talk to the police," he told me sternly.

Eddie glared a moment more, and then we all sat there, dazed and still, until we heard the sound of sirens. The patrol car arrived first, and Eddie got out again to talk to the police. One of the officers looked in at Noel.

"Has he been unconscious all this time?" he asked.

Bobbi said yes. He felt for Noel's pulse and then turned and spoke into the phone on his shoulder. Minutes later, the ambulance arrived. We all got out and watched the paramedics carefully remove Noel from the SUV and get him onto the stretcher to load him into the ambulance. One of the patrolmen began to take down our names, addresses, phone numbers, and information about Noel. While he did that, a tow truck arrived and began to hook up Eddie's SUV. The elderly man, whose name we learned was Mr. Morgan, was able to drive his car back onto his driveway and out of the street.

"My father's going to skin me alive if they don't rule this was the old man's fault," Eddie said. "My insurance is high enough as it is. Damn."

"I think we should be worrying more about Noel," I said.

No one said anything, but I could see they all agreed. Eddie asked the policemen about helping us follow the ambulance to the hospital. The police told him one of us had to call his or her parents.

"I'll call my father," Kent volunteered. "Let me borrow your phone."

Eddie handed it to him, and Kent moved off
to speak privately with his father. I wanted to call
Cassie, but I was afraid of what she would say. I
would have hated to have my father come out, too.

Kent's father arrived pretty quickly after the call.
He was concerned first about each of us and thought
Bobbi should have her arm checked out at the hospital immediately. We all fell into an even deeper
silence as Kent's father drove us to the hospital. He
brought Bobbi to the admittance desk, and a nurse
took her to an examination room to check her arm.
Eddie, Susie, Kent, and I sat in the lobby waiting to
hear about Noel. When we saw his parents arrive, we
grew even more terrified. Noel's father came out a
while later. He looked very angry.

"What the hell happened?" he asked Eddie.

Despite all his bravado, Eddie began to cry as he
explained and blamed the elderly man for shooting
out without looking. I heard him tell Noel's father
that he hadn't had much of a chance to avoid hitting him. He said nothing about Susie distracting
him, however. I looked away, ashamed. Noel's father
marched off again.

"What did he say about Noel?" Kent asked.

"He has a concussion for sure. They're checking
to see if his spine was damaged."

"Oh, no," Susie said and began to cry harder.

Kent's father returned to tell us that with the
policeman's help, he had called everyone's parents.
I looked up, terrified. I had hoped somehow to just
go home and calmly explain, but I understood why
Kent's father had felt obligated to make the calls.

Susie's parents arrived first. They talked to Kent's father for a while and then took Susie home. Eddie's father came without his mother. He was much bigger than Eddie and looked angry enough to beat him right there in the lobby. He spoke to Kent's father, too, and Kent's father managed to calm him. He ordered Eddie out to the car and then went to speak with Noel's parents. Just then, Cassie arrived.

I think I shall never forget her reaction. In contrast to everyone else's parents, their face pasted over with fear and anger, my sister looked calm and in a strange way satisfied, and I don't mean satisfied that I was fine. She had an expression on her face that said that everything she believed and told me about other people had been verified. She politely thanked Kent's father for calling our home, asked about Noel, listened, and then nodded at me.

I turned to Kent, who had kept his head down and his hands over his face all the while. "My sister's here. I'm going home, Kent."

He looked up slowly and nodded. "Yeah. I guess we just don't have luck when it comes to being together," he muttered.

"It wasn't your fault."

He didn't reply. He looked down again, as if he wanted to avoid looking at Cassie.

"Call me if you hear any more about Noel," I told him. He nodded but didn't look up.

"Let's go home, Semantha," Cassie said.

I followed her out to her car. She said nothing and looked as if she might not even when we were in the car. When I got in, I said, "It was terrifying, Cassie."

"Of course it was." She started the engine and backed out of the parking spot. "Don't worry. I didn't tell Daddy. He was asleep on the sofa in the living room when Mr. Pearson called the house, and I just left for the hospital. I'm sure he's still asleep. We don't have to say anything until the morning."

"Why is he asleep on the sofa?" I asked. It wasn't that late, and I wondered why he wouldn't be upstairs with Mother.

"He drank too much wine at dinner. We both did, but he drank far more. He needed desperately to relax, so I didn't say anything or try to stop him. We went into the living room to talk afterward, and when he fell asleep, I simply took off his shoes, got him comfortable, and put a blanket on him and a pillow under his head. He's better off sleeping there and not with Mother tonight. She's still obsessing about losing Asa, dreaming she hears a baby cry."

"Maybe it's better that she return to the hospital," I said.

"If she goes back in there, she might never come out, Semantha. How would you like that?"

I started to cry.

"Stop it. That's all we need now is you bawling like some infant."

I sucked back my tears. "How terrible, and now this happens."

"Yes, now this happens. Were you all drinking?"

"No. We had just left the movie and were going to a friend's home."

"To do what?"

"I don't know. Listen to music and stuff."

"Right, stuff," she said. She looked at me and nodded. "Maybe you were lucky you were in an accident."

"Oh, Cassie, how can you say such a thing? Noel might have serious injuries."

"You could have had serious injuries, too."

"Right."

"I don't mean in a car accident, Semantha. I mean in a different kind of accident, a sexual accident."

"I wouldn't," I insisted.

"If I had a penny for every girl your age who said that and got pregnant, I'd be richer than Daddy."

I said nothing more. When we arrived home, she had me keep very still. I looked in and saw Daddy asleep on the sofa. It was so strange to me. No matter how drunk he had gotten on his wine, I still couldn't understand why he wouldn't want to be upstairs with Mother. I started to go into the living room, but Cassie seized my arm.

"Don't disturb him. It took me quite a while to get him relaxed. He might look at your face and immediately see what happened tonight. Just go to sleep, Semantha."

I continued to look at Daddy. Her fingers grew tighter on my arm until I pulled it away and hurried to the stairs. When she couldn't see me, I rubbed my arm. She remained downstairs with Daddy, so I went to see Mother. Although the room was dark, I saw she wasn't sleeping. In fact, she was sitting up. The moment I opened the door, she called, "Teddy? Is that you? Did you hear him?"

How could I tell her Daddy had fallen asleep downstairs and wasn't coming up? Hear him? Hear who?

"No, Mother. It's Semantha. How are you?"

She didn't reply. I walked in farther and saw she had her eyes closed even though she was sitting up. I waited, but she didn't open them. I didn't want to wake her, so I slipped out quietly and closed the door softly.

As I was approaching my room, I heard my phone ringing and ran the rest of the way and practically lunged at my phone. It was Kent. I held my breath.

"He doesn't have any serious spine injury, just the concussion. The head wound wasn't serious," Kent said. "We were all lucky."

When he said that, I thought about Cassie again saying the same thing but for different reasons.

"Eddie's lucky there were no witnesses," Kent continued. "It will surely be considered the old man's fault. But you were right. Eddie would have had plenty of time to see him back out if he hadn't been doing other things."

"I know."

"You won't say anything, will you? You might be asked by some lawyer."

I was silent.

"If you did, no one would talk to you in our school again."

"What about what's right, Kent?"

"What about it? The insurance companies will pay anyway, so there's no sense hurting Eddie any more than he's hurt."

"Eddie's hurt? Noel is in the hospital, and the elderly man is going to be hurt, too, because of all this."

Kent was silent. "I've got to go," he finally said. "Maybe I'll see you tomorrow."

"No, I'm attending my father's gala store opening in Lexington."

"Whatever," Kent said, and hung up.

I held the receiver a moment longer and thought, Cassie was right. Kent Pearson wasn't good enough for a Heavenstone. The second I thought that, however, I felt guilty. No one should be considered better than someone else because of his or her family's wealth and history. I told myself that, but I kept hearing Cassie's warnings and arguments about why we had to remain special.

I didn't think I could fall asleep. The accident replayed itself in my mind. I was afraid I would have terrible nightmares, but my eyelids had other ideas. They slammed shut almost as soon as my head hit the pillow, and as Daddy might say, they were as tightly closed as the vault in the First National Bank.

I overslept. It was nearly eleven when Cassie shook me.

"You should get up, Semantha. Lucky for you, Daddy wasn't a hundred percent himself this morning."

I sat up quickly. "Did you tell him everything?"

"Of course. You want him to find out about it from some stranger? He wanted me to wake you earlier to be sure you were all right, but I assured him you were. I promised him you would call him after lunch, which looks like it will be your breakfast."

I scrubbed my face with my dry palms and shook my head. "It all seems like a dream, a nightmare."

"Someone was watching over you, all right. Most likely, it was the spirit of one of our ancestors. Maybe even Asa."

"How's Mother this morning?" I asked as soon as she had said that name.

"She ate breakfast, but only after I showed her the empty nursery again."

"You did?"

"She kept talking about that weird dream, so I had to. Unfortunately, the sight of the furniture, the decor, the new windows, all of it put her into a little depression again. I knew it would, but there was no choice. I can't have her believing in dreams."

"You need to call the doctor, Cassie," I said, rising. "This can't go on."

"We'll see," she said. "Maybe after the gala, if she's still like this. Get dressed. We need to work on the kitchen today after you have your brunch."

I showered and dressed. Despite the hour, I wasn't as hungry as I thought I might be. I hurried in to see Mother. Cassie had turned the television on for her, but she didn't look as if she was watching it as much as she looked as if she was just looking through it. Of course, I couldn't tell her about the accident. Fortunately, she didn't ask about my date.

"Why aren't you in school?" she asked instead.

"It's the weekend, Mother."

"Oh. I've lost track of the days."

"Do you want anything? I'm just going down to the kitchen."

"No. Thank you, Semantha. You look very nice, very grown-up. I feel like I've been away so long. Have I been away long?"

"No, not long, Mother."

She nodded, smiled, and then looked sad again. "Did you hear anything last night?"

"Hear anything? What do you mean?"

"A baby's cry?"

A chill went through me. "No, Mother."

She nodded again. "He feels betrayed, I'm sure," she said. "I took him so far, so close, and then . . ."

"You can't blame yourself like this, Mother. Please. You have to try, or you won't get better."

She looked at me again and smiled. "You're so grown-up. My grown-up daughters. That's nice. That makes me feel good. You help your father. He has so much to do, and I can't be of any help to him."

"That's why you need to get better quickly, Mother."

"Yes," she said. "Yes."

"You sure you don't want anything?"

"Yes, I'm sure."

I started out.

"Did you see how beautiful the nursery came out, Semantha?"

I paused. "Yes, Mother. But please, don't think about it so much."

"No," she said. "Don't think about it," she recited, and turned back to the television set without an iota of interest in what she was seeing.

I hurried downstairs. I didn't care how much

Cassie knew or how well she and Daddy thought she was taking care of Mother. Something more must be done. I practically charged at her in the kitchen.

"Dr. Moffet should be called today," I said. "She's not right. I'm frightened, Cassie. She actually asked me if I had heard a baby's cry."

"I've already discussed it with Daddy," she said calmly. She was whipping up some cupcakes. "It's the weekend, and Moffet's not here this weekend. He went to visit his son in Boston. His son's a doctor, too, you know."

"I don't care about his son. We should still call him."

"We will on Monday. If she hasn't improved, I'm afraid she might have to go back into the hospital."

"Oh."

"Eat something. We've got work to do."

"How can we leave her tomorrow?" I asked. "She's not going to the gala, right?"

Cassie stopped working and looked at me with a wide smile. "Can you imagine her there? Of course not."

"Well, then, how can we leave her alone?"

"We're not."

"We're not? Who's going to be here?"

"You," she said.

"Me?"

"I would stay, but Daddy needs me at his side. Don't worry. She'll have taken some of her medicine and will sleep most of the time, anyway."

"But—"

"What's more important to you, Semantha,

attending a party in a department store or making sure your mother is all right?"

"Of course, looking after Mother."

"Exactly." She returned to the cupcake batter. "I understand how you feel, how hard this is on all of us, and, like you, I wish Mother had been stronger, but she's not, so we have to contend with it.

"Other families would crumble," she continued, "but not the Heavenstones. We rise to every occasion. People look up to us. We inspire them; we always have. Mother doesn't have the Heavenstone blood in her, so she's not as strong as we are." She paused to spoon out some of the batter. "Daddy's going to love these cupcakes," she said. "They're marble inside. He loves that."

I stared at her until she turned back to me.

"What? Why aren't you having your brunch?"

"Mother is as strong as any Heavenstone," I insisted.

She shook her head. "Yes, Semantha, and there is really a Santa Claus, too."

She returned to her cupcakes.

I knew how Cassie was about our heritage and importance, all that. I had heard it and believed some of it myself, but something was different.

It was as if . . .

As if I, too, heard a baby's cry.

12

Silence

I HAD NEVER been so happy to hear Uncle Perry's voice as I was this particular afternoon. Cassie went to the door before I could. I was still in the kitchen. She had insisted we take everything out of every cabinet and wipe each cabinet clean before putting it all back. We would do the same with the pantry and the silverware drawers. The moment I heard him, I stopped what I was doing and hurried out to greet him.

"Your father's right behind me," he said. "He was just finishing up a few things. How's your mother?" he asked Cassie as I approached.

"She's about the same. You know she's on some antidepressants, right?"

"Yes, your father told me. Hi, Sam. How are you doing?" he asked as soon as he saw me.

"Sam," Cassie said, turning to look at me before I could respond, "was very lucky last night. She was in a bad car accident."

"What? Teddy didn't say anything about any car accident."

"As you can see, Semantha is all right, and my

father has his mind on many important things today, Uncle Perry," Cassie said.

Uncle Perry turned to me. "Are you all right?" he asked, clearly implying that he didn't trust Cassie.

"Yes, Uncle Perry. Cassie's right. I was lucky. One of the boys, however, hit his head on the dashboard and has a concussion. He should be all right, though."

"Wow. So, what happened?"

"Yes, why don't you amuse Uncle Perry with that story while I look in on Mother?" Cassie said. "I'll see how she is and let you know if you can visit when I come down," she told Uncle Perry.

"Why couldn't I visit her?" he asked or, rather, demanded. I saw he was losing patience with Cassie. "I didn't drive out here just to chat with you two. I promised your father I'd visit your mother."

"I didn't say you couldn't visit, Uncle Perry. Chill out. All I meant was I'd see if she was awake. She drifts in and out with this medicine Dr. Moffet has prescribed. You don't want to stand there looking at a woman asleep, do you?"

"I'll wait until she wakes up, even if it takes the rest of the day," he replied firmly.

Cassie smiled and nodded. "We appreciate that, Uncle Perry. Honestly, we do," she said, and walked off to the stairway.

He looked at me, the anger in his face receding. "What happened to you, then, Sam? What's this about a car accident?"

I walked him into the living room. He sat on the sofa, and I described the accident. With him, I told the truth.

"There's probably no doubt your friend Eddie could have prevented the accident if he had been paying attention. All of us, but teenagers especially, should be trained in defensive driving. I don't know all that much about insurance companies, but I can't see how the elderly man won't be held accountable anyway, Sam. If he couldn't back out and drive off without any car hitting him, he should have waited. He was probably not looking enough. But from the way you describe your friend who drove, I don't think this is the end of his getting into trouble."

"I feel so terrible with all that's happening to my mother and Daddy right in the middle of so much."

"It will be all right. Don't worry," he said, and stood up to give me a hug just as Cassie entered.

"How loving," she said. "An uncle and his favorite niece caught in a tender embrace. My mother is awake, Uncle Perry. I told her you were here. She had no reaction, but don't mind that. It's the medicine."

He looked at me with skepticism, then started out and stopped. "Why don't you come up with me, Sam," he said.

"I'll wait here for Daddy," Cassie said, as if he had asked her and not me.

I joined him, and we went upstairs. Mother was in a robe and sitting in the oversized chair in the bedroom. I made a mental note to work on her hair as soon as Uncle Perry left. Right now, it looked like a rat's nest. She wore no makeup, and sitting in the afternoon sunshine pouring through the windows, she looked quite pale. When she saw Uncle Perry, she began to cry.

"Arianna, please, don't," Uncle Perry said, rushing to her. He knelt beside her and took her hand in his. "You can't blame yourself."

"I came home without my baby. Teddy's male heir," she said. "His Asa. I know how much he dreamed of him."

"He's got heirs."

"The Heavenstone name, Perry. It's so important to him."

"Not more important than you are to him, Arianna. Besides, I've always told him that this Heavenstone thing is over the top. We're just people who happen to have a thriving big business. Everyone has a history. This isn't some kind of royal dynasty, and Teddy isn't Henry the Eighth."

If Cassie were there and heard him say that, she would pounce on him and scratch him from ear to ear, I thought. He glanced back at me as if he heard what I was thinking.

Mother nodded slightly but without any enthusiasm. "I know it's just my imagination," she said in a voice barely above a whisper, "but sometimes . . . sometimes I hear a baby's cry, and I think maybe he was born. You know what I mean?" she asked Uncle Perry, her face brightening with some hope.

It was as if she really did expect him to say she was right. She had heard her baby. What did she think he would tell her? That all of this was just a bad dream, or she had suffered so much difficulty giving birth that she had lost her memory?

"Now, now, Arianna, you're only making yourself sicker with this sort of talk. You've got to get hold of yourself, get strong and well again. Please," he begged, still holding her hand.

Her face sank with disappointment, but she nodded. "I know. I know just how much of a burden I've become for everyone."

"No one says you're a burden. That's ridiculous. Everyone wants you to get well and is anxious to help you do so. C'mon. Let's see that joie de vivre again. You're my inspiration, Arianna. Just knowing you're around spurs me on to try harder and do better and better things. You've always been my best cheerleader. I'd be lost without you."

Mother gave him a quick smile.

"Now, that's the sister-in-law I remember."

We turned toward the door when we heard Daddy's voice from the stairway. He sounded very excited and happy. Cassie's laughter followed, and moments later they both entered.

"Arianna, you're up and about. How wonderful," Daddy said, hurrying to her.

Uncle Perry stepped back so Daddy could kiss Mother. Then he took the newspaper out from under his arm and held up the pages that had pictures of our new store. Both pages were dedicated to the story. There was a good picture of Daddy and, next to him, a picture of the governor, who was definitely coming to tomorrow's opening gala.

"Cassie suggested we hire a band and set them up near the entrance," he said. "I just hired them. And look at this, Arianna. Look at what else your daughter came up with." He pulled out a key chain that had an angel attached. It read, *Heavenstone's. Where angels shop.* "We're going to give one to each of the first five hundred customers." He handed it to Mother.

She smiled and looked at Cassie. "Very clever, Cassie," she said.

"Thank you, Mother." Cassie glanced at Uncle Perry, but he said nothing.

"We're blowing up hundreds of balloons, and we've constructed a small stage area with seating for four hundred people," Daddy continued. "I'm sure there will be another few hundred standing. We'll have the mayor, the governor, and," he said, digging into his pocket to come up with a letter to wave, "Senator Barry is flying in from Washington. With the suppliers, retail salesmen, and employees, we're sure to have an overflow crowd."

"I'm happy for you, Teddy," Mother said.

"It's for us, not just for me, Arianna. Don't worry. I'm videotaping all of the festivities, and I'll be able to play it for you tomorrow night."

"Maybe she can go," Uncle Perry suggested.

Cassie stepped forward instantly.

"It would be too tiring, and she's not ready to listen to people offering their condolences. They'll drown her in an ocean of pity. Daddy and I and you, too, will be too occupied to care properly for her."

"What about Sam?" Uncle Perry nodded toward me.

"My sister isn't equipped for such a responsibility yet."

"What?" Uncle Perry smiled incredulously. "Not equipped? Why not, for Heavenstone's sake?"

"She's barely able to look after herself," Cassie

muttered, glaring at me. "Other teenagers will distract her attention, and she won't know how to keep people from badgering Mother."

"Other teenagers? You're a teenager," Uncle Perry pointed out.

"Hardly," she replied.

"Huh?"

"Please, don't argue," Mother said with surprising energy. "Cassie's right. Just the thought of walking down the stairs tires me out right now."

"I'd gladly carry you all the way," Uncle Perry said.

"I know you would, Perry. Thank you, but I'd rather Teddy not have to worry about me. I don't want any of you to be worrying about me tomorrow. All of you, go and enjoy."

"Semantha is staying with you," Cassie said.

"Oh, no!" Mother cried. "I don't want her to miss it on account of me. You go, too, Semantha. I'll be fine."

"I could call someone," Daddy said. "Just to be around if you need someone."

"I'll be fine," Mother insisted. "Please, Teddy. Don't make me feel like any more of a burden on you all than I am."

"You're not a burden, Arianna."

"That's what I told her," Uncle Perry said.

Cassie made a show of looking at her watch. "Mother is due to take a pill now, and I'd like her to rest before I bring up her dinner. She has to eat more. I've made those cupcakes you made for Daddy a while back, Mother. I'll be bringing you one."

"Are you staying for dinner, Uncle Perry?" I asked, hoping he would say yes.

"I'm afraid I have to get back. I still have some work on the displays and some arrangements to complete for tomorrow, but thank you for asking, Sam." He glanced pointedly at Cassie, but she looked disinterested and unashamed that she hadn't asked him to dinner.

"I'll sit with her a while and make sure she's resting," Daddy said, moving toward Mother.

Uncle Perry returned to her side just held her hand for a moment and looked at her.

"Please get better soon, Arianna. Everyone needs you back."

Mother didn't speak, didn't smile. She simply stared at him. He leaned over to kiss her cheek and whisper something, and then he started out.

"I'll walk you to your car, Uncle Perry." I hurried after him.

He charged at the stairway and didn't speak to me until we were well out of earshot. He turned at the bottom of the stairs and looked up.

"I don't like it, Sam. I don't want to alarm you, but Cassie is taking on too much responsibility here. Your father should have hired another nurse or had her readmitted. She is in a deep depression. She shouldn't be this way so long after the miscarriage. As I understand it, she hasn't left that room since she was brought home, not even to go out and get some fresh air, right?"

"Yes."

"Well, then, talk your father into getting someone else immediately, will you?"

"Yes," I said. "I'll try." He was saying what I felt and was afraid to say. It made my heart thump and my stomach swirl. We walked out, and he kissed me good-bye.

When he opened the car door to get in, he paused and smiled. "I'm sure it will be all right, Sam. I don't mean to get you overly alarmed. I'm just . . . not used to seeing her like that, and your sister . . . your sister makes me feel like an outsider. I don't want to start any trouble between you, but when it comes to being nice and loving, you're miles above her, and right now, your mother needs a lot of tender loving care."

He got in, started his engine, waved, and drove off. I watched him go, feeling as if I was coming apart where I stood. I wanted to run after him and shout, *Don't go, Uncle Perry. You're right. Stay here and convince Daddy. I can't do it by myself, and Cassie wouldn't like it.*

I actually took a few steps forward, but he was already at the bottom of the driveway and preparing to turn out of the gate. In seconds, he was gone. My heart sank. I stood looking after him until I heard the front door open.

"What are you doing standing around out there?" Cassie shouted. "We haven't finished the kitchen yet."

I didn't turn around immediately. I was afraid that if I did, I might start screaming at her, and who knew what would happen then? Daddy would certainly be very upset if Cassie and I had words. I had no choice. I took a deep breath, lowered my head, and started back to the house.

"Did you see how fast your uncle Perry ran out of here when I mentioned giving her the medicine?" Cassie asked as I drew closer. "I told you he hasn't the stomach for any really difficult problems. He's like a high-strung woman or something. If he had to deal with one-tenth of what Daddy deals with daily, he'd be in a loony bin himself."

"You didn't make him feel all that comfortable, Cassie," I said.

"Oh, pardon me. I guess I should have considered his delicate feelings more than what Daddy and Mother need." She put her hands on her hips and wagged her head as she continued. "If he doesn't have the common sense and the sensitivity to see how difficult things are for us now, I couldn't possibly care less about his discomfort."

When I turned to continue toward the kitchen, she reached out and pulled me around.

"You listen to me. Men like him are very self-centered, Semantha. Don't get caught up in his show of affection. When you scratch the surface of all that, you'll find it's all a façade or, as Daddy says, as phony as a two-headed nickel.'"

"That's not true or fair," I said, turning away again.

"Believe what you want, but you'll see how right I am when it comes time for him to do something for you in a crisis," she insisted, following me.

I didn't respond. I returned to the kitchen to finish the work as she wanted. She went to complete her preparations for Mother's dinner and then our dinner afterward. Before she carried up Mother's tray, she turned to me.

"You heard her before when we were talking about the gala. Mother's not going to want you to stay with her tomorrow, but I still think you should. What you can do is let her think you've gone with us, but stay downstairs and go up to see how she's doing hours later. If she asks you why you're here, tell her you have a headache or something, anything."

"Don't worry, Cassie. I wasn't going to leave her if Daddy didn't get someone to stay here with her."

"Good. He won't," she said with confidence.

"Is Daddy still upstairs with her?"

"No. He's in his office."

"But I thought he was going to stay with her to be sure she relaxed."

"I told him I would do that and sent him to do what was needed. He has a great deal left to arrange, so don't bother him. I'll be back in a little while. Just finish that section and go up to get ready for dinner."

I did what she wanted and then went up to my room. Bobbi called and told me how Noel was doing, but the real reason she called was to tell me that Eddie was nervous about my telling people the accident was his fault.

"The old guy should have been more careful," she added before I could respond. "Don't you agree?"

I thought about what Uncle Perry had said about the insurance company blaming Mr. Morgan no matter what. I decided there was no point in arguing or trying to get the others to see how careless Eddie had been—and with our lives, too!

"Yes," I said.

"Good. Oh, good luck with your new store, too."

"Thank you."

"I'll be there for the festivities. My parents are going, too," she said. "See you tomorrow."

I didn't want to tell her I wouldn't be there, so I said okay and hung up. Later, I went down to help Cassie with our dinner. Daddy was so occupied in his office that she had to go get him and insist that he come to eat. At the table, I felt like some outsider. He and Cassie discussed the details of the gala. Neither paid much attention to me. However, I had to admit to myself that I was impressed with how much Cassie knew about what had to be done. She could be the CEO of our company.

"Should I go up to get Mother's tray?" I asked, finally interrupting.

They both looked at me as if they had just realized I was at the table, too.

"No. Daddy and I will go up. You clean up here," Cassie ordered. "I'll bring down her tray, and you can stay with her," she told him.

It shocked me to see how she was giving all of us orders now and how Daddy just accepted it.

"Cassie told me you insisted on staying here with your mother tomorrow, Semantha. Are you sure? Because I can get someone to stand by. I hate to see you miss the gala opening," Daddy said.

I did want to go very much. Many of my classmates would be there, and as I listened to them talk, it was sounding more and more exciting. Cassie could see I was seriously considering Daddy's offer.

"Semantha and I have discussed it thoroughly, Daddy," she said, looking directly at me when she spoke. "We both agree that strangers don't do well in this house, and Mother is too delicate at the moment to be deserted."

"Oh, it's not really deserting her," Daddy said.

"No, I'll stay, Daddy. Cassie's right. I'll watch the video with you and Mother later."

"Well, it would be nice to have both of my daughters at my side, but if you're really sure . . ."

Cassie glared at me, practically daring me to say I would go.

"I'm sure, Daddy. There will be other events."

"That there will. You're right there," he said, "right as rain. Well, then, let's go see how she's doing, Cassie. I expect she loved that cupcake as much as I did."

I watched the two of them head upstairs. Cassie whispered something in his ear that made him laugh aloud, and then they started up the stairway. My nerves felt like broken guitar strings. I practically attacked the dishware and silverware, nearly breaking a cup. It slipped from my grip, but I caught it before it hit the floor. I was almost finished with the dishes when Cassie returned with Mother's tray. I saw that she hadn't eaten very much, and she hadn't touched the cupcake. When I said something, Cassie told me the medicine hurt her appetite.

"I'll speak to Dr. Moffet about it on Monday," she said.

"You will? Why wouldn't Daddy?"

"I meant I'll tell Daddy to speak with him."

"He should come here to see her."

"Maybe he will. Now, forget this for the moment, and let's talk about tomorrow, Semantha. It's very important that Mother believes you're going. We just told her that again."

"Daddy lied to her?"

"It's not a lie when he's just doing what's necessary to help her relax, Semantha. Please don't talk like a child right now. I need you to be grown-up."

"I am grown-up. I'm not talking like a child. Don't say that!"

"Okay, okay, don't blow a gasket. Your daddy told a little white lie. Satisfied? Now, back to what I was saying. In the morning after breakfast, you get dressed as if you're going. Put on something special. Maybe that blue skirt outfit with the light-blue V-neck sweater, the outfit I bought you for your last birthday. Tie your hair, back and put on some makeup. Look excited about going, too, understand? I'll be with you when you go in to say good-bye."

"I don't like doing that, Cassie. It makes me feel so deceiving."

She rolled her eyes. "Are you going to cooperate or not? I have to know now. If not, I'll go up to Daddy and tell him to find a stranger to babysit. Well?"

"Yes, I'll do it."

"Good. Now, go up and say good night. I'll finish here. Well? Go on," she ordered when I didn't move.

There was so much I wanted to say, but the words just wouldn't come down to my tongue, and everything I could think of suggesting rang like the thoughts of someone selfish. I had no doubt that she would make me look that way in front of Daddy if I suggested any other solution, such as hiring another private-duty nurse just for the day. A private-duty nurse was a professional more than she was a stranger, but I hadn't said anything at dinner, and I certainly couldn't do it now.

I left the kitchen and went up to Mother's room, but I paused in the doorway. Mother was lying back on her pillow, her eyes closed, and Daddy was holding her hand and resting his head gently against her. The moment was so personal and tender I couldn't interrupt it. As quietly as I could, I backed out and walked down to my room. I sat thinking until Susie called me to talk about the gala, too. Her parents weren't going, but she was going to join Bobbi and her parents. Again, I couldn't get myself to say I wouldn't be there. She rattled on and on about the accident and how lucky we were. She told me Noel was hoping to go home in a day or so and that Eddie had been to the hospital to visit him. She said he really felt sorry. I knew she was saying that to reinforce their demand that I not contradict anyone else's story of how it all happened.

"He had to take a taxi. His father has taken away his driving privileges for a month even though it wasn't his fault. Parents," she said disgustedly. "They forget when they were our age."

"Maybe they don't and that's why they do what they do," I said.

"Huh? What's that mean?"

"Figure it out, Susie. I'm tired. Thanks for the call," I said, and hung up.

I ended up dozing off before returning to Mother's room and then decided it was too late. I'd see her in the morning. Cassie must have risen at the crack of dawn, because by the time I awoke, she was already dressed to leave and had brought Mother her breakfast. I had to admit that Cassie looked prettier than ever. She had taken time with her hair and her makeup and wore one of her nicest dresses. In her high heels, she looked years older to me. She came charging into my room to wake me and be sure I chose the clothes she had suggested and did everything to make it appear that I was going.

"Hurry up and dress. We have a lot to do today," she told me. I was jealous of her excitement.

When I went down to breakfast, I was surprised to learn that Daddy already had left hours ago. I had wanted to wish him luck.

"I didn't know he was going so early. I would have set my alarm clock," I whined.

"You can call him later," Cassie suggested, "but don't be upset if you can't get to him quickly. He'll be inundated with people requesting this and that, and he does have to make special preparations for the governor. Let's both go up to get Mother's tray and say our good-byes now. If you have trouble keeping to our story, just look at me, and I'll help you. Okay, Semantha?"

"Okay," I said. My voice cracked. I was that close to tears.

"Get hold of yourself," Cassie ordered, her eyelids narrowing. "Don't screw up this day for Daddy."

I took a deep breath, nodded, and followed her

up the stairs. The first thing that struck me was that Mother had not eaten much of her breakfast, and she had not eaten much of her dinner the night before. She was lying there, looking up at the ceiling.

"Mother," Cassie said sharply, "we're getting ready to leave for the gala."

She barely turned her head, but then, when she saw me, she smiled and looked more awake. "You look lovely, Semantha. You both do," she said. "I'm very proud of the two of you."

"Thank you, Mother," Cassie said.

"Don't you want to eat more of your breakfast, Mother?" I asked, going to the tray. "You hardly touched your eggs and didn't eat much toast."

"No. I ate what I could this morning."

"But you haven't eaten enough to get you through the time we're gone," I stressed.

"I'll bring her a sandwich wrapped in wax paper and something to drink," Cassie said, looking at me and sounding as if she was trying to make me feel better rather than Mother.

Mother said nothing. She reached out for me, and I took her hand. "You must do what you can to make your father happy, Semantha. He's had a great disappointment. I'm sure he'll be proud to have the two of you at his side today. Don't think about me. Think about him," she said. "Promise?"

I pressed my lips together to keep myself from sobbing. My heart ached. All I could do was nod.

Cassie moved quickly to my side. "I'll make sure she does, Mother. You just eat what I bring you and rest. We'll head back the moment the festivities end."

"Thank you, Cassie. I have always been proud of how strong you are and how dependable."

Cassie simply stared at her. I saw a struggle going on in her face, and for a moment, I thought, She's going to tell the truth, she's going to say something warm and loving, but she pulled back her shoulders and looked at me instead.

"I'll go get Mother's lunch prepared," she said, taking Mother's tray. "You get those flyers I prepared with Daddy and bring them out to the car."

What flyers? I thought, and then realized she was making it up to get Mother to believe I was going. I didn't say anything. I leaned down, kissed Mother on her cheek, and turned away, comforted to know I would soon be back up there and taking care of her. Maybe we would have a good talk without Cassie around to interrupt.

"Enjoy the day," Mother called to us. I started to turn back, but Cassie nudged me to keep walking, and I did.

"I'll get the sandwich made quickly. You wait in the living room," she ordered.

"She's not eating, Cassie. She looks worse to me."

"We'll call the doctor. Just concentrate on what we have to do today," she insisted.

I went to the living room and sat on the sofa to wait. About twenty minutes later, she came in. I thought she suddenly looked very agitated. She began to pace, as she often did when she was giving me some lecture or instruction.

"What's wrong?" I asked her.

She shook her head. "Nothing's wrong. Now,

you listen carefully. You'll only make things worse for Mother and yourself if you don't do exactly what I'm telling you to do."

She looked at her watch.

"It's a little after nine. Don't dare go up there until two. By then, it will be too late for her to make a stink about your not going to the gala. If you go up earlier, she'll be very upset and try to get Daddy on the phone or something, and that will cause great problems for him right in the middle of everything. Do you understand me?"

"Yes, Cassie, but what if she calls out or something?"

"She won't. She thinks no one's here. Don't imagine anything, either, Semantha. You're making me very nervous. Are you going to do this right or not? If I have to take you with me, Daddy will be very upset thinking no one's here with her."

"I'm doing it," I said. "I'll do what you say."

"All right. You can call me on my cell phone, but be sure you call from down here, so she can't hear you if you call before two, okay?"

"Yes."

"And make sure you're as quiet as a ghost. If she hears you moving about or talking to someone or watching television, she'll get frightened. Here's the program Daddy and I designed for the gala," she said, handing me a copy. "We should keep to the schedule, so you can imagine what's happening by looking at the clock. Just sit and read it quietly. Understand?"

"I understand, Cassie."

"Good. Good. We're going to be all right. Everything is going to be all right, even better," she added.

"Better? How could it be better if Mother doesn't improve?" I asked, but she didn't reply. Her mind had already taken her to the gala.

"Wish us luck," she said instead, and left. When the front door closed, the house seemed to grow ominously quiet. I looked up at the family portraits and imagined an expression of concern on all of their faces. No one smiled in any of those portraits, anyway. Back then, they didn't believe smiling was dignified or something. At least, that was what Cassie had told me, but right now, I desperately needed a smile.

Instead, I had only these somber faces. I sat there sinking deeper and deeper into my own troubled thoughts and staring at the grandfather clock. Mother always said, "A watched pot never boils." Well, that seemed true for time, too. Hours seemed more like days. I dozed off once or twice and rose on tiptoe to the windows to look out. Fortunately for us, we were having a beautiful Kentucky day. There were only a few scattered clouds, and the breeze looked as gentle as could be.

I looked at the program Cassie had given me and tried to pretend I was there at the gala. I heard the music when it was scheduled to begin. I imagined the crowds, checked off the list of speakers as the hour passed, and envisioned Daddy standing there looking like a president. I could easily see Cassie at his side, making sure every little thing was done correctly. And then I thought about Uncle Perry and imagined his disappointment in my not being there. Maybe when he complained, Cassie said something nasty to him.

I got a little hungry just after one and went to the kitchen to eat some cheese and crackers. I hoped Mother had already eaten the sandwich Cassie had brought her. When I went up in about an hour, I would make sure she ate it if she hadn't. I would insist and ask her to do it for me.

The last hour seemed to take the longest. I thought about calling Cassie and even Daddy but decided not to interrupt anything, and besides, they probably wouldn't hear their cell phones ringing. When the grandfather clock bonged two, I rose quickly from the sofa and headed to the stairway, rehearsing all that I would say to calm Mother down and then even apologize for having had to fool her like this. I would justify it by explaining, as Cassie had, that Daddy would have been too upset to enjoy his gala opening otherwise. I was sure she would understand.

I moved as quickly as I could so she would not be frightened at the sound of footsteps. When I looked in on her, I saw she was lying and staring up at the ceiling just as she had been doing when I had first seen her this morning, and, just as I had suspected, she hadn't eaten her sandwich. In fact, it was still wrapped.

"Mother," I called, and started toward the bed. She didn't reply or turn to look at me. "Mother, I'm here. I didn't go," I began. "I see you haven't eaten, either."

I unwrapped the sandwich and put it on the plate.

"You have to eat something, Mother."

She didn't turn to me. I paused. Something was different about her. I put the plate down and touched her arm. It felt cold. I shook her.

"Mother!"

She didn't move.

It struck me first in the stomach and then moved up my body like a sheet of ice, freezing me so that I couldn't move. I couldn't speak, either. Gradually, by inches at a time, I lowered myself to lean toward her and put my lips to her cheek. It was like kissing a statue. My eyes went to the night table and the bottle of tranquilizers. It was over on its side. I picked it up and looked in it.

It was empty.

And Mother was gone. She had taken them all at once. It felt as if someone or something was beating on my bones. The reverberation shook my very brain.

I looked at Mother's tranquil face and her glassy eyes staring at nothing. Her mouth was slightly opened.

The screams I heard sounded as if they were coming from outside the room, coming from someone else.

When they were actually coming from me!

13

Sorrow

I FUMBLED FOR the phone. My fingers seemed detached, but I managed to tap out Cassie's cell-phone number. It rang and rang and rang until her answering service came on. I didn't want to talk to some machine, so I tried to call again, and again it rang and rang, and again the answering service started. I sat there for what must have been close to a half-hour, calling continuously, crying, hanging up at the sound of the answering service, and calling again. Finally, she answered, and for a moment, all I could say was, "Cassie."

"What is it, Semantha? Daddy has just introduced the governor. We're running a little late. Semantha?"

"It's . . . Mother . . ."

"What about her? Hey, don't move that, please. We want that there!" she shouted at someone. "What, Semantha? You didn't go up too early and get her upset, did you?"

"No, I waited, Cassie. Cassie . . ."

"What, already? By the time you tell me why you're calling, I'll be on social security."

"She's not moving; her eyes are open, but she won't move, and she feels cold."

Cassie was silent.

"Cassie, did you hear me?"

"What are you saying, Semantha?"

"I think . . . Mother's dead. The pills are all gone. The bottle is empty. She took too many pills!"

"Now, listen to me, Semantha. Don't go in there. Go to your room and wait."

"Are you going to tell Daddy?"

"No."

"What?"

"I can't tell Daddy that now. Are you crazy? He's on the stand with the governor of Kentucky, a senator, and a mayor. I'll tell him after it's all over. Maybe you're wrong. Maybe she's just in a deep sleep."

"Cassie . . ."

"Do what I said, Semantha. Don't call anyone else. Just go to your room. Semantha! Are you listening to me?"

"Yes. Oh, Cassie . . . Mother . . ."

"Look, as soon as I can, I'll call Dr. Moffet. Stay in your room. I'll call you when I reach him. Okay?"

"Okay."

She hung up. I sat holding the receiver for minutes, not moving, afraid that if I did, I would fold up on the floor as if all my bones had turned to jelly. I looked back at Mother, who still hadn't moved a muscle. I couldn't just stay there staring at her, so I ran from her room to mine, throwing myself onto the bed. I sobbed and sobbed until my ribs ached. Then I curled up in a fetal position and held myself tightly.

Maybe Cassie was right, I hoped. I supposed I could be mistaken. *What she said made sense,* I told myself. *Mother's just in some sort of a coma or deep sleep. Mother can't be . . . gone. The doctor will be here soon, and he'll make her better. Surely, it was all just a misunderstanding. I'm such a fool to panic like that. I deserve to be blamed, bawled out. I'm no doctor. Just because someone feels cool doesn't mean she's gone.* Yes, I convinced myself, *I made a mistake, a terrible mistake. It's good that Cassie hasn't called back yet. I'll have time to do something, and then, when Mother shows she's all right, I'll call Cassie again and tell her not to worry.*

I leaped up, wiped my cheeks dry, and headed back to Mother's bedroom. Seeing that she still hadn't moved at all sank my heart again, but I charged forward and seized her hand to pump her arm and wake her.

"Mother, it's Semantha. I'm sorry I left you. You've got to try to wake up. Please, please."

I was shaking her whole body now, but she didn't move. Her eyes remained opened, locked in that ghastly gaze. How could she be in a deep sleep with her eyes open? I asked myself, and then remembered seeing someone in a coma on television, a woman who had her eyes open. The medicine simply had Mother out cold. I had to get her to hear me, to come back. I dropped her hand to the bed and started to unwrap her sandwich.

"Listen to me, Mother. You have to eat something. That's what's wrong. You lack energy. Just take a small bite. Please, Mother," I begged, holding the sandwich close to her mouth. I stood there holding it for a few more moments, and then I nodded, imagining that I knew what was wrong.

"Oh, I know. You don't like what Cassie made. Yes, it looks dry. There's some freshly made chicken. I'll go make you a new sandwich. It's no problem. I'll be right back." I charged out of the room, practically running down the hall and down the stairway to the kitchen.

"Maybe I'll cut it into the perfect four squares Daddy likes. You like it that way, too, sometimes, don't you, Mother?" I muttered as I prepared the sandwich. "Cassie does it so well, but this doesn't look bad. Oh, I'll put a slice of pickle on the plate. You like that."

When I was finished, I held it out and admired it as an artist might admire his newest painting or sculpture.

"Very good. As good as Cassie's sandwiches, if I say so myself," I declared, and went back up to her room.

Cassie had still not called back to tell me about Dr. Moffet. I wished she would now, so I could tell her I had prepared a new sandwich for Mother and was making new efforts to get her to come out of her coma. I hurried to her bedside.

"Look, this is a better sandwich, Mother. See the perfect four squares? You're still not hungry yet? That's all right. I'll wait," I said.

I put the plate down and pulled a chair closer to the bed.

"Actually, I'm glad we're alone, Mother. I have

so much to tell you, things I've been a little afraid of telling you. I never told you everything about my first date with Kent Pearson and what happened. I wanted to tell you, but Cassie made me feel as if I had done a bad thing, and I was a little ashamed. I know we should have had more mother-daughter talks like this. I wanted them, but Cassie always seemed to be between us. She's not here now, so we can talk. Oh, I have so much to tell you about school, about my crush on Kent, about . . . oh, about the car accident. I wasn't supposed to tell you, but I'm fine, and I learned a lot from it. It's not right to hide things from you, anyway, Mother."

I reached out and took her cold hand into mine, hoping mine would warm hers. As I held it, I went on and on until my throat ached. I don't remember how long I sat there or what I actually got to tell her before I leaned forward and fell asleep holding Mother's hand, but suddenly, I felt some strong hands waking me and lifting me out of the chair. I turned to see Daddy and Dr. Moffet. Daddy's eyes were flooded with tears. Dr. Moffet rushed to Mother's bedside and began to examine her.

"Semantha," Daddy said. Once again, I felt as if all the bones in my body had turned into jelly. I collapsed in his arms, and all went black.

When I woke up, I found myself in my bed. The door was open, and I could hear the voices of Dr. Moffet, Uncle Perry, Cassie, and Daddy. There were strange voices, too. A short time later, I heard footsteps drawing closer and saw Daddy come in with a short, stocky man in a jacket and tie. Daddy looked exhausted, so drained he seemed barely able to stand. His face was gray with sorrow.

"How are you doing, Semantha?"

I didn't answer. I looked at the stranger instead.

"This is Detective Reynolds. The police had to be called. Can you tell him what you know about what happened?"

"How's Mother? Did Dr. Moffet get her to wake up?"

Daddy shook his head. "She's gone, honey. I'm afraid we've lost her."

"I made her a better sandwich," I said. "I thought if she ate something . . ."

I felt a trembling in my face. It was as if my body was in its own earthquake. Daddy sat on my bed and embraced me. He rocked me, and my tears flowed over my cheeks onto his shoulder. Then he lowered me to my pillow again and wiped my hair back from my forehead just the way Mother would.

"Can you tell Detective Reynolds what you remember, Semantha?" he asked. "Tell him what happened."

I took a deep breath. "I don't know what happened. I was downstairs waiting until it was two o'clock before I went up to see her."

"Why did you wait until two?" Detective Reynolds asked.

"We didn't want Mother to know I was home."

"But why not, Semantha?" Daddy asked.

Before I could answer, Cassie came to the doorway and stood looking in at us.

"I waited until two, just as Cassie told me to," I

said. "I did, Cassie." I looked at Daddy. "Cassie said it would upset Mother if she knew I hadn't really gone to the gala, and she would call you, and you would be upset, and you had so much to do."

"I didn't mean for you to neglect her so long," Cassie said. "I just told her to stay away long enough for Mother to think she had gone, Daddy."

"But you said . . . I thought you said to wait until two, Cassie."

"She's just confused, Daddy."

"Oh, God," Daddy said, bringing his right thumb and index finger to his temples. "I should have insisted we have someone here."

"It's not your fault, Daddy. It's mine," I said.

"No, no, it's not your fault or Cassie's, Semantha. Both of you were doing what you thought best," Daddy said. "I was simply too distracted with this opening."

"And when you finally came up and looked in on her, what did you see?" Detective Reynolds asked me.

"She hadn't eaten her sandwich. She hadn't eaten much of her breakfast or her dinner the night before, so I tried to get her to eat something. I thought . . ." I looked past him at Cassie. "I thought maybe she didn't like the sandwich Cassie had made, so I went down and made her a new sandwich with fresh chicken. I cut it in four equal parts. That's the way Daddy likes his sandwiches, and sometimes Mother does, too."

"She was talking to you?" he asked.

"No. She was just looking up at the ceiling and not moving."

"Then how did you know she didn't want the first sandwich?" Detective Reynolds asked me.

I started to cry again. "She wouldn't eat it."

"She's not making any sense," Daddy muttered. "I'm sure she's in a bit of shock. Let her rest. I'll bring her around, or you can return if necessary," he told Detective Reynolds.

He nodded and turned to leave.

Daddy stroked my hair and smiled. "You stay here and rest a while, Semantha. Cassie will stay with you. I have things to do."

He followed the detective out, and Cassie came in and stood by the window looking out.

"You did tell me to stay away from her until two o'clock, right, Cassie?"

"It was such a wonderful day for us," she said instead of answering. "Daddy has the DVD to play back, so you'll see. How horrible for this to have happened today of all days. She just couldn't let him have his day."

"It's my fault, isn't it? I should have gone up to check on her earlier."

"Stop it. You heard Daddy," she snapped at me. "It's no one's fault."

"Was it an accident, Cassie?" I asked.

She just stood there looking out without speaking for a few moments and then finally turned and shook her head. "An accident? Emptying all those pills into her stomach? How could that be an accident, Semantha? What have I told you about not facing realities, about fantasizing and pretending things aren't what they are? You're almost an adult now, Semantha. You have to put away this childish behavior. Things are going to change radically for us. We all have to be stronger, and we have to support each other, protect each other, and especially you and I have our work cut out for us to help Daddy get through this and go on. Do you think you can do that without moaning and whining and fantasizing your way out of difficulties? Well? Do you? I'd like to know."

"Yes, Cassie," I said. "But Mother . . ."

"She's broken all our hearts. Now, we must mend then," Cassie said.

She came toward me slowly and put her right palm flat against my forehead.

"Don't worry. I'll give you as much of my strength as I can so that you can be stronger." She closed her eyes and kept her hand on my forehead. Maybe I was imagining again, but it did feel as if something electrical, some energy, traveled down her arm and into my head. I closed my eyes, too.

When I opened them, she had taken her hand away, but had brought her face close to mine and kissed me on the cheek.

"Haven't I always been more like a mother to you? Haven't I always stepped in to do the things she neglected to do? Rest, little one," she said. "There's much to be done."

She straightened up quickly, adjusted her dress, and walked out to join the others. A little while later, Dr. Moffet came in to see me.

"How are you doing, Semantha?" he asked. He sat on my bed and took my hand. "Your father's very worried about you. It's a shocking thing to have happened, for a child to see."

"I waited too long," I said. "I shouldn't have waited."

"Your father told me everything. You and Cassie thought you were doing the right thing, Semantha. I'm sure your mother thought she was doing what was best for all of you. It's unfortunate that none of us fully understood how depressed she was, but it won't help now to blame yourself. You want me to give you something to help you sleep?"

"No," I said quickly. I hoped I would never take another pill again.

He nodded. "I understand. Well, I'll be only a phone call away. You take care of yourself. You girls have to look after your father now. It hasn't fully hit him yet." He patted my hand and stood. "I've very sorry about all this." He looked as if he might cry himself.

Later, when Cassie returned to my room, the thing that seemed to bother her the most was that the police were calling Mother's death a suicide, so we couldn't tell people it had been an accident, a mix of medicines, or something unintended.

"It will be treated like some sort of a scandal," she said, "and just when we were getting all this positive press for our stores and Daddy. You can't imagine how difficult it's going to be for him to face his employees and the public. I'm sure they'll find a way to blame it on him."

"Why?"

"Why? They'll say he made his wife feel terrible about losing Asa."

"She did feel terrible, Cassie. Dr. Moffet said she was very depressed."

"But not because Daddy made her feel that way, and don't you ever say otherwise," she said with her eyes wide. After a moment, she calmed. "You saw how loving and devoted he was to her, how he tried to get her to get better."

"The other students in school will look at us the same way, then, when we return, won't they? They'll make us feel guilty or strange."

"Don't worry yourself about it. We're not returning to school," she said.

"What? What do you mean? Why aren't we?"

"You're going to have home schooling, tutoring, and then next year, you'll go to a private school."

"What about you?"

"I told you I was quitting to be with Daddy. Now it's definite. He needs me more than ever."

"Does he know what you intend to do? Did Daddy say I should be home-schooled?"

"No, he doesn't know any of this yet. He's too much in mourning right now to hear anything. At the right moment after the funeral, I'll speak to him and get everything arranged for you. Don't say anything about this to him until I have the conversation with him. For now, I have to prepare for people who will start calling to give condolences. Of course, most of them will come out of sick curiosity, but there's nothing we can do about it. We can't shut them out.

"What we will do," she continued, "is be strong and not let anyone see us being weak. Be somber, but Heavenstones don't cry in front of strangers, understand? I'm hiring some help to prepare and serve during the period of mourning. I'm not cooking and baking for a bunch of strangers."

"When will they come?"

"It will start tomorrow. It doesn't take long for bad news to whip through the community. I'm going to work on that right now."

"Where is Daddy?"

"He's waiting for the ambulance."

"Ambulance? Isn't it too late?"

"Oh, Semantha. You'd think you would know more, at least from those novels you read. There will have to be an autopsy. There's little or no question about the cause of her death, but the law requires it, so she'll be taken to the hospital morgue and examined. In the morning, Daddy and I will go to the funeral parlor and start arrangements."

"Won't I go?"

"It's going to be difficult enough for him without your sobbing and wailing," she said. "And what if you faint again when we go to the funeral parlor?"

"I won't."

"We'll see," she said.

"Is Uncle Perry with Daddy?"

"Yes, but he's not much help. He's as white as a bedsheet and looks like he'll faint, too. He's already had two shots of whiskey, thanks to me," she added. "Frankly, I wish he'd go home."

"But he's Daddy's brother. He should stay with him, with us."

She smirked but then said, "The only good thing about it is that Daddy's worrying over him keeps him distracted from his own deep sorrow for now. I'm going down to make something simple to eat in case anyone's hungry tonight."

"I can't imagine ever eating again."

"Eating is comforting," she said. "You'll see. Sorrow is exhausting."

"Is that why Asa's father drank himself to death?"

"Yes, I'm sure it was."

"Just think, Cassie, the first Asa dies, and the second dies in a miscarriage, and—".

"Stop talking about it," she snapped. "It's not the same, anyway. The first Asa died in a war. He had lived with his family for years. Our Asa was little more than an idea. We don't even have a picture of him."

We heard people talking in the hallway.

"That's the ambulance personnel," she said. "I don't think you should come out and see this." She walked toward the door.

"If you're going, I'm going," I said.

"Suit yourself, but don't dare faint or anything."

Just warning me about it put it in my mind. I was a little dizzy when I stood up, but I closed my eyes and then opened them to follow her into the hallway. The sight of Mother covered with a sheet and being wheeled out of the bedroom was like a blow to my stomach. I started to dry-heave, but Cassie spun on me with those fiery eyes, and I caught my breath.

"I'm all right," I said.

We walked behind the ambulance attendants and watched them lift the gurney and carry Mother carefully down the stairway. Daddy walked right beside them as if he was afraid they might drop Mother. Uncle Perry waited below. The attendants lowered the gurney again and wheeled it to the front door. Daddy followed them out, but Uncle Perry stood back, watching with us. Then, without a word, he turned to me and put his arm around me. Looking pointedly at Cassie, he said, "You must not blame yourself, Semantha."

Cassie turned away from him and headed toward the kitchen. Afterward, he went with Daddy to Daddy's office to call our minister and what relatives they thought they should call, and I joined Cassie in the kitchen.

She was right about us being hungry, after all. When I looked at Daddy, even though he was eating, he seemed more stunned than sad. Every once in a while, I caught him looking toward Mother's chair. Cassie was sitting in her own place again. We had just gotten seated at the table when the phone started to ring. Cassie took it on herself to handle all phone calls. She reported each and every one to Daddy. He smiled at some names and nodded, and then returned to his far-off look.

Later, he and Uncle Perry sat and talked. Cassie kept busy in the house but walked in and out to ask Daddy if he needed anything. I tried to stay up with everyone, but my eyelids wouldn't cooperate. They kept shutting, and I kept dozing off until Cassie shook me and told me to go up to bed.

"I'll come up to look in on you in a little while," she said.

How she could be so strong and so helpful when I was nothing but a wet noodle amazed me. Once again, I thought how Mother had been right about her, how she would be a leader and would always have strong self-confidence.

Despite all that had occurred and all I had seen, I still couldn't get myself to believe that Mother was gone, had literally been carted away under a sheet like something to be kept hidden from curious eyes. I had to go back to her bedroom and look in at the empty bed, praying to myself that this was all just a bad dream and I would soon wake up. No one had touched the bed. The blanket was still pulled back, her pillows showing where her head had been. I started to cry again and hurried back to my room. I cried in the bathroom. I cried when I got dressed for bed, and I sobbed into my pillow until I felt Cassie's hand on my shoulder and turned to look up at her.

"Now, don't cry, Semantha. Don't worry. I'll always be here for you. We're the Heavenstone sisters. We can overcome anything together. I want you to be strong over the next few days. I want you to help me with Daddy, be at his side to give him the strength he will need, okay?"

I nodded.

"Just try to get some sleep. Remember, the sun in the morning is the kiss of life," she said, which was something Mother always said. Then she kissed my cheek, stroked my hair, and fixed my blanket. "I'm right across the hall," she said, "as always."

I watched her leave and closed my eyes again. It bothered me a little for reasons I couldn't quite understand yet, but Cassie was as comforting as our mother had been able to be.

In the morning, she was up ahead of me as usual and had done quite a bit before I ventured down. She had the table set and our breakfast prepared.

"I'm sorry I didn't get down early enough to help you, Cassie," I told her.

"That's all right. You needed more sleep than I did. You went through a more trying time. I'm going up to see about Daddy. We must be sure he eats a good breakfast. He needs his strength. I know it will be hard for you, but try not to cry in front of him, okay?"

"Yes."

I waited at the table, and when Daddy came down with Cassie, he looked as if he had aged years overnight. He wasn't dressed as impeccably as he usually was, and his hair was not as neat. Surely, sleeping in the bed in which Mother had died was very difficult and very emotional for him. I was positive that he had not had a good night's sleep and had probably woken up many times to convince himself that she wasn't there and would never be again.

On the other hand, Cassie was as buoyant and energetic as ever, urging Daddy and me to eat, clearing dishes, pouring coffee, and serving her special egg omelette. She spoke to Daddy as if he was her child and not vice versa. He nodded and gave her whatever smiles he could. Somehow, she got him to finish his breakfast, and then I helped her clear the table so we could get ready to go to the funeral parlor. Daddy suggested that he would go himself, but

Cassie insisted that we accompany him. She assured him that we would be fine and looked at me sharply to remind me how to behave.

Uncle Perry met us at the funeral parlor. I was grateful for that, because he held my hand and stood by me the whole time. Even so, I think the one thing that saved me was the feeling that none of this was real. Even when I looked at the choices for a coffin, it seemed as if I was watching a movie about someone else. The only time I reacted to anything was when Daddy asked us if what he had chosen was appropriate. Cassie assured him it was, and I quickly nodded. After all of the arrangements were made, we headed back home. Amazingly, Cassie already had organized the caterers and staff to handle the mourners who would visit.

Our days of mourning seemed to run into each other and become one very long, dreary, dark day. Although Cassie was polite to people, I could see she didn't appreciate anyone's sympathy or look grateful for anything except being left alone. She never tired or failed to be at Daddy's side for one moment. The stream of mourners didn't faze her one bit. On the other hand, their tears, words of encouragement, and dark faces draped in heavy gloom exhausted me. I slept on and off and fell asleep early each night.

Mother's funeral was attended by so many people that the church overflowed, and people had to stand outside and listen to the minister on a speaker. There were many dignitaries. The governor sent a representative, and both of our state's senators did as well. A great many of the mourners followed the hearse to the cemetery, too. Daddy stood between Cassie and me as the minister said his final words and prayers. I cried but held on to Daddy, who simply stared at the coffin. Cassie, on the other hand, seemed strong enough to be holding him up. Uncle Perry stood beside me and took my hand. After the graveside ceremony ended, we returned to the house for the final greeting of mourners.

I saw very few students from our school at the church and none at the funeral. When I mentioned that to Cassie, she smirked, nodded, and said, "The hypocrites told their children not to mourn someone who committed suicide, I'm sure. Who cares? Who wants their empty sympathy, anyway?"

I did. I wanted to see a friendly face. I had hoped Kent would come, but he didn't, and neither did any of the girls who had become my new best friends. Cassie's decision for me to stay home and then attend a private school seemed very sensible to me now. I hoped she hadn't forgotten and would convince Daddy.

When everyone was finally gone, Cassie sent Daddy up to bed and took care of the caterers and locking up our house. She sent me up to bed as well. Before he left, Uncle Perry came to me and asked me please to call on him for anything at any time. He hugged me and kissed me.

"It's all right to cry now, Semantha," he said. "You've been a good soldier for your father, but don't hold your grief in your heart. Let it spill out."

I thanked him and went up to my room. I was still moving in slow motion like someone in a trance myself. After I got into bed, I heard Cassie come up the stairs, but I didn't hear her go to her bedroom. I waited and waited but still didn't hear her. Curious, I got out of bed and looked down the hallway. I didn't see her for a few moments, and then suddenly, she emerged from Daddy's bedroom with an armful of clothing.

Now she was the one moving like someone in a trance. She seemed not to see me standing in my bedroom doorway and almost walked past me and into her room before I called out. She turned slowly.

"Why aren't you asleep?" she asked.

"I was just getting to sleep when I heard you. What are you doing with those clothes?"

"These are some of Mother's things that I want to keep and wear," she said. "We are about the same size. Daddy was always fond of these outfits."

I just stared.

"Actually, I can fit into everything that was hers," she added.

I didn't know what to say.

She smiled.

"Good night, Semantha," she said, and went into her room, closing the door behind her and leaving me shivering in the darkness of my own bedroom.

The Deal

DADDY WAS GOING to return to work the next day right after a little breakfast, but Cassie asked him to leave later so we could have a family meeting.

"Then you don't want to return to school yet?" Daddy asked.

"No. This is why we must meet and have a family discussion," she told him.

The idea of it being a family meeting without Mother seemed strange. I winced at the sound of it, but Daddy agreed, so right after breakfast we all went into the living room, where Cassie could discuss important matters. She would say nothing until Daddy and I were seated. Even then, she paced back and forth for a few moments, looking as if she was taking great care about how she expressed herself.

I couldn't take my eyes off her, and I was holding my breath in anticipation, but Daddy looked quite subdued, his gaze on the floor. I didn't expect him to be himself, of course, but he looked as if all of his strength, his love of life, and his energy had been buried alongside Mother in her grave. Maybe that was why he was so willing to agree with Cassie, why he presented little opposition to her requests, which sounded more like her usual faits accomplis.

She began. "You might have noticed, Daddy— although if you didn't, we understand, of course—that few, if any, of our classmates were at the church for Mother's funeral services." She turned to me. "Am I right, Semantha?"

I looked at Daddy and nodded. He said nothing, but the sadness in his face deepened.

"As you know, Daddy," Cassie continued, "both Semantha and I have never been happy in public school. For me, it's been little or no challenge, and as some recent events proved, it's not been a happy time for Semantha, either. It's not your fault, but because you are so successful, because the Heavenstones are so well known and respected here, Semantha and I are often resented at school. So many are jealous of us and eager to criticize us or see us have misfortune. Even our teachers look at us though green eyes of accusation, accusing us of thinking we are better than anyone else."

"Have any of them said such a thing?" Daddy asked.

"No, but it's not hard to see the thought rolling around in their heads and hear it in their tone of voice whenever they speak to either of us."

I nearly smiled when Cassie said this. Why was she making it sound as if that made her unhappy? She certainly believed we were truly better than everyone else and had not failed to tell me so one way or another practically every day of my life.

"I do know what you mean," Daddy said,

nodding. "It's often more of a burden to be held in high regard in your community. I can sympathize, because when I was growing up, I felt much the same way you two do, but—"

"But we have a solution, Daddy," Cassie interrupted.

He nodded. "What's that?"

"Well, as regards me, I'm dropping out of school for now. I'm putting my formal education on hold for a while."

"Oh, I don't think that's—"

"You have often told me how Grandfather Heavenstone only went through the eighth grade, but his business acumen guided him to slip into his father's shoes and continue to build a successful enterprise. Whenever you talked about him, I could see in your face how proud of him you were."

"He was an extraordinary man," Daddy agreed.

"And I don't think I'm being immodest by saying I have proven to be somewhat beyond my peers and even most of my teachers. You know that's true, Daddy."

"I've always said that, Cassie, and so did your mother. We're very proud of you and your accomplishments."

"Which is exactly why you shouldn't be worried about my hiatus from formal education."

"But what will you do?"

"I have a lot to do here now, and I'd like to become more of an assistant to you, learn more and more about our business. You're carrying the whole load on your shoulders, Daddy. Don't pretend you're not, and don't pretend that Uncle Perry can shoulder much or any of that responsibility."

"Perry has other talents," he said as a way of agreeing with her.

"But not executive talents," Cassie insisted. "You're still a young man, Daddy, but you're not Superman. With all that's happened, you need someone upon whom you can safely and comfortably rely. I know I can be that someone for you. Mother never took much interest in the Heavenstone Stores. I'm not faulting her. I know it just wasn't her cup of tea, but she was at least supportive, and you need someone like that on a daily basis. You need reinforcement. I'm not saying you're not up to your responsibilities, but it's good to have someone you can trust watching your back."

Daddy nodded and then finally smiled. "You are truly a very bright and thoughtful young woman, Cassie. I wish your mother was here to listen to you."

"Thank you. So, that's settled," she concluded, even though Daddy had not actually said so. Then she looked at me. "Now, we have Semantha to consider. She isn't doing spectacular work at school. She's actually average or even a little below average in her grades. And that's not because she's not trying. It's because she's so unhappy." She said it with a firmness that made my denying it impossible.

Daddy looked at me and nodded. "Your mother and I often discussed that. Even though she didn't say anything, I knew she was just as concerned. Of course, I know you always helped her as much as you could."

"Which is why I think we should do what I suggest for now, Daddy," Cassie said.

"What is that, exactly?"

"I think Semantha should withdraw from public school, too. There are just too many obstacles for her there, too many unnecessary challenges now in light of what's happened. I have found . . . I mean, I know of an excellent tutor for her home-schooling."

"Home-schooling?"

"Just until the end of this school year. With our great family tragedies, it's best we are all together, supporting each other for a while. After that, we can enroll her in a good private school where she will attend classes with other boys and girls who come from similar successful families, although few as successful and important as ours."

Daddy looked at me for a reaction, but I kept myself stone-faced and said nothing. I was afraid I would say something that wouldn't please or support Cassie, and the truth of it was, I was nervous about returning to school and seeing my classmates. I knew by now we were the big topic of all the gossip. Mother's suicide would stain me indelibly. No one would look at me without thinking about it. They would make me feel freakish. Surely few, if any, would want to be my friends anymore, not that so many were knocking down my door. I could only guess how Kent would view me. Eddie, who was afraid I might undermine his fabricated explanation for the car accident that had injured Noel, would probably gloat at my isolation. Who'd listen to anything I said?

"And you know someone good enough for her?" Daddy asked Cassie.

"Yes, I do, Daddy. I learned about her through an acquaintance at school who told me how successful this woman, Mrs. Underwood, had been with her invalid cousin. Mrs. Underwood, a widow, is a retired high-school librarian with expertise in all subject matters. She has the proper certification. Her children live in New York, so she has the time to take on jobs like this, and she needs to supplement her meager teacher's retirement pension."

"I see. Apparently, you've done some research on it." He shook his head. "I'm not surprised." He turned to me. "Your sister is always a mile ahead of most of us, always prepared. That's a good quality to have, in business especially."

"Exactly why I'd like to be more of a part of your work, Daddy."

"Yes. Well," he said, pressing down on his knees to get himself standing. "I think you have it under control, Cassie. Why don't you get the ball rolling? I'll sign whatever papers need to be signed."

"I'll get on it right away," she said. "Don't you give it any more thought, Daddy. You have enough to think about."

"Thank you, honey. Call me if you need anything."

"No, Daddy, thank *you*," Cassie said, going to him. "Thank you for being so perfect."

Then she did something I rarely saw her do. Cassie embraced him and pressed her face against his chest. He looked at me, a little surprised, and slowly brought his hand up to stroke her hair. When she pulled back, he kissed her forehead. I didn't move a muscle.

He smiled at me and started out

"Have a good day, Teddy," Cassie called.

He turned, a bit surprised.

"I know Mother always said that to you," she told him. "I know how much you would miss it."

Daddy looked as if he would burst into tears for a moment, then swallowed hard, nodded, and quickly left. Cassie stood looking after him. She stared so long at the doorway I thought something was wrong, but she finally turned to me.

"Well, now, I have a lot to do today. I'm going to the school to see the principal and inform him of Daddy's decisions and mine. Then I'll go see Mrs. Underwood and make the arrangements for you. In the meantime you should start on the house. With all of those hypocrites traipsing through it during our period of mourning, we have a lot of cleaning to do. Every room, every floor, every window needs to be cleaned. The vacuum cleaner will probably be filled up. Throw out all these flowers, too."

"The flowers? But they're still quite alive."

"They're flowers for the dead, Semantha. Get rid of them. It makes the place smell like a funeral home. Just do a good job cleaning up. Don't touch Daddy's bedroom, however. I'll do that myself."

She started away, paused, and turned back to me.

"You know, Semantha, it wouldn't be so terrible if once in a while, you thanked me for doing so much for you. I don't desperately need thank-yous, but it wouldn't be so terrible."

"I'm sorry, Cassie. Everything is happening so fast. Thank you."

"Yes," she said. "When something terrible happens, it's always best to take strong, quick, decisive action. You should make mental notes. I'm going to arrange for your tutor, but your real education comes from what you will learn here in this house."

I was surprised she hadn't added *from me,* but she paused and thought again, and then she suddenly smiled.

"Daddy looked so pleased, didn't he? He was so down, so defeated when he came to breakfast this morning, but he left with some bounce in his step, didn't he?"

Bounce in his step? When she had said good-bye to him the way Mother used to, he looked terrible. What bounce?

"Didn't he?" she repeated, her eyes wide.

"Yes, Cassie."

She smiled. "I knew this would all work out. We'll be fine. We'll never stop being the Heavenstones."

With that, she left to get dressed to do her tasks, and I, still quite stunned by the lightning-quick changes about to occur in our lives, moved like a snail to begin the chores Cassie had dictated. I didn't resent it. Having something to do, so much to do, kept me from crying all day.

I lost track of time and even forgot to eat lunch. Hours later, I was in the dining room polishing the furniture when I heard Cassie call to me. I stepped out and saw her standing in the entryway with a very tall, thin woman. Her hair, the color of pewter, was sharply cut at a length just under her ears. She wore no makeup, not even a touch of lipstick, and the one-piece dark-blue dress she wore was ankle-length. It had a high collar with prominent pearl buttons down the middle. As I drew closer, I saw that she had a pretty face despite her thinness. I thought she had an interesting color of blue in her eyes, too. In the brighter light, they looked silvery.

"Mrs. Underwood," Cassie said, "this is my sister, Semantha. Semantha, I wanted you to meet Mrs. Underwood today. She will begin with you tomorrow, but I wanted her to become familiar with our home and you. I thought it would be best if you worked in our den, Mrs. Underwood. Semantha will show you to it, and you two can get acquainted."

Cassie turned back to me. "Mrs. Underwood will consult directly with me about your progress, Semantha. Please remember that your father and I are making these arrangements to give you an opportunity to improve your work and avoid all the unpleasantness at the public school. Don't disappoint us."

I stared at her. Between the time she had left the house and when she had returned, Cassie seemed to have undergone a complete change. I didn't notice that she had put on one of Mother's dresses. Now she had her hair even more like Mother's, and if I was not mistaken, she was carrying one of Mother's purses. Was it because of all this that she tried to sound more like my mother than my sister?

"Okay," I said. Mrs. Underwood smiled at me, and I smiled back. "I'll show you around the house," I told her.

"Yes, you two get acquainted," Cassie said. "I'll be down in a while, Semantha, and we'll start preparing dinner for Daddy. I called him twice today, by the way. He's doing all right." She turned to Mrs. Underwood. "My father comes from a family in which all of the men had grit, strong backbones. We're very proud of who and what we are. That's why we're hoping Semantha makes some significant improvements working with you. In fact, we expect it."

"I'll do my best for her," Mrs. Underwood said, but I sensed a discordant note, a slight darkening in her eyes as, if she thought she had just been threatened.

"Sometimes," Cassie said, now looking directly at me, "we have to do better than our best. See you both soon." She went to the stairway.

"This is quite a house," Mrs. Underwood said.

"My triple great-grandfather built it."

"Triple great? How quaint. It is a bit much to say great-great-great-grandfather, I suppose."

"Cassie made that up."

Mrs. Underwood nodded and continued to look around. I gave her a tour, pointing out the ancestral portraits and identifying some of them for her. She was very good at identifying our style of furniture and really appreciated many of the artifacts, figurines, and such that Mother had collected over the years and those that had been collected by our grand- and great-grandmothers. I could see Mrs. Underwood was quite impressed, and without fully realizing it, I began to behave more like Cassie. I had to correct myself when I thought I sounded too arrogant.

"The den is perfect for us," Mrs. Underwood said. "Well, I don't need to take up any more time today. I'll arrive at eight A.M. Monday through Friday and work with you until two. To begin, I will bring you these good tests I've been using with other students."

"Tests? Already?"

"Not that kind of test," she said, smiling. "These are analytical. They'll give me a good idea of where you are in your educational progress. I don't like to waste time teaching and reinforcing things my students have already mastered. I will expect that whatever homework you're given, you do on time. I've had students who were lazy or procrastinators, and they were not only wasting their parents' money having me but wasting time I could have spent elsewhere with other young people who needed me. Understood?"

"Yes."

"I do appreciate how difficult it is for your sister and you to get back to a normal life after . . . after such a tragedy in your family. I just don't want you to use that as an excuse for poor study habits."

"Exactly," we heard, and turned to see Cassie standing in the den doorway. "I'll make sure that doesn't occur as well, Mrs. Underwood."

"Very good. Then you do want me to start tomorrow? You are sure it's not too soon?"

"It's never too soon for any of us to improve, right, Semantha?"

"Yes," I said.

"Now, if you'll just step into my father's office

for a few more minutes, Mrs. Underwood, I'll discuss our financial arrangements. Semantha, would you please start preparing the salad? Remember, your daddy and I hate seeing brown stains on the lettuce. Right this way, Mrs. Underwood."

Mrs. Underwood nodded at me and followed her.

"Your daddy and I hate seeing brown stains on the lettuce?" I don't like that, either. Whether she was doing it deliberately or not, she was making me feel not only a lot younger but almost like a stranger, some hired servant. Even her voice sounded different to me. It made me a little angry, until I thought that perhaps this was all just her way of coping with our great tragedy and new difficulties. It wouldn't help things much if I started to complain, anyway, I decided, and went to the kitchen to begin preparations for dinner.

While I was working, I heard Cassie and Mrs. Underwood come out of Daddy's office. I couldn't believe Cassie wouldn't know I could hear her, but maybe she was just not thinking clearly. I heard her tell Mrs. Underwood, "My sister is a little spoiled. Our mother spoiled her, but don't put up with any back talk or any snide remarks about the work you prescribe. If she gives you even the slightest trouble, please come see me immediately."

"I think we'll be fine," Mrs. Underwood said. "She seems like a very nice young girl."

"We don't put blinders on our eyes in this house," Cassie said. "It's a Heavenstone trait to be objective and, if necessary, brutally honest. It's part of what has made us successful."

"I'm sure," Mrs. Underwood said.

They walked on to the front door, and Cassie let her out and said good-bye.

My heart was thumping, and I could feel the heat in my face. I had to say something when she entered.

"I'm not spoiled, Cassie. Why did you tell her that?"

"Psychology. Of course, she believes you're spoiled, that we're both spoiled. She lives in a two-by-four low-income apartment and walks into this mansion where she sees all we have. It's only natural, expected, that she would think we would be spoiled, rich young women. When will you learn that people beneath you, with so much less than you, instantly harbor a resentment?"

"But why make her feel that she's right?"

Cassie smiled. "Simple. When she sees how we really are, she'll hate herself for having had such thoughts, and we'll get along much more easily." She paused and stared at me so long I didn't know what to do. "I would think that by now, Semantha," she continued, her eyes now those Cassie narrow, angry eyes, "you would have confidence and faith in what I say and do, especially for you and for our family, and you wouldn't challenge me or be critical."

"I wasn't being critical. I was just wondering why you would tell her such a thing."

"Well, now you know, so forget it. We have too many other things far more important to do. I'm going to do the meat loaf Daddy loves. Why don't you go upstairs and put on something nicer for dinner tonight? I laid out something for you on your bed."

"You did?"

She smirked at me as if I had asked something very stupid, but putting out something special for me to wear was often something Mother would do.

"Go on. Don't dilly-dally. I want tonight's dinner to be a little more special. We'll use the better dishware. Go on!" she snapped when I didn't move quickly enough for her.

I turned and hurried up the stairs. Everything had suddenly become even more complicated to me. I felt as if bees were buzzing in both my ears. No more going to school, a tutor, Cassie behaving as if she had suddenly aged twenty years, while treating me as if I had become younger. How much of this was the result of our family tragedy? It seemed I couldn't even ask a question now. Maybe when Daddy came home, things would be different and not as tense and even frightening.

As I turned to enter my room, I gazed through Cassie's open bedroom door and stopped so fast anyone would have thought I had walked into a wall. The furniture looked rearranged. What was going on? Slowly, I stepped through her bedroom doorway and looked around. It was shocking. Cassie had moved Mother's vanity table into her room, and it was covered not with Cassie's things but with Mother's. Even the gilded oval vanity mirror that had hung above Mother's table was now hanging on Cassie's wall. I could see Mother's bathrobe hanging on the door of Cassie's bathroom. By the bed were Mother's pearl-colored fur slippers, the ones with the light pink ribbons. Cassie's own vanity table was gone, as were many of her other things, including the pictures she had had hanging on her walls. I even recognized that the bedding had been changed, replaced with a set of Mother and Daddy's. How strange.

I turned and hurried to Mother and Daddy's bedroom. Without Mother's things—her vanity table, mirror, pictures—and with her closet stripped, the room looked half-naked. I couldn't help it. I started to cry. I didn't even realize I was crying until I felt the tears on my cheeks. Now my own temper started to pound. I turned and hurried down the corridor and the stairs. Cassie was absorbed in her meat loaf when I stepped back into the kitchen. She didn't hear me at all. I was taken aback by the happy tune she was humming. A week hadn't even passed since our mother died, and she was humming a happy tune?

"Cassie!" I cried.

She turned, a look of confusion on her face. "What's wrong? Someone idiotic call you, one of those stupid girls from school? I didn't hear any phones ringing."

"No, no one called me. How could you . . . how could you take all of Mother's things like that and put them in your room, even her wall mirror?"

She stared for a moment and then wiped her hands with a dish towel. "Ordinarily, I would be very angry at you for constantly questioning everything I say and do, Semantha, but I understand what you're going through," she said calmly. "You see all this only from your own pain. It's typical of an adolescent to think, feel, and act as if the whole world revolves around her, but it doesn't."

She sat at the kitchenette. I thought she wasn't going to say anything more, but she nodded and continued.

"Can you stop thinking about yourself for one moment and think about Daddy? Can you shove your personal worries and thoughts out of your mind and imagine, try to imagine, what it must be like for him to go into that bedroom and look at Mother's things and know she is gone forever? Can you even feel a little of that pain for him?

"Do you know what he told me last night? He told me he turned and for a moment thought he saw Mother at her vanity table brushing her hair, and it filled him with a rush of hope that everything had been a bad dream. Of course, that image popped, and there was no one sitting at the table, but the table haunted him. Why, her perfumes, colognes, everything that has a scent was still in the air of that bedroom. He smelled it every night when he went to bed. He told me he still smelled the scent of her hair spray on her pillow beside him, and he told me he took her hairbrush and took some hairs from it and put them in his wallet, the wallet he carries in the inside pocket of his sports coat, the pocket closest to his heart. You mention the mirror. Do you know he told me he thought he saw her face in the mirror?"

"But . . . we're not getting rid of those things. You put them in your room," I said in defense of myself, even though her words had taken the air out of my anger.

She smiled. "Exactly. Soon, he'll see them as my things and not Mother's, and besides, Semantha, we're not out to rid this house of every reminder of Mother, are we? Should we?"

"No. Of course not. I didn't mean—"

"In time, Daddy will see that I'm . . . we're . . . more grown-up, and he won't be so worried about us. My wearing some of Mother's things, having some of those things, lets him see me as older, more mature. I know most of this is quite beyond you, but—"

"No, it's not."

"You understand, then?"

"Yes," I said weakly. I didn't understand it completely, but I knew I couldn't stand her making me feel like some vapid adolescent.

"Okay." Her face hardened. "I'll let this outburst pass, but the next time you come at me for something, you had better think a few times first and not be so judgmental. It's unbecoming for a Heavenstone to act solely on impulse and not based on reasonable thought. You have a ways to go, Semantha, but don't worry. I'm going to make sure you get there."

"Where?"

"To Heavenstone perfection, of course, where else?" She rose. "Now, please go up and put on the clothes I chose for you, and let's have a nice dinner with Daddy tonight. He'll want to know all about Mrs. Underwood. Even if you have some reservations about her, keep them to yourself for now. We want Daddy not to worry about us, okay?"

"Yes, Cassie."

"Good. Pin your hair back a little so the strands don't fall over your eyes so much," she added, and returned to her meat loaf.

I went up to my room. I had no complaint about the dress she had chosen and the matching shoes. Mother would have chosen it as well, but if I had ever thought Cassie was bossy before, she was an ogre now. For a while, I just pouted in front of my vanity mirror. As soon as I heard Daddy come home, I hurried to dress and go down. By the time I descended the stairs, he had gone up to his room. The silence was curious. I was surprised not to find Cassie in the kitchen and went looking for her in the living room. She was standing by the window, gazing out.

"Cassie?"

She didn't answer, but I could tell from the way she was embracing herself that she was very unhappy. When she turned, I thought she wasn't as angry as she was sad. She shook her head, and then, for the first time I could remember in a long time, Cassie's lips trembled and she started to cry. The tears moved uncertainly down her cheeks, as if they were in unknown territory and unsure of themselves. They didn't streak straight down and off her chin as mine did when I cried, but instead went to the sides of her cheeks and toward her nose. With her right thumb and index finger, she snapped them off, sending them flying. It didn't occur to me until this moment that Cassie had not shed any tears at our mother's funeral, not even at the gravesite. She had looked as devastated as I had, but as she often told me, "A Heavenstone doesn't cry in public. We're like the Kennedys." Cassie, however, rarely cried in private, either. This sent shivers of fear up and down my spine.

"What's wrong, Cassie?"

She took a deep breath, bringing her shoulders up. "Daddy."

"What about him?" I asked, now clutching my hands and pressing them between my breasts.

"He said . . ." She had to gasp for the air to speak. "He said he had a terrible day after all, and he was too exhausted to eat dinner. He apologized and went up to his room. He looked awful, just awful."

"But I thought you told me and Mrs. Underwood that you had called him twice and he sounded good."

"I said that just for her benefit, so she would know what sort of people Heavenstones are."

"Well . . . what should we do?"

"There's nothing we can do at the moment, Semantha," she replied, her voice losing any softness and returning to her Cassie voice. "Not in light of what Mother has done." She looked toward the door and upward. "He's suffering. I was hoping I could ease that pain quickly, but it will take more time."

"It is too soon to expect our lives to return to normal."

She narrowed her eyes. "Our lives were never quite normal, Semantha. What I hope to do is bring that about as quickly as I can."

"I don't understand. Why weren't our lives normal?"

She shook her head at me as if I were far too young and unsophisticated to comprehend what she was saying. It was a waste of her time to try. Instead, she turned and looked out the window again.

"Cassie?"

She raised her right hand to shut me up and

dismiss me. I stood there anyway and waited. Maybe she thought I had left, but I was positive I clearly heard her say, "He'll forget her as soon as I can fill the empty place in his heart."

It was as if someone had thrown a pail of ice water over me. I actually shivered.

And then I turned and fled the living room.

15

Holes in His Heart

CASSIE AND I never sat down to eat the dinner she had made. She was so disappointed about Daddy that she dumped the meat loaf into the garbage. Then she told me to make myself something else to eat. She said she wasn't hungry and, with her head down, charged up the stairs to her room. It reminded me of when she was very young and went into tantrums, not speaking to anyone for days sometimes. No one could shut herself up as quickly and as completely as Cassie could. Daddy used to say she cut herself off so tightly that it was amazing she could breathe.

I made myself a sandwich and ate alone in the dining room. With both Daddy and Cassie shut up in their rooms, the house was cemetery-quiet. The stillness toyed with my brain. It was as if some normally heavily locked door was thrown open, and my imagination came rushing out, gleeful that it had no restrictions, no limits. Suddenly, I saw Mother sitting at the table. She was much younger, too, and so were Daddy and Cassie. Daddy had just surprised Mother with a gift for their anniversary.

"But our anniversary isn't until Sunday, Teddy. Today's Friday," she said as she turned the small gift-wrapped box, looking at it from every angle as if she wanted first to guess what was in it.

"If I gave it to you on Sunday, it would be less of a surprise," Daddy said. "Here it comes out of the blue, so to speak. You never expected it."

"See how clever your father is?" Mother told us. She looked especially at Cassie, but Cassie didn't speak. She looked upset, in fact, making that small tightness in the corners of her mouth. Funny how I never thought about her reaction, I told myself now. What annoyed her? Did she think Daddy was being too corny or something?

She tried not to look as Mother opened the small box and took out a beautiful gold locket shaped like a heart with a small diamond at the center. She held it up so Cassie and I could see it.

"Oh, how beautiful, Teddy."

"Open it," he said with that wide smile of his that warmed me so when I was little. His eyes would sparkle. It was as if I could actually smell his love. It was that great and comforting.

Mother worked the latch and looked. Even more surprise blossomed in her face.

"Teddy, where did you get these?"

"I have my ways," he said, winking at me. He looked at Cassie, but she didn't change expression.

Mother turned the locket so we could see. "This is a picture of me when I was your age, Semantha, and this is a picture of your father when he was your age, Cassie."

"You didn't know each other then," Cassie said sharply. It was clear she thought the pictures were silly, especially in such a locket.

"Oh, but we did," Daddy said. "Not very well, but we had met, because your mother's father, your grandfather Brody, was a salesman for Carter and Smith and just happened to have brought your mother on a call to our store in Kenton when I was there with my father. We spent a little time together waiting for our fathers. Remember, Arianna?"

"Not as well as you do, Teddy."

"I think I fell in love with you that day," he said.

"How can you fall in love with someone when you're that young?" Cassie asked. She asked it in that hard tone of voice that made you think what you had said was very stupid. When she did it to me, it was cutting and painful, but Daddy always held his smile and never changed his tone with her.

"You can when you meet your soul mate, Cassie," he said, and reached for Mother's hand.

"That's romantic nonsense," Cassie muttered.

"When you meet yours, you'll change your mind," Daddy told her.

Cassie didn't reply. She simply started to eat, her gaze far-off. I knew she had shut the door on any further discussion.

The whole scene, that memory, played itself before me as if I were watching a television rerun. When I heard Cassie's footsteps on the stairway, the memory popped like a bubble, and that door in my brain locked tightly after it and pulled my imagination back inside.

"Are you going to have something to eat, Cassie?" I asked as soon as she stepped into the dining room.

She didn't answer. She continued into the dining room and walked slowly around the table, pausing at Daddy's seat. She looked at it as if he were sitting there. Slowly, she extended her hand and held it in the air as though she were caressing Daddy's head lovingly. Then she turned to me with a strange, deep smile on her face. I had never seen her eyes so bright. They seemed to illuminate her whole face, giving her an excited glow.

"I understand," she told me. "I sat up in my room and thought and thought and thought, and suddenly, I understood."

"Understood what, Cassie?"

"Daddy's pain. Think of it as two holes in his heart, Semantha." She sat in what had always been Mother's seat and leaned toward me. "Mother's death is one hole, and Asa's is another."

"Asa's?"

"The Asa that could have been, Daddy's Asa. One hole is so deep it won't close, but the other will in time."

"Which will close?"

"Mother's death," she said without hesitation. "Men lose their wives, and most, sooner rather than later, remarry and close the hole, but no parent can close the hole created by a lost child. The child has to be brought back to do that."

"Brought back? How can a child be brought back?"

She didn't answer. She continued to look at me, but the way she was looking at me gave me the eerie feeling that she was looking through me and not at me. And she was smiling, smiling at her own thoughts.

"Cassie? How can a lost child be brought back? No one can bring someone back, Cassie."

She snapped out of her thoughts, stopped smiling, and said, "Jesus raised Lazarus, didn't he?"

"But that was Jesus. He performed a miracle."

"There are other ways," she said.

"What other ways?"

"Don't keep asking the same question. We can, and we will."

"But I don't understand."

She was frightening me now. I could feel the terror gripping me at the base of my spine. There was this new, even stranger look in her eyes. She blinked, and it was gone as quickly as it had come.

"It doesn't matter. Just do what I tell you to do. Get along with Mrs. Underwood, and do your house chores. I'll take care of everything else," she said sharply.

I was still confused, but I didn't say so. Her expression changed again, this time returning to a warmer, more sisterly look. She nodded at my sandwich?

"You made that with the chunky chicken. Very good. I'm hungry now. Why don't you make me the same sandwich."

This was another surprise. The only other time she let me make her anything was recently, after I had gotten in trouble in school. She didn't mind me in the kitchen helping clean up or gathering what was needed to set the table, but she rarely liked me participating in the actual preparation of any food, except for slicing salad ingredients. It was always so important for her to receive all of the compliments, and if Mother ever started to show me some recipe, Cassie always reminded me of some other chore I had. She would tell Mother that she would teach me whatever it was later, but she never did.

"Food preparation requires almost as much concentration as a work of art," she would tell me whenever I complained, "and you don't have the ability to concentrate on something like that, Semantha. In fact, you almost have attention-deficit disorder. That's why you're doing only mediocre work in school, even with my help."

She told me that so often and with such conviction that I started to believe it myself. This was another justification for her deciding that I should have a private tutor after all. It had come to that, she said. Deep down, I wanted to disagree adamantly, but the truth was my grades were nothing special. Next to her, I was like a small flashlight beside the sun.

I rose quickly to make her the same sandwich.

"And cut it in perfect quarters," she added before I entered the kitchen.

Little did I realize it that night, but it was only the beginning. Every day for weeks afterward, Cassie insisted that I learn all of the recipes she knew, recipes she had learned from Mother, and I prepared them for our dinners. At first, I worked with her at my side until she was satisfied, and then she began to have me do all of the preparations myself. I thought she had finally come to see me as old and smart enough, but she had another reason for giving me the responsibility.

"I have to spend more time with Daddy," she explained. "You will simply have to take on more and more of our housework as well."

Spending time with Daddy didn't only mean going with him to work in the morning or following him in her own car. It meant sitting at the dining-room table and talking to him while I prepared our dinner. Mostly, I heard her voice and her laughter. Daddy was still not fifty percent of his former self, and even with Cassie talking excitedly about something, he would stare blankly and drift away. It was easy to see how much that bothered Cassie. Her commands were sharper and full of frustration.

"Clean up. Wash the kitchen windows tonight. Clean out the refrigerator. Polish the stairway banister tomorrow." On and on and on.

With these new responsibilities, my home-schooling, and my usual house chores, I had little time for myself, not that there was much for me to do for myself, anyway. The few friends I had made at school quickly forgot me once I stopped attending. I heard only once from Kent, but that was early on, merely to confirm that it was true that I had withdrawn from public school. None of the girls called me. Despite the fears I had about returning and facing the other students after Mother's death, I couldn't help but feel a constant emptiness. Aside from Mrs.

Underwood, who avoided any conversation other than what was necessary for schoolwork, Cassie, and Daddy, I spoke to no one for weeks and weeks.

And Daddy was still quite different, much quieter, rarely smiling or laughing, even with me. He seemed only vaguely interested in my progress with Mrs. Underwood, too. If he said anything about it, it was to tell me Cassie had told him I was doing well. In my mind, I wasn't really doing much better than I had done attending school, but Mrs. Underwood appeared satisfied. Her compliments, if any, were never exuberant. The best words I heard from her lips were "Good, continue."

So, despite all I had to do, I still felt a terrible sense of loneliness and boredom. Cassie kept telling me how time softens the pain of loss, but I missed Mother even more. I thought it was just as true for Daddy, but Cassie insisted otherwise. When I told her what I thought, she became impatient and annoyed.

"I told you about the two holes, Semantha. It's the deeper one, the deeper one!"

I didn't argue, but I still didn't understand or believe what she was saying. In the weeks that followed, Cassie became so different. She no longer wore any of her own clothes but only Mother's. She would put on some of Mother's jewelry as well, and Cassie was never one for wearing lots of jewelry. In fact, I recalled how much she had complained about Mother's jewelry. No matter what Mother wore, it was always too much, too gaudy. Now she was doing exactly the same thing, never leaving the house without wearing a necklace, earrings, four or five rings, bracelets, and watches, even a jeweled pin. And this was the sister who had often said, "What Mother's wearing today could feed a third world country for a week."

One other thing that truly surprised me even more was Cassie's sudden use of makeup, all Mother's makeup too. Once someone who hated even to put on lipstick, Cassie would now spend hours on her hair and face while she sat at Mother's vanity table and looked into what had been Mother's mirror.

When I asked her about it, she snapped at me. "Don't you see how I'm trying to brighten things up here for Daddy? Can you even begin to imagine what it must be like for him every day to finish his work and start out for this house, knowing how empty it is for him? The holes, Semantha, the holes!"

She didn't have to shout about it. Of course, I could imagine how hard it was for Daddy; it was still hard for me, and I wasn't completely oblivious to the other change in him as well. I noted how he drank more, especially after dinner. I was very worried about him, and when Uncle Perry paid a visit, I brought it up the first chance I had. Actually, I was the one responsible for his visiting. I realized I hadn't seen him for a long time, and I called him to invite him to lunch on a Saturday. When I told Cassie, she had another fit.

"Why did you do that without checking with me?"

"It's only lunch, Cassie. What's the big deal?"

"The big deal is Daddy and I are going to Lexington on Saturday, and I'm not going to change our plans to accommodate Uncle Perry."

"Well, I suppose I could cancel and tell him to come some other time if we're going to Lexington."

"I didn't say *we're* going, Semantha. I said Daddy and I are going. It's a business trip, not an outing. We won't have time to entertain you."

"I don't have to be entertained. I haven't gone anywhere in weeks, Cassie."

"I'll take you out for dinner one night this week. I think Daddy's having a dinner meeting with some retailers. Thank goodness for the business. It takes his mind off the holes in his heart for a while, at least."

"Maybe Daddy will be upset that he won't be here for Uncle Perry," I said.

"Hardly," Cassie said. "Don't give it a second thought."

She smiled and walked off with that Cassie confidence that she wore like a dress. I had to conclude that she was probably right, because when Uncle Perry arrived, he was surprised that neither Daddy nor Cassie was home.

"I left a message for Teddy that I'd see him this weekend. He never called back to tell me about any trip to Lexington, or I would have stayed home and joined him." He thought a moment and then added, "But I imagine he had a lot on his mind."

I had prepared us a nice lunch, and because it was late spring, I had set the table on the patio. Uncle Perry was genuinely delighted and insisted on helping me bring everything out.

"This is a terrific shrimp salad, Sam," he remarked as soon as he tasted it. "I had no idea you were so clever in the kitchen."

"I hadn't been until recently, but we're doing everything we can to help Daddy cope."

"That's good."

I told him about Daddy's drinking and how it worried me.

"I'm concerned, too, but I'm sure he'll be all right in time."

I almost expected him to add, *We're Heavenstones, after all,* but he stopped short of that.

"So, how did you learn to be a gourmet cook overnight?" he asked.

"Cassie's been tutoring me. There isn't much I can't make that she can anymore."

"Oh?"

"Actually, I do most of the cooking now, Uncle Perry."

"Really?"

He nodded and looked away for a moment to sip his iced tea.

"I notice Cassie has made a number of changes," he said, not looking at me, and then he turned quickly to see my reaction. "She's wearing different clothing, jewelry, makeup. Has she found a boyfriend?"

"I don't think so. She doesn't go anywhere at night."

"Hmmm." He sipped some more tea and ate. "Do you like this home-schooling thing, Sam?"

"It's okay for now, but I do miss being with other kids my age."

"Yes, I would think you would. To be frank, Sam, I don't understand why my brother agreed to such an arrangement. Did you want this?"

"I did for a while. It was going to be difficult at school for us."

"I'm even more surprised that your scholar sister took this hiatus, but then again, there's little Cassie does that doesn't surprise me. I guess she's good for my brother right now. I have to admit, she's everywhere in the offices and the stores. I never thought she would take to it. She was never very excited about the stores, the merchandise, customers. But everyone responds differently to personal tragedy. This might just be her reaction. Perhaps it won't last, and she'll return to being the Cassie we know, huh?"

"I don't think so," I said, and he raised his eyebrows.

"Oh?"

"That would be like admitting she had been doing something wrong, and Cassie never does anything wrong."

Uncle Perry roared with laughter. "I always wondered how you two came from the same parents. I still do," he said.

After lunch, we took a walk around the property, and he told me he thought he hoped I was not going to continue the home-schooling much longer.

"You do need to be with young people, Sam. I know you do a lot here, but you need a normal life as soon as possible. Your father should hire some household help, too. I'll bug him about it."

"Please don't, Uncle Perry."

"Why not?"

"Cassie would think I put you up to it."

He stopped and stared at me. "You shouldn't be so intimidated by her, Semantha. I think she bullies you too much. From what I've seen, at least."

"She only means well, Uncle Perry. She's very worried about Daddy."

"Um. So am I. So am I," he said.

At his car, he hugged me and took my hand in his.

"You're weathering a terrible time quite well, Sam. I can see how much you've grown, how it's rushed you out of your adolescence. I'm sorry about that, but I'm proud of you, proud of what a support you are for your father, too."

"Thank you, Uncle Perry."

"I'll call you soon," he promised. "Thank you for a wonderful lunch."

I watched him drive away. As his car disappeared around the turn at the base of the driveway, an overwhelming sadness rushed over me, and I just started sobbing. I cried so hard my chest ached. Never had our house and our property looked so empty, so depressing, even in the sunlight. It was as if Mother's death had hollowed out the heart of what it had been. There's a third hole, Cassie, I thought, and it's in my heart and goes right into my very soul.

After I cleaned up the kitchen, I went up to my room to read and, perhaps because of my emotional stress, fell asleep. The next thing I knew, Cassie was shaking me to wake me up.

"What's wrong with you? Why are you sleeping now? Don't you realize what time it is? You should be thinking about dinner."

I sat up, still groggy. She stood back with her arms across her breasts. Her blouse was unbuttoned down to her cleavage, and for the first time, I saw she was wearing Mother's special locket, the one with her and Daddy's pictures in it, pictures from when they were both very young.

"I was reading and just fell asleep."

"How was your lunch with Uncle Perry?"

"Very nice. He wants to take me to dinner one night."

"I wouldn't hold my breath. Your father and I had a big lunch, so just do the light chicken salad," she said. "We had a very busy day. I made some suggestions for changes at the Lexington store, changes your uncle Perry won't like, but they'll save money."

"Why won't he like them?"

"We're cutting back on the teenage clothing displays, and I'm reducing the store space."

"Why? I thought Daddy said Uncle Perry's creations were successful."

"He said it to make him feel good. They're not that successful. It doesn't fit the business model to keep it as it is," she said. "Don't worry about it, Semantha. It's just another little thing annoying Daddy, and he's still in a very dark, unhappy state of mind."

"But—"

"Just worry about dinner," she said, and left before I could ask anything else.

At dinner, when I mentioned to Daddy that Uncle Perry had come for lunch, he seemed totally surprised.

"He said he left you a message, Daddy."

"He did? I didn't get any such message. Do you remember such a message, Cassie?"

"No," she said quickly.

"Well, that's odd."

"Maybe he thought he had left a message but actually forgot," she said. "I showed you how he's running his accounts."

Daddy shook his head. "Well, I'm sorry I missed him. We could have put off the trip to another day. I spend so little time with him these days."

"Semantha entertained him well, I'm sure," Cassie said.

Daddy nodded. In fact, it brought a little more light into his eyes. "I'm glad, Semantha. We need to hold on to what little family we have." He went back to eating silently. Cassie threw me a knowing look.

Later, in the kitchen, she hurried over to me.

"You see," she whispered. "You see how much deeper the Asa hole is? It weighs on his mind."

"What does?"

"Not having as much family, not having a son," she said, and left me with the cleanup to join Daddy in the living room. It was the way we finished every night lately: I was in the kitchen; they were relaxing in the living room.

It was just the way it had been for Daddy and Mother, and Cassie's excuse for it was always, "I'm trying to help him close the hole."

After I was finally finished with the dining room and the kitchen, I went into the living room to join them. Cassie was sitting on the settee across from Daddy, who was in his favorite chair, the oversized-cushion one in which I would sit sometimes when I was very little and pretend I was on a magic chair that could take me to one wonderland after another.

Cassie was staring at him and didn't hear me enter the living room. Daddy was apparently asleep. When she realized I was there, she turned in two jerky moves and looked at me. I was surprised, because she looked as if she was about to cry and that was one look that rarely dared plant itself on Cassie Ann Heavenstone's face.

"No matter what I say . . . I was in the middle of telling him some wonderful new ideas for the stores. He just . . . closed his eyes and drifted off."

"Maybe he drank too much, Cassie."

"*No!* No," she said more calmly. "It's not the drinking. It's the pain in his heart."

I looked at him again. Our voices didn't stir him, and while he sat there with his face so gray, his eyes closed, his upper body looking limp and weak, I had a terrible foreboding and fear. What if he couldn't stand all this sorrow and did what Mother had done?

Cassie saw the terror in my face. "Go up to your room, Semantha. Do some homework or watch some television or something. If he takes one look at you, he'll fall into an even deeper funk. Go on. I'll stay with him. You did a very nice job with dinner," she added.

"Thank you," I said.

She smiled and then held out her arms. "Come here."

Come here? How odd, I thought. She kept her arms out until I walked over to her. Then she embraced me and kissed me on my cheek.

"Good night, little one," she said. Those had often been Mother's good-night words. For a long moment, I couldn't move. She was wearing Mother's clothes and Mother's perfume and makeup and jewelry. She was wearing Mother's smile.

It took my breath away.

I hurried out and up the stairs. When I walked down the hallway, I paused at Cassie's room. I was drawn to Mother's vanity table. Maybe it was Cassie's way of remaining close to her even though she was gone, I thought. I wanted some of that, so I went in and sat at the table. I looked at myself in the mirror. My eyes began to tear, and then I looked down and saw that wonderful locket. I took it in my hands and just ran my fingertips over it softly, lovingly, smiling to myself at the memory of that dinner when Daddy had given it to her. How happy, bright, and young she had been.

I flipped it open to relive that moment.

And my heart did a flip-flop.

Where Daddy had placed the picture of Mother as a young girl, Cassie had placed a picture of herself.

16

Porter

I STARED AT the open locket with such amazement that I didn't realize how much time had gone by. Cassie had come up to change into something more comfortable. She intended to return to the living room and wait for Daddy to wake up. I had no idea how long she had been standing in her bedroom doorway watching me, but suddenly, as if a cold shadow had slipped over me, I realized she was there and turned abruptly.

"What are you doing in my room?" she asked softly, calmly.

Immediately, I closed my fist over the locket.

"I just felt like sitting at Mother's vanity table."

"That's no longer Mother's vanity table, Semantha. It's mine. If we don't think in those terms, we'll be crying and beating our chests all over this house. What's in your hand?"

"Mother's locket. Why did you replace her picture with yours?"

"Precisely for the same reason, Semantha, that I don't call that vanity table Mother's. It's no longer Mother's locket. Mother is gone. It's my locket, so I put my picture in it."

"Does Daddy know?"

"Of course. I showed it to him."

"What did he say?"

"He said how remarkable it was that he could look at my picture and think he was looking at our mother. It pleased him, and it's not easy finding things to please your father these days." She walked in and took the locket out of my hands. "I would appreciate it if from now on, you didn't rifle through my things."

"I didn't rifle through anything, Cassie. It was right here on the table. And why is it your locket, anyway? Why isn't it just as much mine?"

"Mother gave it to me the morning of the day she died. She told me she wanted me to have it."

"You never said anything about that."

"Don't be a child, Semantha. Why isn't this yours? Why isn't that? You don't fit into the clothes, and you don't have the same complexion and hair color, so it makes more sense that I have the makeup and other things, doesn't it? Well?"

"I suppose. I remember the morning Daddy gave her that locket for their anniversary. I was just thinking about it today, in fact. I didn't think you liked it."

"Why wouldn't I like something Daddy bought? He has impeccable taste when it comes to those things. He has a sense of style, classic style. Too bad his younger brother didn't inherit that love and appreciation for what's classic instead of flitting about from fad to fad."

She opened a small drawer, dropped the locket in, and closed the drawer quickly. I got up, but as I started out, she put her hand on my arm to stop me.

"I thought you should know. I've met someone at work," she said.

"What someone?"

"A nice young man, bright, ambitious. He's working his way up to be manager of one of our stores. His name is Porter Andrew Hall. The Halls are an old family here, too, but not as old or as important as ours. I'm going on a date with him this Friday, so you'll be totally in charge of taking care of Daddy."

"A date?"

"A date," she said. "Yes, a date."

Not only had Cassie never gone on a date, but she had never spoken of any romantic interest in any boy in school or elsewhere. I knew there were nasty whispers and rumors about her because of that, so this was more than just a surprise. It was a happy surprise.

"That's nice, Cassie."

"I'll let you know if it's nice or not. Anyway, I'll give you the menu to prepare for Friday."

"Maybe Daddy would want to go out to dinner," I suggested.

The idea seemed to shock her. Her eyes widened. "Don't you dare pressure him to do that, Semantha Heavenstone. He'll be coming home from a hard week. We had to make so many adjustments in how we do business, and he's carrying terrible sorrow day in and day out. The last thing he needs is to come home and go right out again, especially to face people, restaurant owners, managers, waiters and waitresses who were accustomed to seeing him with

Mother. They'll kill him with their pitiful, sad looks of compassion, which is just what he does not need right now."

"I won't pressure him. I just thought—"

"Don't think. I'm doing all the thinking for you. Now, I'm going to get out of these clothes, put on my robe, and see how he is."

She nodded at her doorway as if to give me permission to leave, and I started out. Her robe, I thought. It's Mother's robe. Those are Mother's slippers. And I didn't care what she claimed, that was Mother's locket and always would be to me. I couldn't do what she was doing, erase Mother from all of these things just so I wouldn't feel sad.

She closed the door behind me as soon as I stepped into the hallway. I heard her lock click. How odd, I thought. I couldn't recall a time when she had locked her bedroom door. It was as puzzling as so many other things she was now doing, but I just shrugged and went back to my bedroom to finish the homework Mrs. Underwood had given me.

Much later, I heard her come up the stairway with Daddy. He sounded groggy, and when I looked out, I saw she was helping him along to his bedroom. He looked wobbly. He is drinking too much, I thought. I made a mental note to call Uncle Perry to tell him. I waited for quite a while in my doorway after Cassie had brought Daddy to his bedroom and then returned to my homework. Finally, I heard her come out, and I rushed back to the doorway.

"How is he?"

"Suffering," she said, and went into her

bedroom, locking her door again. The click echoed down the hallway.

How different everything in my life seemed now. I knew it was my overworked imagination, but after Mother's death, the house changed. Shadows were deeper, darker. The faces on the ancestral portraits were gloomy, foreboding. Suddenly, they all looked like Daddy, depressed, with a sadness that flowed inside them with their blood.

Every sound in the house was different now, too. Footsteps echoed longer, spidery creaks formed webs of sound that vibrated in the ceilings and through the walls, sometimes resembling groans and moans. All of the lights were dimmer, and the windows filtered and weakened the sunlight that had once brightened our rooms and our lives. For the first time, I thought I could smell the age in the walls. It was as if our ancestral home was decomposing like the skeletons of our relatives.

The once beautiful and comfortable, classically styled living room had become a funeral parlor in which my father sat to suffer through his reminiscences. The sound of my mother's voice was still fresh in his ears, the whiff of her perfumed hair still lingered in his nostrils, the feel of her soft skin remained on his fingertips, and the taste of her lips coated his. Surely, she stood before him, a shimmering ghost so close and yet a world away.

I feared he toyed with ending his own life like some modern-day Romeo challenged by the realization that all that had once been wonderful and beautiful was gone. The death of his soul mate was like a sword through his heart. Why go on? Every pleasure would be half a pleasure, every joy half a joy, even the joy he took in Cassie and me.

Perhaps Cassie felt this even more strongly than I did, and that was why she was so adamant about protecting him, pleasing him, helping him. She would never admit it as quickly or as easily as I would, but she might be as afraid for him as I was. I have to be a little more understanding, I thought, a little more forgiving, even when she seems to be so mean to me.

Because of these thoughts, I had trouble sleeping. A string of disturbing visuals streamed under my closed eyelids: Cassie's angry face at the sight of the locket in my hand; Daddy's darkened sad eyes; him asleep in the chair, his face ashen; Mother's glassy eyes focused on the ceiling, that empty pill bottle on its side; Uncle Perry's worried look. Every vision was like a needle stuck in my heart. By the time I actually fell asleep, it was nearly morning and time to get up. I wouldn't have woken if Cassie hadn't slammed her bedroom door. That sound was followed by her clicking footsteps on the tiled hallway floor. I hurried to get up, dressed, and down to breakfast.

I was surprised to see Cassie sitting by herself at the table. Dressed for work, she was sipping coffee and looked very deep in thought, so deep, in fact, that she didn't realize I was there. I saw her reach out toward Daddy's chair and place her hand on the table as if his was there as well.

"Where's Daddy?" I asked.

She pulled her hand back and spun on me. "Why are you sneaking up on me like that?"

"I'm not, Cassie. I was—"

"Never mind. He's having breakfast with the CEO of our public-relations firm. Neither of us is happy with their presentations lately."

"How come you didn't go along, too?"

She pinched the bridge of her nose and looked up at me. "I guess you don't have the ability to realize just how quickly I've become important to your father. I have to cover at the office."

I felt the back of my neck stiffen. I was tired of hearing *your father.*

"Why do you say 'your father'? He's your father, too, Cassie."

She put her coffee cup down and rose, ignoring what I had said. "Make sure you have a good day with Mrs. Underwood. I've seen some of the results, and frankly, I could do just as well tutoring you. If there's no improvement, significant improvement, I can't see keeping her."

"But I thought I needed a licensed tutor."

"Whatever. We'll deal with that when the time comes. Right now, we have far more serious concerns than your high-school achievements."

She started out and then paused, turning back.

"Look. You're no brain, Semantha. I could almost predict every moment of your future. You'll get a high-school diploma and maybe attend some community college or something, but you'll surely end up marrying and having a small herd of kids. Just keep up your good looks."

She walked out, leaving me standing there, unsure whether I should be angrier at her or at myself for not being bright enough to shove those words down her throat. Whether she intended for it to happen or not, my anger turned into more determination to improve with Mrs. Underwood. By the end of the week, my tutor gave me a real compliment.

"I see you do have more ability than you've demonstrated so far, Semantha. Keep your focus. I'm not only proud of you but flattered that I'm having so good an effect. Your sister will be happy to see these results."

Cassie made it a point to come home earlier on Fridays so she could have a quick review meeting with Mrs. Underwood. This Friday was no different. She always conducted the meeting in Daddy's office with the door closed while I started on dinner. When I heard the office door open, I went to the kitchen entrance and peered into the hallway, anticipating both of them emerging with smiles on their faces. The dark, angry look on Mrs. Underwood's face surprised me.

"Mrs. Underwood?"

She continued walking with her shoulders stiff and never turned around before she left the house. I looked back at the office. Cassie was still in there. I wiped my hands on a dish towel and hurried to see why Mrs. Underwood had left in such a huff. Cassie was still sitting behind Daddy's desk. She had just closed the family checkbook, so I knew Mrs. Underwood had been paid.

"Cassie?"

She looked up. "What is it, Semantha? Something about dinner?"

"No. Mrs. Underwood looked upset. She wouldn't

even speak to me. She barely looked at me before she left."

"Really? How unfortunate," she said dryly. "Well, I'm not paying her to make her happy here. I'm paying her to get you up to speed so you won't look foolish when you're sent to a good private school. There's nothing more embarrassing than to be told you will have to be in some remedial class. At a private school, especially, you would be treated like something inferior, and you'd be even more unhappy than you are at the public school."

"Didn't she show you my work?"

"Of course she did. Why do you think I'm home this early? Why do you think I leave your father every Friday this early when there is so much to do at the office?"

I waited to see if she was going to add something nice, but she went back to sorting through some papers.

"Cassie, Mrs. Underwood told me I was doing a lot better."

"Yes, she told me the same thing. I looked at what she calls 'a lot better.' It's on the upper end of the average scale, but far from what I would call 'a lot better.' I let her know it, too. In fact, I told her that if there wasn't a real improvement soon, I'd have to let her go. Maybe that's why she didn't look so happy leaving. But we're not going to throw away Heavenstone money. I want value for what I pay for, real value, not window dressing."

I stood with a mix of emotions swirling inside me. Cassie's words were hurtful, but even more hurtful to me was my disappointment. I had been looking forward to a compliment from her as well as Mrs. Underwood. Cassie's opinion was very important to me, but that disappointment turned into anger, too.

"I'm trying, Cassie. I really am. I thought you would appreciate that."

She looked up at the portrait of our grandfather, just the way Daddy often did, and then looked at me. "I do appreciate that, Semantha. That's why I'm so upset. I don't think she is doing well by you. I'm only looking out for you. I can't believe you don't see that. I can't believe you have so little appreciation for my concern. That hurts me more than anything."

She looked away again, as if she didn't want me to see her eyes tear over.

"And with all we've been going through," she added, almost under her breath.

My indignation wilted. Maybe I was misinterpreting her concern for me. After all, why else would she be so critical of Mrs. Underwood? She was the one who had raved about her and arranged for her to be here.

"I'm sorry, Cassie. I just thought you'd be happy about the progress I've made with Mrs. Underwood and—"

"Well, I'm not, and I don't hesitate to tell people what I really think, Semantha. As you know, I never have." She smiled. "Daddy says that's because I was born under the sign Sagittarius. Same as Mother, by the way, only she was more reticent about speaking her mind, especially in public—whenever she was in public, that is. Anyway, don't concern yourself about all this right now. Do the best you can, and we'll see."

She rose.

"I have to prepare myself for a date with Porter. He's booked Le Jardin Francais, which, as you know, is an elegant restaurant. We were taken there last year."

"I remember. I remember how much Mother liked it."

"Of course, she would. I remember you weren't too happy with anything on the menu."

"I don't like the thought of eating snails," I said, and she laughed. It was the first time in a long time that something I said had amused her so much. "Well, I don't! I keep seeing them crawling over the tiles outside. Ugh."

"You'll get used to those things someday, I hope." She started out. "It's the world we both belong in, Semantha, little Semantha."

She suddenly kissed me on the cheek.

"I'll get your opinion of what I wear and how I look. Try to think beyond Uncle Perry's idea of what's in style and what isn't."

I returned to the kitchen to finish the dinner preparations.

A little more than a half-hour later, she appeared.

"Well?" she said, standing in the hallway.

I put everything down and went out to her. She was wearing one of Mother's more elegant and expensive dresses. I remembered when Mother had bought it and the first time she had worn it. It was an Oscar de la Renta strapless, cherry silk, sponge crepe column dress, ankle-length. When I had seen Mother coming down the stairway, I thought to myself, my mother is as pretty as, if not prettier than, any movie star. I had dreamed of becoming as beautiful, but as it turned out, Cassie was the one who continued to resemble her more and more.

In fact, right now, Cassie looked more beautiful than I had ever seen her. It took my breath away, because her wearing this dress, fixing her hair to be like Mother's, wearing Mother's makeup just the way Mother had worn it, and wearing Mother's beautiful pearl necklace and matching pearl earrings made it seem as if Mother had been resurrected.

Before I could say anything, however, Daddy came in, and the expression on his face said it all. He stood there stunned.

"Cassie," he said. "For a moment . . . my God, you look beautiful, as beautiful as your mother."

The expression *She was exploding with happiness* had never fit anyone as well as it did Cassie at that moment.

"Thank you, Daddy," she replied.

"I'm jealous of Porter," he said, smiling. It was a real Daddy smile from before Mother's passing.

"You don't have to be," Cassie said. "You don't ever have to be jealous of anyone when it comes to me."

"I know, honey." He hugged her and kissed her cheek. Then he looked at me. "Your sister's something, huh, Semantha?"

"Yes, Daddy."

"Semantha has been working on your dinner,

Daddy," Cassie told him. "She's making you a rack of lamb."

"Is she? Well, I actually have something of an appetite tonight," he said. "Seeing you in this dress, Cassie, stirred the old juices. I'll be down in a little while, Semantha." He started away. "Oh. Have a good time, Cassie."

"Thank you, Daddy." She watched him go up and then turned to me. "Remember, now, he's very fragile. Be careful of what you say to him. Mention nothing about Mrs. Underwood or anything that could add to his tension and burden, okay?"

"Yes, Cassie."

"I'm depending on you to take care of him."

"I will, Cassie. I promise."

"Good. Good. I'll stop by your room when I return and give you a report, just the way you gave one to me when you went out with that . . . what's his name."

"Kent?"

"Right."

She hugged me just as the doorbell sounded.

"That's Porter. Come. You can say hello," she said, fixing my hair and straightening my blouse. She took my hand. "I want him to see that both of the Heavenstone sisters are beautiful, Semantha."

Suddenly, she had become my older sister again and not some guardian ogre.

When she opened the door, I thought I was looking at what Daddy surely had looked like when he was younger. Porter Andrew Hall was my father's height and had a similar build, but he also had stunning black opal eyes, what Mother used to call jewels in a face. He had ebony hair as well, and the contrast with his almost caramel complexion was as striking as his eyes. I thought he was one of the handsomest men I had ever seen, and that included movie stars. His strong, firm mouth and straight, perfect nose completed a face that would make the Greek gods jealous. When he smiled, everything came to life in that face, as if there was some little magic lantern inside him. I actually felt a tingle beneath my breasts and knew that I was blushing. He was looking so intently at me.

"So, this is Semantha," he said, before Cassie could introduce us.

"This is Semantha," Cassie replied.

"Your sister has told me all about you, Semantha. I used to think she was so arrogant, that she thought she was above everyone and wasn't interested in anyone else, but she's put you on a pretty high pedestal. She never stops talking about you."

I looked at Cassie. Never would I have imagined her bragging about me. What could she brag about? I wasn't Miss Popularity when I was at the public school, and my grades, as I had constantly been reminded, were average at best. I had no real musical talent and had struggled with the piano lessons when I'd had them and the dance lessons as well. I didn't think I looked especially beautiful. Now, I could cook and bake almost as well as Cassie. I kept the house as clean as she could, but to make me the center of her conversation? It was quite a surprise to hear it.

"Never mind all that now, Porter," she said. "Let's just go."

"I'd love to see the house."

"Some other time. It's not ready for visitors. Be sure you look after Daddy," she told me.

Porter hesitated, still smiling at me. Then he winked and said, "Wish me luck, Sam."

I almost lost my breath. "How did you know to call me Sam?"

"Cassie told me. How else?" he said. He winked again and turned as Cassie closed the door between us.

I stood there as if I expected it would open again and Porter would be there to say one more thing. It didn't, and I soon turned away and returned to the kitchen. A little more than a half-hour later, Daddy came down to dinner.

"It all smells wonderful," he said watching me make the final touches in the kitchen.

"Just go sit at the table, Daddy. I'll take care of everything."

"You don't need any help?"

"No, I'm fine."

I brought out our salads, poured him his water, and opened his bottle of red wine just the way Cassie always did, standing by his side and pouring a little in the glass for him to taste. He smiled at me and nodded. I poured the rest and took my seat.

"So, how's it going with this home-tutoring business?" he asked immediately.

"Fine," I said, and then wondered how Cassie would ever explain our letting Mrs. Underwood go if I told Daddy it was fine. It all made me so nervous.

"I know I've been quite occupied with the business and other things, Semantha, and I haven't paid proper attention to you. However, Cassie has been keeping me up-to-date. Your mother always told me how good Cassie was at details, and after having her with me these days, I can tell you that's absolutely true. I have more confidence in her judgment about things than I do in some of my so-called trusted advisors of many years.

"But I'm proud of both you, Semantha, the way both of you have handled yourselves after this . . . this terrible family tragedy. I know most other girls your age would be emotional wreckage and into therapy for years and years, maybe their whole lives."

"Cassie says that's because we have Heavenstone blood in us."

He smiled. "Maybe she's right. You know most of the stories about our family's past hardships and how well they were weathered." He paused and leaned toward me, smiling. "Don't tell her I said so, but Cassie should have been born to royalty somewhere where royalty still matters. She's a true aristocrat."

He sat back and thought a moment.

"Maybe she's just what the doctor ordered right now. Later, we'll calm her down a bit." He smiled again.

After I brought in the rack of lamb, he poured me some wine.

"You're old enough for it, at least at home, and I don't like drinking wine alone."

I wasn't crazy about the wine. Cassie enjoyed it with him and had even drunk it with him and Mother. I sipped it slowly. Before we were finished, he had emptied the bottle himself. I saw how often he glanced at Mother's empty chair, and I thought to myself that maybe Cassie was right to sit in it and take his attention away from Mother. Without her blocking out that great emptiness, filling that hole in his heart that she had described, he grew despondent again no matter what I said or did at the table. He ate everything but told me he didn't want any dessert.

"Can I help you clean up?" he asked.

That was all Cassie had to hear, I thought, me having Daddy clean up.

"Oh, no, Daddy. It's easy. You should just go relax."

He nodded and withdrew to the living room. I heard him go to the liquor cabinet and pour himself an after-dinner drink. By the time I was finished with everything and had put everything away, he was slumped in his chair again. I spoke to him, but he didn't respond. He had drunk himself into unconsciousness, which was now his way of dealing with those holes in his heart. I didn't leave him, however. I sat and read and watched him moan in his sleep. Eventually, I dozed off myself and then woke when I felt Cassie nudge me.

"What happened?" she demanded, nodding at Daddy, who was slumped even more.

With my small fists, I ground out the sleep in my eyes and sat up quickly.

"Nothing, Cassie. He enjoyed the dinner and then came in here while I was cleaning up. By the time I came in, he was already asleep. I stayed with him to—"

"To do what? Fall asleep. You can go up to your bedroom. I'll take care of him."

I stood. "I didn't fall asleep right away, but he gave me some wine, and maybe it made me tired."

She shook her head. "I knew I shouldn't have left him. It's too soon."

"How was your date, Cassie?"

"I'll tell you about it later," she said quickly. "Go get ready for bed."

I glanced at Daddy and then went up. I was tired and moved in slow motion. Finally, in my pajamas, I pulled back the blanket and crawled into bed. I heard a door close and then Cassie's high heels clicking in the hallway. They grew louder as she drew closer. I could tell she had paused by my bedroom door. Maybe she would wait until tomorrow to tell me about her date with Porter. I was actually hoping she would. It was late. But to my disappointment, she turned into my doorway. For a long moment, she simply stood there looking in at me. I had not yet turned off the night table lamp, so she knew I was still awake. Why was she just standing there?

"Cassie?"

"He's getting worse," she said, coming closer to my bed. "He was sobbing as I walked up the stairway with him. It broke my heart to see him like that. My chest feels as if it's filled up with gravel. I can hardly breathe."

She pressed her hand to her breast and closed her eyes. I sat up quickly.

"Are you all right?"

"No," she said. "And neither are you, as long

as he isn't all right. We're more connected to one another now than ever. What makes one of us happy will make all of us happy, and what makes one of us sad or angry will do the same for all of us. How can you or I laugh in this house again? A smile is as comfortable on our faces as a moth is next to a candle flame. It can come close, but it can never settle on it without being destroyed. It makes it very hard to enjoy ourselves."

"I was hoping you would have a good time tonight, Cassie, and be able to put all of this out of your mind for a while."

"I tried. You liked Porter, didn't you?"

"Oh, yes. He's very handsome."

"And very intelligent, very clever and witty. But mostly, he is very ambitious."

"Isn't that good?"

"Oh, yes, very good," she said with a wry smile on her face. "Very, very good. Ambitious men are more . . . more cooperative."

"Cooperative?"

"More agreeable, easier to get along with, because they're so careful not to offend."

"So, you like him, too, then?" I pursued.

"Yes, I like him."

"Then he'll be asking you out again?"

"Oh, we'll see quite a bit of Porter Andrew Hall. You can count on that," she said. "But I can't go to sleep thinking about him anymore right now, Semantha," she added, changing her expression to a more serious look instantly, "not after these last few moments with Daddy. He was beside himself. I helped him into bed, but he was mumbling and sobbing something awful."

She looked down, her head lowering like the head of someone resigned to a great defeat and disappointment, like the head of someone simply helpless.

"Oh, no," I said, the tears quickly flooding my eyes. "How terrible it must be for him. How terribly he misses Mother."

She raised her head quickly, her eyes brighter. "No, Semantha," she said. "Mother's name was not on his lips as he sank into what will surely be a night of dark dreams."

"What do you mean? Why wasn't her name on his lips? What did he say?'

"He said . . . Asa . . . Asa."

"He did?"

"Yes. He's not selfish. He's not suffering just for himself, for his own personal loss. He's suffering for the entire line of Heavenstones. He needs his Asa, Semantha. The Heavenstone blood in him is boiling with that need."

"What can we do, Cassie?"

"We can give him his Asa."

"What?" I shook my head. "I don't understand. How could there be any Asa Heavenstone now? Mother's gone. Our children will have their fathers' names."

She smiled.

Then she turned and walked toward the doorway.

"Cassie? They'll have Heavenstone blood because of us, but they'll have their fathers' names, won't they?"

She paused in the doorway and turned back to me, that smile still there.

"Not if there is no father," she said.

"But how can there be no father?" I asked.

She didn't answer. Instead, she kept her wry smile and left.

And left me hanging by a thread over a pot of boiling confusion.

17

Overhaul

IN THE MORNING, I expected to see a face of sadness and defeat on Daddy, the same face he'd had after dinner the night before, but instead, he looked bright and energetic. He was going to visit one of the stores, the one in Fayette. I didn't know it until then, but he was going to stay overnight for a meeting the following morning. My second surprise came when Cassie told me that neither she nor I was going with him.

"We have things to do here," she told me.

She didn't tell me what they were until after Daddy had left. She had been keeping a big secret. On her own, she had contracted with the decorator Mother had used to redo some rooms in our house, and together they had planned out a major renovation of Daddy's bedroom. Less than an hour after Daddy left, the trucks began to arrive. Cassie, with the decorator, had planned a top-to-bottom renovation. There would be new flooring, new wallpaper, new curtains, new lighting fixtures, and then, even more shocking to me, an entirely new bedroom set. By now, every article of Mother's clothing that Cassie had not taken had been given to charity, so her closet was completely empty, but Cassie had the decorator redo the walls, floors, and drawers in that closet as well. I stood by and watched the parade of workers, electricians, even plumbers, because she was redoing some bathroom fixtures.

I couldn't believe how much was accomplished before the end of the day. When we sat down to dinner, I said so.

"For the right price, you can get anything done, Semantha. Believe me, I made it worth their while. I wanted it to be completed by the time Daddy enters the house tomorrow."

"But why did you want to do all this, Cassie?"

"Often, when a husband loses his wife or a wife loses her husband, there is a need to get away. The house has too many memories. It takes on the personality of the woman and the man living in it, their taste in everything. It's painful for the bereaved survivor.

"Now, Daddy could and would never leave this house, Semantha. This house is part of who and what we are, so I did the next-best thing for him. For him, it will be like moving into a different world, at least when he is alone in his bedroom. He won't feel Mother's presence so strongly and miss her so intensely."

She smiled as if she had come up with the most wonderful thing. While I understood her reasons, I didn't feel as good as she did about it. I didn't want Daddy to forget Mother so quickly, and I certainly didn't want to forget her at all. Yes, it was painful to wake up every day and realize she was gone and that

I would never hear her voice, or feel her kiss on my cheek and her fingers caressing my hair. I wouldn't have her smile to soothe me when I was unhappy or in pain. If anything, her passing made me feel more alone in this world than ever, even though I still had Daddy and Cassie. But that didn't mean I wanted to find a way to get her out of my mind. I was sure Daddy didn't, either.

I wanted to say this to Cassie, but I could see how much it would hurt her. Once again, she would accuse me of not appreciating her and the good things she did and had done. Once again, she would make me feel ungrateful.

"Do you understand?" she asked when I said nothing.

"Yes, but it makes me feel bad, Cassie. I can't help it."

"That's all right. I feel bad, too, but I'm not thinking of myself. I'm thinking of Daddy. He has to go on, for himself and for us."

I nodded. I certainly didn't want to feel selfish.

"How do you know he'll like what you and the decorator have done, Cassie?"

"Why shouldn't he like it? Everything was suggested by the same decorator Mother used. He knows Mother's taste in things, a taste Daddy appreciated, and as it turns out, I have the same taste in most things." She looked very annoyed at my question. "It's not brain surgery," she added sharply.

"I'm sure you've chosen the right things," I said. "I didn't mean to say you didn't."

She calmed and then smiled at me. "I do apologize

for not taking more interest in you and spending more time with you, Semantha. I know how hard it is for you now, too. How are you feeling? I mean, health-wise? Any problems, female problems, especially?"

"What do you mean?"

"Well, young girls sometimes have little difficul-ties. Take your period, for example. Is it still regular? Because emotional trauma can have a serious effect on all that."

"Yes, I'm still regular. Remember? Mother used to say she could set a clock by me."

"I remember. As I recall, yours comes around the first of the month, doesn't it?"

"Yes, Cassie."

"So you should be having one any day now."

"I guess so," I said.

"Don't guess so, Semantha. Take more interest in your body. I want you to let me know when it starts."

"Why?"

"Just do. Can you do that?"

"Yes, sure."

"Good. Now, let's clean up and watch some tele-vision together. We haven't done that in a long time."

"Okay," I said. She was right. We hadn't done much together for quite a while. Actually, I hadn't seen Cassie in this good a mood for just as long. She and I worked side-by-side in the kitchen, and as we cleaned up, she talked about the Heavenstone future, how she envisioned our stores moving to other states and eventually becoming as big as the most famous national chains.

"Soon we'll start considering a good private school for you," she said. "I want to visit them and interview. We're not placing you in just any private school. As Mother would say if she were here right now, most of these places are just dumping grounds for spoiled children. Their parents are simply searching for a clean place to dump their kids and get them out of their hair. We won't do that with you."

"What about your own education, Cassie? You're really not going to just stop learning, are you?"

"Of course not. I learn something new each and every day. Right now, it all has to do with our business. When I feel Daddy is back on his feet one hundred percent, I'll think about continuing my formal studies."

The way she sounded when she said it made me think it was something very far off in her planning. She saw it in my face, read my thoughts easily as usual.

"Don't worry about me, Semantha. I have everything well planned out. Everything is going to be all right."

She gave me a hug and a kiss, and we went into the den to watch television. After only ten minutes, I recalled why I wasn't especially fond of watching television with Cassie. According to her, nothing we turned to was worth our time. She especially ridiculed the reality shows.

"They just pander to voyeurs. It amazes me how willingly people will make fools of themselves in front of millions of viewers. Self-respect is becoming as rare as perfect diamonds."

That didn't end her critique. She flipped through channels, but every sitcom and even some of the dramas were "stupid." It occurred to me that Cassie never had any favorite actors or actresses or singers. She had never put up a poster in her room or collected anyone's CDs. She knew classical composers and famous classical music, but she didn't include any music in her daily life. I had never seen her buy an entertainment magazine or even browse through one in a dental office waiting room or anyplace like that.

What, I wondered, were her conversations about with other students, the ones she deemed worthy of her attention at school? By her own choice, she didn't participate in any social events. Were all of their discussions only about schoolwork?

On a number of occasions, I tried to get her interested in the music I liked or a movie I had seen and actresses and actors I liked, but she showed no interest and, if anything, ridiculed my choices as being silly, insufficient (whatever that meant), or just poor choices. She often ended the conversation by saying, "You have to be who you are, I guess," and left it at that. Somehow, she always managed to make me feel stupid.

Finally, frustrated with everything that was on television, she shut it off. I thought that would be that. We'd go up to our respective rooms and go to sleep, but she surprised me by talking about Porter Andrew Hall.

"I promised I would tell you about my date," she said, and sat back on the sofa. "I like to watch the faces of other women when I enter a room with a man, not that I have done that much. Anyway, when we entered Le Jardin Francais, I could see the envy on the faces of other women. Porter is quite an elegant-looking man, don't you think?"

"Yes, very handsome."

"More than just handsome," she corrected. "He has an air about him, a demeanor that suggests self-confidence. He doesn't come off as arrogant. He's very much like Daddy. You can actually feel his strength. A man like Porter Andrew Hall is rare today. He has that Old World elegance. Simply put, he could easily slip into the shoes of any prince and be treated with the same adulation his subjects express."

She paused, but I didn't know what to say. I had never heard Cassie speak so well of anyone, certainly not of any man.

"Did you see how understated his style was, his clothing, his hair? I like someone who doesn't feel the need to announce himself through ostentatious cloth-ing or some outlandish new fad. He doesn't have to be the center of attention, simply because he already knows he will be. Understand?"

"I think so."

"Well, when you get to know him better, you will definitely understand," she said. "I've decided to in-vite him to dinner."

"Really?"

"Yes, really, Semantha. I haven't decided the exact night yet. I'm waiting on Daddy's decision about some events and meetings he might or should attend over the next few weeks and then I'll schedule it. But, I'll give you plenty of warning so you can think about your own hair and clothes. It will be a special night, a very special night. Is that okay?"

"Oh, yes, Cassie," I said quickly. Surely, she must know how I craved some company, some social activity of any kind, even if it was just to entertain her prospective new boyfriend. Someday, I thought, she would be doing the same for me.

"Good. Well, let's go up and look at Daddy's new room again," she suggested.

It was still painful to hear her refer to Mother and Daddy's bedroom as Daddy's solely, but I nodded and went up with her. We stood in the doorway to take it all in. Cassie walked in and ran her hand lovingly over the headboard of the new bed. It was quite different from the canopy bed Mother had chosen just a few years ago.

"This is a Victorian Eastern king," Cassie began, speaking as if she was selling it to me. "It's done in a terra brun finish and made of solid hardwood. Isn't it beautiful?"

I nodded but still wondered if Daddy would like it.

"I made sure to have one of those newly engineered mattresses, too, the kind that keeps someone from developing aches and pains. You probably don't recall Daddy asking Mother if she would like him to get one and replace the mattress they had. He was always complaining about it."

"No, I don't remember." I really didn't, and I thought that was odd, especially if Daddy had frequently complained. In fact, I never saw or heard him complain about any aches and pains in the morning.

"Well, take my word for it, he did. He asked her, and she hesitated. You remember how reluctant she was to do anything different, change anything. It was like pulling teeth to get her to allow him to put in that new dining-room table four years ago. You were probably too young to see or remember all that," she concluded, flipping her hand, "but I wasn't. I can recall silly little arguments between them when I was barely four. Anyway, now he has the mattress."

"You replaced all the pictures of Daddy and Mother," I realized aloud. "Their wedding picture is gone, too."

"They're put away for now," she said. "It's still brutally painful for him to look at them, Semantha."

"But he'll be upset."

"Let me worry about it. He'll be upset only because he'll feel guilty for not being upset."

I felt the folds deepen in my forehead as I squinted my skepticism. It annoyed her.

"You'll just have to trust me about this. I know what I'm doing. I think I know him better than anyone now."

I knew him just as well, I thought.

"I don't mean you don't, too. It's just that because I'm older and more acquainted with these problems, I'll make better decisions. As you see," she continued, "I have all of his personal things out and arranged just the way he likes them. Go look in the bathroom."

I glanced in and saw how neatly everything had been arranged and how anything remotely reminiscent of Mother was gone. Suddenly, seeing the room this way, seeing how thoroughly and completely she had removed our mother from our father, I felt sick. I actually had a wave of nausea. For a moment, all of the blood drained from my face, and then a surge of heat rose up the back of my neck.

"What's wrong with you?" Cassie demanded.

"I don't know. I'm just . . . feeling terrible about Mother, I guess."

"Well, maybe you should go to bed, then, Semantha. Get yourself together, stronger. I want you to be at my side when Daddy sees all this. I want him to think you were part of it, too, that you cared just as much about him."

"I do, but . . . I miss Mother."

"As you should, but as I also told you repeatedly, if you show your sorrow and pain so emphatically, you'll make him feel his own sorrow and pain more deeply, and sorrow, as we know from what our triple great-grandfather did, can kill. Do you want to kill him, drive him further and further into his dark places, drive him away from us?"

"No, of course not."

"Then get stronger, and do it quickly," she commanded. She smiled. "Just look at me when you have those moments, especially in his presence. I'll help you, okay?"

I nodded. "Sorry, Cassie."

"Just go to sleep. Tomorrow . . . tomorrow is the beginning of a new day for us. In many, many ways," she added, and then kissed me on the cheek.

She held me, too.

When she let go, I turned and left the room.

She remained in there long after I had gone to bed, first to do battle with my own twisted thoughts and fears and then to welcome sleep as I would have welcomed my mother's comforting embrace and kiss.

"I won't forget you, Mother," I whispered to the darkness. "I promise. I won't."

I couldn't help but be a ball of nervous tension all morning, anticipating Daddy's midday arrival. On the contrary, Cassie was loose and happy, singing to herself as she moved about the house and put the finishing touches on the bedroom. The moment I heard Daddy enter, my heart began to pound. I was in the living room trying to read, but my gaze continually slid off the page and my mind fell back into anxious thoughts.

"Hey," Daddy said, smiling, when I stepped out to greet him. "How are you doing, Semantha?"

I ran to him, and he hugged me and kissed my forehead. Just as I lifted my eyes to meet his, we heard Cassie call from the top of the stairway.

"How were your meetings?"

"They were good. I got them to drop the so-called energy fees."

"Wonderful," Cassie said, coming down the stairs. "I knew you would convince them. If anyone could, you could."

I stepped back so she could hug him.

"I'm tired and hungry," he said. "I had a crummy breakfast because there was so much talk."

"I figured you would be hungry, so I prepared a shrimp salad, and we have those rolls you love."

"Great. I'll just run up, shower, and change. Then you two can fill me in on what you've been doing to amuse yourselves while I was gone."

"Oh, I think you'll know pretty quickly," Cassie said, winking at me.

"Oh?" He looked at me and then at her. "No hints?"

"You don't need any," Cassie said.

He kept his look of suspicion and started for the stairway. Cassie glanced at me, and then, when he started up, she seized my hand and pulled me along to follow him as soon as he turned the corner to his bedroom. I looked at her as we hurried up behind him. The excitement in her face was infectious. Maybe this would be a wonderful present for him.

When we turned the corner to his room, however, we found him standing outside looking in. He looked more stunned than pleased. Cassie paused. He didn't turn toward us and didn't enter his bedroom. Finally, he looked our way.

"What have you done, Cassie?" he asked.

"I had your bedroom completely redone, Daddy. I wanted it to be fresh and new. I planned it all with Casper Flemming, Mother's decorator. He had many of the things she had wanted on record. You know how she was torn between that shag carpet and this cut pile plush. How many times did she wonder if she had made the right choice?"

"But our bed . . ."

"It was the bed she died in, Daddy," Cassie boldly reminded him. "It wasn't a happy place for you anymore. I knew what it was like for you every night to come up here and face the scene of . . . of our tragedy. We knew," she added, turning to me.

Daddy looked at me, and I nodded.

"I'm not saying I don't appreciate it. I'm just . . . overwhelmed. You even had the curtains changed, I see."

"Well, you know how it is with decorators, Daddy. Once you substitute one thing, they talk you into coordinating it with another and another, until you've redone everything."

Daddy nodded and finally entered his bedroom. We followed but remained in the doorway. He stood at the foot of his new bed and looked around.

"Where are my pictures?"

"They're all on the shelf in your closet, Daddy."

"I don't want them hidden away," he said. His tone was sharper, even a bit angry.

"Oh, well, I . . . we just thought . . . but do whatever you think with anything."

He looked into the bathroom. "I can't believe you had all this done in a day, Cassie."

"I was planning it for a while. I coordinated everyone."

"No question you could do that," he said. "Well, let me change and freshen up, and we'll talk about it at lunch."

"Okay," Cassie said, and turned to leave.

I stood there looking at him a little longer. I thought he was visibly shaken, and although he was containing it well, he was disturbed and far from as happy about it as Cassie had anticipated.

"C'mon, Semantha," she ordered.

I followed her down the hall and the stairway.

At the bottom, she turned to me. "You could have been more supportive, said more, agreed more, so he would know it was something we both thought of doing."

"But we . . . I didn't."

"We're the Heavenstone sisters, Semantha. What one does the other does, what one suffers the other suffers, and what makes one happy makes the other happy. We always defend each other and support each other. We're two parts of the same person."

I had never heard her put it that way. It suggested that we were equal, but in Cassie's mind, I was surely not her equal.

"He didn't look pleased."

She gazed up the stairway. "He will be pleased after a while. Mark my words, one night he'll just come out and thank us profusely. But you have to understand, Semantha, his deeper sorrow can't be cured with the things we do to ease his pain over Mother's death. His loss of his Asa remains. For now," she added, and headed for the kitchen. I hesitated, thinking about what she was saying. What did she mean, "for now"? Still confused, I followed her.

Later, at lunch, it was easy to see that despite what Daddy had said upstairs, he wasn't terribly happy about the changed bedroom. He ate silently. Finally, Cassie leaned toward him and, in a soft tone, asked, "Are you upset with what's been done, Daddy?"

"No, it's just too soon," he said. Then he smiled. "I know you two are just trying to help me get through this. It's not that I don't appreciate it. Give me some time."

Cassie extended her hand, and he took it, and then I extended mine, and he took mine. The three of us sat silently around the table holding hands. I was the first to cry. Daddy took a deep breath and looked down. Cassie held her face firmly and looked at me with annoyance. I pulled back my sob and rubbed off my tears, and then we finished our lunch in silence. For me, it was almost a religious experience, but for Cassie, it was obviously a deep disappointment.

Despite the passage of time, Daddy didn't express any greater joy at the changed bedroom. In fact, over the next week and a half, he seemed to do everything he could to avoid going there. He came home later and later and stayed up later and later. There were a number of mornings when he was gone before either of us rose and got down to make breakfast. It was as if he couldn't wait to get out. I was afraid to ask Cassie about it or even make a comment, even though I could see the disappointment deepening in her face. This was, after all, the first thing she had done in a long, long time that hadn't completely pleased him. It wore on her. She was cranky and short with me. When I told her I had gotten my period, as she had asked me to tell her, and I described how it was, she looked very annoyed.

"You asked me to tell you," I said, thinking she would be pleased I had followed one of her orders so well.

"Yes, but not to give me a blow-by-blow

description, Semantha. It's a disgusting event as it is without your elaborating on your flow."

"Sorry," I said, and made up my mind never to share my period with her again.

She was irritable with Mrs. Underwood as well and continually snapped at her, criticizing her techniques and what subject matter she emphasized while working with me. She implied that Mrs. Underwood hadn't kept up with what was important in education today and suggested that she visit a public school. The look on Mrs. Underwood's face by itself could have sunk a battleship. I could see that Mrs. Underwood was losing her patience with Cassie, and I didn't anticipate her staying on much longer as my tutor.

Finally, one morning, after Daddy had left before Cassie again, she surprised me by greeting me with a much brighter and happier face. She looked more energetic and fresh as well.

"I have a surprise for you," she began.

"What?"

"We're having the dinner for Porter Andrew Hall this Saturday night. Daddy is off to a convention in New Orleans and will be gone for four days beginning Friday, so we have our work cut out for us. I want the house gleaming from top to bottom. I'm going to design a special dinner, and I'm taking you to buy you something more glamorous to wear."

"Me?"

"Of course, you. I can't have you looking like poor Cinderella or something while I look dressed to the nines, can I? How many times do I have to repeat that we're the Heavenstone sisters, Semantha? What that means is that when anyone looks at us, they look at us as descendants of the most established historically important families in this state. Imagine if a king had two daughters, and one was a slob or something and the other was elegant and royal."

"I'm not a slob," I said.

"No, but you want to look as bright and as imperial as I do, especially to Porter. I'll take you to Mother's beauty salon as well. I've already made the appointment for both of us, for that and a manicure. You should have your nails done by a professional."

Cassie had gone to a beauty salon only a half-dozen times, if that, in her whole life and only because Mother made her go. From her childhood into her teen years, she had carried her dislike of anyone touching her hair. I was now even more impressed with her feelings about Porter.

"Couldn't we get something Uncle Perry created for our stores?"

"Are you brain dead? Do you think Porter Andrew Hall would even look twice at those teeny-bopper or whatever you call them fashions? I'm talking about spending real money on your first real dress, Semantha. As you know, I have Mother's entire wardrobe at my disposal, because we are the same size, but it's different for you. For you, we need something special."

Special? For me? At times over the next few days, I thought she was more interested in how I looked than in her own appearance. She dragged me from one upscale store to another, from one designer to another, until she was satisfied we had found that special dress, special because it emphasized my "best qualities."

What surprised me here was what Cassie thought were my best qualities. She never complimented me on my figure. Mother used to remark how lucky I was that I had developed so perfectly proportionally. I had a metabolism that wouldn't permit me to grow too heavy in my waist or my legs, and my breasts were firm, perky. Cassie had a nice figure, too, but Mother had never spent as many compliments on her as she had on me. Daddy had been more economical with his praise, but I would never forget one summer day when we were all out at our swimming pool.

I had come out in a new two-piece Mother had bought me the day before. Daddy, Cassie, and Mother were already out at the pool on their chaise longues. Cassie always wore a one-piece, never a two-piece. Everyone was reading when I strolled over, and then Daddy lowered his paper and whistled.

"Well, look who's become a beautiful young woman," he said.

Cassie, who always wore tons of sunscreen even though she kept herself mostly in the shade, looked as if she had an instant sunburn.

"Yes," Mother seconded. "She is."

"I tell you what, Semantha," Daddy said. "You're pretty enough to be dangerous now."

"What does that mean?" Cassie asked sharply.

Daddy smiled at her and nodded at me. "She can give a man a heart attack."

Mother laughed, but Cassie returned to her

book. I did feel like a little princess that day. Cassie never said another word about it, or anything about my figure, but the dress she settled on for me now was far more revealing than I would have ever expected.

The saleslady described it as a "Sweetheart hourglass minidress." It was a strapless style with built-in bra cups, giving me extra uplift. It had a seductive front leg split. It was made in a jet-black animal-print leather mixed with satin panels that shimmered as I moved. It was finished with a sexy lace back. When I tried it on, I saw other customers, women and men, stop to look at me.

"Perfect," Cassie said. "Let's pick out some shoes to match. I have just the right string of pearls for you, too."

Although I would never have dared say it, it was tickling the tip of my tongue. *Aren't you afraid, Cassie, that I will steal away all of Porter's attention?* I almost did say it when I saw the dress she had chosen for herself. It was one of Mother's plainer one-piece dresses in a light gray that did nothing for Cassie's figure and complexion. It made me even more self-conscious, but she didn't seem to care.

Late Saturday afternoon, she came into my bedroom to give me another present, a bottle of one of Mother's expensive perfumes.

"Everything you have smells like candy," she said. "This is perfume for a woman." Then she said a strange thing to me. "Don't look so surprised at everything I do for you, Semantha. When I do it for you, I do it for myself.

"And," she added before she left, "what you do for me you do for yourself."

It was something that should have made me feel happy, reinforced our being sisters, close and loving, but like so many things Cassie said and did, it left me standing with my heart skipping beats.

18

Hangover

WHEN THE DOORBELL rang, I felt as if I were about to step onstage as the curtain was raised. Cassie insisted that I answer the door and start showing Porter the house. She was still very busy in the kitchen. Porter was wearing a beautiful black silk sports jacket with a light wool black V-neck sweater and black slacks. He wore no jewelry aside from his gold watch. In his right hand, he had a bouquet of red roses and in his left a box of candy wrapped in a pink ribbon.

"Hi, Sam, this is for you," he said, handing me the box of candy. "Your sister told me chocolate mints were your favorite."

"Thank you."

I was more surprised at Cassie telling him what I favored than I was at receiving the gift. I couldn't get used to the idea of them spending much time talking about me.

"You look beautiful. That's quite a dress, and I love what you had done to your hair."

The way his eyes moved over my body and the way he smiled made me very self-conscious. I held the box of candy against my breasts, covering my cleavage because his gaze seemed locked on that. When he widened his smile, I felt silly being so modest. What did I expect when I put on this dress? I blushed, and my heart did little flip-flops when I looked at myself in the mirror the first time I put it on. It still amazed me that Cassie, who was so critical of the way girls dressed to go to school, would have chosen this dress for me.

I stepped back so he could enter.

"Something smells really good, and I don't only mean your delicious perfume," he added, which only made me feel more nervous.

"Cassie's been preparing all day. She finally decided on surf and turf. She likes to marinate the filet for hours and hours, and she's made special couscous. No one steams vegetables as well as she does, and there's this dessert . . ."

I saw from the amused look on his face that I was babbling, and stopped.

"Your father told me what a great cook she is. I skipped lunch today so I could make a pig of myself." He looked around. "This is an amazing house."

"Cassie wants me to start you on the tour. She'll be right out," I said.

"Thank you."

I led him into the living room first and began to explain the portraits. I told him the story of Asa Heavenstone but didn't mention how his father had died. After I described our furniture and why Mother loved this style, I showed him her artifacts, her collected pieces from Spain, Hungary, and England. He seemed very impressed and told me I was as good a guide as any he had met.

"After all, this house is historic. I do feel as if I've entered a museum, although," he added quickly, "it does have a warm, lived-in feeling. Your mother made wonderful choices."

"She spent most of her time in this room," I said, gazing at the settee on which she would sit for hours and hours reading. "Let me show you the den."

"This is my kind of room," he said when I took him to the den. He admired all of Daddy's electronics and told me it was all high-end. He loved the leather furniture and thought our collection of movies and CDs was quite extensive.

"My mother only liked to see films here. She loved this room as much as my father does," I told him.

"I can see why."

As I took him toward Daddy's office, Cassie joined us, and he gave her the roses. I showed her my box of candy.

"How thoughtful. Thank you, Porter. Semantha, why don't you put these in a vase for me and put it on our dining-room table? You can get the salad ready to serve and open one of the bottles of wine I have out so it can air."

I nodded, and she led him on to see the rest of the house. They were gone for a good fifteen minutes. The moment I heard them coming down the stairs, I brought out the salad.

"What a beautiful dining room and table," Porter said, standing back to admire it. "Where was the set made, Semantha?" he asked with a tight smile, as if we shared secrets.

"Spain."

"I thought so," he said. "We don't sell furniture this expensive, of course, but I know something about it."

"You'd better. We're slowly going to upgrade our merchandise," Cassie told him.

Cassie had set her place where Daddy normally sat and had me on her right and Porter on her left. When she moved to her seat, Porter rushed to pull her chair out for her and then mine.

"May I?" he asked, reaching for the wine.

"Please do," Cassie said. "Semantha is having wine with us tonight."

"Good," he said, and poured our glasses and his own.

Cassie leaned over to whisper. "I forgot to tell you to bring out the bread. And bring the olive oil, too."

I jumped up and quickly fetched them. She had the bread all sliced, with a touch of garlic, in the bread warmer. Porter was up again to pull out my chair as soon as I had returned. Cassie nodded at me as if to say, *This is what a gentleman is like. Get used to it.*

I had wondered what we would all talk about, but Cassie answered that almost immediately when she continued to talk about the Heavenstone Stores, especially the one Porter was in. She praised him, but I could see that he was far more pleased with how critical she was of the store's manager. Porter was his assistant. When she started to discuss her financial analysis of the store in dry details and he responded, I felt invisible. I drank my glass of wine before Cassie and I went into the kitchen to bring out the surf and turf.

When we returned, I saw that Porter had poured me another glass of wine, and I looked to Cassie to see if she had noticed or cared. She said nothing. Porter raved about the food. Everything was wonderful, but I was surprised that I was beginning to feel the effects of the first glass of wine so soon. It actually slowed down my eating. I didn't want to say anything and look like a little fool who couldn't hold two glasses of red wine. I could just imagine my friends at school laughing at me. Wine was probably like soda to most of the girls. Most important, I didn't want to embarrass Cassie. This was, after all, the first time she had invited a young man to our home. All I had to do was ruin it for her.

Neither Cassie nor Porter seemed to notice how I was feeling, anyway. They talked on and on about the business and Cassie's plans for changing this and that. Their voices began to drone in my ears, their words merging until I couldn't distinguish one from the other. I felt myself waver and put my right palm down on the table to steady myself. It was as if the room was tilting first to the right and then to the left. I envisioned everything sliding off the table. Finally, their words were distorted, slowly pronounced, deeper in tone. I realized Cassie was talking to me, but I couldn't respond. I was only vaguely aware of Porter rising and coming around the table. I thought I shouted as I slipped off my chair and fell into his arms.

The rest of the night seemed to be one long dream. I was floating like an astronaut in space. My body had lost all of its weight. Like a helium balloon, I drifted up over the stairs, bounced off a wall, and floated into my bedroom. I thought I could hear Cassie and Porter talking, but their voices were very far off, and I couldn't understand anything they said. I do remember Cassie's fingers on my clothes and laughed to myself, imagining that I was a banana being peeled.

In my dream, when I turned my head to the right, I saw Porter totally naked. He seemed to take forever to come toward me, but finally he did, and I could feel his hands over my now-naked breasts before he ran his palms down the sides of my hips and gently lifted my legs so he could fit himself comfortably between them. When he entered me, the shock sent me reeling backward into some dark cloud. My whole body seemed to undulate like a wave in the ocean. It went on and on, pushing me deeper into the darkness and then, when I began to emerge, pushing me back.

I could hear their voices again. They sounded different this time. Cassie's was higher-pitched, as if she was angry. Soon after, I felt Porter moving over me again, fitting himself into me and turning me once more into that undulating wave. I thought I moaned and cried out, but I couldn't be sure. My own voice sounded far off, outside my body. It was as if I had completely left my body and was watching some erotic scene played before me on my bed.

I would never be sure, but the same scene was replayed. I had no idea of time, how long it went on.

I no longer had any sense of myself, any control. I felt whipped about, turned, and prodded, then finally deserted and left to linger in this dark space, where I drifted and drifted, until finally, I bumped into something that led me to light and consciousness. I realized I was in my bed, so that part hadn't been a dream. I was naked, too. When I tried to sit up, my head started to pound, so I fell back onto my pillow. The slight illumination seeping around my window curtains told me it was nearly morning. My throat felt so dry that when I swallowed, it was as if I had a mouth full of sandpaper. All I could do was close my eyes again, and again I fell asleep.

This time, when I opened my eyes, it was bright in the room, and Cassie was standing by my bed looking down at me. She was in her robe—Mother's robe, I should say.

"How do you feel?" she asked.

"What happened to me?"

"You passed out at dinner, and we had to bring you up to bed. I undressed you and let you sleep. You shouldn't have gulped the wine so quickly on an empty stomach. I'm sorry. I wasn't paying attention to what you were doing."

"I didn't gulp it."

"Please. You drank four glasses. That's a whole bottle by yourself, Semantha."

"I did?"

"I'll show you the empty bottle if you don't believe me. You should have known your limit."

I started to sit up and groaned with the pain in my temples.

"You're having your first hangover," Cassie said. "That's good. It will teach you a valuable lesson. I hope."

I fell back onto the pillow again.

Then some moments from my dream started to return.

"Was Porter here when you undressed me?" I asked.

"Why would you ask such a thing?"

"I had . . . dreams . . . I saw him."

"Please, spare me your erotic fantasies, Semantha. You're going to be worthless to me all day today. I'll bring something up to you that is said to help people with hangovers, although most of these recipes are tall tales. It's like all the different solutions guaranteed to cure the hiccups."

She started to leave and then turned.

"You nearly ruined one of my more spectacular dinners, but fortunately, I was able to rescue the situation."

"I'm sorry. Was Porter upset?"

"Like any man, he was more amused than upset, although I reprimanded him for encouraging you. Let's not tell Daddy about any of this. He'll be the one who's upset, and he'll be mostly upset at me for letting you drink wine."

"No, he won't. He gave me wine at dinner when you went out with Porter. Just one glass."

"Apparently, you didn't take advantage of him as you did of me. We'll have to get you up and looking at least half-awake by the time he comes home." She thought a moment. "Just tell him you're having a period if he asks. That works all the time with men."

"But I had my period two weeks ago."

"Really, Semantha, I strongly doubt your father noticed or knew." She thought a moment. "Unless you told him. Did you?"

"No."

"Good, because I don't think he would be comfortable hearing about it, or any female problems, as far as that goes. You just talk to me if you have any, okay?"

I nodded.

"I'll bring you the drink, and then you should take a shower and move around to get your blood circulating."

"Thank you, Cassie. I'm sorry."

She shook her head and left. I lay there struggling with my memory. Why didn't I remember drinking so many glasses of wine? Was what I saw and felt in my dream really my own sexual fantasies, as she had said? My legs ached a little, and when I peeled away my blanket to look at myself, I saw what looked like a thin scratch on my right thigh. There was something else that confused me. The bedsheet was different from the one I had put on the bed. I felt pretty sure about this, because the one I had put on had some frills at the edges.

The first thing I asked Cassie when she returned with the hangover drink was, "Did I throw up?"

"Yes," she said. "Don't get me started. I had to wash you down and change your bedsheet. Fortunately, not the blanket. You don't remember any of that?"

"No," I said.

"Just drink this and forget about it for now. Take that shower and get dressed. Go outside and get some fresh air. Put some color back in your cheeks."

"What about Porter?"

"What about him?"

"Is he . . . are you going to see him again?"

"We'll see," she said. "I don't throw myself at men, Semantha. It takes a while to see what someone is really like. That's why I was always trying to get you to go slowly, especially with that Kent. Now that you've seen a man like Porter, you can understand the difference, at least, can't you? Well?"

"Kent's only a high-school boy. He's not as old as Porter Andrew Hall."

"Makes no difference. You either have something of quality in you or you don't. Never mind all of this for now. We'll talk about it again when it's time. Finish the drink."

I did, and she took the empty glass. She stared at me a moment.

"What?"

"I want you to start taking some vitamins, Semantha. Mother never believed in them, because we always ate so well, but there are nutrients you can't get from the food we buy and eat. There's too much processing. I'll get some for you tomorrow."

"You don't take vitamins."

"I'm going to start. We'll start together," she said. She smiled. "Like sisters should, okay?"

"Okay."

"Good."

She left again, and I went to take a shower, dress, and go outside as she had prescribed. Although it made me feel better, I was still very confused and disappointed in how little I could remember. I tried so hard that it hurt my head again, so I stopped and went in to complete the homework Mrs. Underwood had assigned for the weekend. That wasn't easy. It was hard to read with a dull, pounding pain above my eyes, but I managed to get most of it done by the time Daddy came home.

I was nervous when he saw me, but he was so interested in Cassie's dinner for Porter Andrew Hall that he didn't pay all that much attention to me. I suppose I should have been happy about that, but I was also jealous of the interest he took in whatever Cassie did as compared with whatever I did, even if it wasn't something of which I should be proud. Was this the sibling rivalry Mother described, only in me instead of Cassie?

To keep him from asking too many more questions, she began to fire questions at him about his trip, and before long, they were into a detailed discussion about the Heavenstone Stores. I didn't have much of an appetite at dinner, but I was afraid that might attract Daddy's attention, so I forced myself to eat as much as I always did. As soon as I could, I pretended I still had lots of homework to do and excused myself.

"Semantha," Daddy called as I started toward the stairway.

"Yes, Daddy?"

"You didn't tell me your opinion of our Porter Andrew Hall."

I glanced at Cassie. There was no way to tell from her bland expression what she expected me to say.

"He seems very nice," I said, "and very interested in our stores." That pleased Cassie.

"Your sister has been advocating a promotion for him. I guess I'll have to give it some serious thought. How are things going with this Mrs. Underwood?"

This time, Cassie knew I was looking to her for help.

"The jury is still out on that, Daddy," she replied for me.

"Um," he said. "Well, we'll do what's best," he concluded, and went into the den for his after-dinner brandy.

Cassie nodded at me, which was her stamp of approval, before she followed Daddy into the den.

The days that followed seemed to run into each other until one became indistinguishable from the other. Cassie and Daddy were very busy with what Cassie called a full restructuring of our chain of stores. Sometimes, the two of them were so occupied that I was told to eat dinner without them. Aside from Mrs. Underwood, who was never the same since Cassie criticized her, I had nearly complete days without anyone else speaking to me. I watched a lot of television, ate junk food out of boredom, and slept a lot. After three weeks, I noticed I had gained some weight. My face looked bloated, and some of my jeans felt tighter at the waist. Neither Cassie nor Daddy noticed, or if either did, neither said a word. Even Mrs. Underwood didn't mention anything, but at this point, she wasn't looking at me as much as she was looking through me. At least, that was the way I felt.

She became far more mechanical, dictating my work, explaining things almost as if she were speaking into a tape recorder and not to me, and made little comments about the work I completed. I had the sense that she was afraid to give me a compliment now, afraid that Cassie might jump down her throat for praising work that was not really exceptional. On a few occasions, while I was working on a math problem or completing pages in a workbook, she looked as if she was falling asleep.

Finally, one day, she paused and said, "I really don't understand why you're not enrolled in either a public school or a private school, Semantha. You're not an invalid or homebound by any illness. Don't you miss being with other kids your age? Doing school activities, clubs, teams?"

"Yes," I admitted.

"Then why . . ." She held her hands up.

I gave her Cassie's stock explanation, but she shook her head.

"First, you shouldn't be running away from difficulties. You should be facing them and solving them. Hiding in your home like this is no solution. Second, I'm sure that's all a bit of an exaggeration. I don't want to sound like I'm diminishing your family's tragedy, but there are many, many young people your age who have suffered similar things but don't hide out.

"Listen," she said, getting softer in her tone, "I'm giving you advice that takes money out of my pocket, but I have to confess that I'm beginning to feel somewhat guilty about it. I don't like taking advantage of people, especially young people. What do you do here all day after our lessons? Do you have any friends visit? Because I've never heard mention of any."

"No, no one."

She shook her head. "And your father approves of this?"

I shrugged. How was I to explain to someone who wasn't a member of our family how Daddy was so attentive to Cassie's wishes and ideas? How was I to tell her that my sister, only a few years older than I, had stepped so completely into my mother's shoes, at least when it came to parenting? My father was an important and influential businessman in the state. He was on a first-name basis with senators and congressmen, as well as the governor, but when it came down to my education and even Cassie's, he seemed incapable of opposing her.

Mrs. Underwood shook her head. "I think it's time I had a conversation with him," she muttered. "I don't want you to think I don't like you. It's nothing like that, Semantha, but I've been in education all my life, and I have always placed the interests and needs of students ahead of my own. You're doing the work I assign, but you're only going through the motions. You're not inspired by anything. You don't show any special interest in any one subject, as you might if you were in a classroom with a good teacher. But," she said, ending her little speech, "these are things I should be telling your father and not you."

I didn't say she shouldn't. Everything she had

told me made sense and was what I believed in my heart, anyway. Besides, I was beginning to get cabin fever. Except for the grounds workers, I didn't see another person. My longest walk was to go down the driveway to get the mail. Twice I asked Cassie why Porter hadn't returned or why she wasn't going out on another date. The first time, she ignored me completely. The second time, she said she was simply too busy right now. I didn't follow with the next question, but it was on my lips. *How can you be too busy to take a few hours out of a week and enjoy yourself?*

Because Mrs. Underwood didn't say any more on the subject, I assumed she was just talking about doing something but never would or had, but two days later, before Cassie followed Daddy to the office, she came into the kitchen while I was cleaning up after breakfast and told me Mrs. Underwood would no longer be my tutor.

"What?"

"Just what I said. Mrs. Underwood is finished here, Semantha."

"But she gave me assignments for today."

"We paid her off late yesterday afternoon. She had the tenacity, the nerve, to go to your father and tell him everything I had suggested we do for now was dreadfully wrong. Daddy called me in, and I had it out with her right in front of him. He saw what a weak, insecure, stupid woman she was after all.

"I'll tell you what I think," she continued. "I think she jumped at this job, this opportunity, because somewhere in that rotting brain of hers, she fantasized about winning Daddy."

"Winning Daddy? What do you mean?"

"Christmas trees, Semantha. She's a widow. Daddy is a recent widower and a tremendous catch for any woman."

"Mrs. Underwood? But she's . . . isn't she older than him?"

"What does that matter? There are thousands of men out there being seduced by older women, especially when those men are vulnerable after suffering a loss. I saw the way she looked at him when she saw him in the house. I'm sure she thought that if she went to see him and gave him this story, which would result in her losing income, he would be so impressed he'd want to see her again or maybe even beg her to stay on, and then pay more attention to her. I could hear her thoughts, but I smothered them quickly. You can be sure of that," she said.

"What did you do?"

"I agreed with her. She's not the right tutor for you right now. I explained to Daddy right in front of her that you have not grown as a student, that your work is about as mediocre as it ever was, if not worse, and that she wasn't moving you forward at a fast enough pace. If we continued with Mrs. Underwood, you'd be behind when you finally attended a good private school, and you'd have to go to remedial classes."

"What did she say?"

"She sputtered and protested and tried to argue, but I was too much for her. Daddy saw the light. He thanked her and paid her an additional month's salary. While he wrote the check, I stood at his side and stared her down. She couldn't leave quickly enough.

Starting tomorrow," she said, "I'll take over the tutoring until we find someone else who's qualified."

"When will that be?"

"The school year's almost over, Semantha. There's no reason to panic."

I didn't know what to say. With Mrs. Underwood gone, I would see no one else but Daddy and Cassie. At least, Mrs. Underwood had been some company.

"How are you feeling?" Cassie asked, suddenly changing the subject. "Have you been taking the vitamins I brought?"

"Yes. Why were they in a medicine bottle? Didn't you buy them in a store?"

"No. These are special, Semantha. The average person doesn't get these. They can't afford them. What's the point of having all this money if we don't use it to our advantage?" She looked at her watch. "I've got to go. Enjoy your day off."

"Day off? Except for the hours I spent with Mrs. Underwood, there's nothing different about it."

"I promise. We'll do more now. I don't have to be at the office as much. Things are under control, and changes are up and running." She smiled. "A good executive, a really good one, knows whom to assign the work to and whom to depend upon. Take out the pork loin roast for tonight. You know how to prepare it now," she ordered, as if to illustrate her point. Then she smiled and left.

During the weeks that followed, Cassie kept her promise. What I thought at first would be a dreadful situation actually became something wonderful. We were finally behaving like two sisters. She was with me from morning until bedtime. We went shopping together, ate lunches out, and, of course, worked on my school material. Rarely had I seen her so patient with my difficulties in understanding various problems in math or my mistakes on the questions in science and social studies. Cassie enjoyed tutoring me in English the best. She loved grammar and made a game of it by illustrating the lessons when we were out. She would turn to me after a waitress or waiter said something and ask me when they were gone, "Okay, what was the grammatical error?"

Our work in the kitchen preparing dinner was more enjoyable, too. Usually, if I made a mistake, even as small a mistake as cutting the bread unevenly or putting too much of one vegetable on the plate and not enough of another, she was all over me, claiming I wasn't paying attention to what I was doing. Now, though, she seemed truly to enjoy teaching me a new recipe or a new technique for making something we always ate.

Every day, I expected her to tell me she was going out again with Porter, but that wasn't happening. I was afraid to ask, afraid she would get angry and it would all go back to the way it had been between us. She never mentioned him to me, but I did hear her talk about him with Daddy, and when she did, she was always very flattering. It was clear that she was pushing Daddy to promote him and get rid of the man who was the store manager now. If she liked him that much, why didn't she want to go out with him again? Finally, I took the chance of asking.

We were at lunch again at a small Italian

restaurant near our store in Lexington. I had wanted
to ask Uncle Perry to join us, but again, I was afraid
that would upset Cassie, even though we always went
to nice places and never fast-food stops. Our lunches
usually ran an hour or so. I hadn't realized how much
I had been eating during the last two weeks, but at
every lunch we had out together, I finished everything
I ordered, and she barely ate hers. I saw it put a soft
smile on her face.

"What?" I asked.

"Nothing," she said. "Well, maybe it's just that
I enjoy watching you eat. You have a healthy appetite."

"Maybe it's not so healthy. I know I've gained
weight, especially here," I said, pressing my right
palm against my breasts.

"You're maturing," she said. "Boys will like you
better. Don't most young girls squeeze and push until
they finally show cleavage? I see how they flaunt
themselves, trying to be a magnet for the eyes of
boys. They should simply wear signs on their forehead, *Notice me! Notice me!* Remember what I told
you. In their heart of hearts, boys admire the girls
who are self-confident enough not to have to go chas-
ing after them. They look special."

"You've always been that way, Cassie."

"Of course."

"But you haven't done much dating."

"My standards are too high for the boys at our
school. Porter has been the first young man who interested me at all."

That gave me my opening. "Can I ask you why he

doesn't come around, then, or why you haven't seen him since that first date, Cassie? I know you're still fond of him. I hear how well you speak of him with Daddy."

"That's business," she replied, bristling. "One thing has nothing to do with another. Porter happens to be a far better executive than the man running on only one cylinder who is currently the store manager."

I smiled. That was one of Daddy's expressions, one of his ways of describing someone he thought wasn't living up to his expectations or putting out what he should for the business, "running on one cylinder."

"Anyway, I'm not ready for such a relationship," she continued. "I have things to accomplish yet, and I don't want someone else's mood swings and needs to complicate my life. I don't want to make the necessary compromises just to please someone else."

She said all that in her usual sharp tone, so I quickly changed the subject and talked about the new book she had bought me two days ago. Since we hadn't replaced Mrs. Underwood yet, she was still in charge of my reading and designed what she said was the proper foundation to prepare me for my formal schooling when that started again.

"Don't I have to have a certified tutor?"

"Stop worrying about it. You'll be fine. Believe me, you'll do well now with your entrance exams and be better prepared than most of the rich kids who attend whatever school we choose."

"So, when are we going to visit the private schools, Cassie?"

"Soon," she said. "There's no rush. They're not going anywhere."

Neither was I, I thought, but I swallowed it back. Little did I know then, but there was a big reason I need not rush developing inside me.

19

Expecting

THREE DAYS LATER, I woke in the morning with a terrible wave of nausea and had to run to the bathroom to throw up. Cassie heard me and came quickly to see what was wrong.

"I think I have food poisoning," I said, and moaned, holding my stomach.

"I heard there is a stomach virus going around. Make sure you drink a lot of liquids."

"Should I go see Dr. Moffet?"

"Just because you threw up once? It's probably one of those twenty-four-hour things. Take it easy today." She put her hand on my forehead. "You have no fever. It looks like the stomach flu. Are you tired, too?"

"Yes."

"And a little achy?"

"Yes. Especially my lower back," I said, pressing my hand to it and bending over like an old lady.

"Go back to bed. I'll bring up some tea and toast for you."

"You will?"

I could never in a million years even imagine

Cassie serving me in my room. She had used to make fun of Mother for doing it when I was sick, and when she was sick, she had never let Mother bring her food or even give her the medicine. Whether she had fever or not, she would get up and go downstairs.

"Of course, I will. Go on. Back to bed."

I did, and she brought up the tea and toast. My stomach calmed down, and I soon felt better enough to get up and dress. To my surprise, my appetite quickly returned, and I ate a big lunch with Cassie out on the patio facing our pool. Spring was, as Daddy might say, cut off at the knees this year, with summer galloping on its heels. The weathermen were talking about record-breaking summer temperatures coming and the possibility of a drought. Our skies were almost all blue every day, with lazy clouds drifting so slowly they looked more like patches pasted over holes in the heavens.

Mother had always had our pool heated by now, and Daddy, even though he hardly used it, had continued that practice. It did look inviting. It was a large oval-shaped pebble-tech pool with an overhang on the deep end that provided shade in the afternoon. Mother had always avoided the sun. She had said she did that to protect her complexion, but Daddy had always teased her and said it was evidence of snobbery. Rich people, Cassie had explained to me afterward, avoided tans in the old days because day laborers always had tans. Of course, Mother had insisted that wasn't her reason.

Cassie had never been fond of swimming or doing much of anything outdoors. She said she got enough exercise taking care of our big house. She was always moving about, doing something, and did continue to enjoy a nearly perfect figure. In fact, looking at her and then at myself now got me a little depressed. Neither Daddy nor Mother was overweight, but I could see that my face was bloated. My little forays into the food pantry to nibble on crackers and cookies were showing results. I made a New Year's–like resolution to stop.

"I'd like to go swimming today," I told Cassie.

"So, go. You look like you're over what hit you this morning."

"I tried on some bathing suits yesterday."

"And?"

"They all looked too small or felt too tight." ,

"So, we'll get you some new ones."

"I think I should go on a diet, Cassie."

"Oh, please. Don't become like those anorexic, narcissistic bubble-heads and end up being a mannequin. That's all Daddy needs now, something else to worry about. Just eat normally."

"That's the problem, Cassie. Lately, I'm not eating normally. Look at today. I throw up and then suddenly get so hungry I could have had double what I had."

"Symptomatic of a short-lived flu," she said with confidence.

Maybe she's right, I thought, and stopped talking about it, but the following morning, I was nauseated again, and again, I threw up. I had a more painful lower backache and was too tired to go down to breakfast. Again, Cassie brought me some tea and toast.

"I should go to the doctor," I told her. When she didn't say anything, I added, "You said what I had was short-lived."

"We'll see. Flu does that sometimes, comes and goes."

"There's something else," I told her before she started out of my bedroom.

"What?"

"I should have had my period two days ago."

She stood there thinking. "Sometimes, when you are sick with a flu or something, you lose your regularity. Let's wait before we let our imaginations run wild."

"What do you mean? How can mine run wild about my period?"

She squinted. "Let's wait," she said firmly. "And don't say anything to Daddy. He's having something of a crisis at the office."

"What?"

"At one of our stores, one of our idiot salesmen left a rack sticking out too far, and an elderly woman tripped and broke her hip. Her family is suing us."

"He didn't say anything about it last night at dinner."

"Don't you remember? He doesn't like to talk about the business at dinner. Mother hated it, and I don't like it, either," she said.

"But I've heard you—"

"Semantha, please don't be a problem for us right now. Just deal with your problems like a mature young woman, like a Heavenstone. Show some spine, some independence and strength. Dip into your heritage, your blood, and overcome your fears and weaknesses," she lectured.

I tried to do as she said. I kept my headaches, my backaches, and my morning nausea to myself for the remainder of the week. The nausea subsided, but the backaches were always there. When two more weeks went by and I still hadn't gotten my period, I began to panic. Something strange was happening to me, all right. Left alone, I thought again and again about the night Porter had come to dinner and I had drunk too much wine. Those dreams seemed like more than dreams. The images, and feelings were all still too vivid, too strong. Dreams tended to thin out and drift away like smoke, but these memories were actually becoming stronger, clearer.

I was spending more and more time alone now, too. Cassie said she had to visit the office more. There were other problems, and Daddy needed her. She still spent more time with me than she usually had, but I had longer periods during the day when I simply fell asleep or was too tired to do anywhere near what I used to do.

And then I began to notice other changes in my body. I was going to the bathroom more often, and when I took off my clothes and looked at myself in the mirror, I noticed there was a darkening around my nipples, a darkening I had never seen. My breasts were bigger, and I was sure I had a little pouch developing in my abdomen. I felt a hot flash through my neck and face and went to my computer. My fingers trembled as I searched for the information I dreaded to read, but it was there, and it took my breath away.

Late that afternoon, Cassie found me waiting for her in the living room, sitting in Daddy's chair. I had done nothing about dinner, nor had I done any of my usual chores. I didn't open a book, either. I had spent most of my time just sitting and thinking and shivering under the dreadful weight of what I now believed.

The moment she entered and saw me, she paused. "What are you doing? Why are you sitting there like that?"

"Cassie, I think . . . I'm pretty sure I'm pregnant."

To my surprise, she didn't laugh or start to ridicule me. "Oh, really?"

"I've read about it, and I have every symptom."

"And how do you explain being pregnant, Semantha? Are you going to tell me it just happened, an immaculate conception?"

"No. Listen. Here's what I think. That night . . . when Porter was here and you brought me up after I had drunk too much wine . . ."

"What about it, Semantha?"

"Was he out of your sight for a while? Did you leave him and go clean up after dinner?"

"Why?"

"I think . . . he might have raped me."

"Porter Andrew Hall raped you? Please. Besides, how could you not know you were raped?"

"When we were in the kitchen getting the food, he might have slipped one of those date rape drugs into my wine. Our health teacher explained them to us and warned us about them. Some are tasteless and clear and give you amnesia."

She stared at me as if I had gone mad. "Maybe

you are spending too much time alone. Your imagination is running away with itself."

"Well, I have no other explanation for this,
Cassie!"

"Really? Will you swear that while I was away
working with Daddy, all these past months, that Kent
didn't come around and talk you into doing more than
you wanted? He tried it on your first date, didn't he?"

"Absolutely not. No one's been here. None of
those kids called me again or anything. I have to see
a doctor."

She nodded slowly. "Well, it can't be our doctor,
Dr. Moffet. He would tell Daddy, and we don't want
Daddy knowing any of this."

"Why not? I need him to know."

"Are you crazy? You would do that to him now?
Why don't you just sneak into his room late at night
and stab him in the heart, Semantha?"

I started to cry.

"That's perfect. Act like a child just when we
need you to be grown up the most."

"Well, this is hard for me, Cassie. I didn't have
anything to do with Kent or any of them. I swear."

"Well, don't you make any wild accusations
about Porter. All we need now is another lawsuit."

"What will we do?"

"It's not brain surgery, Semantha. I'll get one of
those pregnancy test kits, and we'll see. I'll do it tomorrow."

"What if . . . if it shows I am pregnant?"

"I'll find another doctor, and I'll bring him here
to see you."

"When?"

"Right away," she said. "Stand up."

"Why?"

"I want to look at you. Stand up and take off your robe. Go on."

I did as she asked, and she drew closer, studying my body, my breasts.

"Since Daddy won't be looking at you naked, we'll be fine for now. You don't look big enough for anyone to think anything more than that you gained some weight. If Daddy says anything about that, admit you've been a little pig these past weeks, and promise you'll have more control. Put your robe back on. Go get dressed, and let's think about dinner." She left me standing there, still naked, still terribly afraid.

I did the best I could to hide my nervousness from Daddy at dinner. Cassie helped by distracting him with some suggestions about the landscaping, pool furniture, and some other minor problems on the property that she thought needed attention. She pointed out that he had hardly been home and probably hadn't noticed. She complained about our maintenance people and got Daddy to agree that he could do the things she thought necessary. She thanked him and said I would help. It was only then that he really looked at me and gently suggested I might do with a little exercise. Cassie promised to make sure I did. Her little glances kept me mute.

Late the following morning, she came home with the test kit.

"All right," she said. "Go into the bathroom and get some of your urine in this cup. This is a good test.

The pharmacist told me it's the same one they use in clinics, and it's ninety-nine percent accurate. Go on."

She handed me the cup, and I did as she asked. I stood by waiting as she tested with the strip. The grimace on her face alarmed me.

"What?"

"According to this, you're not pregnant, Semantha."

"I don't understand."

"Me, either."

"I should see Dr. Moffet, then."

"No. I still want us to leave Daddy out of it. We are old enough to handle this ourselves. It's a woman's issue. I'll get another doctor, as I promised."

"When?"

"Tomorrow. I'll bring him here. I've already done some research and have spoken to someone."

"Another doctor will come here? I thought only Dr. Moffet made house calls and only because of us."

"Christmas trees. When will you learn? Everyone has a price. Medicine is just another business," she said. "Now, let's not think any more about this until then."

Early in the afternoon on the following day, while I was working on some math problems she had left for me to do, Cassie returned with a man she introduced as Dr. Samuels. He was a short man, not more than an inch or so taller than I was, with curly dark brown hair and a dark brown mustache that I thought was poorly trimmed. His hazel eyes weren't especially big, but they bulged a little, making it seem as if he was astonished all the time. I was never good at guessing ages, but because he had some graying at his temples and some deep crow's feet and creases in his forehead, I thought he was in his late fifties or early sixties.

"Let's go up to your bedroom, Semantha," Cassie said. "Dr. Samuels will examine you, and we'll see what's to be done."

He didn't smile or say anything comforting as Dr. Moffet would have. His silence made me a little uncomfortable, but I did as Cassie asked.

"Just sit on your bed," he told me, and opened his doctor's satchel to take out a stethoscope. Before he did anything, he asked me questions about my nausea, my backaches, and my period. His face didn't reveal anything. He simply nodded at my answers and descriptions and then finally asked me to undress. I looked at Cassie. She stood right behind him and nodded.

He studied my breasts and touched my stomach. His look of astonishment grew even more emphatic when he listened to my stomach with the stethoscope. He asked me to go into the bathroom to take another quick pregnancy test. After he checked the strip, he spoke quietly with Cassie outside in the hallway while I waited on my bed. When they returned, they both wore very serious looks of concern that frightened me.

"What's wrong with me?"

"Well, for one thing," Dr. Samuels said, "you are not pregnant in the normal sense."

"I don't understand. How can you be pregnant abnormally?"

He looked at Cassie before continuing, and she nodded.

"You are suffering with what we call pseudocyesis. We don't see it that often in young girls as much as in mature women."

"What is that?"

"With pseudocyesis, women have symptoms similar to true pregnancy. They have morning sickness, tender breasts, gain weight, suffer abdominal distension, and many actually claim they experience the sensation of fetal movement, known as quickening, even though there is no fetus present. Some actually go into false labor."

"The most famous case of that is Mary Tudor, the queen of England, who believed she was pregnant more than once when she wasn't. She needed an heir," Cassie said.

I wondered how she could know so much about everything, even this very unusual female condition.

"Yes, that's a good example," Dr. Samuels said.

"But why would I have this?" I asked. "I don't want to be pregnant."

"I'm not a psychiatrist, but subconsciously, you might," Dr. Samuels said, and looked at Cassie again. "Your sister has told me about your mother losing her baby and how that led to a larger tragedy."

"And deeply disappointed our father," Cassie added. "He hasn't been the same since that aborted pregnancy."

I shook my head. "I still don't understand."

"In your subconscious mind, you're having the baby who was lost and giving your father a

wonderful gift," Dr. Samuels said. Cassie nodded
when he looked at her again.

"No," I said. "I never—"

"It's like any mental aberration. You're not in full
control of it, but in time, you'll get better," Dr. Samuels said. He finally smiled. "There's nothing really to
do about this. No medicine to take. Some people go
to a therapist, of course."

"We don't need to do that," Cassie said quickly.
"We'll handle this ourselves."

Dr. Samuels nodded.

"I don't do anything else?" I asked.

He shook his head. "In time, you'll begin to lose
the symptoms. You'll go back to being a normal teenage girl." He patted my hand and closed his bag.

"I'll walk you out," Cassie said. "Just wait here,
Semantha," she told me.

I couldn't move, anyway. I was as solid as a
statue and just as cold.

Cassie returned ten minutes later. She began to
pace in front of me as she often did when she was
doing some serious, deep thinking.

"Okay," she said, pausing and turning to me.
"Here's what we'll do. If this continues and you do
indeed grow larger, you'll wear a girdle."

"A girdle?"

"Yes. It's something women used to wear often.
It will hold you in so that Daddy especially will not
notice anything."

"But maybe we should tell him, Cassie. He'll be
angry."

"I doubt it. He'd only find a way to blame

himself for something else. It's enough that he thinks he can't be a good father without Mother at his side. Your condition will only reinforce that guilt in him and make him even more unhappy, as hard as that is to imagine. When it's all over, we'll tell him, and he'll be proud of you and me, proud that we handled a serious situation ourselves without troubling him."

"Maybe this will stop," I said hopefully. Then I realized something else. "What about school, Cassie?"

"What about it?"

"We've got to arrange for my attending a new school after the summer."

"Not while you're in this condition."

"But . . . if I don't get better, Daddy will wonder why I'm not going. We've got to tell him about this."

"No!" she shouted. She immediately calmed. "I mean, we'll hold off as long as possible, especially while he's under such pressure."

"What will we say?"

"We'll say you decided you wanted to continue home-schooling. I'll tell him we visited some schools and none was very attractive to you or to me, for that matter. Don't worry. I can convince him as long as you tell him the same thing."

"But . . . I want to go to school."

"You will, as soon as this is over."

"How do we get it to be over?"

"I spoke with Dr. Samuels a little more about it when I escorted him out. He suggests a little tough love."

"What's that mean?"

"You already know what that means. I explained it when we had the problems with Mother."

"But how does that apply to me now?"

"It means don't expect me to be sympathetic to your aches and pains and complaints, Semantha. I'm not going to stay home and babysit you, either. However, you are not to leave the house now. Our little trips are ended until this situation changes. I don't want the grounds workers seeing you, either, just in case you forget to wear your girdle or something. Understand?"

"I'll be like a prisoner."

"You're a prisoner of your own condition."

"But I don't feel that way. I don't want to have any baby, for Daddy or anyone. I'm not doing this to myself!" I cried.

"Yes, you are!" she screamed back at me. She looked angrier than I could ever remember. "You're doing this for the Heavenstones."

I was speechless at her rage and also confused. She made it sound as if she were angry and approving simultaneously. I shook my head.

"Just do what I said," she added in a calmer tone. She could turn her moods on and off like a hot and cold faucet. "I've got to go to the office. Watch yourself," she warned. "Remember. Don't embarrass the family."

I remained in my room for almost an hour after she left. Her words had made me tremble, and the trembling didn't want to subside. I was still in shock from what the doctor had said. Every once in a while, I stopped at a mirror and looked at myself. How could my subconscious mind, my own imagination, be doing this to me? For a while, I wandered about aimlessly, disinterested in anything and everything. Then I went to my computer and looked up pseudo-cyesis. It was exactly how Dr. Samuels had described it, and there was even a reference to Mary Tudor, whom Cassie had mentioned.

Even though I read this and understood, I couldn't stop myself from experiencing all of the symptoms of pregnancy during the days and weeks that followed. I tried not to have a bigger appetite, but my resistance was weak, and I ate more than I should have. Every morning, I weighed myself and saw that I was still gaining, and my waist and stomach were expanding. Cassie saw this, too, and one morning, she had left the girdle for me to wear. It was very uncomfortable, so I wore it only when Daddy came home, or at least I tried to restrict it to that. Cassie would appear, see I wasn't wearing it, and go into one of her rages.

"You'll make a mistake and go outside when the workers are around or something is delivered. Unless you stay only in your room, you put it on."

I couldn't disagree. Uncle Perry had appeared at the door unannounced one afternoon, and I had almost neglected to put on the girdle.

"Hey," he said when I went to the door. "How are you, Sam? I was visiting a manufacturer not far from here and thought I'd stop by."

I stood staring out at him stupidly. In the back of my mind, I was worried that Cassie wouldn't approve of my inviting him in right now.

"Hi. I'm fine," I said.

"Can I come in? I've got a little time," he said.

"Of course." I stepped back, but I was very nervous and afraid he would see it.

"It's pretty hot today," he said, gazing around but eyeing me suspiciously. "Got something cold to drink?"

"Oh, sure. I made some lemonade this morning."

"Perfect," he said, and followed me to the kitchen. "I've been asking about you. Sorry I haven't come around, but Teddy is making some major changes, and we've all been quite busy. If I ever needed a vacation, now is the time."

"Are you going anywhere soon?" I asked, pouring him a glass of lemonade and pouring one for myself.

"I'm supposed to go to Greece. A friend has a friend in Athens, and from there we're going to some islands, Mykonos, Crete, and a less known one, Chios. His friend has a yacht."

"That sounds wonderful. I want to travel like you someday, too."

"You will," he said. "I'm sure." He sat at the kitchenette. "So, tell me, what have you been doing with yourself besides the home-schooling?"

"Lots of reading, cooking, taking care of the house."

"Still no having friends visit or doing things with them?"

"No. But," I added quickly, "I'm sure I'll make new friends soon."

"Really? I understand from Teddy that you want to continue home-schooling."

"For a while, yes."

"Why?"

"I'm just more comfortable with it now. I'll be all right."

"It's not healthy for a girl your age to be cloistered like this. Is it because of your mother, what she did?" he asked, his eyes narrowing. "Do you still feel you can't face people?"

"Maybe. I suppose," I said, appreciating the reason. For now, it got me off the hook.

"Perhaps you should see a therapist, Sam. There's nothing wrong with that."

I nodded. "I'll see. Actually, Cassie and I have been talking about it."

It wasn't a total lie. I had been talking about it. She had just not responded with any enthusiasm.

"I hope you don't mind me saying you look like you've gained some weight."

"I know. I'm on a diet," I said.

The look on his face told me he was just as good as Cassie when it came to reading my face. I had to look away.

"You're eating out of boredom, aren't you?" he asked.

I breathed relief. At least, he hadn't thought of any other reason.

"I suppose."

"This is so unhealthy for a young girl as vibrant as you, Sam. Would you mind very much if I nagged my brother about it?"

"Yes," I said a little too emphatically. I calmed quickly. "Please don't, Uncle Perry. I would hate myself if I added any new worries to Daddy's list right now. I'll be fine. Maybe I'll do what you suggest and see a therapist soon. Please don't bother Daddy about it."

He drank his lemonade and stared at me with skepticism.

"Besides, I've been doing a lot with Cassie," I said. "We go shopping and out to lunch and to movies. It's given us a chance to get to know each other better."

He nodded. "Well, I hope more of you will rub off on her than vice versa," he said, and downed his lemonade. "Okay. I just wanted to be sure to stop in to see how you were." He rose. "When I return from Greece, I'll take you to dinner and tell you all about it."

"I'd like that."

"In the meantime, watch for my postcards."

"I will," I said, and followed him to the front door.

He looked intently at me for a moment and then put his hands gently on my shoulders and kissed my cheek.

"Don't ever hesitate to call me if you need anything, Sam. I'm always there for you."

"Thank you, Uncle Perry."

"Think seriously about the therapy, Sam. You've got to get on with your life."

"I will. I promise."

"Good. See you soon," he said, and left.

I couldn't help wondering if he had left with more concern and suspicions. When Cassie came home, I told her he had stopped by.

"You didn't greet him without your girdle on?"

"No, but he remarked about my weight."

"He did, did he? A gentleman wouldn't be so crude."

"He was just worried."

She thought a moment. "You didn't say anything to make him suspicious?"

"No."

She nodded.

"He thinks I'm staying home because of Mother and what happened. He thinks I should see a therapist."

"Oh, he does, does he? Good. Let him think that."

"I asked him not to say anything to Daddy, but he might."

"Don't worry about him. I'll know if he says anything to Daddy. Just keep doing what you're doing," she advised. "And don't forget that girdle."

I did as she said, frightened that she would appear suddenly at any time and catch me without it. It worked until I started what was my seventh month of this imaginary pregnancy. I had begun to experience the "quickening" Dr. Samuels had described, but I was afraid to mention it to Cassie. She made it clear that she still didn't want to hear anything relating to my condition, whether it be pains, frequent urinating, or this.

Finally, I went into her bedroom late in the afternoon one day and told her I couldn't wear the girdle. She had to listen whether she liked it or not. She was sitting at her vanity table, Mother's vanity table, and

brushing her hair slowly. Lately, she had been wearing more makeup and spending more time on her
appearance. She didn't turn from the mirror. She kept
brushing her hair, either ignoring me or locked in
some trance.

"Cassie, didn't you hear what I said? It's too difficult!" I cried.

The one thing she had done was buy me some
dresses a few sizes too large. So far, we had been
successful in keeping it all from Daddy. He was involved in some major new real estate ventures and
expansion of the Heavenstone Stores. He was working on going public and raising millions through
stock. It was all quite involved and over my head. I
had so little patience for anything these days, anyway, even reading and watching television. Finicky,
achy, and deeply unhappy about my imprisonment,
I wandered about like some lunatic in an asylum.
Anyone who had known and seen me seven months
ago would surely wonder what was happening
to me. I wasn't taking care of my hair and didn't
bother to put on lipstick. What was the point? No
one except Cassie and Daddy, when he was around,
would see me.

"Nonsense," she replied, still looking at herself
in the mirror and still brushing her hair. "You'll—"

"No!" I shouted. I couldn't stand it anymore.
"I can't. I won't. And there's more. I am feeling the
quickening. It's more than a feeling. I feel a baby
inside me . . . kicking. You've got to call Dr. Samuels
and have him return, or else . . . or else I'm telling
Daddy everything."

She finally stopped brushing her hair and turned
to me. She stared at me a moment. I thought she was
going to go into one of her rages. I was prepared for
it, but instead, she suddenly smiled, and for some reason, that smile was more frightening than any look of
anger on her face.

"You feel the baby kicking?"

"Yes, and don't go on about how it's my subconscious. I can't stand all this lying and avoiding
Daddy's eyes and everything. I want to tell him. I
can't live like this. I'm like a trapped animal."

She was silent, but I didn't budge. This is one
time Cassie will not intimidate me, I thought. I'm not
leaving this room until I get her to agree, and I will
make it clear to her that even if she doesn't agree, this
is what I will do.

"Yes," she said, surprising me. "It's time to tell
him, time to tell him everything."

Her agreement had an effect on me that was the
opposite of what I had expected. Instead of being satisfied, I was suddenly frightened. Maybe I shouldn't
be forcing this. Maybe I should wait, I thought.

"What about Dr. Samuels?"

"There's no point in that man coming here, Semantha. He can't change anything."

"But he said I should go to a therapist. Can't we
arrange that secretly, too? I'll do it."

"There's no point in that, either."

"Why not? How do you know so much? You're
not a psychiatrist, Cassie."

"I know enough."

"No, you don't. Mother used to say you were full

of self-confidence, but too much self-confidence can be bad. It can make you arrogant, Cassie."

"Really?"

"Yes, really."

"Well," she said, continuing that now annoying smile, "I have just enough self-confidence to know there's no reason for you to see a therapist."

"And why not?" I was practically screaming now. I could feel the heat in my face and the strain in my neck.

"Because you really are pregnant, Semantha. You don't have any mental condition. You're having a baby, and soon, too."

20

A Plan

WHEN A CHARACTER in the novels I read, especially my romance novels, had a shock, the author would write, "it was like a clap of thunder." Well, it was like that when I heard Cassie's words. The air seemed to snap around me and be filled with electricity. It jolted me. I felt my entire body recoil and my heart sink in my chest.

"What? What are you saying, Cassie?"

She turned and looked at herself in the vanity-table mirror. "Daddy needs his Asa," she said, "and very soon now, you're going to give him to Daddy."

She spun around.

"It will be a wonderful day, a wonderful gift, and our world will return, our Heavenstone world. Just think. I'll take care of him, be his mother. You can return to school, and no one will know what happened."

"What are you talking about? Dr. Samuels said I wasn't pregnant. He said—"

"He said what I wanted him to say. He was someone I hired to play the part," she admitted. "He did a very good job, too, with my coaching and preparation, of course."

"He wasn't a real doctor?" She didn't answer. "Why would you do that?"

"Why? If you knew you were really pregnant, you would have wanted to abort. Don't say no."

I stared at her, the words tripping over my paralyzed tongue.

"Oh, don't be upset, Semantha. You're doing a wonderful thing for our family. In time, you'll not only understand. You'll realize just how clever I've been and thank me."

"Thank you?" Realizations were striking at me like meteors zooming down from outer space. "Then I didn't dream about Porter raping me. He did rape me. All that I thought, that you told me were fantasies . . . what I saw happening, the date-rape drug . . . it was true, and you knew it."

She turned back to look in the mirror. "Porter is intelligent and capable and, most of all, ambitious. He's going to be the manager of the store starting next week, and in time, I'm sure he'll become one of our top executives, maybe Daddy's right-hand man, especially since I'll be so occupied now with Asa. He has the right genes to father a Heavenstone. Believe me, I made a thorough study before I engaged him. He's the youngest of four boys, and every one of his married brothers has had only boys."

I had to catch my breath to speak. Every word she said quickened my heart even more. My legs felt wobbly. I leaned back against the wall. She continued to brush her hair as if we were speaking about the most trivial things.

"All that time you pretended to be interested in

my health, my female problems, those special vitamins you said you got for me, all of it was just planning for me to get pregnant?"

"A healthy mother has a healthy child," she said.

"And getting rid of Mrs. Underwood . . . that wasn't because she was doing a poor job. You wanted no one else here, no one to see what would be happening to me."

"She was incompetent."

"No, she wasn't. I was doing better."

"You'll do better. Stop worrying about that."

"I'm not! That's not what I mean, Cassie. All that business with Porter, making me attractive for him. At the right time, you asked him to rape me, and now you're rewarding him? How could you trick me like that?"

"You were too young to understand, and you wouldn't have agreed."

"Why did you do this to me? Why didn't *you* have a baby if a baby is so important?"

She didn't answer. It made me even angrier. I took a step toward her.

"Don't worry. You don't have to explain. I know the answer, Cassie. You're afraid of being pregnant. You're afraid of sex. That's why you've never had a boyfriend. You're right, Cassie. I shouldn't see a therapist. You should be the one seeing a therapist."

She turned again but not with the face of anger and rage I anticipated. She looked quite calm. "I understand your anger, but that will pass, Semantha."

"I'm right, aren't I?" I insisted. "You're afraid

of sex. You're terrified of getting married and having children."

"No. I actually envy you for being able to get pregnant, Semantha. I've been trying to get pregnant for some time, and when I was obviously unable to, I went to see a specialist. I have a condition known as endometriosis. That's a big word for you, I know."

"What?" She was right. It was a big word, big enough to choke on. "What is that?"

"It's simply misplaced tissue that supposed to be in a woman's uterus. In my case, it's growing outside my ovaries."

"I don't understand."

"I'll give you a little lesson in female anatomy. Every month, hormones cause the lining of a woman's uterus to build up with tissue and blood vessels. If a woman does not get pregnant, the uterus sheds this tissue and blood. It comes out of the body through the vagina as her menstrual period.

"Each month, the growth adds extra tissue and blood, but for me and others who have this problem, there is no place for the built-up tissue and blood to exit the body. As the misplaced tissue grows, it can cover or grow into the ovaries and block the fallopian tubes. This can make it difficult, if not impossible, for women with endometriosis to get pregnant.

"It's not that uncommon. It's uncommon for someone my age, but that's my burden. Everyone has a burden. For your prurient information, it actually causes me to have pain during sex, but I endured that hoping to bring Asa here. In other words, I was with Porter before he was with you, so you can toss your theory out the window. When I began to experience other symptoms, I saw the specialist and was told."

"Couldn't he cure it?"

"There is no cure. There is only treatment for the pain. Eventually, I'll probably have an operation, but in the meantime . . . no babies, no Asa growing in my body."

She looked in the mirror at herself again and fiddled with strands of hair around her ears.

"So, he grows in yours," she continued. "We're the Heavenstone sisters," she added in one of her whispers. "It's the same thing as if he was growing in me."

"I don't care that we're the Heavenstone sisters. He's not growing in you; he's growing in me!"

She was silent.

"How are we . . . are you going to explain this to Daddy now?" I asked as the next realization struck my brain.

"Simple. I'll tell him I didn't know you were pregnant until very late in your pregnancy, and we decided to hide it from him and everyone so that you could give birth here without anyone knowing you were so promiscuous."

"You'll make me look terrible in his eyes."

"For a little while," she admitted, "but once Asa is born and I convince Daddy to keep him and I agree to take care of him, he'll change his mind and his feelings about you. You'll have given him the one thing he wanted most."

"No, I won't, Cassie. I'll tell him the truth, that I was raped. I'll tell him what Porter did, what you got him to do."

She smiled. "If you do that, "I'll back up Porter. I'll tell Daddy you seduced him, and then you'll be exposed as just another pregnant teenage girl. Good luck in your new school or your old one, because I'll see to it that you go back there. I won't help you with anything. And most of all, I'll hate you forever."

She glared at me.

"Let me tell you something more, Semantha. Men, including Daddy, never look at a girl who's been a rape victim the same way. No matter what, they can't think of her as anything but partly responsible. It's unjust, I know, but that's the way most men think."

She shrugged.

"In some countries, the girl, the victim, is even ostracized by her own family. They don't do it as openly here, but it's in their thoughts, in their eyes. Wait until the young man you want, you fall in love with, learns you were raped and had a child. You'll think he was born to walk backward."

Despite my determination to fight back and defy her, Cassie's words were sharper than darts and all aimed at my heart. I couldn't keep my eyes from filling with tears.

"There is absolutely no reason for any of that to happen to you, if you just follow my plan and do exactly what I tell you to do. First, I want you to wear a face of shame. Daddy won't be able to stand it, and he'll eventually be sympathetic and concerned for you. You'll see. He'll make you feel better. Second, you'll have the baby secretly, as I said, and we'll get this over with quickly. And third and final, as soon as you're up and ready, I'll make sure we get you into a good school, and this will all be behind you.

"Well?" she asked.

The pounding under my breast reached into my ears.

"I'm afraid," I said.

She smiled. "Don't be. I'll be there right beside you the whole time. I'll make sure nothing bad happens to you. I'll protect you the way Henry the Eighth would protect one of his wives who could give him a male heir. For the rest of your pregnancy, I'll make sure you're treated like a queen. I'll pamper you and hold your hand whenever you like. In fact, I won't leave this house again after we tell Daddy. I'll send out for everything we need. I'll never leave your side.

"Tomorrow," she said, turning back to look at herself in the mirror, "we'll open the nursery and make it spic-and-span. Did you know that Daddy had all sorts of boy's baby clothes bought? I know where they were placed in storage. We'll wash it all and get it all organized. He'll want a nurse, of course, but I'll convince him it's unnecessary with me here. Look," she said, rising and going to her bookshelves. She ran her hand over the binders of a half-dozen books. "These are all books written by baby experts describing how to care for an infant from day one on. I practically have them memorized."

She turned and waited for my response.

"You don't have to wear the girdle anymore, Semantha," she added, granting it to me like some sort of bonus.

The air around me still felt too hot to breathe.

"I'm going to lie down," I said. "I don't feel so good."

"Of course. Go on. I'll bring you something to drink, some warm milk."

She approached me and ran her right palm gently, lovingly, over my cheek. "When you're hungry, I'll bring up your dinner. That will make Daddy curious. I'll tell him our story and ask him to be kind to you. I'll explain how upset and frightened you are. You'll see. I'll get him to accept it and be concerned for you, too. You know I can, so be relieved. Rest."

Before I could prevent it, she hugged me and kissed my cheek.

When I looked into her eyes, I saw only love and hope.

However, it didn't reassure me. It only made me more afraid of what was to come. I said nothing.

I hurried to the sanctity of my own bedroom. Now more in a daze than anything, I lay back on my bed and stared up at the ceiling. It began to swirl. I felt as if I were looking into a whirlpool. Images slowly rose as the swirling sped up. I saw Mother's loving smile, but that was quickly followed by Daddy's face of tragedy. I saw Cassie choosing my sexy dress, and I saw Porter Andrew Hall handing me the box of candy. Then I saw him naked, approaching me in my bed, and I quickly turned over so I wouldn't look up. I slammed my eyelids shut. If only I could wish hard enough for all of this to be untrue.

As if my baby inside me could hear my thoughts, he kicked. I turned on my back and put my hands on my stomach to feel his movement. Despite what that phony Dr. Samuels had told me and what I had read, in my heart of hearts, I had known I was really pregnant. I had let them fool me. I had wanted their story to be true so much that I had convinced myself as well as, if not better than, they had convinced me. I had never told Cassie, but I'd had dreams, night-mares, in fact, about my baby. In them, I had heard him cry. Was that impossible? Did babies cry in the womb? Did the baby inside me know he was being denied? Did he want to announce his existence, de-mand to be recognized?

The avalanche of emotions that had begun when I entered Cassie's room and heard the truth exhausted me. I couldn't keep my eyes open and soon fell asleep. I woke to the sounds of Cassie's and Daddy's voices in the hallway. Daddy was very upset. I had never heard him speak so sharply and angrily to Cassie. And I had never heard her words so muffled by sobs. That was something usually reserved for me.

Moments later, Daddy entered my room. He stood gaping at me. Cassie drew up gingerly beside him.

"Then this is true?" he asked me.

Lying there without the girdle and my hands still on my abdomen, I was sure I presented a clear pic-ture of a pregnant girl. He approached slowly, his lips pulled back tightly, looking like someone who had just swallowed something very rotten. He grimaced with pain and disgust. I looked past him at Cassie. She wasn't looking devastated or even upset. She wore a slight smile and nodded to tell me that all was as she had planned.

"If you would have had the courage to tell me about this immediately, Semantha, I would have done something. Now look at the mess we're in."

"We're not in any mess, Daddy," Cassie insisted, stepping up beside him again. "I told you what we'll do, and we'll do it."

"How could you have done this, Semantha? How could you have been so stupid, and so soon after . . . so soon?"

Everything in me wanted to burst out with the truth. I couldn't stand to see the pain on my father's face, pain he believed was solely and wholly my fault, all my fault. All I could think was that he was going to stop loving me or would never ever love me the same way he had.

"I didn't . . ." I started to say, but Cassie stepped up quickly.

"She didn't mean for it to happen, Daddy. No girl actually plans such a thing. It happened. She was in a precarious emotional state, as we all were after Mother's tragic death. People do unexpected and foolish things when they're like that. Things they can't explain afterward or defend. Surely, you understand."

He wilted and sat at the foot of my bed, lowering his head into his hands. "I let you girls down," he muttered. "I let Arianna down by not stepping up to be twice the parent when it was necessary."

"Oh, no, don't blame yourself, Daddy. You were under great emotional strain as well. Neither of us blames you for anything, right, Semantha?" she said, looking intently at me.

I shook my head, but Daddy didn't see.

"Right?" she repeated.

"Yes, right. This is all my fault, Daddy. I'm sorry."

He sighed deeply and lifted his head from his hands.

"Please don't worry, Daddy. I'll handle all of this," Cassie told him.

"How can you handle all of this?" he snapped at her. The immediate expression on her face told me how shocked and disappointed she was. "She needs medical attention now. She has to see an OB and be set up for a delivery this late in the pregnancy."

"People have had babies in their homes forever, Daddy. Many still insist on it and don't want doctors. They have midwives. I've done some research on it. Unless there are reasons for complications, giving birth in a hospital isn't any safer than at home. Birthing is really a natural process. It doesn't need all this medical paraphernalia. That's just window dressing so doctors can charge large fees."

"I'm not risking Semantha's life," Daddy said firmly. "Tomorrow, we're taking her to see Dr. Moffet, and he'll refer us to an obstetrician. And that's that!" His words fell like thunder.

Cassie didn't wince. She held her ground. "You'll be making a big mistake, Daddy. First, you'll be branding Semantha a whore for the rest of her life. No matter how you get people to swear to secrecy, it will leak out. A secretary, a nurse, Dr. Moffet's own wife or the OB's might let it slip, and you know how quickly any story about a Heavenstone will be spread. What are you going to do, send her away, maybe to Europe? How can she return to school and face other girls and boys her age?

"No, the best way to do this is to involve only one person besides me. We'll get a midwife from out of the area to oversee this, and we'll pay her enough to shut her mouth about it forever. As I told you, until then, I'll stay with Semantha here in the house, and she won't be seen by anyone. No one will see me, either."

"What does that do for us?" he asked skeptically.

Cassie actually smiled. "We can tell people it's my baby," she said.

Even I gasped with surprise

"Your baby?"

"Many women don't show until the late months. You didn't realize Semantha was pregnant. The same thing could easily be true for me."

"But why—"

"I'm not rushing back to school, and I'm much, much stronger than Semantha. I can carry the burden of having given birth. Semantha, as Mother often said, is much more fragile than I am. You know it's true. So, she gives birth. No one knows about it, and very soon afterward, we enroll her in the private school."

"What about the baby?"

"The baby has Heavenstone blood in him. He belongs with us. I'll care for him as well as any mother could. He is, despite everything, your grandson, Daddy."

"But your own life, your future . . ."

"Is here, with you, with our business. It always

has been. I just didn't realize it as clearly as I do now, thanks to Semantha," she said, nodding at me.

"I don't know," he said, but I could feel the resistance lowering in his voice. He turned to me. "What about the father of this child? Who is he?"

"What difference does that make now, Daddy?" Cassie quickly responded. "If we involve him or another family, we'll defeat ourselves. The truth is that the boy involved doesn't even know Semantha is pregnant."

"Really?" he asked me.

I couldn't answer. I just looked at him.

"I don't know," he said. "He should bear some responsibility here. He—"

"We don't know who he is," Cassie added quickly.

"What?"

"There was more than one," she said, "in a very close period of time."

He looked at me sharply. Despite my new size, I felt as if I were shrinking beneath his outraged and disgusted gaze. He got up quickly. "I'm sick about this," he said.

"Of course you are," Cassie said. "Semantha is sorrier about that than anything. That's why she insisted we keep this from you so long."

I know my mouth fell open. I had insisted?

"Well . . . I still wish you hadn't, Semantha," he said, looking back at me. "I can trust Dr. Moffet. I'll speak with him about this and see what he recommends. I'm sure I can get him to deliver the child here in the house."

"If you're absolutely confident about that, then speak to him. But if there is even the slightest doubt, Daddy—"

"Enough! I think I know whom to talk to and whom not to, Cassie."

"Okay, Daddy. I'm sorry. I'm just trying to be extra careful now."

"Now? Seems to me being careful should have been something prominent at least seven months ago," he said, and left my bedroom.

It was as if he had taken all of the air out with him.

Cassie, on the other hand, wore a big, happy smile. "See?" she said. "It will all work out just as I planned."

She came to the bed and put her hand gently on my stomach.

"I want to feel him move," she said, and exploded with happiness when she did. "He's coming, our Asa is coming. I'll go down and prepare a dinner platter for you. Just rest," she said. "You're not to do any work anymore, either, Semantha. You're not going to be like Mother and lose this baby."

"He is so angry at me, Cassie. He's so upset."

"He's going to get over it, Semantha. You'll see. He's on his way to forgiving you. I wouldn't stand for any other conclusion. Trust me."

She smiled, then turned and left me.

Trust her?

How could I ever trust her again?

But then, what choice did I have now?

When she returned nearly a half-hour later with my dinner tray, she was even happier.

"We talked some more, and I persuaded him not to go to Dr. Moffet. I told him I had located a very experienced midwife and already had contracted with her."

"Have you?"

"Yes."

"How could you be so sure he would agree to that?"

"Do I know him better than anyone could, better than even Mother knew him?"

She fixed my pillows and brought over the bed table I hadn't used since I was eight and had a terrible ear infection.

"Her name is Mrs. Chapman, and she'll be here to see you soon. Don't worry about eating too much anymore," she added, nodding at the big piece of chocolate fudge cake. "We're not hiding anything from Daddy any longer.

"I want you to be happy," she added, "as happy as I am."

She spent the rest of the night working on the baby clothes Daddy and Mother had bought for the Asa they had thought was coming. In the morning, she wanted to bring my breakfast up to me as well, but I insisted on going downstairs.

"Well, you do need to exercise," she said. "But I want you to be extra careful on the stairway. In fact, always call me before you go up or down, okay?"

Suddenly, now that my pregnancy was out in the open, she was going to be a real mother hen. It should have made me feel better to know she cared so much, but I knew what she was really worrying about was the baby, not me.

"Look, Semantha, I'm not going to be looking over your shoulder every minute of the day, but there are many things you should avoid and should not do. Don't dare sneak any of Daddy's alcohol or drink any wine with dinner anymore."

"I wish I never had," I said.

"Before you take anything for anything, check with me. No aspirin. Aspirin can cause bleeding and you remember how Mother hemorrhaged. I don't want you drinking coffee until after Asa's born. Caffeine might cause a child to contract diabetes. Be careful when and if you go outside. Avoid insect bites."

"I would even if I weren't pregnant, Cassie."

"More so now," she emphasized. "Don't go scavenging for food. You'll eat the wrong things. Just eat what I give you. If you're still hungry, tell me. Stay away from the microwave. You probably didn't notice, but I took away your electric blanket. You wouldn't use it now, anyway, but you have on cold, rainy days. I don't want you near the cleaning products anymore, and no more long, hot baths."

"All this came out of the books you read?"

"Yes, and they're all written by experts."

"It only makes me feel like more of a prisoner, thank you."

"It's for Asa's sake. Think only of him now," she said.

"I thought you were thinking of me, too."

"Of course, I am. If you're unhealthy, he's going to be."

"That wasn't what I meant."

"What did you mean?"

"Forget about it, Cassie. I'm tired."

"Then go to bed. Always lie down when you're tired."

"How often should I breathe?" I asked under my breath. If she heard me, she ignored it.

My rage at Cassie didn't subside over the next few weeks, no matter how much she pampered me. At times, just to see her work harder, I pretended to be in some sort of pain or greater fatigue. I flew into my own little tantrums, rejecting the food she made, complaining about the taste, and forcing her to make me something different. She blamed it on my pregnancy, claiming my emotional ups and downs were typical of a pregnant woman.

Nevertheless, it did my heart good to hear her running up and down the stairs. I could see that the effort to please me, to make sure I was comfortable and well, was taking a toll on her. She looked more tired at times than I was, and if she hadn't cared about her appearance before, she looked as if she wanted to destroy it deliberately now. Her hair was straggly. She didn't change clothes for days. I thought she neglected bathing as well and told her she smelled and it was nauseating.

Almost daily now, I said and did everything I could to upset her, but nothing stopped her, and she rarely permitted herself to lose her temper or even show any anger for fear it would upset me. After all, as she told me often during the past days, stress was unhealthy for a pregnant woman.

What did upset me and give me great stress was

to see that Daddy wasn't in any way forgiving me. He rarely smiled at me, and if I did catch him looking at me, it was always with a face full of disappointment and sadness. It made my heart ache. Where was the miracle Cassie had sworn she would create when it came to him? Not only did that never happen, but one night, I overheard her talking to him in the living room when they both thought I was sleeping upstairs. I was about to join them when I heard Cassie apologizing for not telling him about me sooner.

"Please don't be angry at me," she pleaded. "I didn't keep her secret to protect her, Daddy. I did it to protect you, to protect our family."

"I know," he said. "It's just that I'm so deeply disappointed in her."

"Don't you think I am, too? All these years, I tried to be a big sister to her, tried to educate her about boys and sex, tried to guide and protect her. I feel just as betrayed as you do. Thank God Mother's not here to see this."

The hot tears were streaming down my cheeks.

And when Daddy said, "Yes, thank God. She would have killed herself over what Semantha has done for sure," I turned and ran up the stairs. I threw myself onto my bed and started to cry, and then I stopped.

A strange new feeling came over me. It was as if all the sadness turned hard and filled me with a new and more satisfying emotion.

I was filled with hate, hate for my sister. All I could dream of that night was getting my revenge and getting Daddy to see the truth and love me again.

Little did I know that the way to get all that accomplished lay waiting for me where it had been ever since Mother's death.

And in a real sense, it was as if Mother herself brought me to it.

21

Downfall

WHEN I SAW Cassie's Mrs. Chapman, my supposed midwife, I thought for sure that she was another phony like Dr. Samuels. First, she looked about as old as Grandmother Heavenstone had on the day she died, and second, she was more interested in seeing the house than she was in seeing me. Instead of asking questions about my pregnancy, she asked one question after another about paintings, vases, furniture and appliances. It was as if she was really a real-estate agent and not a midwife. If Cassie saw my skepticism, she ignored it.

We didn't go up to my bedroom for any examination. She felt my stomach and pulled a pressure cuff out of her satchel to take my blood pressure. Then she finally asked me questions about my pregnancy. When she started to recite what I should expect during the last weeks, I stopped her.

"Cassie has given me things to read about that. I know all that," I said petulantly. I was still suspicious of her. In the back of my mind, I harbored the thought that Cassie probably believed she could deliver the baby herself, anyway. That damn self-confidence

Mother had so admired in her was showing its face constantly these days. Often, I found her reading her books on birthing. She told me she just wanted to be sure everything went all right. If I didn't know better, I'd say she was trying to experience what I was experiencing, imagining it so hard and so well that she would have labor pains when I did.

For my part, I hoped she would. To my way of thinking, she deserved the pain more than I did, anyway. She should have been the one to throw up, not me. She should be the one waddling like some duck around the house, not me. And she should be the one gaining all this weight and looking like a stuffed hog, which was how I felt now. I hung a dress over my full-length mirror so I wouldn't have to see myself every morning.

"We'll deliver the baby in my bedroom," Cassie told Mrs. Chapman, and then she brought her upstairs to see the room, as if that mattered. "I want the baby born in my bed," she whispered.

Mrs. Chapman looked at her and shrugged at me.

"A bed's a bed," she said.

"Hardly," Cassie told her. "Let's go to my office now and discuss the finances."

I didn't follow them. I returned to the living room to wait. Nearly twenty minutes later, Mrs. Chapman emerged and stopped by the door of the living room.

"You're getting close," she said. "I'll be by every other day about the same time. Your sister has my phone number. Do you have any questions?"

"How many babies have you delivered?"

"Oh, too many to count," she said. "Now, mind your sister," she added, and left.

When Cassie returned to the living room, I told her I thought Mrs. Chapman was a phony.

"Why do you say that?"

"You call what she did an exam? I asked her how many babies she has delivered, and she gave me the dumb answer, too many to count."

"It's probably true."

"No, it's not."

"Do you think I would risk Asa's birth by bringing in a charlatan?"

I looked away. I didn't want to tell her what I really thought, but I was very close to doing it.

"I don't want to lose my baby," she added.

"Your baby? I'm the one having the baby."

"He will be my baby, Semantha. We've established that. I'm going to be a mother afterward, not you. You'll be off being a teenager again, going to parties and dances, dating. I'll be the one stuck in this house raising an infant."

"You want that. You made this happen because you want that."

She simply stared. She was wearing another one of Mother's dresses and had once again brushed and kept her hair just like Mother had kept hers. I noticed she was wearing Mother's jewelry, too.

"Why do you keep wearing her things? Why don't you wear your own things?"

"You're getting yourself upset," she said. "What did I tell you about stress and pregnancy?"

"Well, why do you do it? And don't tell me you

don't want to see it all go to waste or be given away. You have nice things to wear."

"I'm not going to stand here and talk about such nonsense." She turned to leave.

"It's not nonsense!" I screamed. "I don't want you wearing Mother's things."

There, I thought, I said it.

She turned very slowly and glared at me. "That's a very unkind thing to say to me, Semantha. I'm doing everything to restore you in Daddy's eyes."

"No, you're not. You're making yourself look good and me look bad. I hear things."

"I do what I have to do to get us through this."

"Through this? You caused it. I think you've convinced yourself that it's all my fault."

"This discussion is over," she said, and this time, she marched out. I heard her go up the stairs, and followed.

"I won't stay in this house another minute if you don't take off Mother's clothes!" I screamed.

She paused on the stairway and looked down at me. Then she smiled.

"Okay, Semantha. We'll cater to your tantrums. I'll go and change into something of my own. Satisfied?"

"And take off her jewelry."

"Fine," she said, and continued up.

My heart was beating so hard I had to take hold of the banister to steady myself. The baby kicked and kicked. He hates when I'm upset, I thought. He can hear the shouting. I went to get myself a glass of cold water. As I stood in the kitchen drinking, I realized just how much I relished bossing Cassie. As long as I

was pregnant and she had to be very careful with me,
I could face her down. When I saw her come downstairs again in one of her own dresses and without
Mother's jewelry on, I enjoyed the sense of power, a
sense I had never felt.

"Satisfied?" she asked.

"No. I never thought it was right that you took
Mother's locket. I should have been given a chance to
wear it sometimes, too."

"You want it with my picture in it now?" she
asked, smiling slyly.

"Yes. I'll put my picture in it."

"Fine," she said, taking it off and handing it to
me. "Here. Put your picture in it, but don't lose my
picture. It goes back in after . . . after you've had
your turn. Now, are you satisfied?"

"Yes. Don't put any of her things on again," I
added.

I could see the battle with herself in her face, the
struggle to restrain herself and the urge to come at
me as she usually would.

"I have some paperwork to do. Go upstairs and
take a nap. Calm yourself down," she ordered, and
walked off to Daddy's office.

I smiled and congratulated myself. My success
gave me more courage and a burst of energy I had
not felt for months. Drunk with my newfound power
and filled with determination, I went upstairs and into
Cassie's room. I threw open her closet and began to
take out each and every one of Mother's dresses, skirts,
and blouses. It was easy to tell which had been hers.

I'll make sure she doesn't wear Mother's things

again, I vowed. I formed small bundles with the garments and carried them one at a time to the stairway at the end of the corridor that led up to our attic. The light switch was on the right just inside the door. There were only naked bulbs hanging from the ceiling, but they illuminated the space well enough. I would put Mother's things in an old armoire at the far right corner. The door had a key in the lock. I remembered the piece well, because I had been up there often when I was younger, pretending it was my own little house. In fact, some of my dolls were still set where I had placed them years ago. They were the witnesses today, watching my every move. I even spoke to them, the way I used to when I was a child.

"I've got to do this. I've got to stop it. Cassie is not our mother and never will be. It's too painful for me to see her wearing Mother's things."

It took me three trips to get all of the clothes up and into the armoire. I was tired but still quite energized, so I returned to Cassie's room and began gathering what I knew to be Mother's jewelry as well. I could take it all up in one more trip. The armoire had some drawers in it. I pulled open the top drawer and paused. There was a pill bottle in it. How odd, I thought. All these years, there was a pill bottle in it. I didn't remember it. How could I have missed it?

Slowly, I put the jewelry down on the floor and then took out the pill bottle and turned it in my hand to read the label. It was a prescription for sleeping pills Dr. Moffet had written for Mother.

Why was the pill bottle up there? It felt empty. Why keep it?

I opened it and looked inside. There were capsules. How strange, I thought. I emptied some into my palm and stared at what was there. They were all empty capsules. There was something familiar about them. I plucked one between my fingers and studied it a moment. The realization of what it was, what they all were, brought so much heat into my face I thought I might go up in flames.

They were Mother's sleeping pills, emptied.

How . . . why empty them? Like another clap of thunder, the possibility ripped through my brain, and then, suddenly, it was as if a cold breeze caressed the back of my neck. Slowly, I turned and saw Cassie in the attic doorway. With the light behind her and the illumination weaker in the attic, she was in shadows. She didn't move. She looked more like a ghost. I blinked to see if she would disappear, but she didn't.

"What are you doing up here, Semantha?" she asked, still not moving in.

I started toward her slowly. "I was bringing up Mother's clothing for storage," I began, "and her jewelry, when I opened the top drawer in the armoire and found this."

I held out the palm of my hand.

"So?"

"These are Mother's sleeping pills, aren't they?"

She didn't answer.

"They've been emptied. Mother wouldn't have emptied them to take them. She would have just taken them. Why are they hidden up here?"

She was still silent, but now I clearly envisioned the horrendous scene that was emerging in my mind.

"You emptied them into her drink."

I could see her face clearly now. She looked different, not angry, not sad. She looked like someone who was hearing voices and not hearing me.

"Cassie!" I cried.

She lowered her head a little and looked at me. "Mother was in terrible pain," she said. "She had failed Daddy, failed the Heavenstones. She wasn't getting any better, and she would never get any better, and she would never bring Asa into the world. She wanted to sleep, to sleep forever and ever."

"No!" I screamed, cringing. Tears were streaming down my face, tears for my mother, for my father, and for me. "You did a terrible, terrible thing!"

She shook her head and smiled that smile of damn Cassie self-confidence again. "No, I didn't."

"You know you did. Deep inside you, you know you did, otherwise you would have buried these, buried the evidence. Maybe you hoped they would be found. You hate yourself, Cassie Heavenstone. You'll always hate yourself. Daddy will hate you forever!" I added, much louder.

That wiped the smile off her face. "No," she said, shaking her head. "He can't. I love him too much, and everything I do is all for him. He can't ever hate me. He loves me."

"Not anymore," I said. "Not after he sees this."

Now anger rose to the surface of her face. "Give me those pills and that pill bottle. Do it now, Semantha," she ordered holding out her hand.

I shook my head. "He's got to know everything, Cassie. You've got to tell him everything, even how

I got pregnant. Everything. I'm going to call him," I said, and started to the left of her.

She blocked me and seized my arm. I formed a fist around the pills and the bottle.

"Give it to me!" she demanded, and started to pry my fingers open, digging her nails into my palms. We struggled, but she was stronger than I was. She managed to get my fingers up. I pulled back as hard as I could, and she grasped the pill bottle, but she was pulling hard in the opposite direction, and when I let go, she went backward and flew off the top step. I saw her hit the edge of a step with the back of her neck and then flip over twice before slamming onto the floor below.

I froze in disbelief. It had all happened so quickly that there was nothing I could do to stop it.

Blood trickled out of the corners of her mouth and began to zigzag down her chin.

"Cassie!" I screamed, and hurried down to her.

Her eyes were open, and she was looking up. They seemed to glaze over as I watched. Her mouth opened just a little more, and I thought I heard her whisper, "He loves me."

In a panic, I hurried to my room to call Daddy. He was out of the office, but his secretary located him quickly for me and transferred me to his cell phone.

"What is it, Samantha?" he asked. The tone of his voice had not softened when he spoke to me all these weeks, and it had that sharpness in it now as well.

"It's Cassie," I said. "She's fallen down the attic steps, and she's hurt badly."

"What? Did you call for an ambulance?"

"No, not yet."

"Okay. I'll call," he said, and hung up before I could tell him anything else.

I returned to Cassie's side. First, I picked up as many of the emptied pill capsules as I could find, and then I found the bottle itself. I put the capsules back into it and sat beside her, holding her hand. It grew cooler and cooler in mine. I don't know how long I was sitting there with her until Daddy arrived. He came right behind the ambulance. The paramedics flew up the stairs behind him, and one of them lifted me out of the way gently.

Daddy waited while the other checked Cassie and then looked up and shook his head.

"Oh, my God, no! No!" Daddy screamed. "Not my Cassie! She can't be dead! Give her CPR! Do something!"

Whether they did it to calm him or they really believed it would help, I do not know, but they tried. The one who had helped me told Daddy they had to call the police. He barely nodded. Then he grabbed my left arm and pulled me toward my bedroom.

"Tell me exactly what happened," he said. "How could she fall down this stairway?"

From the tone of his voice, I understood he was blaming me even before he heard anything. The day he had learned I was pregnant, he had swept me off the pedestal on which every father sees his daughter. I was the fallen angel who had cracked his shattered heart even more, and nothing I could do would ever mend it. Because of that, he would never have any trouble seeing me as being at fault or believing I was the cause of more trouble, more pain. Yes, I could be evil. I could lie. I could do illegal things. He wasn't an objective parent. He had been moved from one who could never see or believe his child was evil to one who could see little else. Forever and ever, I would be guilty until proven innocent, and not the vice versa it was for almost all parents and their children.

I sat at the foot of my bed and looked at the floor. He stood over me, breathing so hard I thought he was going to have a heart attack. I was almost too frightened to speak, and I was still crying.

"Semantha," he said.

"It all started when I told her to stop wearing Mother's things."

"What?"

"She was always acting more like my mother than my sister."

"You're not making any sense, Semantha. What's that have to do with the stairway, the attic?"

"I made her change her clothes, and then she went to your office, and I went to her room and began gathering up Mother's things. I thought I would put them in the attic, in that armoire you said belonged to Grandmother Heavenstone. I put all the clothes in there."

We heard someone running up the stairway and turned toward the doorway.

Uncle Perry appeared.

"What happened, Teddy?" he asked, and looked down the hall where the paramedics remained beside Cassie's body. We could hear one on his cell phone talking to the police.

"I'm trying to find out."

I began crying harder.

Daddy grabbed my shoulders and shook me hard. "Stop this and talk. Talk!"

"Take it easy with her. This is a huge shock for her, too, Teddy," Uncle Perry said.

Daddy took his hands away. "You said you put your mother's clothing into Grandmother Heavenstone's armoire in the attic. So?"

"Then I went back to Cassie's room and got all of Mother's jewelry to put in there as well. I opened the first drawer and I found this," I said, opening my fist.

Daddy hadn't noticed that my fist had been closed the whole time.

Uncle Perry moved closer to look.

Daddy took the pill bottle out of my hand, looked at it and then at me. "What is this?"

"That's Mother's sleeping pills," I said.

"So?"

"Why were they up there?" Uncle Perry asked.

Daddy looked at him. "Yes, what is this?"

I took the pill bottle from him and opened it. "Hold your hand out, Daddy," I said, and he did. I emptied some of the capsules into his palm.

He looked them and then examined one.

"They're empty," Uncle Perry said.

Daddy nodded. "Well?"

"Cassie . . . Cassie emptied them into Mother's drink."

"What?" Daddy grabbed the pill bottle and emptied all of the capsules into his palm. Some fell off.

"They're all empty," Uncle Perry said.

"Why would she do that?"

"She said Mother was in too much pain having lost your Asa and wanted to sleep forever."

"My God," Uncle Perry said.

"She said that?"

"Yes. She came up to the attic just after I found those, and then she told me, and then she tried to get the pill bottle from me, and we struggled . . . and . . ." I started to cry again. "And she . . . fell backward . . . when I let go."

We could hear a police siren in the distance.

"Excuse me, Mr. Heavenstone," one of the paramedics said, coming to the doorway. "We can't move your daughter until the police arrive. Your younger daughter will have to speak to them."

Daddy said nothing. He barely nodded. The paramedic returned to Cassie's body.

"Are you pregnant, Semantha?" Uncle Perry asked, just realizing.

"Yes, Uncle Perry."

"She got herself in trouble," Daddy told him. "Cassie was helping to keep it quiet."

"That's not what happened, Daddy," I said. "I never got myself in trouble."

"What? What are you saying now?"

I began to tell him, but before I could finish the whole story, the police arrived. However, what I had told him of it so far was enough to drain all the blood from his face and weaken his knees so much that Uncle Perry had to hold him up to face the police. They told me to stay in my room while they went to talk to the paramedics.

In the end, it was Uncle Perry who was more concerned about the Heavenstone reputation. He came back to me before the police did.

"Don't tell them about the pills and your mother," he said. "That will turn this into a circus. The tabloids will have a field day with us. Just tell them you were both bringing things up for storage, and she lost her footing and fell backward."

"I'm not good at not telling the truth, Uncle Perry. Cassie will tell you that—" I stopped myself. The realization that Cassie was gone forever still hadn't set in.

"Do the best you can," Uncle Perry said. "Your father and I will handle it from then on. Don't worry."

When the police came in to speak with me, I told them Cassie and I had been taking things up to the attic, and when I had taken some clothes from her arms too quickly, she had lost her footing and fallen backward. I thought I saw doubt in their faces, but Uncle Perry stepped in quickly and told them I was too upset to talk too much, and as they could readily see, I was pregnant. Maybe because of who we were or maybe because they really didn't see any reason to continue, they left me alone and continued to work on getting Cassie's body out to the ambulance.

I literally fell over on my side on the bed and closed my eyes. Sleep was truly an escape. Later that day, Daddy and Uncle Perry came into my room and sat beside my bed to hear the rest of the story. They barely spoke or asked a question. Daddy told Uncle Perry to call Porter Andrew Hall and tell him to come directly to our house immediately. I remained in my room. Uncle Perry brought me something to drink and a little to eat and told me to rest. He said he and Daddy would be back up to see me as soon as they had met with Porter.

When they did return, it was apparent that Porter had confessed to everything. Daddy was devastated, but he was finally more concerned about me than himself. Despite all that had happened and all he had learned, he was able to hold himself together and get busy on what had to be done about Cassie. Since there was no longer a reason to try to keep my pregnancy hidden, Daddy had his secretary, Mrs. Hingen, come stay with me while he and Uncle Perry went off to speak to the police. Uncle Perry said he would get started on the funeral arrangements.

For the first time in a long time, my father and my uncle were behaving like real brothers. Later, Daddy would tell me that nothing cements a family tighter than family tragedy. That's when they are reminded that their blood shares mortality and lives only as long as they do and their children do.

Late in the evening, Daddy came into my room. I was in bed but hadn't been able to fall asleep for very long. I'd doze off and then wake up and be awake for long periods of time until I dozed off again. Anyone who's been through so traumatic an event would say he or she wondered if it had all been a dream. Every once in a while, I'd listen hard for Cassie's footsteps to confirm it had been a nightmare and nothing more, but those footsteps never came.

When I woke after one of my short dozes, I saw Daddy sitting in the shadows carved by the moonlight flowing through my sheer cotton curtains. The sight of him sitting so still startled me. I sat up slowly.

"Daddy?"

"How are you?" he asked softly.

"I'm okay. I have trouble sleeping."

"I don't expect to sleep at all," he said. "I'm sitting here wondering how I let all this get by me, wondering why I was so blind, deaf, and dumb. She always seemed so perfect to me, or maybe I wanted her to be perfect. I suppose most parents are blind to their children's faults or want to be. It's just that I always thought of myself as . . . wiser, I guess. I believed my own publicity."

"I should have told you more, talked to you more. It's mostly my fault."

"No, hardly. I'm sure I would have found some excuses or ways to disregard whatever you said. When I lost your mother, I lost my clear eyes. But there's something that frightens me even more as I sit here beside you and think, Semantha. I wonder if you know anything about it."

"What, Daddy?"

"Cassie was so in charge, especially after your mother became pregnant. I remember how upset she was to learn it when we announced it at dinner. It comes back to me now. A lot comes back to me now. It's as if I had videotaped this past year or so and can play back troubling moments, so I can't help wondering . . ."

"Wondering what?"

He leaned toward me. "Did Cassie do anything to cause your mother to have the miscarriage?"

His question didn't surprise me, because somewhere deep inside myself, I had the same fear. I recalled how just recently, Cassie had warned me against taking anything for a headache or a backache, especially aspirin. She made the point of saying it causes bleeding, and she was, as Daddy said, taking care of Mother so often when Mother was pregnant.

"I don't know, Daddy. I know she very much wanted you to have your Asa. She talked about it all the time."

He nodded, but I knew that, like me, he didn't really want to know.

"I guess that's something we're not going to know and shouldn't think about anymore. Not now, not after all this," he said.

"No."

"We both have a lot to forget."

He rose and stood there a moment. Then he leaned over to kiss me.

"Try to get some sleep."

"You, too."

"Okay. We've got a lot to do tomorrow." He paused near the door. "As soon as I can, I'll take you to see Dr. Moffet. Let's do something right."

"Okay, Daddy."

"It's just you and me now," he said. "But don't be afraid, Semantha. I'll be here for you. I promise. What happens to you happens to me."

He left, his words hanging in the air.

And I thought, those were almost Cassie's exact words, too.

Only she would have added, "After all, we're the Heavenstone sisters."

Epilogue

THERE IS SOMETHING about the nature of unwitnessed accidents in homes that stirs suspicious minds. Perhaps it's because the things that cause the accidents and deaths are apparently so common, so shared with everyone, that everyone hopes there's another explanation. No one wants to know that the everyday things he or she does can be fatal if some mistake is made. We're not on battlefields when we're in our own homes.

Or are we?

Not every war has to have bullets and guns and bombs. The war that raged in our house was practically invisible. There were constant explosions in the air, in our minds, and in our very souls, but we didn't see them or feel them or want to see them and feel them. After all, we had so much camouflage to rely on, such as our wealth, our fame, and our well-guarded privacy. Ironically, it was Mother who enabled all this by refusing to have servants— witnesses, in fact. And it was both Mother and Daddy who built an image of Cassie that put her so high up, making it impossible to see not only her weaknesses and faults but, most of all, perhaps, her desperation.

She was so desperate for love that she would harm those she loved to put herself at the front of the line when affection was to be expressed. No wonder she was so fond of whispering. It enabled her to live just under the radar. She moved freely in and out of her own world, always shutting the door behind her so no one could enter that world or even see into it.

I did finally. I think I always did, but, like my parents, I refused to believe in what I saw and what I heard. So, when I told Daddy that much of this was my fault, I meant it. I understood why it was, why I should have tried harder to get my parents to see as well. I was young, yes, and afraid, but as I have come to believe, we are all in a war in our own homes in one way or another, and wars cause you to lose your youthful innocence faster.

I guess I lost mine completely the day Cassie fell on the stairs. I buried it with Cassie.

Cassie was always so proud of how big and elaborate the Heavenstone tombstones were. They did dwarf the monuments around them in the cemetery. There was no doubt in any mourner's mind where the Heavenstone plots were located. They could be seen practically on entering the cemetery.

I kept thinking Cassie would have been so pleased with it all: the large crowd, the tons of flowers, the parade of limousines. The only thing that would have displeased her was where her plot was located. It was to the left of Mother's. Daddy's would be to the right, so that Mother separated her from him. It almost made me smile that day to see her coffin lowered into that plot. I imagined her screaming and complaining, insisting it was a mistake, and demanding that a new grave had to be dug immediately.

I think there were just as many eyes on me being pregnant as there were on Daddy and on Cassie's coffin. I could feel the questions buzzing around us just as clearly as I could have felt a hive of bees circling. Uncle Perry was right beside me, holding my arm the whole time. In the church, he held my hand, and he did so in the limousine as well.

Some parents and students from my public school attended, but I felt they were there to gawk at me more than they were to pay respects to Daddy and Cassie. I was happy that Daddy kept the visitors afterward to a very close group of business associates. I kept thinking that Cassie would like this, at least. She had hated it when we'd had all those curiosity seekers at Mother's funeral.

Afterward, the house had never felt as empty. Sometimes, I would pause to listen, because I thought I heard Cassie's familiar footsteps on the stairway or in the hallway. For days and weeks, whenever I entered the kitchen, I half expected to see her working on a meat loaf or making a pasta. I did the best I could in my condition, but Daddy now talked about hiring a cook and some maids. Uncle Perry practically moved in. He was here so often. I saw he was just as concerned about my father as he was about me. It brought me continuously back to that idea that tragedy cements a family.

In fact, it was Uncle Perry who rushed me to the

hospital the day my water broke. He had gotten to the house before Daddy, and just turned around with me in his car. Dr. Moffet was there to greet us. Daddy arrived before I went into the delivery room. He held my hand as they wheeled the gurney, but he turned down Dr. Moffet's invitation to be in the room. I didn't blame him. I wished I could turn down the invitation.

The last shock came when my baby was born.

It would have killed Cassie again. She had been so confident.

I gave birth to a girl, not a boy.

Daddy and I hadn't discussed what would be done with the baby. Without Cassie around to shove reality and decisions in our faces, we both ignored the question for as long as we could. We did discuss my going to a private school as soon as I could, but the baby's destiny was left hanging in the air just outside our lives.

Daddy came to see me as soon as I could have any visitors after the delivery. He hadn't gone to see my baby yet. After he was sure I was fine, he grew silent. We both did. The words hung like apples ready to be plucked.

"Neither of us is equipped to be a mother right now," he began. "The circumstances that have brought the child to us will always be a stain on our minds, Semantha. It's unfortunate, and it's not the child's fault, but it's there nevertheless."

I couldn't disagree.

"Obviously, although we haven't spoken about this, I have been working on a solution. I couldn't see us just giving the child up for adoption to total strangers, so I've been in contact with your mother's cousin Royce. You might remember that she and her husband, Shane, lost their daughter, Vera, in an auto accident five years ago. There's an older boy in college, but Royce is only in her early forties. They've agreed to take the baby. Is that all right with you?"

"Yes," I said.

What else was there to say? I didn't know Royce and Shane well. They had come to Cassie's funeral but hadn't spent all that much time with me. Considering what Daddy was now telling me, I thought that was odd, but then again, I thought maybe Royce wanted to feel more like the baby's mother. To do that, it was better not to think of the baby's real mother.

"I told Royce and Shane they could give the baby a name. It's not Asa," he said, almost smiling, "but it's close enough. They chose Anna. I've gone ahead and had it put on the birth certificate, Anna Norman."

"That's a nice name, Daddy."

He nodded.

"Are you going to go see her?"

"I'd rather not," he said. "I hope that's all right. I'm making sure Anna has everything she needs," he quickly added.

"It's all right," I said.

I knew Daddy was right about it all, but it still made me terribly sad. What Cassie had done, the pain, lived on long past her and always would.

But that would be another war in another home

to come. What role I would play in it lay out there in the future, like some egg yet to be hatched.

A day before I was to leave for my private school, I asked Uncle Perry to take me to the cemetery. He surprised me by telling me that my father had been there often. Daddy had never mentioned it. When we arrived, Uncle Perry remained in the car, and I walked out to look at what was now another impressive tombstone. It seemed so unreal to read Cassie's name on it. For a while, I simply stood there looking at it. Then I went down on my knees and took out the spoon I had brought in my purse. I dug as deep a hole as I could in her grave. When I was satisfied, I reached behind my neck and undid the clasp. I held the locket in my hand for a moment and then dropped it into the hole, quickly covering it.

Was that an act of forgiveness?

Was that an act of love?

Or had I simply come to believe that the locket was hers after all?

It would take me years to learn the answers.

I didn't say a word. I stood, looked again at the tombstone, and walked away.

But in my heart, I knew I wasn't leaving her behind.

I would forever hear her whispering in my ear.

For after all, as she had said many times, we were the Heavenstone sisters.

And nothing, not even death itself, could change that.